Pressed Together

The Buckeye Lake "Together" Series
Book One

Kim Garee

M✝ Zion Ridge Press
Books Off the Beaten Path

www.MtZionRidgePress.com

Mt Zion Ridge Press LLC
295 Gum Springs Rd, NW
Georgetown, TN 37366

https://www.mtzionridgepress.com

ISBN 13: 978-1-962862-21-9

Published in the United States of America
Publication Date: May 1, 2024

Copyright: © 2024 Kim Garee

Editor-In-Chief: Michelle Levigne
Executive Editor: Tamera Lynn Kraft

Artist: Addison Stewart
Cover art design by Tamera Lynn Kraft
Cover Art Copyright by Mt Zion Ridge Press LLC © 2024

The Buckeye Lake "Together" Series:

Pressed Together
Packed Together
Patched Together

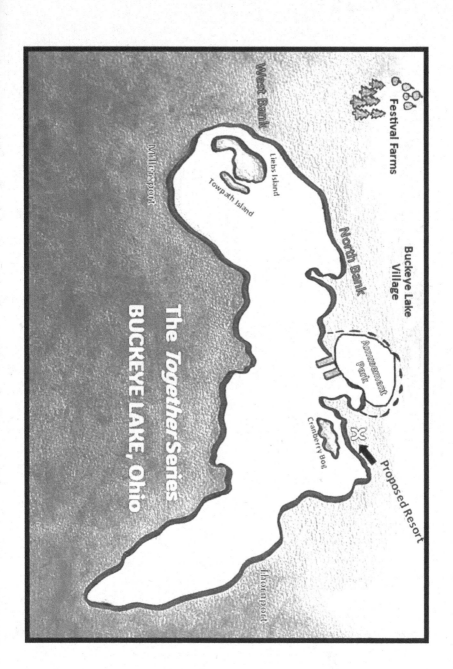

The *Together* Series
BUCKEYE LAKE, Ohio

Festival Farms

West Bank

Millersport

Liebs Island

Towpath Island

North Bank

Buckeye Lake
Village

Amusement
Park

Cranberry Bog

Proposed Resort

Thornport

DEDICATION

Dedicated to Brent.
Of course.

AUTHOR'S NOTE

I love history and research, in general. I've especially been enamored with the history of Buckeye Lake for decades, since working there right out of college and covering the opening of the historical museum. I was careful to incorporate some historically accurate aspects of the amusement park that was the "Playground of Ohio," *but* I also played fast-and-loose with some facts for the sake of the story. For example, Buckeye Lake was incorporated as a village less than fifty years ago, but I've got them holding a town council meeting in 1946. For a complete list of what's true and what's fiction in *Pressed Together*, please visit the *Books* page on my website at www.kimgaree.com

Acknowledgements

So many had a hand in the project of this story.

First, thanks to Charlie Prince who took the time to turn a regular English major into a reporter, and thanks to the whole staff of the *Buckeye Lake Beacon* for handing all the "fluff" assignments to me. Those shaped me (and this book), for sure.

Thanks to my very earliest readers, Dan and Karen, for their guidance, as well as Rebecca, whom I tricked into reading the first draft while she recovered from surgery (I think I dropped off a tray of homemade mac 'n cheese with a rough manuscript as dessert). Later, I was very grateful to my ACFW Ohio Chapter critique group, as well as beta readers Cameo, Leah, and Heidi. Thank you to my launch team and my family and friends who "prayed me through" big changes.

The ladies at Mt. Zion Ridge Press have been such a blessing: thank you for allowing me my creative freedom even as you made my draft better. I can't wait to drink tea with you when we're all in the same place at the same time.

Research-wise, thanks to Mr. John Long of the Free Press Museum. John was working for his father as a "printing devil," lining type from the age of three, so his eight decades of experience proved invaluable to me as I sorted through what "going to press" might look like for Emily Graham in a small town in 1946. Another helpful resource was Mr. Gene Policinski, Senior Fellow for the First Amendment Freedom Forum.

Thank you to J-me and the ladies at the Buckeye Lake Museum for research help and for some of the most memorable Friday evenings of my life. I'm indebted to the late Donna Braig before them (and to her invaluable book, *My Buckeye Lake Story*). Thank you to Brad, of course, my favorite poet farmer.

Any mistakes in this book are entirely my own (but please check my website for an account of the ones I made on purpose).

I'm also very grateful to my mom who took us to the Ohio Historical Society Museum so we could imagine things on the weekends, even when we had no money. I adore her so much, along with Jim, who never complained about going along after we all fell for him.

Special thanks to Graham, Emma, and Kora for blindly believing in their mama's stories and for always making me laugh at the table. And especially to Brent, who was *the* early encourager, sounding board, and reader who can often be heard saying, "I've got this. You go write."

Thank You, Lord, for walking me through things that got me trusting You with both my eternity *and* with my day. And for Your Word. *"For I am convinced that neither death nor life, neither angels nor demons, neither the present nor the future, nor any powers, neither height nor depth, nor anything else in all creation, will be able to separate us from the love of God that is in Christ Jesus our Lord."* Romans 8:38-39.

Prologue

Reno Daily Star
March 22, 1946
24-year-old Philadelphia soldier shot behind Fox casino

Gilbert Reese trembled as he ducked deeper into the rank shadows of the bus terminal and leaned against the walls. Only one thing mattered to him at the moment. The Conti family did not leave witnesses alive. That was how the "uncles" had survived and thrived for so long in Reno.

So when, twelve hours earlier, one of the three Contis in the alley had glanced up at him over Jamie Mathison's body — through the smoke from his Model 19 classic — and made eye contact, Gil had run for his life. And now here he was.

He'd made two mistakes in the confusing moments that followed the murder of his best friend.

He never should have run to Betsy's dressing room in the neighboring casino. Now she was involved in the whole thing, too. That was the first mistake. She'd be hunted now, as he was, but he hadn't been thinking clearly. The dancer had listened to him blubber and gasp out the story, tears streaming and hands shaking. Really, she already knew how Jamie used his brains to move numbers around for the Contis, and everybody knew Gil had been all too happy to come in on it during their time as privates at nearby Stead Air Force Base.

Everybody knew they'd made plenty of money in the deal.

Had everyone known it would never be possible to end their relationship with the Contis once they'd been discharged at the war's end?

Gil winced. He and Jamie had learned that lesson the hard way.

Especially Jamie.

In the bus terminal, staring hard at the oversized clock around the corner, Gil bargained with God. Was God anticipating it? Maybe. That is, if the Man Upstairs hadn't given up on him entirely at this point. *I'll clean up my act, I promise. But I need to be alive to do it, Lord. Please don't let me get killed.*

Gil's hands shook. The image of Jamie's blood running out in an alley was always with him now. Maybe God had gotten tired of both their antics.

Just like most everyone else had. Gil's father. Their First Sergeant. Emily.

That was his second big mistake. Gil clenched the bus ticket to Ohio in his sweating hand. Looking down, he saw the fresh ink had smeared.

His knees shook, too. The woman at the window would be able to identify him, wouldn't she? Just as Betsy would be able to reveal his plans under the right kind of pressure, the scrutiny of the pin-curled matron who'd sold him the ticket would yield an impression as clear as footprints. She would easily recall Gil's bright red buzz cut, shifting eyes, sweaty forehead, shaking, shaking, shaking. Pin-curl knew exactly where he was going because she'd printed his ticket.

Back to Buckeye Lake.

Back to Emily Graham, who seemed so far from the hot mess of Reno. Emily ran the newspaper at the lake now, and she owed him one, didn't she? For letting her out of their joke of an engagement with so little fuss? For covering for her after they'd soaped Mr. Byrd's windows in primary school? For allowing her the honor of covering for him all the other times?

Gil squeezed his eyes shut to see if he could make the burning go away. He'd been awake too long and had cried too hard, but he could not sleep on the bus, no way. He had to stay alert. He focused on breathing in and breathing out, but his lungs burned, too.

He had to hide. Emily would know what to do. She always knew what to do. She was a hundred times smarter than Gil, always had been, and for some reason she'd never completely given up on him. Emily would hide him.

He just had to stay alive until he made it back to Ohio.

2

Chapter One

The Buckeye Lake Beacon
Saturday, June 1, 1946
High wire cyclist! Beach opening! MORE planned for Decoration Day Weekend

Drew Mathison had never been particular about clothing. He'd worn nothing but a uniform these past four years, but this small-town cop getup wasn't sitting right on either his shoulders or his conscience.

"This feels wrong, sir," he told Buckeye Lake Park's aptly named police chief, Harley Gunn. As a decorated MP detective, Drew might have more experience with firearms and combat than old Gunn would ever have, but the lanky scarecrow of a chief was far more in his element out on this sunny boardwalk pier this morning. And he was the only person Drew trusted with his real purpose here at the lake.

"You're fine, you're fine. You can move around freely now, as one of my officers, y' know?" Gunn nodded to a couple about his age, but rather than stopping to talk, the pair veered away, confirming Drew's suspicion that he needed to work on his friendly demeanor. "You may have lost your little brother, son, but you can still find justice." Gunn's hand landed on Drew's shoulder in a fatherly gesture, mingling the scent of cherry pipe tobacco with nearby French fry grease. "I'll help you any way I can, y'know."

"I'll honor the uniform and your trust, sir. First thing I'd better do is just ..." Drew paused to confirm that five nearby children were playing a game of keep-away with a *carved coconut head*. "... Just figure this place out, I guess."

The middle of Ohio was decidedly not coconut country. In fact, this lake was a shallow valley surrounded for miles by oceans of nothing more exotic than cornfields. The postcards in all the boardwalk shops boasted "The Playground of Ohio," a dizzying amusement park built at the end of the Interurban railway decades before. In recent years, it was the family car, rather than the railroad, that dumped the landlocked and war-weary at the isolated Buckeye Lake Park by the tens of thousands. The park didn't disappoint, either. Its carefully constructed beaches, its charming boardwalk, its rides, and the piers supporting dance halls and skating rinks were all filled to overflowing on this first day of June. And it sounded like they would stay that way until September.

3

What a perfect place for a coward to hide.

Drew Mathison squinted up at the roller coaster, scanning its segmented seats for one man. The "click-click-click" of the cable meeting the cog on the first hill was followed by a beat of silence, then screams as the cars plummeted and raced out over the water.

"Day like this, the coaster alone brings in 5,000 bucks and more, y'know," Gunn told him proudly.

Drew nodded and scanned, rehearsing ways to get information without giving any away. He chewed on a sliver of wood he'd used to stir his coffee, impatient with the air of celebration that had been getting in his way since he'd arrived two days before. He pushed to the background the pulse of a jazz band, that chorus of squeals raining down from The Dips coaster, and the crack and fizzle of a midday firework. Just beyond the coaster but still overhead, a man in pea-colored tights rode a high wire cycle over the midway. As people poured in, they gawked at him, eager for the distraction of the unexpected.

Drew resented distractions. They got in the way of what he wanted: to haul the man who could identify his kid brother's killer back to a courthouse six states away.

Gilbert L. Reese's black and white Army photo was tucked in Drew's uniform pocket, and he had the face memorized. He'd stared at the image as he'd fought sleep along the interstate and fueled himself with sandwiches and Coca-Cola from roadside stands. Having mapped every freckle, though, wasn't helping much in this crowd. With the morning sun gleaming orange on the lake water, the wooden boardwalk itself looked like a melting popsicle alive with ants. Instead of ants, people moved in and out of crowded candy shops, fortune teller booths, jewelers shops, and arcades. More of them crowded the long pier fifty yards to the west. Gilbert Reese's hair was a bright orange, as well, Drew had been told. Shouldn't that make this easier?

"Get yourself all settled in at the inn, then?" Gunn asked. "Have any trouble finding a room?"

"No trouble." It was more a closet than a room, but it suited him fine. "And thanks again for putting a word in."

"Yeah ... sure." His pause was uneasy, as though something else had caught his eye. "Sure thing. Thank me while you can because you won't be doin' it for long," the chief said, his tone of both amusement and warning pulling Drew's attention back from the next load of riders on The Dips. He followed the chief's nod and apologetic gaze toward an approaching woman. "I was going to warn you, but here she comes. Already. Woman beats me to near everything, y'know."

She was clearly aimed right for Drew, set apart from the crowd not just in her focus but in the fact that, like him, she was obviously not a

4

vacationing tourist here for the summer kickoff. This woman was working.

She wore a white blouse with a little blue bow tie that matched the belt on her flat-fronted beige skirt. A wide satchel strap crossed her chest. Her shoulder-cropped hair was blonde, nearly yellow, and she wore an eager smile. *Here she comes.* Gunn's phrasing echoed in Drew's head over the rattling of the roller coaster's latest pass.

The final thing he noticed about the woman — too late — was the notepad in her hand, gray and boasting the words "field notes" across the front: a reporter's tool.

"She insisted on running a little story on you," Gunn explained, arm out in an almost defensive gesture.

"There's no story," Drew heard himself say. What could the chief have been thinking? She had already arrived, though, and overhearing his statement only seemed to make her smile broader. The assessing sweep of her eyes felt like a mild electrocution, neither a good nor bad thing, and then she turned to Gunn.

"They're at it again, Chief," she announced. "This time they've soaped the newspaper's windows with a *highly* unpleasant word. Looks like I'll be filing another complaint."

But she said both the words "unpleasant" and "complaint" in the bright, delighted way a girl might boast about winning a Best Legs contest. Or something. What had his head going there? Drew had never even been to a contest like that, and he was *not* staring at this woman's legs. Not for more than a second, anyway.

Gunn sighed. "You know there's nothing I can do about it, Emily, 'cept for documenting. And don't think I don't know you just want the police report on record so you can put it in the paper."

"Until you solve these crimes, all I can hope for is shaming them in print." She shrugged, still cheerful, and turned again. "Is this the new Officer Mathison you mentioned?" Her hand, covered in a summer-knit white glove, was narrow as it found his for a shake. "Emily Graham."

"Call him Sergeant in the story," Gunn corrected, shooting Drew another apologetic look. "I told him he could keep his rank in our department. A man doesn't go from being a decorated Army detective to 'officer' back stateside, you know?"

"Officer is fine," Drew mumbled. *Publicity? A story?* This couldn't be happening. Mama Mathison's ear-twisting manners had him adding, "Nice to meet you, ma'am."

"Great. Good. Leave you to it, then," Gunn said even as he walked away. "I'll just be, ah, checking in with George about the barge for the fireworks. Got that quote I gave you, Emily? Make me sound good and all?"

5

"You know I always try, Chief," she called affectionately, with a grin at Drew.

She was not a short woman, in those strappy heels, and he only had to look down at her a little as he told her, "There's no story." He could only imagine how disastrous a feature in print would be: his name plastered across the paper for a Conti hitman to find.

Drew had to get to the witness before there was no witness. Publicity was his enemy, of course, as was wasted time. He nodded and started to move away, happy to have made himself clear.

"If you won't let me interview you, will you at least take my complaint report, Officer? I mean, Sergeant?"

Oh, right. Soaped windows. Unpleasant word. *Highly* unpleasant word, for all that she seemed more amused than frightened.

Curiosity mingled with impatience. Plus, this was the work he'd agreed to. And this was about her, not him, so it was fine to turn back.

Now it was his turn to pull out a notebook. It didn't feel quite as reassuring in his hand as a gun, but somehow the job did settle him.

They faced one another on the pier, pencils ready.

"This is like a Wild West draw," the newspaper woman observed. She was chewing gum, something he had always found unattractive. "You can take the first shot, soldier."

"What's your complaint, ma'am? Who are 'they' and why do you suppose they soaped your windows?"

"I don't know who they are, for sure, but I know what it's about," she answered. When he just stared, she continued, "It's my coverage of the proposed resort project. Or, rather, the editorials I've published. I'm trying to protect the bog. So far, I've been able to slow down the zoning. It's making a few people angry, to the tune of about five threats in the past couple of weeks."

He had no idea what she was talking about, of course. On his note sheet, he dutifully scribbled "resort project" and "zoning" and "bog." Sounded like small town politics and every low-budget political film ever written. "So, you're a newspaper reporter who is being threatened because of what you've been writing?" It was predictable, but what didn't quite fit was her apparent glee about being threatened. He studied her as she confirmed with a nod. Her eyes were the same blue-green color as Buckeye Lake.

"My turn," she announced. "Fair's fair."

"You can't publish a story about me, ma'am." Nor did he have the mental energy to invent a false one for her.

"Emily."

"Emily. Please don't publish anything about me."

"I'll just ask to satisfy my own curiosity, then? You have my word.

Entirely off the record."

Gunn seemed to trust her, and the chief understood the peril of the larger situation. Drew's small nod was all she needed.

"What brings you here to Buckeye Lake, Sergeant?"

"Just looking for ... what comes next," he said gruffly. It was a type of lie, sure, but Drew had taught himself to justify a lie in defense of justice. That's what a detective did. He felt satisfied when she didn't write it down.

"'Next' as in after the War?" She angled her head, her hair a mop of gold. "How long have you been back stateside, then?"

"Not long. A few weeks." As an MP, he'd had to help get the rest of the boys home from the vast European theater. It hadn't been a smooth project. On the trip back across the Atlantic, he thought he'd known exactly what came next. As the second son of Hank Mathison of Mathison Construction, he was supposed to manage the business alongside Sy, the eldest. Jamie would do the books, and Michael was the sales guy. The four Mathison boys, back together again now that the war was finally over.

But then there'd been the telegram waiting for him as soon as he'd returned. Instead of arriving back in Philadelphia, Jamie had been killed. Not in battle, ironically, because the war was well over. Just when Mama Mathison's boys were at last due to return to her miraculously whole, Jamie had been gunned down behind a casino. A *casino*. No hero's death, and no witness to confirm the identity of the killers. No one in Reno was doing anything about it, either, so Drew had taken about thirty seconds while his mama cried to decide that *he* would. The last few weeks had been spent in his beat-up construction truck, driving across the country to a murder site, to a barracks, to a dancer's dressing room, to a bus station, and then back through the Midwest to this lake. He made promises to his family without really caring if this was what they wanted from him.

It was what he needed to do.

"My turn," he insisted to the newspaper girl, wanting to finish her police report and move on. He would take these notes back to the station further up the boardwalk, where a secretary apparently worked to make sense of scribbles. This vandalism report would be the first he would file here at Buckeye Lake. "What have some of the other threats been, ma'am?"

"Oh. They painted a big, sloppy message on my car the other day. Not funny."

"No." He wrote it down. "What did that one say?"

One side of her lips twitched like she might, in fact, grin again. "It said 'Swamp Rat.' With a heart shape. What does that even *mean*? That I love swamp rats or that I am one?"

What indeed? Drew could not be less interested. "Seems to confirm your suspicions regarding the motive, ma'am."

"Emily is fine." She quickly scribbled something on her own notepad and turned it toward him. "That's the word they soaped all over my windows at the newspaper office, by the way. That was this morning."

She didn't blush. Drew grunted and added the word to the report.

"They slashed my tires first. That kind of thing. But I filled out separate reports for the rest. Gunn's got it all on file." She talked a little like the way a typewriter sounded.

Drew wrote. Flipped one of the small pages. Looked up. "Miss Graham, I have to ask. Is there a reason you seem so ... happy about these incidents?"

"Because it means I'm making a difference," she said. "The resort would destroy a natural landmark and the only beach access point the local kids have. Rare bogs and poor kids don't have a chance against a hotel development company, but I do."

This time a small, pale pink bubble of gum blossomed from between her lips. Drew reminded himself that gum chewing had always seemed a little crude. There was no reason, then, that the sharp pop of that tiny bubble should ricochet around his ribcage like a gunshot.

~~~~~

Emily Graham was growing disappointed. This new police officer was not as impressed as he should have been. Not by the magic of Buckeye Lake's amusement park.

Nor by her role as heroic victim.

She, on the other hand, was enjoying both so thoroughly that Drew Mathison was beginning to frustrate her. "The way I see it, plenty of folks have motives for these pranks," she explained, trying to be helpful. He really hadn't written much down.

He eyed the word she'd scribbled again. "Vandalism isn't a prank."

In general, his voice sounded like he hadn't spoken to a soul in years.

"Dottie's been flipping her wig every time I publish something about it because her family — the Berkeley family — owns the land the park is on and all that land on that side of the north shore. So, they're looking to make money on selling a chunk to the resort," Emily said. "Wait. What are you doing there?"

"Writing down suspects. Isn't that what you wanted?"

"Don't write *Dottie* down!" *Now he decides to take careful notes.* "We grew up together, for crying out loud. I just said she's been mad at me, is all." At his exasperated look, she decided to forge on. "I mean, it could be any one of a number of contractors who wanted to bid on the job ... or a couple of crooked council members looking for a kick-back."

"A lot of people hate you, then."

That took her aback. That wasn't right. *Was it?*

Emily blinked. She studied him, and he studied her, like some kind of contest to catalog details that would point to the truth. Cop eyes and reporter eyes, she realized, were the same. She was about to explain to him, more slowly this time, how it all just meant she was doing worthwhile work when she heard her name shouted in an Italian accent from the skies.

"Emmmmily!" Shielding her eyes from the sun, she knew who she'd find up above, balanced on a bike and a high wire.

"Morning, Toppy!" Maybe a wave was all he wanted. Half afraid Drew Mathison would dart away on the pretense of some altercation, Emily invisibly linked the police officer to the cyclist. "Toppy, this is Officer Mathison! You'll be seeing him policing the boardwalk here!"

Her voice needed to be loud enough to reach him, so dozens of people on the pier also heard and shouted a cheerful welcome to the new police officer. Drew grimaced and waved with such poorly concealed annoyance that Emily laughed out loud. He was a nice-looking man, she supposed, and some people looked longer than she'd expected. High above, Toppy returned the gesture with a half-wave.

"I am hungry," he called down. "Dottie did not feed me this morning!"

"Didn't she?" That was unlike her. Emily scanned the crowd briefly, half expecting Dot Berkeley to be striding toward the ballroom tower with a tray of food. Still squinting up at him from under the flat of her hand, Emily called, "I'll bring something up in a bit, Toppy! Okay?"

"Thank you!" He twirled the spiraled ends of his mustache. "You are beautiful today!"

When she turned back around, the new guy was regarding her with confusion. "The park and the Chamber of Commerce work together on these things," she explained.

"These things?"

"Yeah. The Free Acts, the gimmicks. The stuff that gets people to come in and then to stay." Drew Mathison nodded, glancing around again, so Emily gave in to her inner show woman. "It's an amazing lineup this year, you know. At two today and again later tonight, you'll see a horse jump off that platform up there. See? From that platform and into that tank of water."

His gaze followed her gesture, and he raised his brows. Could he finally be impressed? *That* was more like it.

"Sometimes we set the tank of water on fire. Pour gasoline on the top, right? Then a man dives down into it, doing a backflip off the platform, and *splash!* He puts the fire right out! We call him Aerial Man. You should *hear* the crowd on that one!"

Drew's eyes, gray and shadowed, tracked back up to Toppy, who had

9

pedaled away and was performing a stunt on an empty stomach. Emily needed to have a talk with Dot and her crew. Hadn't they determined breakfast needed to be served before opening? "Toppy is up there on the high wire for the *whole summer* starting two days ago," she revealed. Mathison blinked. "You can read about it in *The Beacon*. That's why we have to take his food up to the platform there. Even sleeps up there. Can you imagine?"

"That doesn't sound safe."

"They strap him to the bike while he sleeps, so he doesn't fall. Perfectly safe." Drew looked skeptical. "No, really," Emily pressed on. "Sometimes these things even make us money, and we split it between the chamber and the park. Like Submarine Man or the block ice bets."

"I'm sorry?"

"I need to give you a copy of the newspaper. At the end of the pier there, see that line?"

"Which line?"

"The one past the Dips. At the far end. There's a French-Canadian man camped out in a first war sub on the bottom of the lake all summer. You can pay a quarter to talk to him on the phone for two minutes."

"And people *do* that?"

"Sure. We published a picture of him in the paper, and let's just say the ladies would spend more than just a quarter for the chance to flirt with him. And the accent doesn't hurt. We send his food down a chute. Dot's dad buried a guy underground last summer. He made it to the first of August in a glass box you could pay to look through. You'd see him just sitting there, reading magazines and the like. He'd look up and smile and wave. A few summers ago, we had live seals down at the end of the pier. A dime to feed them a fish. We made thousands on that one but even more in publicity when they escaped all over the lake."

By now, Drew Mathison appeared more baffled than impressed, but Emily was still enjoying herself. She was proud of both her lake and her park. Creativity was every bit as much at play here as the visitors still pouring in the front gates.

"I do have another question," he said, turning back to her. She nodded, happy to answer. In that way, this conversation was not unlike the strange back-and-forth game going on nearby involving a coconut carved like a human head. "Do you *make* the news or report the news, Miss Graham?"

Emily laughed off the mild insult. "I make the *fun*. And then I report the news, of course."

"Excuse me. Officer?" This time, it was his turn to be interrupted. A teenage girl with a paper cone of bright pink cotton candy placed a hand on his arm and looked up at him from beneath her lashes.

10

"Yes?"

"I was just wondering." Her voice was high and breathy. "Is your gun real?"

"Yes."

Emily noticed a pair of the kid's friends standing slightly off to the side watching, close enough they could be heard giggling. One of them audibly said "dreamboat." Emily recognized them as school-age locals but couldn't remember their names. The assertive one was batting her lashes and rubbing the officer's arm. Drew looked to Emily for help, but she just grinned. This couldn't be the first time he'd dealt with this.

"Is there something else I can help you with, Miss?"

"I'm lost," the kid said dramatically. The Dips clattered by again, and Emily hoped it covered the sound of her accidental snort-laugh. The girl's perfume warred with the scent of grease from the rides and the fries.

"Uh. Where do you think you're supposed to be?"

"I can't find my parents. I figured I'd better stay with you so I'm safe until they find me. You'll keep me safe until they get here, won't you?"

The two friends were still holding one another upright and fanning themselves. The girl from whom Drew was trying to step away winked up at him now, and Emily decided that was enough for his first day.

"There's a reunion tent over by the beach house," she put in helpfully, shoving her notebook into her satchel. "I can walk you—and your friends—over to wait for your parents."

The girls united to give Emily a comically violent look.

"We'll find it," the leader said spitefully. She offered a final glare for Emily, a blown kiss for the new officer, and a sashay she probably hoped made her look years older.

Emily watched them leave. "Now you owe me a real interview, Mathison."

He blew out a breath. "I have to keep reminding myself that all that is what we were fighting for."

That got Emily's attention. "I'm sorry? *What* were you fighting for?"

He shrugged a broad shoulder. "So that a botched flirtation like that is the biggest challenge a young American girl has to face on a sunny June day."

Chapter Two

The Buckeye Lake Beacon
Saturday, June 1, 1946
Zoning hearing scheduled for mega resort proposal

Emily tripped over a tin bucket of chalk in front of her sister's photography studio.

As the rainbow of chalk stubs clattered across the walkway, she realized her nephew, Charlie, must have left his collection behind. He had been sulky when she'd seen him earlier, having been made to spend most of the holiday weekend with his grandfather at the marina rather than running up and down the boardwalk.

Instead of grinding the chalk bits to powder, Emily nudged them out of the way with the toe of her pump and willed her sister to come unlock her studio door.

"Rosie," she called once more and rapped hard on the door jamb. A "closed for now" sign taped to the door's center didn't necessarily mean Rosie wasn't holed up in the darkroom within.

There was no answer.

Emily needed the prints from this morning's film rolls. She had a deadline. She also supposed it was past time to stop avoiding her perceptive sister. Squinting up the boardwalk, which was beginning to clear out a little as the crowds zeroed in on the ballrooms and the evening lights of the midway, she scanned for Rosie. Then she tried the door handle again and huffed out another breath.

Emily had been urging her sister to house her dark room in the back of the newspaper office one street off the lake, but she had to admit the arrangement would serve herself better than it would serve Rosie, who did far better business here with her tiny showroom. Even the far end of the boardwalk was better than being tucked away at the back of an office full of chain-smoking pessimists.

Still, though. Emily could be typing even now as she waited for Rosie to return from wherever she'd been. She didn't have time for this delay.

So, she considered the bucket of chalk and the great slab of slate that served as a walkway between the wood of the boardwalk and the stoop of the studio. She'd seen little Charlie cover that gray slab with sketches of Captain America's adventures over the last few years while his mother worked. It occurred to her that if it could accommodate a little boy's

13

drawings, it could pass as a layout board for this week's paper.

Who ever said she needed an office of chain-smoking pessimists to get a little work done?

Propping her satchel against the concrete stoop, Emily hiked her skirt up a little to kneel on the cool of the rock. An older couple sauntered by on their way down to the busy pier, but she ignored their curious looks as she let her front page take shape in the gray space before her.

She sketched her title flag — *The Buckeye Lake Beacon* — across the top of the rectangular stone. For kicks, she indicated the little lighthouse that was the paper's signature logo alongside the broader *Beacon* letters. Rosie had claimed most of the artistic talent in their family, but no matter. As long as Emily had her on staff, along with Sammy and his sketching skills, it all kept coming together.

Leaning back on her ankles and then forward again every few seconds, she planned the banner headline and where the big photo would sit. The photo would be the parade, most likely, and maybe one of Toppy on his high wire just under that. A story about Sub Man's first week of submersion on the bottom of the lake would go under the fold. Diving horse, page three.

And there was no getting around running the zoning story, the proposed resort, on the front, even if it was Decoration Day weekend. The year-rounds had been closely following the story of a group called FH Resorts that was trying to tempt the Berkeley family — mostly managed by Emily's pal, Dot Berkeley — into selling off the land near Cranberry Bog for development. Just east of the amusement park, Cranberry Bog was a natural anomaly, a chunk of Canadian marsh that had been deposited in the lake when glaciers receded centuries ago. Its spongy moss ground was home not just to cranberries each autumn but to dozens of other plants not native to the U.S.

Only Emily's desperate fight in the paper had so far kept the commission and council from approving the resort that would destroy a unique piece of nature with its extensive docks.

She scribbled out a headline for that piece. *Resort proposal slated for Thursday ZB meeting.* Emily reconsidered, then sent the fingers of her right hand through it until it blurred and she could rework it.

Her sister interrupted with an apology for running behind.

"Shhh. Thinking."

"I hope that makes sense to you." Emily felt Rosie squat just beside her. *Hearing scheduled for mega resort proposal.* Nearly satisfied, Emily nodded over her sidewalk work. Rosie's index finger landed on the square under the flag. "What photo do you want there?"

"I'd have to see the photos you took to know."

"Yeah, yeah. I got tied up." Rosie shifted her own bag of supplies and stood, beautiful and comfortable as always in an embroidered, flowing skirt. She considered the chalk scribbles again. "You want a shot of the parade there?"

"That's what I figured. Did you get one of those diving clowns on the float?"

"I did, but I think you'll like the one of the band better. It was a great angle."

"Didn't I run the marching band last year?"

"Shriners."

"Oh." Emily sat back and cringed over the tingling pain in both feet. Dusting chalk off her hands, she eased further back to join Rosie on the stoop, the metal door cool against her shoulders. She let her eyes droop shut and lungs fill with fresh, sweet carnival air. "It's high time the season started. That was one long winter."

"That was *a few* long winters. You've been desperate for this place to fill up again."

"The whole lake has been desperate." The war had changed so many things, amusement park summer holidays being the least significant of them.

"It's not about the money for you, though."

"Don't be so sure."

"June through September you have an excuse not to hold still."

Emily, eyes still closed, hated that she could sense Rosie still staring at her.

"Something's bothering you, Em. And the start of the season helps you pretend it away with all the busy. Acting like your deadline is looming when it's days away." Rosie's knee bumped Emily's.

"Hmmph." Showed what Rosie knew. The deadline was perpetual.

"I know I've got you cornered when you stop making words."

"And look at you, just full of them."

"It's not that ridiculous graffiti or vandalism bothering you either, so don't try that." Another family walked by, heading toward the pier. Rosie, waving in her usual pleasant way, waited for them to pass. "Are you hiding something, Em?"

It mattered how someone asked a question. Every reporter knew that. And Rosie had asked hers in the wrong way, which gave Emily just the leeway she needed to tell herself she wasn't lying to her favorite person in the world. People and people's secrets weren't technically "things," after all.

"Of course, I'm not. The paper's getting bigger, that's all. Lots of seasonal ads." She sat up, stretched, and employed the smile she knew fooled people. Then she nudged Rosie's knee in return. "A bigger paper means more photos, you know, staff photographer."

Just a playful, carefree gal, enjoying peacetime and saving a Canadian bog from the bad guys.

"You're more frenzied than ever, for some reason, and what's with that fake smile? What's nipping at your heels?"

Emily rose, letting the smile fade into the twilight. Five hundred yards away, the ballroom was throbbing and gushing with the strains of a lively orchestra and the stomping of thousands of jive bombers who'd paid ten cents a dance.

"Do you ever think about Mom?" She looked back over her shoulder at Rosie to gauge her reaction. They never called Lillian Turnbull Graham "Mom," partly because they never talked about her at all.

Rosie stood up, too, her movements cautious. This was clearly not what she'd been expecting, and Emily figured it served her sister right for pressing.

"No, not really."

"You're lying."

"I don't think about her, not anymore. Not since God gave me Charlie."

"What's Charlie got to do with our mother?"

"When he turned a year old, I looked at him and thought that's how old *you* were when she left. When he turned two, I thought that's how old *I* was when she decided to hit the road. That's about the last time I made time for a thought about her. I mean it."

Rosie was a gentle person, not given to anger. Emily blinked in surprise at the steel under her sister's words. "She was grieving. Her husband had just died suddenly, Rose. She was a professional dancer living on a little island in the middle of a lake surrounded by corn country."

"We were her babies, and she left."

"Raising kids by yourself is hard, and you know it."

"I do know it's hard, and that's why I spend my time with Charlie rather than wasting it thinking about her." Rosie took a breath that somehow managed to sound apologetic. She pushed her hair, bright like Emily's but with red in it, behind her ear. "Why this, Emily? Why is it getting to you now?"

In truth, it had always been "getting" to her, but Rosie's reaction confirmed that Emily was still alone in that. That was why she would keep the telegrams and her dwindling bank account to herself, as she had been all year.

And she'd go on wishing that were still the biggest of her secrets.

"No reason," she said, shrugging. "I guess sometimes I wonder about her. Maybe it's just that we're the age she was when she was making those choices, you know? That's probably what it is."

16

Rosie squinted at Emily as though she were sizing her up through a viewfinder. Whatever she saw in her face now must have reassured her. "Here we are, though. Meeting our obligations." Rosie pressed into Emily with a hug. "Together."

"We sure are." But Emily felt more alone than ever as she followed her sister into the tiny gallery area of the studio.

The walls there were lined with matted and framed shots of the lake, both in and out of season. Rosie, a nature lover, was always far more likely to shoot the sunrise over the lily pads or the nest of a blue heron than she was squealing children on the Dodge 'Em cars.

Emily let her sister fiddle around in the dark room beyond the store for as long as she needed, knowing better than to disturb her there unless expressly invited to do so.

Taking advantage of the moment alone, she folded her arms on the display counter and let her forehead rest there. Just for a moment. She was terribly afraid that this summer season, which had promised to revive the lake and the park and the businesses after the long war, was going to be awfully complicated.

The soft "plop" of early summer raindrops outside the door seemed confirmation. It increased, inevitably, to a splattering downpour.

There went her chalk plans.

"About how many inches?" Rosie called from beyond the door. "For the parade photo?"

"Three" — that was columns — "by four" — that was inches. Emily called it out without raising her head. She'd crop the print with crayon before it went to the engraver's, anyway.

Rosie's studio kitten made her jump to attention, though, when it head-butted Emily's right ankle and then leaned hard as it rubbed itself across the bone there. It tried its impossibly small teeth against that bone, and Emily was reminded of her sister's question a few minutes before. *What's nipping at your heels?*

"Hello." Emily scooped her up and shoved her like a small, gray scarf against her neck. "Bitsy, you smell weird."

"She upset a tub of chemicals this morning," Rosie called by way of explanation from the other side of the door.

"Sheesh, Bits. You may be glowing green this time tomorrow." Emily considered the kitten's face and sniffed her again. "Your eyes already look radioactive."

"She's fine!"

Emily smiled. "Her eyes are the color of green slime. And I think there's a buzzing sound coming from her skull."

"It's called purring. And many, many cats have green eyes."

"Wait till I tell Charlie. Bitsy'll be the star of his next comic strip. Cat

Captain America. Indestructible and on the cover of every issue of the *Beacon*." Developing chemicals or not, Emily buried her lips on the puffy little head, just between warm, paper-thin ears, and gave the cat a kiss. Bitsy pushed her head against Emily's arm, and Emily couldn't help but think of the teenager who had pressed herself just as persistently against the arm of the new police officer at the park.

Sergeant Mathison. Recently out of the Army, looking for "what's next." Emily's thoughts had strayed back to him off and on all day. Perhaps, she thought, she was no better than that shameless kid, though she couldn't identify why the man had stayed there in a corner of her mind.

Emily might have dozed off for a bit before Rosie summoned her to the darkroom. It smelled a lot like the kitten's chemical-covered fur in there, where a print of the marching band glowed, taking form in darks and lights. Rosie hung another beside it on the line, this one of the clowns Emily had requested. Emily stood, arms crossed, and watched it develop. Rosie stood beside her.

Finally, Emily said, "You were right. The angle on the band is superb."

She wished she'd never brought up their mother. Even as she wished she could talk through everything else.

"Sorry I pressed earlier, Em." Rosie regretted it, too, it seemed. They stood together in the dark, breathing the scent of processing fluids. "I have to admit, I have a strange feeling today, too."

"Mmm?"

"Like something's about to happen. Do you ever feel that way?"

"Yes." But Emily knew why her sister was feeling it. Because something — *things* — already were happening.

Chapter Three

The Buckeye Lake Beacon
Tuesday, June 4, 1946
Obituaries

The second time Drew Mathison met Emily Graham, it was on a piece of newsprint, cut out and framed on the wall of the little inn on the north bank where he pretended to sleep at night.

Mostly, he paid a few bucks a week to toss about between nightmares in the only room open for the holiday, which turned out to be part utility closet.

What caught his attention about the clipping in the frame, though, Drew couldn't really say. It wasn't large or ornamented with fancy matting. It was the "Obituary" heading, maybe, that had stopped him on his way out that evening. It seemed like an unusual decorating move.

Also, the last obituary he'd read had been his brother's.

Now that Drew paused to consider a newspaper's brief memorial to a life, he realized he'd never even seen Ronnie's or Coop's or Trigger's obituaries after their bodies had been shipped back from France. In that way, these tidy words on newsprint were an aspect of death he struggled to pair with those other aspects of death. The ones keeping him awake at night.

At any rate, the framed obituary in the hallway was for a sixty-six-year-old woman named Louisa. At first, he skimmed.

She *"went to be with Jesus on March 10, 1937."*

Eight years ago. Nothing to do with the war, then. Jamie had also died in March. He'd been shot late in March, Drew thought randomly, as he read on. And then, as he slowed down ...

Louisa brewed sun tea on the porch and chewed spearmint gum. She was known for her crocheted kerchiefs in every color. She dried and canned and jellied everything that grew. Right up to this past winter, Louisa could be found skating on the ice any time the lake froze. Not the plodding kind of well-meant skating you normally see here on Buckeye Lake, but something like an actual art, like a complex dance executed in a fur-lined coat. She glided in a cloud of frozen breath and loud laughter, which surely is how she arrived in the arms of her Savior last Tuesday morning.

The words blurred. Standing here in the creaky hallway of someone's lakefront rented rooms, Drew felt his brother's death wash over him in an entirely new wave of loss.

Jamie's laugh, after all, had also been loud. He'd usually thrown his head back with it. It was the kind of laugh that could be recognized in a crowd and the kind their mama tried so hard to hush during church.

How long, Drew wondered, before he forgot the sound of it?

"Coffee?"

Startled, Drew did not quite manage to stop the single tear he'd lost before meeting the eyes of the woman called Cookie who ran the place. He straightened from where he'd ended up leaning on the wall, his hands balled into fists. If he took the offered coffee from her, he knew his hand might shake.

"My sister," Cookie said simply, nodding at the frame but keeping her eyes on his. Drew noticed her own eyes glistened, though it had been eight years since she'd lost her sister. He did not find that encouraging. She pressed the cup into his hand without checking to see if his hand shook. "She was something, Louisa was. She was like the sunshine."

That seemed right. Drew had not finished reading, but the image of a sixty-six-year-old ice fairy spinning across the lake seemed to be in keeping with this sister Louisa had left behind. Standing alive before him, Cookie sported dyed orange hair, a mouth caked with red lipstick, and an inner glow that made it feel like a privilege to sleep in her utility room.

Drew cleared his throat. "I've never read an obituary quite like this," he said, and it was true. Mama had given the family each a copy of Jamie's. There'd been nothing in it about his brother's laugh, and they'd spelled his name wrong twice, in two *different* wrong ways.

"My niece wrote that," Cookie said, beaming at the frame. "She was just fifteen at the time her granny died. Burt and I ran the paper back then, and she walked in with those words on a sheet of school paper. Not only did we print it, but I hired her to write up all our obits from that point on. Made *The Beacon* almost famous for it. In fact, we turned the paper over to her not so long ago."

The back of Drew's neck tingled. He glanced back at the obituary. The late Louisa had chewed spearmint gum. She was like sunshine. Louisa *Graham*. Suddenly he was certain he'd already met the granddaughter of the deceased, who must also be Cookie the innkeeper's niece.

"Emily Graham," he said, taking a cautious sip of coffee.

One of Cookie's drawn-on, clay-colored brows arched. "Yes! Emily." She still considered the framed newsprint alongside him. "Somehow you've managed to meet already, then?"

"She wants to write a little story about me or something."

"She's good at it. Might as well let her while you're still above ground to read it."

Drew shook his head because it could not happen.

"Emily took over the whole operation once she finished school. Burt and I were tired, and you already know we're booked solid with this place in the summer. This is plenty to do, I'll tell you." She paused, and Drew understood she was, at root, a storyteller herself. Detectives liked storytellers. "Louisa and Hickory—Hickory is Emily's grandfather, you know—they raised Emily and her sister, Rosie, from the time they were wee little girls. Sad story and not really mine to tell. But they stepped right up and gave those girls the best life they could. The loss of Louisa left them just each other. Emily and Rosie, I mean. And Hickory." She seemed to run through the unspoken parts of the story silently, in her head, like a film flickering behind her eyes. "Anyhow, Louisa's illness and passing … it was a hard time for all of us."

What was Drew supposed to say to that? Was this Cookie's way of convincing him he should allow himself to be interviewed? Poor Emily Graham was an orphan nearly twice over, it seemed. Still, even if pity were enough to move him, there simply could not be a story printed about the newest patrolman at Buckeye Lake Park.

There was still a chance Don Conti wasn't here yet, that he hadn't found Gil Reese yet, that there was still one witness alive who could point to his brother's killers.

"Anyway, you seem like you're no stranger to hard times," Cookie observed with a smile and a brief pat on his arm. Drew could not think of a way to steer the story back toward others again, so he thanked her for the coffee and went back to work as though she hadn't just seen that tear.

Buckeye Lake Beacon
Wednesday, June 5, 1946
BLPD adds seasonal officers

The bright-haired, bright-lipped Cookie Strout would always think of Wednesdays as Deadline Day, no matter how much time had passed since she and Burt had handed *The Beacon* off to Emily.

At first, it had been nice to piddle around her home-turned-inn, taking care of clean sheets and guests. "Retirement," they called it. No copy to type up, no linotype text to set, no ads to sell, no equipment breaking at midnight, no phones to answer, no headlines to write, no distribution to worry about. A welcome change of pace. She had taken to arranging vases of flowers in the sitting room window. She'd added two dogs, Pyramus and Thisbe, to her new life.

Indeed, Cookie had absolutely luxuriated in the freedom of not living on deadline ... for exactly one week.

After that week, she'd marched over to *The Beacon's* office and informed Emily Graham in no uncertain terms that she, Cookie Strout, was going back on the masthead as Office Manager, whether the new owner liked it or not. As the new owner, Emily had laughed joyfully and obeyed her aunt and mentor.

Today Cookie marched, in much the same manner, through the alley that led to the paper. She already had a roast cooking in its own little lake of small potatoes and carrots, so she decided to allow herself a pleasant hour in the office, meddling in her niece's love life.

Deadline Day, she thought as she pulled the back door of the newspaper office shut behind her. The day had its own flavor inside these walls. The back of the office was filled with the usual smoke cloud streaming from the desks of Walt and Sammy. A phone was ringing, and Cookie was familiar enough with Walt to know he'd just made some joke that had the other man chuckling and then sitting straight and muffling his laughter as she strolled through.

"Hail the Queen," Sammy, the ad guy, cheered in her direction from his position at his drafting table.

"Empty your ashtray," Cookie told him. "And no, I didn't bring banana bread for you today."

"Aw, come on, Baby!"

"And be respectful of your elders while you're at it." Cookie kept marching past the hapless sports and general reporter to find Emily sitting cross-legged on top of her desk in a pair of cool linen slacks, looking a little rumpled and talking rapidly into the telephone as she balanced a pen over a notebook on her knee.

There might have been a time when Cookie would have worried about a young, pretty woman holed up in an office with two men, but several factors negated that worry these days. One, Emily was their boss. She was miles smarter and quicker than Walt and Sammy put together, and the boys knew it. They had always known it. And secondly, those clowns in the back were deep-down decent human beings under their raucous laughter, smoking, and half-hearted struggle to behave like gentlemen. Cookie wouldn't have hired them if they hadn't been, nor would her niece have kept them on.

Also, Emily didn't seem to worry overly much about etiquette. If someone had dared to suggest she spent her time in an unfeminine atmosphere, she'd have blinked and gone on with her to-do list. Now, the publisher with a degree, whom Cookie would always think of as a kid, slid the earpiece of the black telephone back into its cradle, scribbled something, and flashed one of her sudden smiles.

"Cookie, Cookie! Please tell me you brought something sweet for those monsters back there."

"Too hot to bake today," Cookie declared wickedly from the chair still reserved for her.

"That's a cop-out," Walt called up. "I bet your guests are getting some kind of pie for dessert tonight."

"They're paying me. All you fools do is annoy me."

"I'll second that," Emily said.

"Em doesn't cook for us at all," Sammy whined. "She's a *career* woman."

"You got that right," was Emily's response. "But I do sign your paycheck, DeNune. Go buy yourself some grub."

"You're never gonna catch a husband with that attitude, *Miss Graham*," Walt put in with a wink, and Sammy laughed.

"If baking sweets catches husbands like you, I vow to stay out of the kitchen all my livelong days," Emily declared, and the men hooted all the louder. She was tattooing a rhythm against her notebook with the end of her pen. Cookie considered her the most lovable and exhausting human being on the planet.

The husband talk made a nice segue, though.

"So, what's up, Cookie? Did you bring any tidbits I need to get in before we put a lid on this thing tonight?" Emily was sliding off her desk and rolling a clean sheet of paper into the typewriter that took up the left side of the desktop. Cookie understood Emily wouldn't bother to pretend *not* to be busy. It was Deadline Day, after all.

"Chief Gunn hired himself a seasonal deputy to pick up some of the slack," Cookie said as casually as possible. The sight of the fellow engaged in some invisible battle in her hallway had been gnawing at her for a full day. She hoped he'd like the pot roast tonight. Pot roast could uphold a man while Jesus worked on his heart.

"Yeah. I met him."

"That's what he said."

"I wanted to add a few sentences about him next to the council story, but he's not having it. Unless you convinced him otherwise, somehow?"

"Drew Mathison is his name. Still looks military. Handsome," Cookie crooned, wiggling her carefully designed brows at her pretty niece. A pretty woman, she thought, might be another kind of healing, if it happened to be the Lord's will. *Pot roast plus a pretty woman could equal a cure.*

"Not a talker."

"He's a good man. I can tell from his eyes. He has kind eyes."

Emily rolled her own. "The fact you're still talking about him makes me think you've got some plan. Tell me it doesn't involve me getting married and settling down with a passel of kind-eyed, gray-eyed babies."

"Interesting you noticed the color of his eyes, dear. I didn't say they were gray."

Emily flashed her a grin. "Just because I'm an official old maid doesn't mean I can't appreciate a good-looking man, Cook. He somehow came all the way here from Philadelphia, you know, for a part-time gig. Strikes me as odd." She blinked twice, slowly, then closed her eyes and yawned expansively. She swiveled her head in Cookie's direction. "These dummy days are going to start getting longer and longer for the summer. We jumped an extra broadsheet page this week."

"Dummy days" was a new term for Emily's regime here at *The Beacon*. While Cookie and Burt had literally cranked out a small, simple tabloid on the Mergenthaler linotype machine in the back, Emily had returned from college insisting on photos and illustrations ... and more time spent gathering stories than setting type. For the past two years, she'd contracted with her fellow weekly in Pataskala for the actual printing. Which meant Emily would be working tonight until she could drive a box of dummied layout pages, typed stories, ad sketches, and zinc photo engravings down Route 40 before dawn.

"Want me to come back over after dinner, lend a hand?"

"I wouldn't send you packing," Emily said with warmth. "I'd like to squeeze in a couple hours of sleep before I have to be out at the new bait shop for the grand opening first thing in the morning."

"Hook, Line 'n Sinker, right? That Wally's place, from church?"

"That's the one. Hey, when you come back, Cookie ... maybe you could sneak me a piece of leftover pie from dinner? You always make a pie, so no excuses."

"Honey, you know there are never any leftovers of my peach pie."

"You're killing me."

"Me too," Sammy called from his fog of smoke.

~~~~~

Emily slid a piece of chewing gum into her mouth and hammered out an updated Community Calendar. She spared Dot Berkeley a quick glance when the bells on the front door jingled her entrance.

"On deadline, Dottie," she grumbled around the fresh piece of gum.

"What's up, sweetie?" Cookie asked, rising to intercept Dot at the door, but the young woman strolled casually beyond the counter and back to Emily's desk, surprising no one. It could be said she walked around like she owned the place, which wasn't far from the truth. Her family owned most of the north shore and park. She was dressed, as usual, in a pencil skirt, lightweight jacket, and heels. Her dark, curly hair was pulled back in a bun. This was how she oversaw Buckeye Lake Park every day on behalf of her family, even now that the war was over. None of the other

Berkeleys, after all, were half as efficient as Dot.

"When are we getting together for that story about the Crystal Ballroom expansion, Em?"

"Don't know." Emily offered her a piece of gum, but Dot shook her head in mild disdain. "Pitch it to me again."

"You said you'd run the lineup of bands for the summer, and we'd frame it with all the new lighting. Improvements, updates. But the season's already underway."

"Let's do it for next week, then."

"Can Rosie shoot a photo?"

"Friday night. The Graham sisters will head out there, if you can meet us. Rosie can get pics of … what? Those new updates you're talking about. Folks dancing?" Dot nodded at that. "You can fill me in while she does it," Emily added, already back to work.

"Also, here's an ad about a military discount to the park for next week." Dot pulled a tidy sketch out of her narrow briefcase. "Is it too late to get it in this week?"

Emily managed to finish typing a sentence and glare at her friend simultaneously. "Sammy!?" she shouted back into the space behind her.

"Yeah, boss?"

"Miss Berkeley doesn't think ad deadlines apply to her. Do you have time to work this up for Pataskala? Looks like it'll just need a flag from the archives. Simple."

"You got room for that somewhere?"

"I'll make it work if you can draw it up."

"Bring it back here."

Dot's heels clicked back through the office, and Emily took the opportunity to pound out three more calendar listings before her friend's inevitable return. "Stop telling people we're threatening you over the whole bog thing, Emily."

Emily grinned and looked up, still typing.

"You know threats aren't my style," Dot insisted.

"I can't help it if people assume you're heartless. I haven't said a word. You know I just …"

"'Publish the facts.' Sure."

"Listen, Dottie." Emily gave in to her friend's presence, sitting back and massaging her own shoulder. "I noticed you never rented the old woodworking shop on the boardwalk for this season."

Dot arched a brow. "You want it?" At a nod, she quoted a price that made Emily growl.

Now that it belonged to her, Emily had been trying to move *The Beacon* up to the shore for a year.

Several years before, Dot had helped Rosie out with that very affordable studio space for her photography business. Rosie, after all, had been a single mother trying to support herself and Charlie in a town that judged everything and forgot nothing.

Despite the fact Dot had been closer to Emily than to Rosie, she had never compromised with any similar deal for her old buddy, owner of the town's newspaper. For a year, they'd been doing this dance, and for a year the rent quoted was too steep.

"I just need a fair price to move the operation up there, Dottie."

"I'm always fair."

"You're punishing me for the editorials about the resort proposal, aren't you? You can't sell the beach property as long as the zoning commission drags its feet, and you're blaming me for that."

"Maybe I am blaming you. But I'm *not* painting threats on your windows and car. The beach will sell, irregardless of your published arguments against the development."

"'Irregardless' isn't a word. It's just 'regardless.'"

"When was the last time you slept, Emily? You don't seem like yourself lately."

Emily ignored her and turned back to the Lion's Club pancake breakfast listing.

"Also, why can't you afford that rent? You should be able to."

"I can't."

"The paper is flourishing," Dot said. This was as close as she came to a compliment, Emily knew.

"Of course, it is," Cookie put in. "It's her bridegroom."

"So, why can't you afford boardwalk rent?" Dot pressed.

Emily typed two "e's" instead of one, her neck hot. "I just can't."

"Want me to look over your books?" Dot liked to remind people of her accounting skills at every opportunity.

"I'm not mismanaging or anything like that." Emily pretended Cookie wasn't watching her suspiciously. The former owner of the paper knew Emily, with double the ads and subscribers, should absolutely have enough revenue for two boardwalk rentals, even with the cost of contracting out the printing.

And her aunt knew Emily's neck got red when she was uncomfortable.

But Cookie didn't pry like Dot or Rosie, for which Emily was grateful; after all, when it came down to it, her aunt had always been the hardest of all to dodge when she meant business.

Taking a deep breath, Emily leveled a look at her business tycoon pal and reminded herself that a little building in an alley was a fine place from which to publish a quality newspaper. "I'll see you Friday, Dottie. I have a paper to build tonight."

Chapter Four

The Buckeye Lake Beacon
Thursday, June 6, 1946
East Bank home to new bait shop

A hand-painted sign reading "Hook, Line 'n Sinker" had been hung above a canvas Grand Opening banner. Unfortunately, Drew noticed "opening" had been painted with two "n's" instead of one.

After a few days, he had determined he would get further gathering information with a fishing pole than he was getting with his local police badge. He just needed a few supplies.

The illusive Gilbert Reese, it turned out, was a PK. A Preacher's Kid. And his dad, commonly known only as Pastor Skip, led the lake area's First Community Church.

Church, therefore, was the *second* place Drew decided to search for his witness, after first checking the poker tables in the back of Wright's Drug Store on Saturday night. When no one matching Reese's description was visible at either spot, the parsonage seemed like the next possibility. Word on the street was that Pastor Skip's boy had not yet come home from the Army, but Drew knew better.

How, he wondered, *do you go about interrogating a preacher?*

During Sunday's sermon, Drew learned Pastor Skip loved to fish off his dock. This had not come as a surprise, since both church and parsonage were positioned on the north shore of Buckeye Lake, and fishing itself was such an apparently biblical pastime. It stood to reason the man might be honest and forthcoming by nature—even if his son hadn't turned out that way—so Drew decided it was time to fish off the church's dock, himself. From there, he expected to be able to see who might be coming and going from the parsonage in the quiet hours, and he very much expected the obviously friendly pastor to join him there.

That, he figured, was how to interrogate a fisher of men.

Which was how he found himself contemplating a spelling error on the Grand Opening sign at the Hook Line 'n Sinker bait shop early in the morning. The dewy quality of the air and light reminded him of the slight chill on a construction site while the coffee was still hot and, also, of mornings in France when the dew had soaked his boots on patrol.

He turned when a convertible Cabriolet joined his truck in the small lot, the words "Swamp Rat" painted rather tragically across the back. With a heart. Drew gave himself permission to just enjoy watching the driver climb out of the vandalized automobile. He figured there was only one thing a young woman dressed in a professional but attractive pantsuit could be doing first thing in the morning at the grand opening of an unimpressive looking bait shop … and the reporter's notebook once more flapping out of her leather satchel confirmed it.

Drew's driver's side door squawked as he muscled it shut. Jamming his hands in his pockets, he kept watching Emily Graham and braced himself for a round of early morning questions. He figured it probably wouldn't be him doing the asking.

"Well, well, well," she called merrily. "Doing some fishing on your day off?" He'd been right. Her heels crunched the gravel as she crossed to him and, again, shook a hand he hadn't offered. "Emily Graham. We met Saturday?"

"Yes. I remember." He shouldn't like that *she* remembered. Her golden hair was a little windblown from its trip in the convertible. For a woman whose clothes were so fine, she seemed surprisingly unconcerned about the untidy condition of that wavy hair. She shoved a gloved hand through it and grinned, then gestured with the same hand at the painted words scrawled across her car's trunk.

"What do you think of their handiwork?"

"Anything new, after the soap profanity?"

"No, Sergeant. I figure you've intimidated them into upright living. Thank you for handling it."

He had filed the report at the office after speaking with her on the pier, and that had been that. There was nothing more to do.

The sparkle in her eyes said she knew as much, but she continued, "I just drove this week's edition to the printer early this morning. Sorry to say, there's no story about the new police sergeant in it."

They walked together toward the door. "Well, thank you for that."

"You still owe me. I rescued you from your young damsel in distress, don't forget."

"But then I scared off your soap tormentors. I'd say we're even." Drew watched Emily shake her head a little mournfully, but he wasn't sure if it was in response to him or to the "Grand Openning" typo sign she'd just noticed on the white block building.

"Wally, Wally, Wally," might be what she muttered as she picked her way across the gravel, and then she asked, "You fish much?"

"Thought I'd better outfit myself for it, since I'm living on a lake for a while. Wasn't sure what time this place opened. You?"

"Do I fish? Sure." She yawned. "Just not today. Not on three hours of sleep." As she preceded him a step or two, he noticed a camera in a case slung across her back. It reminded him of his own shoulder holster, mostly hidden beneath his button-down cotton shirt. "I promised Wally a business feature about his new place, see if we can drum him up some customers. He's a good guy. Did you meet Wally at church on Sunday?"

Drew shook his head. Emily Graham had noticed him at First Community, he realized, and he was surprised when this knowledge, too, brought pleasure. Something dead inside of him flopped around like it might come back to life.

When she opened the door ahead of him, though, a gush of water spilled out and over the open toes of her powder blue shoes ... along with a few dying minnows, also flopping around.

Drew stepped back. "What in the ...?"

Emily made some female sound of distress as she poked her head in, while he tried to process why they should be greeted at the door by flowing water.

"Just a second, Wally. I'm here!" she called again through the open door. "Give me just one second!"

With that, Emily backed out and closed the door against the mild current, toeing one tiny fish back over the threshold. She thrust her satchel at Drew and wiggled free of the camera bag. With efficient movements, she kicked off her shoes, shucked her summer gloves off, and rolled her pants legs up above her knees.

Drew usually preferred a skirt to slacks on a woman, but he figured one with legs like this probably had to wear slacks sometimes as a nod toward traffic safety.

"Would you mind just running my things back out and tossing them in the back of my car, Officer Mathison? It seems Wally needs a friend more than he needs a feature story on the day of his grand opening."

And then she was splashing back through the front door of the shop before Drew had time to speak. Or understand what was happening.

Uncertain of what exactly this situation called for, Drew obediently stuffed Emily Graham's reporter tools under the dash of the passenger seat of the Cabriolet. The cop in him resisted the urge to poke around her car out of curiosity.

Maybe he should just drive up the lake road to another bait shop to get the basic fishing supplies he'd started out for in the first place. He really needed to take up his post near the parsonage and cast a line.

Bait the pastor, so to speak.

Curiosity, though, had him heading back into the unfortunate shop with its inexplicable flood. How would this not-so-grand opening be portrayed by the press? Was it some bizarre bait store sabotage, and was this Wally in need of the law?

Drew stood back to open the glass door, again to be met with a tiny but forceful wave of water the color of the cement floor beneath it. This time, he also caught the noxious odor of dead and dying fish. There was no sign of Emily or the shop's owner, but he could hear voices coming from what might be a storeroom in the back. Drew toed off his own shoes next to Emily's heels by the door, stuffed his socks inside them, and rolled up the denim over his calves.

Some detective work, he thought. Just another strange twist in a week of frustration, watching sunburned vacationers blow their money while he haunted poker games after dark. No one looked like the picture in his pocket. He hoped for the hundredth time Gilbert was simply hiding in the parsonage and the pair of them would be on the road back to Reno by tomorrow at the latest.

All he needed was a pole and a pack of worms so he'd look something like a fisherman.

Meanwhile, the water on the cement floor was cold. Though Drew usually had a strong stomach, the smell of death and foul water threatened the cinnamon bun he'd had at the diner. He gave in to a muffled belch and took a deep breath through his mouth. The water didn't quite reach his ankles, and countless bait fish were mostly dead, half-floating around his feet. He waded slowly alongside racks of bobbers, hooks, knives — all the usual wares of a bait shop. At eye level, he was watched accusingly by an enormous bass swimming in a display tank. Probably grateful to have survived the carnage of whatever had happened to the floor, Drew figured.

In the back room stood what must be Wally, a wiry man in his forties with a calico goatee and a hoarse voice. Emily stood close to him, rubbing a hand briskly up and down the black suspender straps on Wally's back.

"We need to just take the sign down," he groaned on a hiccup.. "This isn't gonna work. Not today. We need to ..."

"Nonsense. We just need some mops," Emily said. "Mops, push brooms, buckets, shovels. You still have plenty of merchandise to sell. Let's move! Oh, good. Officer. There you are! This is Officer Drew Mathison, Wally."

"I didn't do nothing illegal!" Wally squawked.

"No, no. Of course not. Drew here just wants to buy bait."

"Bait! There's no live bait here," Wally said with a wild look in his eye. "My live bait is dead. It's all dead!"

"Wally left the hose turned on last night in the live bait tank, Drew," Emily explained in a very calm voice. Something about the way she said Drew's name so casually made it seem like she'd known him forever. He supposed that was just one of the many tricks at the disposal of newspaper reporters.

Detectives did that, too.

"It's the second time I've flooded the place in a week," Wally confessed glumly, pounding the heel of his hand punishingly against his own forehead. Beside him, the ever-resilient Emily blanched a bit. "The second time I've had to restock my live bait. I left the hose running Monday, too. Do you *know* how expensive that is? I'm ruined! And today … today's the grand opening. And it smells *so bad!*"

"The thing to do, Wally, is to post a reminder by the back door that says, 'Turn the hose off before leaving.' Then you'll stop doing that," Emily declared, apparently determined to rally. Drew noticed she was chewing gum again, possibly to keep from gagging. "We'll push this water out of here, along with all the dead live bait, and you'll sell *worms* today, Wally. You'll sell worms and poles and bobbers to all your friends who are coming here to buy bait, and your business will be a tremendous success. And you'll use all the money you get from the worms to buy live bait that's *alive*. And then you'll make that sign to remind you to turn off the hose when you go home. That's what we're going to do."

She'd stopped patting his back and started pushing through the deeper water of the back room toward what might be a broom closet. Drew crossed to help her, trying not to find the way she attacked the water with her ankles so intriguing.

"Your worms are alive, I trust," Emily called to Wally over her shoulder.

"Huh? Yeah. The worms are. I guess."

"Officer Mathison … Drew, here, wanted worms to fish with anyway. Didn't you, Drew? Didn't you want worms?"

"That's exactly what I came for. Worms."

"*Lots* of worms, right?" Emily prodded, the barest of smiles flirting with the right corner of her mouth. She shoved a push broom at him, then looked beyond him impatiently. "Wally, for heaven's sake, people will be here in forty-five minutes. Dry those tears and let's dry this floor. Here. Put the dead fish in this bucket so we can move 'em out of here. My, but they do stink already, don't they?"

So, Wally went to work scooping the remains of his no-longer-live bait into the bucket. The few survivors went back to the tank, probably nervously. Drew imagined shallow water over cold cement flooring was not a habitat they'd enjoyed, for all that they'd made it. Several of the unlucky ones were beached near a drain in the corner, where the water trickled down and out.

Once Wally had those fish carcasses up, Drew started pushing the water from the back room forcefully toward the drain. Emily had taken a bucket into the showroom, where she sang a tuneless but exuberant rendition of "Chattanooga Choo Choo."

As the water levels rapidly went down and Emily's antics rang through the smelly store, Wally began to visibly relax. "It's going to be okay," he said in his husky voice.

"Sure it will," Drew told him, but privately he had doubts. Who killed their inventory twice in one week through carelessness? He made up his mind to buy as many fishing supplies as seemed remotely reasonable today. This man did need help.

"Rosie's on her way over. I just called her," Emily announced to Wally ten minutes later. "She's bringing two huge candles that smell like Christmas and a pan of peppermint puffs. That ought to take care of the smell, huh?"

"They smell … like Christmas?"

"Yeah, pine needles and whatnot." At the business owner's skeptical look, she cocked a hip and planted a fist on it. "It's pine needles or dead fish, Wally. Those are your choices."

"The candles are fine. Thank you," Wally said obediently.

"That's more like it. Also, Charlie agreed to dig up all the worms he can find to see you through until you can restock the wee fishies." And then she whistled the same song she'd been singing before.

The floor was still damp, and the store still smelled off when the first real customers wandered in, but they didn't seem too concerned. Sweaty and armed with brown bags of soil and over-priced night crawlers, Drew lingered by the front door, waiting to walk Emily to her car. He wasn't sure why. Maybe it was that they'd been through something unexpectedly dreadful together. It wasn't quite war-torn France, but there was some dim connection between those experiences and the carnage in this shop.

He imagined her writing an obituary in honor of the fish. Then he imagined himself crying while reading it. In front of a woman named Cookie.

He was still taking in long breaths of fresh air outside the door when Emily came out, armed with two paper sacks of fishing supplies of her own. Her hair, windblown before, was now stuck to her forehead and cheeks and the back of her long neck from the heat and the sweat of their labors. Her face lit with a smile when she saw him standing beside her shoes, and Drew wondered how it was possible to physically *feel* someone's smile. It seemed to reach out and touch. And then she stopped to hold a peppermint puff out to him.

"Open up, hero." Rising on her toes, she popped the bite-sized dessert firmly into his mouth and turned to retrieve her shoes while he chewed. "Wally's doing just fine now, and you've got yourself a week's worth of worms to drown. And one of Rosie's famous peppermint puffs. That's what I call a morning well spent."

It was, he thought, a moment as nice as the weather. He swallowed most of the treat. "What about you?" he asked around the rest of it.

"Hmm?"

They started slowly toward their cars, and she breathed in the fresh air with obvious gratitude.

"What about your story? You didn't get your interview. Or your pictures."

"Oh, that." She waved it away and dropped the sacks onto the floor of her back seat. She handed him the rest of the desserts she'd carried out, wrapped in a piece of wax paper. "I could write that story in my sleep. Coming out here was more to give Wally a kick. I'll come back and get a photo of him after things calm down. Maybe after he stops sweating quite so much. I've got nearly a week to put it together. He needs the advertising."

"I guess he does."

Emily searched for and located her car keys in the glove box. To do it, she had climbed across the seat with one leg like a gangly child, not the least self-conscious, jingling the keys as she resurfaced. She hopped back out, rounded the back of the car, and stopped to shake Drew's hand, which, once again, he hadn't offered.

"It's been a pleasure, Deputy. Thank you."

"I'm not a deputy, but you're welcome."

"Right. Happy fishing, officer. Er, Sergeant. I'm off to proof galley sheets."

And with that mysterious statement, she scooted back onto her seat, flashed him another smile, and sprayed a little gravel as she pulled out of the parking lot. Drew stood there in the company of his worms a few minutes more, eating his peppermint puff in the sunshine.

Chapter Five

The Buckeye Lake Beacon
Thursday, June 6, 1946
Church plans ice cream social Saturday

The sun was high by the time Drew settled onto the end of the empty dock with his surprisingly hearty-looking nightcrawlers. When he'd been here Sunday for church, the three docks reaching into the lake from the church property had been framed with boats. Folding wooden chairs had filled an expanse of grass that was empty now but for two wandering ducks.

A simple, brick building with a bell mounted on a pole out front sat on the other side of the wide lot, where he supposed First Community had their services when the weather didn't cooperate. The adjacent parsonage was painted a cheerful but fading yellow. A gardening shed was across an alleyway with an open window. From beneath his cap, Drew watched absolutely nothing move at the parsonage. Nor the shed. Nor the church.

The two ducks watched him sitting there.

Cookie and Burt, who loved to brag about running the newspaper for decades, were a wealth of information. Even if they hadn't generously cut him a break on the rate for his little closet of a room, he'd have considered his stay there fortunate because they were perpetual talkers. All he'd needed to do was inquire about a place to worship on Sundays, and off they went. From them, Drew had learned the story of the Reese family, listening all the time for clues about where to find the preacher's kid who supposedly hadn't yet returned from the war.

Clemmie Reese had passed away a few years back from a bad heart, Cookie had said, leaving Pastor Skip and Gil on their own. After Gil had joined the Army, Skip had found himself suddenly the guardian of an orphaned great-niece belonging not to his own family but to his late wife's.

"Hopefully Gilbert will get himself home soon," Burt had said, barely disguising a note of disapproval. "To lend a hand."

"Because a hand *is needed*," Cookie put in with an arch of her brows. "The child is a handful. Not that Gilbert, that rascal, is anyone's idea of a good influence."

The report had seemed a little convoluted and morbid. Still, the information turned out to be helpful when, seated on the end of the dock in front of the church property, Drew was slapped upside the head with a dead fish.

It hit more of his shoulder than his head, actually, after flying through the air. As it thumped, heavy and dead onto the decking, there was a distinct giggling from the water below. This giggling was an important clue that this fish was not the work of a gangster hitman.

War had numbed Drew. What did a normal man his age do when assaulted with a fish? As usual, his own lack of alarm was the thing that most alarmed him.

He leaned to the side and regarded the watery shadows just under the dock. His fishing line extended into the sun, but tucked just below him was the source of the laughter, and it had braids. Then he looked back at the fish, white and bloated and stinking beside him. *What was it about this day and dead fish?*

"At least you didn't take that thing off my line, I guess," he said easily. He peered back down to see the braids floating now. Their owner had dropped under the water line, but bubbles of laughter boiled around them.

Behind Drew, the slap of a screen door caught his attention. Pastor Skip was dressed far more casually than he had been for preaching, emerging and tearing across the lawn toward the dock in swim bottoms and no shirt. The white hair curling on his shoulders more than his head must have once been red like his son's.

"*Delia!*"

"Shhhhh," gurgled from below, with some small splashes. Drew looked back down at the bobber on the end of his line and figured it was just his luck that he'd found Pastor Skip's *other* child hiding beneath the dock. Where was the older one hiding?

And then, there was young Delia floating placidly in the center of an innertube just to his right. She had freckles and one front tooth, and Drew understood with just that glance what Cookie and Burt had meant. This child was too much for Pastor Skip Reese, who had now reached the dock, breathless.

"There you are. Why didn't you answer?"

"Did you think I drowneded?"

Pastor Skip ignored that and regarded Drew now that he did know the child was alive. He squinted, and Drew was impressed when he placed him. "Sergeant Mathison." He looked down at his own half-dressed state and at the stinking fish resting in peace between his bare foot and Drew's leg. A toothy smile stretched wide. "I apologize for my attire. I can go put on clothes if you'd rather," Skip said. "I've always been more comfortable in my swim duds than trousers, myself, but I've found folks have trouble swallowing spiritual advice from a dripping wet rag of a fella."

"I don't need spiritual advice." Drew figured that was probably a lie, but he also remembered lies were a necessary part of his work.

"You've met Delia?"

"Not exactly. Though this is her fish." Drew looked down at the kid and nodded. "I'm Sergeant Mathison. A pleasure to meet you, ma'am."

Her smile was like a jack-o-lantern.

Pastor Skip picked up a long birch pole from the edge of the dock. "Where did you get the fish, Delia?"

"The lake," she said simply. "It died. I'm getting out of the tube now."

"No. Stay put." Then the pleasant pastor surprised Drew by stretching out the pole to the innertube and shoving the raft out further into the lake. Delia's braids dragged behind in the water. The tube was tethered to the dock, Drew saw now, with a long, dingy rope. When Delia was pouting and bobbing about twenty feet out, the pastor carefully laid the birch pole down, kicked the dead fish off the edge of the dock, and joined Drew.

"This is the easiest way to keep tabs on her," he said, by way of explanation. "When school's out, she's a full-time job. I make her sit out there so I can have some peace. She's supposed to be thinking about how to make the world a better place."

"I see."

According to this philosophy, little Delia was theoretically thinking about making the world a better place when she'd heaved the dead fish below the dock at his head. He didn't know what to say, so he watched her leaning over the edge of the tube to retrieve something else from the depths of the lake.

"She's your child?" Drew figured this was a fine place to start.

"My ward. A gift from God and my late wife's family. God rest all their souls."

"You have a son, as well."

Pastor Skip didn't seem to think anything of his family being common knowledge. That was probably the way it was for a pastor in a small community. "A grown son, yes. He's out West. Stationed there during the war."

Drew nodded. There was nothing dishonest in the response. In fact, the pastor's eyes were soft and assessing, open and curious, already accepting Drew as a friend.

"And you?" the man asked. "You were in the war?"

"Yes, sir. I was an MP Sergeant, 793rd battalion."

"793rd? Weren't you the fellas doing recon and security for the Red Ball Express?"

"That's right." He and his men had supported the convoys carrying supplies to American troops after the D-Day invasion, unrelieved for days on end with no rations. But hunger had been the easy part. "I served for a time with the Criminal Investigation Division, as well."

"Well, I hope you're not here to investigate this old man." Skip's words were punctuated by a chuckle of delight. Drew sighed. This was not the unease of a man who was hiding his grown kid in the kitchen pantry. *Blast it.*

"Seen Gilbert lately, sir?"

Drew had done it intentionally: casually used the name the man hadn't provided. It caused the pastor's eyes to meet his own. "No. No, I haven't."

From here, it was partly a matter of following a script. "When was the last time you saw him?"

The other man sighed again, low and long. He watched Delia squirming around on the tube, which was slowly drifting back toward them. "I'd like to tell you we shared a delightful Christmas holiday together, but I don't lie. It's been a couple of years." He closed his eyes for a full half-minute. Was he praying? Then he looked back. "Son, why don't you tell me why you're really here? Is Gil ... missing? Dead?"

The bleak confusion in Pastor Skip's eyes deepened Drew's own regrets. It reminded him that the young man he'd been considering as little more than a coward had once bounced on this other man's knee.

"Your son was good friends with my youngest brother, sir. In Reno, 3rd Operational Training Unit at Stead Air Force Base."

"Oh ... Jamie? Yes! Jamie Mathison! Forgive me for not making the connection."

"There's no reason you would have." Drew swallowed, then pulled his cop's voice around him like a cloak to get through the hard parts. "My brother Jamie was killed on March 22nd, Pastor."

The older man's brows slammed together, his eyes immediately compassionate and worried at the same time. "Lord, have mercy." He said it like a real prayer, his hand sliding over his face. Drew steeled himself against that compassion and worry, but he couldn't shut out the comfort in Skip's whispered, "I'm so sorry, son."

"Your own son witnessed the murder, sir. I don't know where he is, and he represents the only way to bring Jamie's killers to justice."

The pastor looked down at the water, shaking his head slowly, trying to take it all in. Was he feeling relief that the dead man wasn't his son? Shame that Gilbert hadn't gone straight to the cops?

Delia, having drifted a little closer, swiveled in the raft and squinted up at Drew.

"Did you figure out what happened to the fish?" When Drew hesitated, she called, "The fish that died. Did you figure out how it died?"

"Um. No."

"Aren't you a police?"

"Yes, ma'am."

Pastor Skip blew out a frustrated breath and reached for the birch pole to send his little blessing from God twenty feet back out into the lake. "Delia, the lake is full of fish. Sometimes they die. Leave Sergeant Mathison alone. One dead fish isn't cause for concern, okay?"

"It's cause for concern if you're that fish," she insisted. "Heeyyyyy!" The pole pushed her back out, still enumerating suspicious aspects of the fish's death from a distance. "I think its eyes were open when it died. Did you see how they're stuck open?"

In spite of everything, Drew fought a grin. He wondered if this little girl would one day be investigating crimes. Or working at the local newspaper with Emily Graham.

Having had time to process, Pastor Skip looked back up at Drew now, his eyes a little damp. "Do you think Gil's still alive?"

"He was still alive after the shooting. I talked to a dancer who'd hidden him immediately afterward."

"I just don't know." Skip was shaking his head now. "I don't know what those boys could've been doing for something like this to happen."

"From what I could tell in Reno, the pair of them started gambling a little at Harolds Club not long after they were first stationed there," Drew said.

"Yes, that much I do know. I talked to Gilbert about it on the phone once, suggested he stop after the first time he went worse than broke. But the only thing he stopped doing was telling me things."

"The Conti brothers, as they're known, went out from New York to make some money through gambling and started The Fox, another casino," Drew explained matter-of-factly. "That would be Crank and Big Joe Conti."

"Crank and ...? Who mixes with people named that, I ask you?"

"Gilbert and Jamie didn't at first. It was a connection from my brother's bookkeeping classes. He'd been taking them to help with our family's construction company." Drew could not allow himself to think of Mathison Construction without Jamie. "He met Don Conti, a nephew of the Contis, there at school, and they met up again out at the casino. I have no way of connecting the dots from there, except the dancer hinted there was some skimming going on at the casino."

"And Gil and Jamie knew about it."

"I'm guessing Jamie more than knew about it. He was a genius with numbers." There was no room for disappointment, not with everything else, so Drew pushed it down. "Gilbert was in on it, too, and apparently, they were making good money by the war's end. It all blew up when the

Contis did some kind of financial injury to someone my brother considered a friend. Tricked him out of a chunk of cash or something. Whatever it was, there was obviously no out for Jamie by then."

"They probably wanted to come home but couldn't," Pastor Skip decided. Drew nodded. It was possible. "And then they just ... killed your brother?"

"The dancer said Gilbert came upon Jamie arguing with Don. Saw him get shot and killed. Don saw Gilbert and chased him afterward, but he did manage to escape."

Pastor Skip was pale beside Drew. They both watched Delia, who was singing some song out on her raft. She looked vulnerable. Had one of the Contis made the connection? Had he been here yet and watched this little girl and old man? There were so many reasons the answers here had to come quickly.

"Gilbert got a bus ticket back here to the lake, Pastor. I need your help to find him before the Contis do."

Surprise flashed in the older man's eyes. "You think he's *here*? At the lake?"

"He bought a ticket, yes."

Pastor Skip looked around a little dazedly, like he expected to see his son peeking out from behind a tree on the bank. He seemed to understand fully now why Drew was here. "I don't know where he is. I would tell you if I did."

"I believe you."

"Do you want to search the parsonage and just make sure? Don't take my word for it."

"Have you looked in your shed recently?"

"Got bird food out of it this morning. But you can look through it. And all through the church." He squinted back out at Delia, as though pondering if she were somehow capable of supplying a grown man with food. Drew thought it didn't seem beyond possibility. The pastor ran a hand over the back of his neck. "What will you do with him when you find him? With Gil?"

"I'll take him back to Reno to testify, sir. We need to keep other people from being gunned down at the whim of a man named Crank. I'll keep him safe."

"I can see he has an obligation to bear witness to the truth. Of course, he does." The pastor seemed sad. "But where would he go?"

"He needs to be well hidden. He'd be very afraid."

"He probably wouldn't come here because he didn't want to involve little Delia and me, right?" The idea seemed to give the father some degree of personal solace, so Drew agreed. "The problem is, he knew *everyone* around here."

"Who was his closest buddy in school? Does that fella have a good hiding spot, by any chance?"

Pastor Skip's brows drew together, then shot up. "Black-Pool Farms."

"Black pool?"

"Smokey Black was a good pal to Gil, and his family owns pretty much all the country to the west of the lake. No end of barns and fields and hiding places. Head out the old canal road, and you can't miss Black-Pool Farms." A restless energy had overtaken the old man. "Smokey's still at an evergreen conference until tomorrow, maybe, or the next day, but then you can head out and ask him. He's a Navy guy, himself." Pastor Skip toyed with the rope that kept Delia from floating away. "I know it doesn't look good that my boy didn't come to me when he needed help. But … we've had our disagreements over the years, I guess. My son and me."

"I'm in no position to judge anyone else's relationships, Pastor." Drew reeled in his empty fishing line. He wouldn't need it anymore. "You'll get word to me at the station if you do hear from Gilbert, right? Even if he tells you it's not safe to tell me. Please know you can trust me."

"I do. I can see why you would do everything you could to keep him safe."

"And be wary of strangers, for the time being. If I traced him back here, you know the others can too, right?"

"I think I understand the danger, yes." Pastor Skip watched Drew pack his gear. "I'm sorry for your loss, son. My profession dictates I reassure you that God has a plan in all this."

"But you're not going to because you know I'm not buying it?"

"No, I *am* going to reassure you of that very thing. But not because my profession dictates it." Pastor Skip winked. "Because I believe it. God will work this out for the good if you stay open to letting Him."

"Okay. Of course."

Chapter Six

The Buckeye Lake Beacon
Friday, June 7, 1946
Pier Ballroom welcomes Carla's Hermanos

The low cloud cover that had plagued Buckeye Lake since dawn seemed to be lifting, almost as if the sky itself understood it was Friday night, the weekend again, and it needed to do its part for ambiance. The last of the clouds reflected the pastels of twilight as they moved east. Emily, satchel slapping its familiar rhythm against her hip, made her way from the boardwalk to the pier, a little late for her meeting with Dot at the Crystal Ballroom.

Dot would accuse her of pouting about their rental standoff, but that was not why she was running behind. She'd simply changed from a lemon dancing dress — Emily jitterbugged with more energy than skill whenever she could make time — into a dress that more suited her mood. And the cloud cover.

This dress was the quiet color of fog, and it would do for an interview with Dot, an early evening, and maybe a book before she nodded off for a few hours. Her one concession to her weakness for the latest fashion: a pair of open-toed opal heels with a dainty strap around the ankle. She glanced down, pleased, careful not to let that heel slide between the planks on the pier. Water lapped a sleepy cadence against the pilings below. She moved by habit toward the ballroom ahead, feeling the pier boards vibrate beneath her feet, signaling, along with the music, that the dancing was well underway by now.

She prayed again as she walked, reminding herself she could talk to someone about all the secrets. God would sort it all out. She could *do all things* with His help. How many times had Grandma Louise reminded her of that? He had made her strong, able to make bold decisions, able to juggle problems, able to keep it all moving forward. She knew it was true. *She* could do it all because *God* could do it all, right?

This was a pep talk she'd perfected in recent weeks.

But she was also perfecting an ulcer, one forming from a suspicion that Granny's biblical reminder might not apply to outright deception.

The laughter of couples spilled out with light from the ballroom onto the pier. There was a little knothole in the wood of one of the lower walls, and the familiar form of little Charlie Graham stood peering through the

43

peephole. Emily switched to tip-toe so her approach was silent, crept in behind him, and surprised her nephew with a sudden and fierce hug. He yowled in shock, but she didn't put him down until she'd planted a kiss on his hair, which smelled vaguely of the lake.

"Where's your mama, Bear Cub?"

"She got tired of waiting for you and went inside to shoot the pictures."

"One of us is always tired of waiting for the other, I guess."

"When she's done, we're going night fishing with Grandpa. Wanna come?"

"Maybe," Emily told him, wrapping an arm around his spindly shoulders and pulling him along with her to the entrance. "No sense in you loitering out here, you rascal. Let's take you in and get you a lemonade."

"Mama said I shouldn't see people dancing the way they do," Charlie warned.

Emily waved at the ticket box and waltzed through, chuckling. A Puerto Rican orchestra, regulars here during the season, had the place hopping. Charlie's eyes were wide. "Trust me, they have lemonade," she assured him.

"What in the world are you doing? He shouldn't be in here. How'd they even let him in?"

"Ah, there's Mama now," Emily called over the deafening music. Rosie had her hands full with the Graflex and bulbs, but she still managed to take hold of her son's elbow. Emily grinned. "I promised him a lemonade."

The three of them made their way back to the manager's office by silent agreement, but Emily swung off to the bar before joining them. Two lemonades later, she considered the remodeled space. The office was half open both to the dance floor and, on the opposite side, to the lake itself. The improvements fit the mood of the place. Dot was perched lakeside on a tall stool, legs crossed, shuffling through papers.

"One for you and one for me," Emily told her nephew, who was sitting obediently at a desk in the middle of the room. She plopped the sweating glass down in front of him. Rosie rolled her eyes at her sister and headed back out to the dance floor with the camera. "Sorry I'm a few minutes behind, Dot."

"I expected it. Figured you got your nose cut off a little over the rent price the other day and you're punishing me."

"Like you're punishing me for the zoning editorials?"

Dot looked up and offered a wicked smile. "Think what you will."

"You do the same." Emily sipped at the drink and plopped her bag down. She felt the cool of the lemonade slide all the way down to her stomach, which had been mostly empty but still churning all day.

"Charlie, do you want to color while your mama finishes working?" Dot asked.

"Do you have any of that chart paper, Aunt Dottie?" The two of them liked to chart things and do math together, Emily knew. She watched Dot scrounge in a file cabinet, determined to find the little guy a sheet of paper, and she felt some of her irritation with her friend fizzle. Dot had stood by the Grahams through all manner of notoriety, never judging, even when they were kids.

Though Hickory and Louise Graham were pillars of the Buckeye Lake community, the abandoned daughters of their scandalous daughter-in-law — shockingly, a dancer — and their late son were always regarded with a degree of suspicion. Emily remembered not being allowed to play with some of the little girls in town, though it had been years before she'd understood what their mothers had meant by the censure. Dot Berkeley, who had grown up collecting rent and balancing the books amidst an amusement park, didn't fit the mold, either. She'd been judged, as well.

And when quiet, artistic, and very unmarried Rosie Graham had produced a baby boy at the tender age of sixteen, all the mothers had felt justified. They had always said those Graham girls had some bad blood in them — "no disrespect to Hickory or Louise, of course" — and this time, Emily and Rosie had heard and understood the talk. Dot, by contrast, had simply brought over a supply of diaper cloth, three receiving blankets, and an offer to showcase some of Rosie's paintings and photos in the park's main office. Upon graduating from college herself in '42, Dot's first order of business had been to move Rosie and her work into the studio space she still occupied.

Now, Aunt Dottie happily produced the chart paper for her darling Charlie. She also pushed a piece of scratch paper from the corner of the desk at him. "Here, kid. Figure out how many more glasses we should order for the summer based on last week's sales. This is current inventory. Chart it."

Charlie's eyes lit up, and Dot returned to her stool.

"I saw the new lighting from way back on the boardwalk, Dottie," Emily said, propping herself beside her friend on the ledge. She noticed the stars peeking out now and watched the water go from gray-green to black in the gathering dark.

She wished the summer evening gave her tingles along her spine like it used to.

Dot needed no additional prompting to talk about the updates and new features of the Crystal Ballroom. Emily scribbled things down. Dot handed her a flier with the bands for the rest of the season listed. Ziggy Coyle. Guy Lombardo. Emily folded it and tucked it in the back of her notebook. Tonight's band took a break, and Miguel, one of the trumpet players, came back to say hello and light an extra cigarette for "his ladies" to share.

"Make sure you dance," he said with a wink.

"Not dressed for it."

"You are lovely," he murmured, tousling Charlie's hair before he made his exit. Emily leaned over and took a dainty sip from the cigarette, imagining herself as Betty Grable.

"Grandpa says cigarettes are unladylike," Charlie preached from the desk, where he'd risen to his knees on the spinning chair.

"So's working seventy hours this week," Emily mumbled, and she heard Dot say "amen" as she obediently tossed the cigarette out into the water below. There would be no corruption of Charlie under their watch.

Emily's eyes tracked the orange tip of the cigarette until it was extinguished by darkness. Glancing back up, she noticed a figure at the far end of the pier, where a few lanterns glowed. The military haircut was common these days, but she knew from the shoulders that this could be none other than the mysterious Sergeant Drew Mathison, the most appealing part of her bait shop cleanup crew.

He was staring off into the night, one booted foot propped on the lower rail. He wasn't dressed for dancing, certainly, and he wasn't in uniform. Emily squinted. Was he … feeding ducks? She shoved a piece of chewing gum in her mouth, feeling a little lighter than she had before.

"Your boyfriend?" Dot asked skeptically, following her friend's gaze, but Emily just smiled and told Charlie she'd be back after a bit.

As she skirted the increasingly crowded dance floor, she convinced herself again her interest in Drew Mathison was natural. For three years, the only men under fifty she'd seen were Sammy and Walt, puffing away in the back of the office and ineligible for the Army due to flat feet and a heart murmur, respectively.

Drew Mathison certainly wasn't the first returned soldier she'd seen. Not by a long shot. But he was the first one who looked at her the way he looked at her.

Chapter Seven

The Buckeye Lake Beacon
Friday, June 7, 1946
Ballroom lighting encourages romance

The crowds didn't come as far as the end of the pier, Drew noted. It was something he appreciated just now. There was nothing out here to draw attention once folks passed the ballroom, really.

He unenthusiastically dropped a tiny blob of bread over the railing. A very ordinary-looking duck smacked its beak, and the bread was gone. Ordinary ducks were everywhere. It occurred to Drew he had yet to spot one of the majestic blue herons everyone talked about.

Drew wasn't spotting a lot of what he wanted to. He would have bet money on Gil Reese being holed up at home. The fact there'd been no trace of him anywhere near the property, nor any real lead for a next step, left him feeling emptied out. And irritated that he was now thinking in terms of gambling and bets. He supposed there were these miles of farmlands and barns to investigate, apparently. Needle in a haystack scenario. One more drop-by at the "big game" had yielded a mention of Reese, but someone had said they hadn't seen him since he'd shipped out for Basic. They had heard, though, he was winning big in Reno.

The end of this pier felt like exactly the right place for Drew to be as darkness fell. A dead end.

Pastor Skip had suggested right away that the two of them should pray. God, he said, would shelter Drew and his family in their grief. God would protect Gilbert and hopefully even use Drew as an instrument in that. They should pray, he said, for justice to be accomplished, for the Spirit to stir Gil to come forward and make his testimony. If they sought His help, Pastor Skip said, God would reveal a way forward.

Drew leaned hard against the smooth wood railing that marked the end of the pier and wondered about that way forward.

"But we should remember, after we ask all that of God, that we also ask His will be done," Drew had suggested earnestly to Skip as he left.

Skip had beamed at that. It was a Gold Star Sunday School statement. "Yes, we will. Of course," the pastor had said. "May God's will be done. Always."

Drew wished for the prayers to come as he stood on the end of the pier. He had no doubt God's will would be done. So, what good did it do for him to ask, really? Drew had prayed a lot to the God of his childhood as he'd learned what it was to really be a man in the burned-out muck of war. He had asked for protection for himself and others. For healing when there was no protection. For no suffering when there had been no healing. *If it were God's will.*

Too often, it had not been.

Drew had been lousy company at the inn's pork chop dinner this evening, annoyed by the company of honeymooners from Marion and an evangelist on vacation from a bank in Columbus who was here to save souls on the boardwalk. All of them made Drew feel impatient, but for different reasons. Cookie, ever colorful and ever perceptive, had tossed a heel of bread off the dinner platter and sent Drew out to feed ducks in the fresh air. It reminded him of his mother shoo-ing one of her boys out just before a fight broke out in her kitchen.

The air hadn't been fresh outside, exactly, until he'd made it this far down the pier. At first it had been tinged with the usual fried dough and sugar smells, the vague scent of grease from the gears of the rides, the spice of bratwurst from a little food booth three buildings to the east.

~~~~~

Emily took a steadying breath as she approached, still trying to pretend she was Betty Grable. She tossed her chewing gum over the edge of the pier. Betty might smoke elegantly, but she sure didn't chomp on gum. This time, Emily told herself, she would pose as a woman who knew how to make herself irresistible to a member of the opposite sex, though she wasn't sure she'd ever consciously tried that in her life before this moment.

How hard could it be?

On top of all the other pressures and confusion she was feeling, Emily had made the unhappy discovery the day before that she was—and she heaved an internal sigh over this—very physically attracted to a man. That was when she'd first tried to explain it away from only having the two guys in the back of the office as a barometer, really.

Still, the discovery was also part relief. She'd spent years wondering why she didn't particularly enjoy her childhood sweetheart's awkward kisses or sweaty hand holding. She'd privately wondered if either she was an exceedingly late bloomer or the movies had it all wrong.

Until yesterday, watching Drew Mathison's shoulder muscles move while he pushed water with a broom, she wasn't certain she had ever felt the tingle of desire.

Now, she had. She simply had to figure out what to do about it. These different feelings, these things she hadn't felt around other men, had her curious. And, like any good journalist, she needed to explore that curiosity.

Approaching him, Emily fell back on the classic and unoriginal tap-on-the-opposite shoulder surprise, wanting to startle a laugh out of him as she had little Charlie earlier.

Only, Drew Mathison was not surprised at all. Which was fine because she'd still accomplished her primary goal of touching one of those shoulders.

He raised a brow and angled a little toward her. "You again."

She liked the way his lips twitched up on one side, like he was always trying so, so hard not to let any happy out. And she liked his voice, a little bit rusty, like he didn't use it very often. Deep. Two words—"you again"—not even nice words, and there was that *different* something going on in her belly.

Too busy analyzing her own response to such a simple statement, Emily realized she had nothing witty to say in return.

"I was just ... working," she said, lamely. She flapped her notebook at him as if required to provide evidence. She shoved it in the pocket of her simple dress, and then she looked down over the edge of the pier to see a family of ducks below, as she'd suspected. Somehow, they seemed to be bobbing along on the rippling water to the precise beat of Miguel's rumba, behind them. "You've been making some feathered friends," she observed, studying the artful grains arranged on the top of a hunk of bread in his big hand. "Is that ... Cookie's bread you're tossing?"

"You can identify people by a piece of bread they made?"

"I go way back with Cookie's baked goods. She's my aunt."

"Anyway, it's just a heel," Drew said. "A heel won't hurt the ducks, right?"

Emily shrugged, unwilling to debate wildlife dietary restrictions with a handsome man who also smelled this good. Carla's voice came flowing from the ballroom now and across the pier. Boy, what Emily wouldn't give to be able to sing like that. Even the ducks seemed to take notice of the pure, sultry sound. She glanced up to find Drew looking down at her in that way that made her want to look back.

"Are you always working?" he asked.

She thought about it. "I guess I am."

"Something with the band or the ballroom, I take it?" At her nod, he asked, "Do you take any time off?"

Maybe he wanted to ask her on a date? "Of course, I take time off. Sometimes it's hard to draw a line with work, in this business. It's just a matter of keeping my ear to the ground even when I'm technically not working, I suppose."

"I get that."

It occurred to her, having done detective work, he probably would.

"Hear anything good lately?" he continued.

49

"A few things. Some curiosity about you and your new badge. Do you like it here at Buckeye Lake?"

"Wait. Is this another interview?"

"Have we had a first? Anyway, why would you think that?"

"Didn't you just say you're always working?"

Emily couldn't help a little huff. "Consider us off record unless I tell you otherwise, okay? Just relax. I'm just Emily talking to Drew."

"Okay." He seemed to visibly recalibrate, which amused her.

"How in the world did you end up here from Philadelphia, when no one here seems to know a thing about you?"

His mouth twitched again in amusement. "If that's not an interview question, I don't know what is."

"Okay, okay. Will you at least tell me how long you plan to stay?"

"Does it matter?"

"Maybe I'm trying to figure out if it's worth my time to ask you to go in and dance with me." She wiggled her eyebrows this time, and the idea took hold. Besides, there was always so much sadness around his eyes, and Emily figured it was hard to be sad while dancing. When there was a conga drum involved, anyway.

Why, why, *why* had she changed out of the yellow dress? Everyone wanted to dance with Yellow Dress Emily. "C'mon, Drew."

But his face clouded even more. "I haven't danced in a really long time." And there was so much pain in the seemingly benign statement that the coward in her almost completely backed away.

Because if there was one thing Emily knew was true about herself, she did not actually do well with *feelings*. Other people's or her own.

"If you're worried you forgot how, I've been told it's just like riding a bicycle," she tried with deliberate lightness. "I'll lead." But still he shook his head. He was impossible, so she dealt with impossible head-on. "You're not attracted to me," she challenged.

She was only bold enough to say it because she didn't think this was the case at all. As embarrassingly inexperienced as she was with romance, Emily had seen a certain something in Drew Mathison's eyes yesterday at the bait shop, when she'd caught him looking at her legs. It was something she'd always shied away from before, but now that curiosity had her wanting to get to the bottom of it.

"Got me," he said without conviction, but his hand reached out, and his fingers ran tentatively along the ends of her hair. He pulled the hand back as quickly as he'd done it, and he shook his head. "Look, I can barely manage a civil conversation. No way I can dance."

"Suit yourself," she said, shrugging. "Though I don't necessarily see what one has to do with the other." She reached over, plucked off a piece of bread and dropped it to the fuzzy ducklings below, lost in so much shadow under the pier that she wouldn't have noticed them there if she hadn't seen them minutes before. "Maybe you've just been trying to have a civil conversation with the wrong people."

A strangled sound of amusement was his response. "You're very perceptive. I think that's spot on for tonight, at least. Um, with you, of course, as the exception."

"There you go."

"I got to eat with an irritating crowd at the Inn."

"Burt and Cookie's dinner table?" She grinned. "You've heard my whole life story at the Inn, no doubt."

"Not your whole life story. But I do have it on good authority that you are a fabulous cook and will make a charming wife and delightful mother someday."

Emily snorted. "Okay, okay. So, it was *your hosts* annoying you."

"Not at all."

"Cookie thinks you're a great catch, yourself, you know."

Another half-smile from the veteran. "I guess I should be flattered."

"I don't know. Her standards aren't that high. You've seen Burt, right?"

And there it was, finally ... a full wattage grin from Drew Mathison. Hard to earn but worth it. His cheeks creased with what might have been dimples on another face but, on his, took the form of grooved lines, instead.

"You always seem a little sad, Drew."

"I'm fine."

Emily had a wild moment in which she imagined showing him all her favorite places at the lake. She couldn't fix her own situation, but could she make him smile more?

"I'm trying to decide if I agree with Cookie's assessment of *you*," she pressed. "You don't give out information about yourself, so you're useless to me on a professional level. And you don't dance, so that rules out everything else. I guess my position is, a pretty face only goes so far, Mathison."

He didn't stop grinning once he'd started. "How's Wally?"

"Making money hand over fist. And the sign is up by the back door."

"Reminding him not to leave the hose running in the tank?"

"Yes, that one. I grabbed a ladder and fixed the spelling on 'Grand Opening.' And a new shipment of live bait comes Monday morning."

"I'm glad things are looking up for him." Drew looked over, and she was close enough to see all the layers of gray in his eyes. She felt seen, and she let herself enjoy it for a minute.

At last, soberly, she said, "I don't want to make you sadder, but I do have other news."

"What is it?"

"Toppy has come down from the high wire. Cycle and all." Then she added, quickly, "Not a fall. He just *got* down."

Drew's eyebrows rose. "I didn't see him when I walked out, but I figured he was just on the other end, eating dinner. Is he all right?"

"Turns out he can see a lot from up on that wire. A *lot*. Including his girl, stepping out with another man."

"No."

"I'm afraid so."

"Who's safe from deception, if not Toppy?"

"He got down quickly."

"What happened then?"

"That's all I know for now, but I'll keep you posted."

"Poor fella."

"See, I knew that would make you even sadder. Sorry."

"Why are you so convinced that I'm sad? What if this is just me?"

Emily shrugged. "I'm glad I'm not a man," she decided out loud.

"I'm glad you're not a man, too." He cut her a sideways look. "You'd be a funny looking one."

She laughed with delight. "That's the nicest thing you've said to me yet, and I want you to think about how pathetic *that* is. No, I'm glad I'm not a man because it seems like a man just has to stand alone in the dark when he's sad. Pretending to have it all together."

She was one to talk, Emily thought suddenly. Was she not a pro lately at pretending she had it all together?

A hypocrite alarm gently sounded in her soul.

Drew turned toward her, but she couldn't read his face. His voice, still a little rusty, was soft. "I don't see you spilling your guts to anyone who would listen, crying in a hankie, whining about things no one can change."

The hypocrite alarm must have been loud enough for him to hear it, then, she thought. "Thank you for calling me out on that. But my point is, I *could* cry and whine if I wanted to, and no one would judge me." She blinked and clarified. "I don't want to, by the way."

"Well, I don't want to, either."

"Still, I could talk about things with other people and not seem weak."

But did she? Had she ever asked for help with anything?

"Speaking of which, any more hostile messages?" Drew asked. "You still a bog rat?"

"Seems like they're moving from name calling to threats, actually."

He turned fully toward her, one elbow still on the rail like he'd slide off the pier without its support.

"I got something in the mail addressed to me today that said, 'Do the right thing or you will suffer,'" she explained.

"Do the right thing …?"

"Yes. Disappointingly vague and subjective, don't you think? I mean, from my perspective I've been doing the right thing all along."

"Did you file a report over that one yet?"

Emily sighed. She didn't want to talk about this. It was getting old, and he was new here, and that was *way* more interesting. "Not yet, and I don't want to right now. There have been a couple of other things these last few days, but all of them are vague. My favorite one was a paper slid under the door at the office that said, 'I know what you're trying to do. Onto you.'"

"Referring to your editorials, I take it?"

"I can only assume. I mean, I try to do *a lot* of things on any given day. It's good to know someone is making sense of it all."

They laughed together, and Emily felt happy for the first time in a month.

"You scared yet?"

"No. Well, yes. But only of one thing."

As a man of few words, he had a way of asking "what" with only his brows.

Emily wished she didn't like it so much. "I have to admit, I'm a little scared of rejection."

"Rejection?"

"I've never asked a man to dance with me before, Sergeant Mathison. Or Lieutenant Mathison or whoever you are. *That's* the story you've left for me to tell. That my very first time asking, I was rejected. Rejected in the name of … let's see, civil conversation, right?"

Mouth twitching with amusement he ran his hand over the back of his neck and looked back out across the lake.

"I feel like," Emily pressed, "you just conversed civilly, proving you are certainly up to one simple dance."

"I doubt anything's simple with you."

"Second nicest thing you've said to me."

Muted trumpets wove a sweet melody that seemed to settle around them with the night.

"Can we do it out here?" he asked, softly and with a hint of pleading. His head gestured toward the vibration and light coming from the ballroom. "I'm not dressed for in there, and I don't …"

"All right, then," Emily gave in cheerfully, turning herself to him. "But be careful with me. I have a habit of ending up in the water at the most inconvenient times. One time I was covering a race down by …" and then her nervous babbling cut off as he briskly took her into his arms and got down to the business of dancing.

This was not an insecure or hesitant man, she thought as she gasped.

It took the two of them no time at all to fall into the rhythm of the music floating through the night. Emily made a mental note to explore this settled feeling of being held close to him, focusing on his neck as she tried to get a handle on a sudden and embarrassing trembling in her torso.

Here it was again … that dangerous and different feeling that she both craved and mistrusted.

In some ways, she'd give anything just then to be clowning around at a school dance with one of the local boys who only made her laugh, boys who were comfortable to be with.

There was nothing comfortable about Drew Mathison, and these arms were not the arms of a boy, and she—for all her big talk and journalistic curiosity—was wildly out of her league.

Where Drew had been afraid he couldn't converse well, Emily was very afraid that was *all* she was actually good at doing. That and writing, and wasn't that just another form of conversing? Otherwise, why would she be trembling?

In a dance with a man, in a romantic moment, she was afraid she was an imposter.

It took several long, shaky breaths and two verses of the Hermanos' current song about a beach in Cozumel before Emily was able to raise her eyes from Drew's neck. Up to his chin. To a hint of stubble.

Where their arms touched, his skin was very warm.

"Your stories about the season opening," he said softly, and she raised her eyes just a fraction more, watching his lips form the words. "They were good."

Emily tried to smile up at him at the compliment but was afraid the face she made looked more distressed than happy.

He cleared his throat and said, "I told you it'd been a while since I danced," with humor and apology in his voice.

She shook her head, trying to clear it. "You're a very good dancer. Thanks for not completely rejecting me." Those miss-nothing eyes were on hers, and she had to struggle not to look away. She thought she heard him swallow. Her own breath shivered out through her lips.

He spun her, and Emily, stumbling a little, decided she didn't care at all if she fell right off the dock. Bringing her back into him, though, he bent his head closer to hers. She realized they had stopped moving to the music and that his lips were right *there*. They brushed hers, her breath hitched, and she leaned in.

~~~~~

Drew had stopped thinking, stopped feeling, at around the time Emily Graham had slid so willingly into his arms.

But he'd had only the barest moment to taste the heat of her lips when the air changed, the loud cadence of beating wings wrenching the pair of them apart in joint alarm. Drew blinked up, a little dizzy, in time to see an enormous blue heron buzz the tops of their heads. He made some sound, ducking at the same time Emily also ducked.

They smacked foreheads. Hard.

There was no time to laugh in the flurry of flapping wings. Their attention was fixed on the heron, who landed only five feet away on the dark pier walkway. From its mouth dangled a fair-sized fish.

"Dinner time," Emily said on a shaky breath, rubbing her forehead with embarrassment. Drew looked down at her, and they both laughed quietly, unwilling to scare away the bird that stood nearly as high as their waists, almost all of it made up of stick-like legs and an impossibly long neck. Drew's arm stayed around Emily's waist, though, as the heron whipped back its head, opened its beak, and worked the fish into its throat.

"Have you ever seen them eat before?" Emily whispered, barely a sound. He caught the lemon scent of her again and felt like he might lose the rest of his mind. Choosing sanity, he casually withdrew his arm.

"No," he admitted. He had never seen a heron, much less watched one dine. But he watched now. The perfect distraction from unwanted distraction, he told himself.

And that was when the dignified blue heron began to choke. Its mighty neck worked spastically, a distinct gagging sound coming from the bird. The bulk of the fish, wedged as a bulge in the neck, wasn't going down.

"Um ..."

Should he be worried? Was it somehow his obligation as a patrolman at the park to open this creature's airway and save its life?

"Wait. Watch," Emily said with childlike zeal, reaching back to put her hand on his forearm.

The heron changed tactics. Drew watched as it flung its head and neck back, whiplashed its beak forward, and spewed out the mound of fish onto the wooden pier. In the blink of an eye, it nabbed the still-live fish by the tail and proceeded to whip it, repeatedly, onto the boards like a dock worker busting up a sack of ice.

"He's breaking the bones in the fish's body," Emily explained, smiling up at Drew. "So it goes down easier, see?"

The pork chop squirmed in Drew's stomach as he listened to the fish bones snap under the abuse. He could not pull his gaze away from the spectacle. Then, just as Emily had indicated, the heron repeated the swallowing procedure. This time, the mound of fish in the long, thin neck — just a sack of smashed bones now — went down successfully.

Drew and Emily watched the heron finish its meal in silence. It spread its enormous wings then, majestic in the darkness even after the scene of violence. Drew looked down and was surprised to find Emily still just as beautiful and as kissable as she'd been before the regurgitation and mutilation of a fish.

"I'm afraid that I'm starting to associate you with dead fish," he told her solemnly.

The laugh, full of joy and genuine humor, exploded from her, and he was helpless but to join in. It felt strange, he thought, to laugh. And then, as though their laughter had drawn him to them, a young boy hollered something from down by the ballroom.

"Hey! Aunt Em!" His feet slapped the pier. "What's going on? We're leaving!"

"That's me," she said. "I should go." She stretched forward, though, and pecked Drew on the cheek. There was the scent of her again and the warmth of soft lips. "Next time I'll do better on that spinning move."

He watched her hurry down the pier and wondered why he'd ever wanted to run away from newspaper reporters.

Chapter Eight

The Buckeye Lake Beacon
Saturday, June 8, 1946
Festival Farms plans first annual harvest bash

Saturday's shift felt long. Drew spent all of it eager to drive out to Old Canal Road to finally track down Smokey Black on his farm. Unlike the night before, today Drew felt hopeful all over again that the man was feeding his old buddy, Gil Reese, alongside some sow in a barn.

He was re-energized.

In no time, he'd be driving back to Reno with his red-headed witness and the gun in his holster at the ready. Sure, the morning's patrol at the amusement park had been tedious: a toddler with a fishing hook stuck in his ear; a drunk college co-ed who'd picked a fight with the worker who ran the high striker, strength-tester game; a pregnant woman who had fainted in the afternoon heat and who had been fine after a half-hour on the substation cot; and, of course, a batch of local boys running around pickpocketing near the concessions.

Through it all had been the constant awareness that Emily Graham was *some*where, doing *some*thing in that way she had of always doing things, within a two-mile radius. He hadn't caught one sight of her, but the knowledge of her presence had still somehow managed to be just as distracting as his need to get out to Black-Pool Farms.

He told himself it would be just fine if he never saw her again. He would certainly have no reason to return to Buckeye Lake after the trial in Nevada. To that end, Drew hoped Emily Graham would be no more than a surprisingly pleasant memory — the memory of a woman he'd laughed with for the first time in what seemed like years. One who had felt right in his arms. One who offered assurance there were still women like her out there, fresh and full of light, waiting for him to finish with all the darkness and get back to normal.

Whatever normal would end up being.

Now, dinner time having come and gone, Drew hoped he could still catch this Smokey fellow on a Saturday night. Having chatted with the guy's mother at the big farmhouse two miles up the road days ago, Drew knew a little about the man he was looking for. Apparently, when Reginald Black Sr. had married Sylvia Pool, they'd joined the two largest landowning, farming families in the county and consolidated everything into Black-Pool Farms. Their oldest son, Reggie, had livestock in a range of barns far out toward the county line, while Levi—or "Smokey"—had established an enormous Christmas tree farm here closer to the lake. Reggie had kept his brother's land up while he'd been away at war, and now that he was back, Smokey was expanding his operation to something he called Festival Farms, which this year would include pumpkins in the fall.

There was a split lane at the entrance of the farm, with a picture of pumpkins to the left and evergreens to the right. Slowing his '39 Dodge, Drew calculated Smokey Black had just returned from a Christmas tree convention, so he turned right. *He'll be more likely to be messing with his trees.*

Emily Graham would say Drew was following some serious detective-level instincts here, he reflected, and he wondered how he could miss someone he barely knew.

Around him were acres of hills speckled with tidy trees and lush vines, colorful farmland that, together with the lake, had been Gil Reese's childhood. Drew, who had been happy enough running wild with his brothers among historic city buildings, still managed to feel a sense of envy. An amusement park, a lake, boats, and fields of crops … what a place to grow up.

And why would the kid have lingered in the stench of Reno after the war ended?

In a stand of balsam trees, Drew at last found a giant of a man, shirtless, armed with hand shears. He shut the truck off and climbed out.

"Smokey Black?"

"The very one." He was already reaching out to grip Drew's hand. Browned from a life in the sunshine, he had a tattoo of an American bald eagle on the bulge of one shoulder. "You must be Mathison. Heard you'd been asking around the farm for me while I was gone. What's with the police uniform, though? You hear Gramps used to make grain alcohol out here in the barns when I was a kid?" He had a boom of a laugh that, like Emily's, made Drew wish he laughed more.

"Just now off duty, is all."

Drew could see where the man, who couldn't yet be thirty, had earned his nickname. Though the five o'clock shadow on his jaw was dark, it was clear that the close-cropped hair on his head was already iron gray. He slid into a light shirt he pulled off a tractor. "Wish I could offer you something, but all I've got out here is the fresh air."

"That'll do. Along with the answers to a few questions I have."

"Questions about pumpkins, I bet." He had a broad, bright smile that matched his abrupt laugh.

"Hoping not to be here in the fall, to tell the truth."

Smokey smacked a deer fly that had landed on his neck, while visibly taking Drew's measure. "Tell me about your part in the War, first."

"Just got back. Army MP. You?"

"Combat diver for the Navy."

"Frogman, huh?"

Smokey nodded. "Operation Overlord." Drew resisted the urge to salute. This man had cleared a high-profile beach of explosives while under fire to help ensure an Allied victory, and today he pruned fir trees. "Strange coming home, isn't it?" Smokey was saying, almost like he read Drew's mind. "Everything seem strange to you, too?"

"You have no idea."

"I'm sure you're right. But that's not the story that's brought you out here to my farm."

"In a way, I guess it is." Drew opted for total honesty, as he had with Pastor Skip. Not only did he respect this man more than almost any he'd met so far, he needed the people closest to Gilbert Reese to understand not just Reese's obligation where justice was concerned but, also, the danger he was in.

He told Black about Gil and Jamie's involvement at the casino, with the Contis. He told him about the shooting and Gilbert's flight, how he'd tracked him back in this direction and was almost certain Don Conti would have, as well.

Smokey's face was disappointingly unreadable through the whole tale. "Sorry about your brother, Mathison," he finally said, shaking his head.

"Thanks. Don't suppose you've seen Gil Reese anywhere?"

Smokey shook his head regretfully and, Drew determined, believably.

"Or maybe you know where I might be looking, from the two of you growing up pals?" he continued.

The man kept shaking his head to that, too. "A bunch of us chummed around together. To be honest, Gil and I weren't any closer than the rest of the gang from high school. Mostly, we were all borderline troublemakers," he said. "Stupid kids. Gil especially. He was always cooking up something crazy." Lost in whatever memories were playing out behind his kind eyes, Smokey sat in silence for a time. In that time, a long-haired tabby cat with three legs hobbled around from the other side of the wagon and moved to weave awkwardly in and out between Smokey's boots.

"Cream Puff," he said simply, introducing the cat. Even petting the fluffball with the ridiculous name, Smokey still managed to look intimidating. "Look, I'll take you around to places he could hide here at the farm," he finally decided. "I'm just telling you that, if he's out here, I don't know the first thing about it."

"Would your mother hide him, by any chance?"

Smokey smiled. "Aw, heck. Yeah. I suppose she would, but she'd tell me about it. I can ask her for you, just the same. My brother, too."

"Thanks. And you could ask questions an outsider can't. In town, I mean. If you don't mind."

"'Course." He scooped up the disabled cat, who nestled against his neck. "Seems funny to me that Gil would even come back here, though, if he needed to hide."

"Why's that?"

Smokey shrugged. "I just figured he wouldn't give up the higher stakes once he found them. It's how he's built." More thinking. "Also, I can't see Gil sittin' still for too long. If he's here at the lake, if he's hiding, I 'spose we'll know before too much time goes by. He's not one for sittin' still, bein' quiet. He likes people, action. Attention, when it comes right down to it. No way he's hiding or sitting still for long."

"Well, that's something."

"You might ask the local newspaper lady," Smokey suggested.

Drew's spine straightened. "Emily Graham?"

"Yeah, Emily. She's easy to find. She might know."

"She does seem to know everyone's business," Drew mused, feeling all over again how soft her lips were in that moment before the heron had buzzed them. Here was an excuse to find her again, he thought with a flicker of joy, to talk to her.

Any excuse would do.

"She'd especially know Gil's business, I reckon," Smokey was saying. "As his fiancée and all."

Chapter Nine

The Buckeye Lake Beacon
Sunday, June 9, 1946
Sweetheart's Canal lit for summer

On Sunday morning, as the evangelist and the honeymooners got ready to go to church, Drew told Cookie he had to check something out over at the park.

Emily Graham would be at church. He really did need to speak to her. The problem was, he really did not *want* to speak to her.

Buckeye Lake Park felt like its own kind of outdoor cathedral, silent and still. The raw wood of The Dips coaster glowed like honey in the late morning sunshine, the colorful canvas tops of sleeping rides their own kind of stained glass. Drew waited for the Holy Spirit to craft some kind of prayer for him as he trudged along the boardwalk. That was what he'd been taught growing up. When someone didn't know what to pray, the Spirit would do it for them.

But he hadn't prayed in such a long time now that maybe the wall inside of him was some kind of blockade. Nothing was getting in or out.

To be fair, something like hope had leaked through for a few hours. He knew it probably shouldn't be the remembered feeling of a woman in his arms that did it, but it sure had felt just like hope. It had finally felt like *some*thing, only now that was all ash and dust again. Burned down like a village in Europe. Or like Jamie's future.

The same fire Emily Graham had ignited had ended up burning out the last of him.

She's engaged to be married.

What had a woman promised to another man *meant* with that dance she'd begged him for at the end of the pier? How had she managed to slide up to him that way, to shoot those lights from her eyes, taste like something new when their lips brushed?

Seeing the empty highwire with no sign of Toppy was a good reminder this morning. Not everyone played by the same rules, he reminded himself. He would learn that eventually. *Toppy had.*

Emily must have also danced with Gilbert Reese, the same Gilbert Reese whose Army photo lived in Drew's pocket now. Certainly, she'd have kissed him. She must have flung herself into the man's arms when he'd proposed, promised to live her life with him. They'd probably

61

already discussed children.

Drew knew Smokey's revelation had moved him closer to tracking down his hidden witness, but he wished he felt happier about it.

He finally decided to make himself coffee in the little substation on the boardwalk, unlocking it and feeling the cool of night still trapped within. Of course, when he glanced down on the desk, there was a newly filed complaint report. Dated and time stamped yesterday after he'd gone off shift, one Emily Graham had called the office requesting an officer at *The Beacon* office. It seemed an old typewriter—not her own, the note said in Gunn's scratchy writing—had been hanging in front of her office door, covered in something that looked like blood but which they had determined to be food coloring, cornstarch, and water. A piece of paper rolled up around the carriage read, in type, "It won't work. Give up." Some of the "blood" had been splattered on the glass at the front of the office. Photos had been taken, but they weren't attached yet.

Drew leaned against the counter and ran his hand over a band of tension at the back of his neck. What had she told him Friday night? That the insults had changed over to threats? *I know what you're trying to do* and *Do the right thing or you will suffer.* He remembered the determinedly cheerful way she'd talked about doing the right thing being a matter of perspective.

But when he could think past that irony, the messages gave him pause. He had only last night made the connection between Gil Reese and Emily Graham. Their romance had to be something everyone around here knew, though. He just hadn't asked the right people the right questions. But what if Don Conti, the Conti family's most likely hitman, *had* asked the right questions?

Emily was almost certainly hiding Gil Reese somewhere.

If Drew knew it, the Contis could, too. Emily Graham was in danger. And if Emily was in danger, so was his witness.

He let the coffee go cold, uninterested in it as he waited for church to end so he could make his way out to the Graham place. It wasn't something to be put off. She thought the threats stemmed from articles she was writing. Drew could only hope that was true because the alternative was very, very bad. Lying awake, he'd been over it all in his mind, and he went over it again now. Why hadn't Pastor Skip mentioned his son's engagement?

Smokey had shaken his head when he'd asked that question. "*Mafia?* Murders?" he had said. "Could be he didn't think for a second Gil would ever involve Emily in something so dangerous. Getting her all caught up in that would be unthinkable for most men."

"And yet, everything I've learned about Reese tells me he wouldn't hesitate to involve her."

"You may never have met Gil, but yeah, you've got a clear picture. The Gil I grew up with would look to Emily to save his hide. She always did, and he would have no reason not to expect her to this time."

Drew had a bad moment, trying to make sense of that intelligent and charming woman choosing to tie herself to a man like Gilbert Reese for life. It just didn't add up. He didn't want it to add up.

Using the report of the bloody typewriter as an excuse, he followed directions Smokey had given him to find the family at Liebs Island, where Hickory Graham owned a marina and reportedly honored Sundays by forcing rest on the whole family. Drew knew his approach with Emily would have to be much different from the way he'd questioned Pastor Skip or Smokey Black. His instinctive belief in the honesty of a man of God and a proven soldier didn't apply here. Emily would have more incentive to lie and would probably be far more skilled at it.

Drew followed a winding dirt road through corn fields, which gave way abruptly to water. On the right side, the road followed the remnants of the old Ohio-Erie Canal, now lined with tiny, homespun docks and the occasional rowboat. Tall trees grew up alongside it, and ramshackle fishing cabins dotted the canal passage just as they did the main lake, which stretched off to the left.

A humble watercraft office with a docked patrol boat in the canal stood watch over a short bridge that connected to Liebs Island. A collection of small homes dotted the island between trees, a circular road framing them. Graham's Marina was on the far side, its drive sloping low to the water, where barn-like buildings in need of paint led to the skeleton of hundreds of dock tie-ups, many with boats currently at rest there.

Hiding places upon hiding places, he reflected, firmly back in detective mode. Drew parked beside the marina office and walked down the lot in the opposite direction, where he could see a bit of what had to be what Smokey called Towpath Island. The canal's towpaths had once stretched across the state, used by oxen to pull barges along the water. Redesigns of the west end of the lake had left a small strip of the path adjacent to this section of Liebs, connected by a little footbridge with space for only two homes. One was a traditional white farmhouse-style home, and the other was an actual barge converted into a cottage.

Drew had almost reached the footbridge when, from the bank below it, two kids appeared with poles and a bucket between them.

"Oh, you." Delia, the little girl Pastor Skip Reese was raising, greeted Drew with squinty eyes. Her hair was popping out wildly from a haphazard braid, and she wore overalls that seemed to match the ones the little boy was wearing. Drew recognized the boy from the pier who had summoned "Aunt Em " after the start of their kiss two nights before ... clue enough that Drew had, indeed, found Towpath Island.

"Hey, there," the kid said, chomping gum like his aunt. "Marina's closed, it bein' Sunday, but you can take your own boat out any time. Just help yourself, sir."

"I've actually come to see Emily Graham. I understand she lives on the towpath."

"Well, yeah, she sure does! I'm Charlie Graham. Emily's my aunt. Who are you, anyway?" The kid's feet were suddenly planted in front of the bridge. The sentinel. The skinny troll with a cracking voice, deciding if the six-foot, two-inch man with the gun on his back could cross over. Delia joined forces with him, sloshing water out of the bucket.

For show, Drew reached into his pocket, pulled out his badge. "I'm Sergeant Drew Mathison. Your aunt knows me from ... work."

Charlie's freckled face lit with pleasure and trust. "Well, all right then! 'Long as you didn't come to arrest her for something." He giggled at his own joke, little knowing his darling aunt was probably guilty of obstructing justice. "C'mon with me, it's just this way."

"We're gonna kill these fish and fry 'em up for dinner," Delia told Drew as he followed them onto the rickety footbridge.

"No investigation will be needed, then," he told her. She looked at him blankly. "Into the death of these fish, I mean."

Apparently having forgotten her preoccupation with the bloated fish in the lake last week, Delia told Charlie, "He's a strange one, this guy."

"We used shiners for bait this time," Charlie was saying to Drew, little caring that he was *a strange one*. "Worked great. I traded about a gallon of worms for a handful of shiners at the new bait store yesterday."

So, Wally's live bait was live once more.

Drew thought back to the way Emily had helped her friend at the bait store, her slacks rolled up over her knees and working that push broom. Every moment he'd had with her was cast now in a different light. She'd belonged to someone else, always. She and her legs *and* her lips had belonged to someone else.

There was a handrail on one side of the footbridge only, and Drew could see through the slats beneath his boots down to the green canal water below. He could also see strange glass sculptures in every imaginable color dangling from the bridge. They formed a vivid garland with no apparent pattern, but it was hard not to be drawn in by them. He stopped to look closer, pondering how someone could let the bridge itself deteriorate to this condition while spending what must have been years to create breathtaking works of art to decorate it. Emily Graham? It didn't fit. He couldn't see her holding still long enough to have formed the kaleidoscope of sunshine faces, lighthouses, moonbeams, abstract insects, and amorphous shapes.

More flashes of color caught his eye in the sunshine, and Drew followed them to realize this short strip of left-over canal was lined on both sides with colored glass creations, sometimes formless and sometimes in the shape of birds or giant flowers. Some even featured wind chimes, tinkling softly in the mostly still afternoon.

"Pretty, huh?" Charlie asked, calling back from the end of the bridge.

Unexpected, Drew thought. He searched for some structural explanation for the breathtaking beauty of the glass installation but knew instinctively that its lack of structure was its point.

"My mother makes them. She's an artist. Folks row out here at night to see them lit up. Gramps lights the canal passage with those flood lights there. See?" Drew followed Charlie's pointing finger. "Mostly it's guys courtin' girls. They call it the Sweetheart's Canal. Kind of gross." Delia punctuated his statement by making a gagging sound. The two were in accord regarding romance and bait. "C'mon, I'll take you to Aunt Emily."

Drew glanced back again at the marina in its disrepair and wondering about these people and their mystical little chunk of canal. The air smelled like some delicious food.

"Moooooom!" The kid belted it out, voice cracking outrageously. "This guy's here to talk to Aunt Em about work or whatever."

"Mom" had wandered up from somewhere in the vicinity of the white house on the southern point of the little strip of land. And she was gorgeous. The two most strikingly lovely women he'd probably met in his entire life, Drew thought ... it made sense for them to be sisters.

"Hello," she said. She had long, caramel-red hair pulled back in a sloppy tail so that strands blew around her face. Same blue-green eyes. And her age—she appeared younger than Drew was—told him that good old freckle-faced Charlie had to have come into her life at a very, very unacceptable age. Intrigued, he shook her offered hand. He noticed she didn't simply insert her hand into his for the shake, as her sister did. She hung back. Friendly yet hesitant, grip gentle. No ring on the left hand.

"I'm Rosie, Emily's sister." She glanced back at the form of another man approaching. "This is our grandfather—everyone calls him Hickory. And you're Drew Mathison."

Had Emily mentioned him to her family? He told himself not to be flattered. She'd probably been bragging about getting one over on him. "Nice to meet you, ma'am."

Rosie turned toward the little, white-haired man hobbling over from the porch. As he got closer, Drew was not surprised to see the same vivid eyes. Beyond that, Hickory Graham could best be described as a shirtless, tan, skinny Saint Nicholas.

"Gramps," she called. "This is Drew Mathison. He's associated somehow with the village or county police force, but it's killing Emily that she doesn't know how or why." Rosie grinned at Drew, confirming that

Emily had, indeed, mentioned him.

The sisters were clearly tight. How much had they shared?

Probably Rosie knew where Gilbert Reese was. They were likely *all* in on it and would stand as guardians here, trying to persuade him to leave the island as quickly as possible. Well, it wouldn't work. He watched the family members carefully for any sign of alarm about his presence, but so far, he'd detected nothing but friendly, Sunday afternoon curiosity.

"Hickory Graham," the old man repeated, coming close to hurting Drew's hand as he took it and pumped. "Welcome, welcome. What can we do for you, besides offer you a cold drink?"

"He wants to talk to Aunt Emily," Charlie provided, dropping the bucket.

"Oh, huh." Hickory shifted his attention to the bucket's contents. "Four more, eh? Not bad. Get 'em cleaned and put 'em on the smoker, Charles. Give him a hand, Delia." Then he looked back at Drew, reached for his arm, and guided him toward the porch of the white house.

"Is Emily home?" Drew pressed.

"Oh, to be sure. My girls are always home of a Sunday. Only time I can keep that one you're after talkin' to still for more than two minutes at a time. But you don't wanna talk to her just yet."

"I don't?" Drew figured there was some truth to that. The way he saw it, if it weren't for the information she had on Gilbert Reese, he'd as soon never talk to her again.

"Nope, you wanna sit down and share some iced tea with me first."

Together, they mounted a porch that wrapped all the way around the house. So much for ushering him off the towpath as quickly as possible. Drew suppressed the urge to whip his gun out and charge all over the island in formal search mode, but he figured this had to be handled delicately if he stood any chance of convincing them to turn Gilbert over to his custody. He had to appear self-controlled, no matter how he felt inside.

Rosie pecked her grandfather on the cheek and offered to run to the fridge. Hickory led Drew to an old glider and commanded him to sit. The old man pulled himself up precariously on the porch rail, one of his dry, brown knees peeking through a hole in his work trousers. Rosie, so fresh and profoundly young next to him, was soon back with glasses of tea.

It occurred to Drew that he was being stalled, that some silent alarm they had worked out must have sounded, and Emily was even now hiding Gilbert away somewhere before joining them. It was like a bad play. For the hundredth time since last night, his stomach went to knots as he imagined her settling Gilbert into his hiding spot with a reassuring kiss.

"Thanks for the tea." Drew took a swig, surveying the property and imagining all the places someone could hide on this little island alone. The marina, too, was easy to see and monitor from here. And there, before him, was that house made from a barge that Smokey had referred to. With more questions than patience after weeks of little sleep, Drew tapped his boot on the porch and considered again an open search. The worst they could do was call the cops on him, and it would take long enough for someone to get out here that he could cover the whole of it.

The bottom line, Drew told himself now, was that he was under no obligation to do this the nice way.

"We'll give our girl another half-hour, see, before we send you over," Hickory was saying, gaining Drew's attention. "You'll find her in a hammock beneath the big old maple yonder, other side of the barge house. She takes herself a good, deep nap there every Sunday afternoon before dinner and, far as I can see, it might be the only time she shuts her eyes all week long. In summer, anyhow."

"Well. I can come back later." *With a warrant*, he wanted to say as he swatted at a fat fly and started to rise.

Hickory waved that away. "Nonsense. Another half hour, she'll be almost endurable, don't you think, Rosie?"

Rosie, who had perched on a footstool nearby, grinned again, and raised one eyebrow to suggest doubt. "Oh, she's a bear when she finishes a nap, no denying it. We'll just let you be the one who goes and wakes her. See how you survive it. Did she finagle an interview out of you, Deputy?"

"She'd better not be working on a Sunday," Hickory warned.

"No, not exactly," Drew said. "I just wanted to check in with her about a report she filed last evening, is all." He took another gulp of tea. Charlie climbed up the porch then, taking the stone steps two at a time. He was covered in dirt and bits of fish scales. Delia was close behind, in both location and dirtiness.

"Wash up and there's juice in the fridge, you two," Rosie told them, the motherly admonishment sounding strange from the face of someone who could have easily starred in movies.

Considering her soft form in her green summer dress, Drew decided Rosie was actually more traditionally beautiful than Emily and lacked the … what? The *motion* that was Emily. Rosie's beauty was quiet, almost peaceful. Emily's was frenetic, abrupt. He felt he could now attest that both were devastating to a man's peace of mind. Poor Charlie, Drew thought as the boy stumbled back out the door with his clean hands, to grow up thinking that was simply what all women looked like. He was in for a lifetime of disappointment.

"I see you eying the barge house, Deputy," Hickory said.

Drew realized he might have been staring at the little ramshackle place but didn't feel it would be right to correct him by admitting he'd really been contemplating his granddaughters' attributes, instead.

"Did Em tell you about the place yet?"

"Emily's never told me much of anything," Drew said. *Like the fact she's engaged to someone.*

"Ah, well then. Better let her tell you about it. No one tells a story like Ems."

"C'mon, Grandpa," Charlie said, wiping juice from his lip with the back of his now clean arm. "You tell stories as good as she does."

"As *well* as she does," Rosie corrected softly.

"You know about the canal system, yeah?" Hickory asked Drew.

"Um … a little. I know it ran through here, connecting Lake Erie to the Ohio River. And pieces are left but not used, like this piece or the one running along the road here to the island. Nice glasswork, by the way," he said to Rosie. She thanked him with a nod.

"Buckeye Lake fed the canal system, like a giant dam. My people, the Grahams, lived here way back then," Hickory explained with pride. "My father, he might have been a little off. In the head, you know? Folks say I'm quite a bit like him, which makes me wonder." He took a moment to chuckle at himself, but the pride was still there. "So, he always told me it was a hand of cards. The barge wasn't being used much, what with the railroad coming through, and the guy who owned it—the same Berkeleys that now own the amusement park over there—lost it to my father playing poker. So, Dad, he already owned most of Liebs Island. He plopped the barge down right there on what folks started calling Towpath Island, and that's where she's set ever since. I grew up in another house on the main part of the island, before the hotels and everything. Back then, we used the barge to clean fish when we caught 'em."

"So, this house wasn't here back then?"

"I built this," Hickory said, gesturing around himself. "At first, my Louise was content to live in the barge after I'd sunk everything I had into starting the marina. That was Oh-Five. But before long she wanted a real home, so I built this a couple years into our marriage. Now the barge is winterized and everything, and it suits Emily fine, coming and going like she does. She should be waking up soon, I'm thinking."

"Charlie, why don't you show Deputy Mathison the way to Sleeping Beauty?" Rosie put in helpfully.

"I wouldn't go kissin' her trying to wake her up, though," the kid said wryly, leaping off the porch. Somehow his knobby knees managed to catch him. "She never wakes up too nice. Probably clock ya."

"Now, Charlie," Rosie scolded. "Don't talk like that about your aunt. Let him make up his own mind. Besides, the man's armed. He might be fine."

Drew turned back toward the porch to nod, stretched his torso and his hand toward the older man for a shake. "Thanks for the tea and the history lesson. It was nice to meet you both." Actually, Drew thought, the jury was still out. They might all be in on Gilbert Reese's disappearance, but if they were, they should be in Hollywood rather than at a marina in the middle of nowhere.

"Oh, it's not goodbye. You'll stay and help us eat the fish!" It was a hearty declaration rather than an invitation. "I caught a whole passel of 'em before service this morning. Come back when you hear Rosie ring the bell."

"Thanks," Drew said, wondering how his conversation with Emily would turn out and what the rest of the day might hold. "I'll have to see about that." Maybe he'd have Gil in custody by dinner and could swing a piece of fish before hitting the road back to Reno, assuming the invitation would stand. He would have to assure these people that he was capable of keeping the red-haired wonder safe before and after he testified.

Drew knew he was up to the task. He only needed to *convince* them he was.

"Maybe me or Grandpa will catch the Golden Bass," Charlie gabbed as he led him along the grassy rise. As another marketing gimmick, the watercraft office had released a bass with a golden tag into the lake last weekend. The winner would claim a large cash prize, or at least that was what Drew had read in *The Beacon*.

"What would you do with the money, if you did win?" he asked Charlie.

"Baseball cards," he said simply. "And a fancy adding machine."

They passed behind the barge house, which looked exactly like the old canal barge it was, but with a raised roof and little flower bed at its base. On the other side and down a slight slope of a green lawn was the maple and, beneath that, a hammock full of sleeping woman.

"This is as far as I go, sir," the kid said. Drew fought an urge to both laugh and to tousle his hair.

"That bad, huh?"

"I woke her up from her Sunday nap when I was five," Charlie said, feigning a shudder. "I don't like talking about it."

Now Drew did laugh. This kid was going to grow up to be okay, either because of or despite a childhood in the shadow of some slightly odd people. "Thanks for the escort. And the warning."

"See ya at dinner." He took off running.

"Maybe." Stuffing hands in his pockets, Drew crossed the lawn until he stood two feet from the broad, corded hammock. It was tethered between the great tree trunk and a thick pole in the ground, easily shaded by the umbrella of leaves overhead.

He looked down for some time at Emily Graham, who was stretched out in a pair of pale blue shorts and a checkered blouse that tied in a little knot in the front. With one arm flung over the top of her head, the shirt bared a creamy patch of stomach. Her lashes lay still against the pink of her cheeks, and her hair was a puddle of sunlight around her head. For one dizzying moment, Drew didn't care about anything he should have cared about—justice, truth, family—and simply *wanted*. Wanted the right to curl up there beside her, stretch his hand across that stomach, feel how soft her skin was …

But then he made himself think of Jamie and whatever had happened behind the Reno warehouse that Gilbert Reese of Buckeye Lake knew all about. The Gilbert Reese who had run like a coward back home to his waiting fiancée. The fiancée with sunshine for hair who, without a doubt, knew exactly where Gilbert Reese was right now.

The one who had quivered in his own arms just two nights before.

Chapter Ten

The Buckeye Lake Beacon
Sunday, June 9, 1946
Graham's Marina offers Evinrude Outboards

Emily often dreamed she was falling.

Sometimes it happened as much as three times a week. In some dreams, she was riding on The Dips coaster, and it flew off the track at the top of the largest hill. In a childhood of cornfields and water, the coaster was the highest place she'd ever been. Other times, she dreamed she was falling out of a tree or off a dock.

So, when her world flipped and she literally fell, she experienced the usual skipped heartbeat and gasped her way out of sleep. Disoriented, she tasted ... *dirt?*

Emily was used to the falling sensation. The dirt taste was new.

"Sorry," she heard a voice say, and Emily felt like a rag doll being hoisted up by a large hand under each of her arms.

"Wha—?" She blinked into Drew Mathison's face.

"I only meant to jiggle the hammock to wake you," he said, his breath close for a mere second before he set her firmly on her feet.

Baffled, Emily looked down to see grass on her leg and palms, her hammock still bouncing in the breeze beside her. She dusted herself off a bit and squinted up to find Drew studying her. Should she be embarrassed? Had he come to finish what they'd begun on the pier two nights before? The unexpected scent of his aftershave took her back, and she remembered she'd been dreaming just now, not of falling, but of being in his arms again.

Then she'd fallen to earth with a thud, and she was terribly afraid she had produced an undignified grunt.

Of course, he wouldn't have dumped her on purpose.

But neither did he *seem* sorry, though she had heard him mutter the word. Shrugging, Emily yawned and smiled, glad to see him anyway. She had fought the urge yesterday to track him down, maybe to just walk his shift with him on the boardwalk. Of course, she had resisted the temptation. But she had perhaps too eagerly called the station in the evening upon discovering the disgusting typewriter threat, hoping it would be Drew who would come by.

"Hi," she said now, patting at her hair.

He reached out, and his thumb found her lower lip. The afternoon grew warmer, and Emily let her lips fall open as she held her breath. She told herself he wanted to kiss her, here on her island under the big maple. Maybe she was still dreaming.

"You've got some …" he began, his thumb coming away with a glob of dirt. The dirt, in fact, was on the verge of being mud, smeared along her inner lip as it had been.

Emily stepped back and scrubbed at her face as she had her knees and palms, laughing a little and warm for a different reason. So, no kissing for now. Unless he was after making more mud. *Ick.*

"You should come with me," she said, motioning for him to follow. "I clearly need a washcloth."

"Sorry again. I tried to grab you."

"I'm glad you stopped by." She let the question hang there … *why had he?*

"I've heard a lot about this place. The marina, the towpath. It's good to get to see it."

"I love it here. I live in this old barge," she told him like a thrilling confession. She opened the back screen door, its springs whining, and gestured for him to precede her inside. "Did you meet the family over at the house?"

"Yes. Charlie escorted me across the canal and to the porch, where I had some tea with your grandfather."

Emily watched Drew take in her little home. Rosie had helped her strip the walls here in the kitchen area so they could paper them over, a project they still hadn't finished. The space was dominated by just a small, green refrigerator, a sink with a pump faucet, and an oven/stove. It was a mere four steps from here to the adjacent dining area, overwhelmed by an antique plank table with benches.

Drew reached up and touched the exposed wood of the ceiling. She enjoyed watching the way his uniform shirt tightened against the muscles of his arm and back.

"This has to be original to the barge," he said.

"Yes. My great-grandfather won this thing in a card game, if you can believe it."

"Hickory was telling me about that."

"We added the little bathing room off to the side over here, thank heavens," Emily said, sliding past him. "I'll go wipe off a bit. I'll only be a minute. Look around all you want."

She knew what he'd see. There was only one other room downstairs, home to her bed with its bright quilt Grandma Louise had made. Emily was glad, not for the first time, that she still bothered to make her bed each morning. When a living space was so small, it had to be tidy.

Years ago, Hickory had expanded the box of a home by knocking out a wall. He'd added a stairway up to a little loft for storage, a closet under the stairs, and a tiny bathroom with sink, toilet, and tub. It would take Drew just about as long to tour it as it was taking her to dampen a cloth and remove the dirt.

Emily rinsed her mouth, dried it, and applied some gloss to her lips in case he felt like touching them again.

He looked enormous in her low-ceilinged bedroom area, his neck bent as he studied framed photos she'd hung on the stairway wall. Inside of frames she'd restored, there were shots of boats they'd decorated for parades through the years. Emily loved one of herself and Rosie, looking like little twins in braids next to a tunnel they'd built in the sand at the marina beach area. She had her grandparents' wedding photo, and it never ceased to startle her to see the pair of them so smooth and fresh.

"Who's this?" Drew asked, pointing to a photo of Lillian on stage in one of the outrageous outfits she'd danced in at the park. "She looks like you."

"My mother." His observation was a compliment, of course, and Emily both loved and hated being compared to her. Certainly, Lillian was lovely. Long, strong legs, a graceful neck, an enormous smile. But the photo failed to show the restlessness, the impatience. Drew could not yet know that Emily battled those traits, too.

"And these? Is this you back in school? Who are you with here?"

Rosie had taken the photo, so she wasn't in it. Spring Formal night, they had gathered for pictures here at the island with the lake behind them. Five fellows from Emily's own class and the year or so ahead, wearing white suit jackets and black bow ties, standing behind the girls who were dressed in white or pastel dresses, all bright in the monochrome shot.

They all looked so gangly, she thought.

"That's Dottie, there. You've met her by now, I'm sure."

"Yes. And I met this man the other day."

"Smokey? His hair was already gray then, believe it or not."

"And who's your date? I don't know him yet."

"That's Gil. Pastor Skip's son, actually."

"He still live around here?"

"He was in the Army," Emily said, purposely vague. "Why don't we sit out front for a bit? It's too nice a day to be indoors."

~~~~~

Drew let his mind process small things as he settled beside Emily on the stone step in front of her little barge house. The smell of smoked fish mingled with the fresh afternoon air, but he hardly paid attention to the boats out on the lake. Sound traveled strangely over the water: distant laughter, happy screams, outboard motors.

The barge-turned-home seemed some kind of extension of Emily Graham, everything bright with happy details. In full detective mode, he turned over that group photo in his mind, a cast of characters maybe six years younger than they were now. Different hairstyles, the narrow attractiveness of youth. There'd been no mistaking Gil Reese with his freckles, his hair thicker prior to enlisting. He and Emily had been laughing, clearly, in the photo.

Her response had confirmed the last of his suspicions. "He was in the Army," was all she'd said before urging him out of the house and changing the subject. If he angled for more information, she would be suspicious.

She was smart. He had to play this carefully.

Outright asking was never going to work. She'd just double down, no doubt about it. His best bet would be for her guard to stay down a bit, to get her to trust him, even if it felt a little dishonest.

But it was the job.

And she'd been dishonest, too, after all.

"I read the report about the typewriter dripping blood," he said finally, after they'd relaxed into the step. It was not very wide, but it was no hardship to let his leg touch her leg, even if it was just the job.

"My least favorite prank yet," Emily said, far less enthusiastic about "the difference" she was making than she had been before. "It was *messy*."

"And scary."

"I guess so. Did you see the photos Chief Gunn took?"

"Not yet. Just the report was on the counter when I got in this morning. Seems like the insults changed to threats and then the threats are escalating."

"It's funny because I haven't even run any letters for the past week. But people need hobbies, I suppose."

"The messages don't seem to be related to Cranberry Bog lately."

"I guess that's true. I hadn't thought about it."

They sat for a moment in silence. Drew imagined her running around putting in a full day of work each day, printing the paper, researching stories, and then managing the care and feeding of Gilbert Reese on top of it all. The coward must be nearby for her to manage it.

Drew swiveled his head to study her, her eyelids still a little pink and swollen from her nap. Lingering fatigue. Spots of red on her cheeks showed the heat of the afternoon. She turned from profile to face him, as well, and he watched her eyes study him as he had her.

"What?" she demanded.

"Who's your best friend?" He wasn't sure where the question came from, but he resented being jealous of the answer.

"My best friend? What do you mean? You mean like Dottie or Rosie or my aunt?"

"I mean who do you unload on when it all gets to be too much?"

She shook her head, looked away. At first, he thought she would just ignore him and move on. Then she finally said, "I guess I don't do that, really."

"You're young. You're running a business in an industry dominated by men. You've got a bottom line, deadliness, and the start of worry lines."

"Hey, now."

"Who do you unload on, Emily?"

She shifted, visibly uncomfortable.

"I'm not even scratching the surface, am I? I don't know half the load you carry."

"You think you've got me figured out after meeting me only a few times."

"I'm trying to."

"Okay. Well, then … I talk to God when it gets to be too much," she said hesitantly. Then, sadder, "But I don't have a person like that. Not really."

"Why not Rosie?"

"She's got her own heavy load that you don't know about."

Drew made a sound to acknowledge that. "I suppose God might put people in your life to help carry all the heavy things."

Oh, he felt like the biggest hypocrite and worst kind of person, using that.

"Not that I'm one to talk," he added.

Emily met his eyes again. "You don't have that person either, do you?"

"No."

"You can tell me things, Drew."

"You've got your own heavy load."

"Touché," Emily said with a grin, but she still looked uneasy.

Drew decided to wait her out in silence. It was an essential skill for a peace officer. Their hands were close. Barely moving, he entwined his smallest finger with hers.

And, just as he'd expected, it paid off.

"I guess there is one thing I'd like some human advice on," she said softly and reluctantly. She glanced around them as if to ensure they were still very alone. "No one else knows about it though."

Could it be this easy? Drew felt his heart beating against his chest and hoped she didn't feel it speed up through their linked fingers.

"You can trust me. I hardly know anyone here. Why would I tell your secrets?" He meant it. He believed he was Gil Reese's only chance for survival, apart from Drew's need for his testimony.

"I'm not sure I'm doing the right thing, is all. I just don't know."

"Things like that are hard to deal with alone."

Emily took a deep breath. "Hickory and Rosie would be so angry with me at this point, if they knew it had gone this far. If they knew what I was doing." Drew waited while she fought some kind of inner battle. "Look, it's probably not going to seem like a very big deal to you, and there's nothing you can do about it anyway."

Don't be so sure. On either count. "I can listen."

He released her finger and shifted to run a hand along her back in comfort. It felt natural to touch her. He reminded himself all over again that she would be Mrs. Reese once the trial was over and her fiancé was safe.

"I have to tell you the background for any of it to make sense," she finally said, apologetically.

"I have nowhere else to be."

"My father grew up here on this island. Jesse Graham. He was my grandparents' only child."

This was not where Drew had expected her connection to Gil Reese to begin, but again, he was patient.

"My mother was a dancer at the park."

"The photo."

"Yes. Lillian Turnbull, practically an orphan when they met. He fell in love with her. They got married and lived here."

"Here in the barge?"

"Yes. He was just back from the first war and was going to take over the marina. They had Rosie and me pretty quickly, but from the sounds of things, Lillian didn't quite know what to do about a family. She hadn't grown up in one, and her only friends were showgirls." He let her pause. "I don't remember because I was just a baby, but my father was killed in an explosion at McCook Field. It's an experimental aviation site over in Dayton that he sometimes worked at after the war. For extra money, you know?"

"I'm sorry."

She shrugged. "I don't remember."

"Still." He kept his hand on her back and felt her deep breath.

"My mother didn't do well with two babies alone, stuck out on this island, surrounded by cornfields. So, she left."

Drew tried to imagine it. This was nothing like his own story growing up.

"She left us to Hickory and Louise. No doubt the best and kindest people you could want to raise your daughters, of course." This all matched with what he'd heard from Cookie when she'd spoken of her

76

sister's death and the devastation it had had on the family. She'd been the only mother Emily or Rosie had known. Drew appreciated that now.

"They did a good job with you," he said stupidly.

Emily nudged him and smiled again. "Lillian missed dancing, I guess. She missed the life, her body before babies. The show. She didn't like to sit still, from what I've heard. That's why my grandparents have always made us rest on Sundays. Well, because of *me*, if you want the truth of it. Because I'm like that, too."

"Don't like sitting still?"

"Right. It's not an exaggeration to say I worry a little about being like her in that way."

"You're not, though. You're incredibly loyal to people," Drew said, and he was confident saying it. Her loyalty, in fact, was ruining his own immediate goals.

"Growing up, I always wondered what it would be like to have a mother like other girls had. Or grandparents who could just spoil you like grandparents are supposed to. I missed my mother, even though I don't remember her. But it wasn't like that for Rosie. Sometimes I'd wish out loud that Lillian would come back. I used to lie in bed the night before my birthday, imagining her just showing up and surprising me. I figured I'd know her right away because I studied that picture all the time." Emily started to chew her fingernail. "When we got ready for that dance, the one you saw a photo of in there? I wished so hard that she would come and help Rosie and me with our hair. Surprise us with a little perfume. Say she was proud of how lovely we looked, all dressed up.

"I even tried taking dance lessons," she said on a rueful laugh. "I thought she'd be very happy about that when she got back."

"But she never came back?"

"No." Emily still chewed her fingernail. Drew temporarily forgot he had hoped for a different story entirely. "I had all my fantasies of some kind of normal family with a mom, but Rosie didn't want to hear any of it. She never has. And Hickory changed the subject any time I brought up our mother. They had searched for her initially, but I think he never quite got over her just abandoning us."

"I can see that."

"This is the first time anyone's let me talk about her," Emily told him suddenly. "Are you sure you don't mind?"

Drew smiled at her. "Unloading does feel good. That's what I meant. And I like hearing you talk."

"Are we friends, then?"

"I hope so." It wasn't a lie. Anyone, he thought with a pang, could count himself lucky to know her.

Emily seemed satisfied. Then she took a deep breath. "So, anyway, when the first letter from Lillian arrived for me at *The Beacon*, I wanted to tell them. Hickory and Rosie." She looked at Drew again now, as though measuring his reaction to what sounded like it should be too happy to be a secret. "But I didn't."

"What did the letter say? And when did it come?"

"Last year was the first one."

Emily explained that there had been some publicity from her college paper and her journalism peers about her—a woman—taking over as publisher of *The Buckeye Lake Beacon*, which was the only way she figured Lillian had heard about it in California. In the letter, Lillian had been slightly penitent but explained she was down on her luck and dreamed of returning to her girls. Her dancing days were done, but she couldn't afford to travel all the way across the country to Ohio.

"When I sent her money for the train and expenses, I kept it to myself," Emily told Drew. "I told myself it would be such a nice surprise for Rosie, for our mother to arrive as I'd always dreamed. For her to get to know her grandson, Charlie, to say nothing of her daughters. I had woven quite a lovely scene in my mind about it."

"The fact there's no sign of her here now makes me think it didn't turn out like that."

"I kept waiting and waiting for a telegram to pick her up in Columbus. I waited for weeks, but I heard nothing."

Drew was not surprised by the rest of Emily's narrative. Another letter had arrived. Another request for funds. The last money sent had to be used to clear some debts before Lillian could leave Fresno, she'd explained, but now she was nearly settled up and ready to come home. Could Emily send more? Emily had remembered to pray for guidance that time, knowing Hickory would tell her she was being taken advantage of and Rosie would advise her, as she always had, to leave well enough alone.

Surely God would want her to help her mother, though, to forgive not just the lifetime of absence but also this recent betrayal. Emily had gone to her Bible and found verses about forgiveness and giving, about turning the other cheek. Pastor Skip had preached about loving the unlovely. The prodigal son could also be a prodigal mother. So, she'd dived into her savings once more.

And once more there had been another extended period of silence. "That was the first time I admitted to myself I was being a fool."

"It's not foolish to forgive people and love them and try to help," Drew said.

"Now it seems she's in some kind of trouble with the law," Emily confessed, letting her despair come through in the words. "She assures me it's 'nothing bad,' but she needs money to pay a hefty fine and get out of jail. She had bought the train ticket to return last time, she says, but she missed the train due to this 'mixup' with her landlord."

"What will you do?"

"I sent it the other day. Almost emptied my savings." She dropped her head on her knees. "It turns out the pretend family I'd constructed with her as the central figure is more powerful than my common sense. I couldn't sleep thinking she's huddled behind bars somewhere, waiting for help."

"How is she communicating with you? I mean, where are you sending the money?"

"Her friend Angelina. She's a dancer, poor like her, so she can't help with bail."

"How will you know if she got it?" Emily looked on the verge of tears, so he moved his hand onto her back again and hastily said, "Actually, never mind."

When Emily leaned into his side as though spent, Drew's heart ached. And finally, he remembered that he'd needed entirely different information from this woman.

"I keep praying."

"Of course, you do." Sitting back and looking at her objectively, this lovely and energetic woman who was a professional success was dealing with quite a mess, indeed. From what he knew and what he suspected he knew, she was trying to take on a zoning proposal that was making half the town furious, she was forking over most of her income to a mother who didn't care about her, she felt like she was betraying the people who did care about her in the process, *and* she had undoubtedly been roped into hiding and protecting a man being hunted by the mafia. Never mind that the man must have promised to love and protect *her* forever.

Looking down, Drew noticed she didn't wear an engagement ring.

A low, sweet ringing echoed across Towpath Island, and Emily raised her head. "That's the bell for supper. You're staying, right?"

Chapter Eleven

The Buckeye Lake Beacon
Sunday, June 9, 1946
Three ways to season your fresh catch

"What on earth is going on?" Rosie hissed in Emily's ear as they plated potato salad.

"Nothing. What do you mean?"

"Some dreamboat just drops in here unannounced for dinner? And you're acting strange. Did Deputy Mathison make some kind of move that made you uncomfortable or something?"

Rosie always expected the worst from men under seventy. Especially the dreamboat versions.

Delia slammed into the kitchen then, interrupting the conversation. "I'll hold the door while you bring the plates out," she said, a piece of raw carrot hanging out of her mouth like a cigar. "Can I stay after dinner a bit longer, Rosie?"

"Pastor Skip said you needed to be home by dark, that's all," Rosie responded. Delia did a strange little dance of celebration. Emily grabbed two plates and skirted out of the kitchen, away from her sister's assessing eyes. Emily felt disloyal, having just laid part of her troubles out for Drew and never for her sister.

Wasn't this particular part of the burden more Rosie's business than his?

Now Drew Mathison was plunked down comfortably at Hickory's right hand for Sunday supper. Emily made eye contact with him as she set a plate of fish, carrots, and potato salad down in front of him. She felt oddly embarrassed, finally having shared her story about her mother with another person. Or *lack* of a story about her mother. Drew was looking at her differently, but she couldn't decide exactly in what way it felt different.

It was almost like he was disappointed with her, but why would that be?

At least he hadn't told her she was stupid and wrong. She knew she was, on some level, but she didn't need to hear anyone say it.

"Thanks," he said in response to the plate of food, spreading a checkered napkin in his lap. Hickory was telling him stories about ice fishing. Emily set her grandfather's plate down now and turned to find her sister had placed her own directly across from Drew's. She pushed her fish around with one of the three-tined forks her grandmother had said had been in the family for ... who knew? Emily wished, not for the first time, she'd paid more attention to those details.

"Father, thank You once more for this good day and for providing for us like the loving Creator You are," Hickory said, head bent. They had all joined hands. Delia's was sticky. "We give thanks for today's good catch that will nourish us so we can be at our best as we work for You. It's in Jesus' name we pray."

"Amen," they said.

"Delia, did you wash your hands?" Emily whispered.

"Yes. Rosie made us."

"Why are you sticky?"

Delia shrugged. "I'm just one of those sorts of people."

"What does that *mean*?"

"Emily has been to Philadelphia," Hickory was saying, pulling her back into the conversation. "With a group in college, wasn't it, honey?"

"Yes," she said.

"It's a beautiful city," Drew said. "Growing up there was fun."

"Do you plan to return?" Rosie asked from beside him.

"Yes, ma'am. Just have to get this law enforcement thing the rest of the way out of my system."

Emily took advantage of an opportunity to watch him pat his lips with a napkin. Then she watched his throat work as he swallowed some tea.

"I'll most likely end up back in the family business. Construction, contracting."

"Ah, you're a builder," Hickory said approvingly. Emily thought of the way Drew had investigated the old beams in the barge house and realized she'd ignored his professional interest while she had studied his arm muscles. "Heavens knows, if you have a minute—when you're not patrolling, I mean—we could hire you on for a few hours here and there at the marina," Hickory went on. "Some of the buildings need work, as I'm sure you noticed. The girls have been urging me to hire more help now that there's help to be had again."

"Grandpa, it should be better now that you've brought that Tom fellow on now and then. He'll hopefully get the docks re-planked out at the tie ups soon," Rosie said.

"*That* guy? He mostly stands around and smokes," Delia offered around a mouthful of fish. "Want me to yell at him for ya?"

"Maybe he's just getting the feel for things, since he only just started," Hickory reasoned gently. "I'll handle him, Sweetpea. What kind of building do you and your family do, Drew?"

"A little of everything, but we work on a lot of the high rises in the heart of the city."

"Not afraid of heights, then?"

"No, sir. My second youngest brother didn't care so much for walking a steel bar fifty feet over concrete, but he was good at the business side."

"Was? Tell me you didn't lose him in the war," Hickory said softly, putting his knife down.

"Not in the war," Drew said, pausing to take a bite. "He was Army, but he was murdered here in the states not long ago."

He didn't raise his eyes as the family expressed dismay. Emily studied him differently. She had wrongly assumed his deep-seated sadness was the result of the war. It seemed to be a heaviness many soldiers carried now, but she knew now she'd been hasty in her assumption. And selfish.

"How did he get murdered? Did someone stab him with a knife?" Delia wanted to know, having forsaken her dinner in a quest for details.

Emily winged an elbow against her.

"Delia, I'm sure he doesn't want to talk about it," Rosie said kindly. "Could you pass the rolls this way, dear?"

"How are you liking Buckeye Lake so far, then, Drew?" Emily asked before Delia could reinsert herself, as she was very good at doing.

"I do like it," he said, taking a last bite of fish. Then he sat back and, drawing in a deep breath, looked around the table. "I don't do many hours at the park, really, so I'd be happy to lend a hand here with the planks if I can. I'll probably be around here a good deal, anyway."

That last part hung in the air as the others turned to Emily. She felt her face heating. What was he saying? *I'll probably be around here a good deal.* Since when did a man make a formal declaration to a girl's family when he simply wanted to go out with her? This wasn't the eighteenth century.

But something girly inside her thrilled at the idea that he was openly interested.

"You're always welcome," Hickory said, still studying Emily. "But may I ask ... in what capacity?"

"As something like a bodyguard, sir, for Emily."

Emily dropped her fork, which pinged loudly against the side of her plate and sent a creamy potato square flying toward Charlie.

"A bodyguard!" Rosie gasped. Or maybe Emily had gasped. She wasn't sure which.

"Is she in some kind of danger?" Hickory had given up eating, too, and blanched. He assessed his granddaughter, and she wilted. "I knew it. I *knew* something was bothering her."

"Perhaps," Drew said with a glance at the children. "That sense that he was holding back some grim truth, in fact, had Emily feeling frightened even though she, of everyone, knew there was nothing substantial to be frightened about. Nothing too very substantial, anyway. Was there? "I'm sure she's told you about the vandalism and threats."

"You mean the 'bog rat' thing on her car?" asked Charlie, clearly worried anyway.

Rosie put her hand on his shoulder as though to soothe him, her brows drawn together when she turned to Emily. "You're getting *threats* now?"

The old farmhouse table was too wide for Emily to kick Drew beneath it. What was he *doing*?

"He's talking about this thing that happened yesterday, but it's no big deal," she said, trying to smile their fears away. "Someone left a typewriter in front of the office with something unpleasant typed on the paper in it."

"What did it say?" Delia demanded with relish. She was enjoying this meal more than she had anything in some time, Emily figured.

"Just reminding me again to stop writing about the zoning for the new resort, that's all."

"There was more to it than that, sir, but we can talk about it later," Drew said to Hickory in a fraternal, masculine way that had Emily's hackles rising. "Anyway, I think she could be in danger."

Emily was silent now in the way a person was when she realized someone she respected was actually deranged.

"What are you proposing?" Rosie asked. "Are you saying you're moving out here? That seems ... extreme."

"No, no. I'll simply watch from a distance, ma'am. See if I can figure out who's responsible and how substantial the threat is."

"I am fine," Emily said at last, trying to toss water on the fire Drew was lighting unnecessarily. She had been saying it in her head for weeks. *I am fine.* "Listen, this is Buckeye Lake. Extremely scary things don't happen here. We're talking about some folks who are angry about news stories, that's all."

Drew crossed his arms, the muscles moving in a way that still managed to distract her. "Bloody typewriters?"

"Bloody?" Delia and Rosie exclaimed together.

"Sorry," Drew said.

"Clearly just a request to stop writing editorials," Emily said through her teeth.

Did the escalating gestures worry her a bit? Of course.

Who was foolish enough to be thrilled with threats involving blood splatter, even if it was fake? But her family certainly didn't need to shoulder this, so she kept owning the incidents like badges of honor.

"Maybe you *should* stop writing editorials," Hickory said reasonably. "There's plenty more to write about here at the lake. Is this really worth it?"

"Stop covering the resort proposal? Grandpa, no. I can't do that."

"The threats are getting worse. I think it's time to get to the bottom of it," Drew said calmly. "And I can. It's what I'm good at."

"This is unnecessary."

"You want to just keep filing reports and do nothing to stop it? The messages are getting bolder, and you know it. Suppose they … take it further?"

"No one's going to hurt me."

"We can't pay you," Hickory said from the head of the table, and Emily groaned because he was clearly convinced. "Except in food. We can feed you."

"No one will be paying him *at all*," Emily said. "Drew, please don't take this the wrong way, because I'm sure you know your profession, but … a police officer cannot just appoint himself someone's bodyguard against her will."

"Why would it be against your will?" This from Hickory. "Seems to me a man offers to watch your back, you say thanks. I *knew* something was off with you lately."

"I certainly wouldn't expect to be paid, sir. Emily and I are friends."

Emily closed her eyes. She imagined herself moving through her life with an armed guard trailing her. What would everyone say? It was ridiculous. She took her work seriously, but she certainly didn't take her*self* that seriously. The guys in the office would never let her live it down.

"Look," she said, deliberately talking to Drew like she would a child. "This all seems rather extreme. How about I just promise to keep you informed if anything else happens?"

She would never breathe another word of it.

"Chief Gunn agrees with me on this. He thinks we need to do more since *they're* doing more."

Hickory's hand came down on the table the way it did whenever their wise leader had made up his mind about a thing. The thud, familiar and final to Emily throughout childhood, sealed her fate. "I will not have you in danger, Emily. If Chief Gunn says it and this upstanding young man says it, there's a choice to be made. Either shut down the paper until this blows over—"

Emily sucked in a loud, outraged breath.

"—or let this capable lawman keep a watch over things."

"Think of it more as surveillance. A stakeout," Drew told her, looking very relaxed now that he'd given everyone else at the table indigestion.

~~~~~

As night fell, Drew was surprised at how different it was, crossing the little footbridge in the dark.

The floodlights had flicked on along the bank of the canal below, illuminating the whimsical glass creations Rosie had arranged down there. They almost seemed to float in the night, the deep red tone of hearts reflected in the canal water.

It was enough to make him forget the reason he'd found his way to this out-of-the-way lake to begin with.

"You do amazing work," he told Rosie, who had offered to walk him out. She'd wrapped a summer sweater around her shoulders and hugged it to herself, nodding thanks for his compliment.

"You're staying at Cookie's and Burt's place?" Rosie asked.

"Or in my truck over here next to the marina. I was serious about the stakeout." He'd certainly not drive away and open the door for Emily to go off and meet up with Gil. He was only moderately concerned about the messages she was getting, but they did give him the excuse he needed to watch her every movement.

To that end, he understood her irritation with him, even as he was angry with her himself. She had lost an important battle at the family dinner table, but more, she'd been right. The idea of her situation requiring an armed guard, at least on the surface, was absurd and unnecessary. Drew was objective enough to admit that manipulating her grandfather's deep love for her was somewhat low.

But he was willing to bet she hadn't considered how hiding the only witness to a murder might affect a grieving family's need for justice or, from a larger perspective, public safety in general. He couldn't appeal to her in that way. Not yet, anyway. She wasn't the type to hand over the love of her life when he was counting on her to keep him safe.

"You're sleeping in your *truck*?" Rosie asked, appalled.

"I can see everything from out here. And I don't require much sleep. The Army teaches you that."

Hickory had slipped him the key to the marina buildings when he'd asked him privately, on the pretense of making sure everything on the island, at least, was safe. Tonight, he'd explore while the Grahams slept.

"I hope you're wrong about there being actual danger in all of this," Rosie said. "But I have a child to keep safe, so I can't see the downside in you making sure."

"I'll make sure. But keep Charlie close for a bit, just in case," Drew said. He thought about the Conti family and what they did to people, and he thought about sweet, trusting Charlie, running free on an island that had always been safe. He wished he could say more.

Emily approached then, sparking annoyance even in the dark. The sisters had retreated to the kitchen after supper, and now tension vibrated between them. Drew had stopped on the bridge, hoping the thing wouldn't collapse. With a separate part of his brain, he calculated it would take a day or two at most to reinforce it.

"I'm glad someone knows the truth about what's been going on with Em," Rosie said.

Emily made a sound like a growl.

"It was a pleasure to meet you, Mr. Mathison." She seemed to debate the wisdom of leaving him with her irritated sister, but then she turned to leave. "Just let me know if you need anything."

"Thank you. I will."

Rosie waved and disappeared into the darkness of Towpath Island. Emily hesitated, then walked onto the bridge, as well.

This was a very different woman from the one he'd stood in the dark with two nights before, even if the scent of her was the same. Drew mourned the loss of their easy camaraderie, their undeniable attraction to one another ... squelched on his own side by the knowledge she was engaged to be married and on her side by the fact she was used to calling all the shots.

When she finally spoke, it was as though she could read his mind. "This changes things, Mathison."

"Does it?"

"I admit I was very attracted to you before. The first time I saw you. At the bait shop. On the pier. Even when you sat beside me on my step earlier."

"And you're not now."

"To be honest, I don't think you're quite right in the head. I know I've been hinting at that all evening, but I'm just going to say it now. I hope it doesn't hurt your feelings."

Drew couldn't help chuckling. He really did enjoy her, despite everything, and he privately understood her perspective completely. "I'm sorry if that renders me unattractive," he said. "But what if I can't help it?"

"Oh, I'm sure you can't. I don't suppose people can't help being deranged."

The sound of other voices crawled through the night and over the canal water below, halting their exchange. Drew peered over to see a rowboat bump its way from the lake into the entrance of the piece of old canal—the lovebirds Charlie had warned him about earlier. He heard more than saw them: oars softly thudding against the wood of the little boat, the low hum of their voices. There was a girlish giggle, an exclamation over the embrace of the swans, lit from behind. Emily watched the pair slide through the night beneath them, as well, standing silent beside him. He wondered if she envied them the romance, as he did—a magical, intimate evening devoid of vomiting herons or secrets.

A prism of reflected light caught the couple, just for a second, as the boat slid beneath the bridge, and Drew would have them forever in his mind like that: a large, awkward young man's hand tenderly caressing a girl's back through her corded sweater. And just as quickly, they were gone, swallowed back up by the night, little ripples trailing back through the sleepy canal.

Drew wanted to imagine the pair of them getting married someday, maybe telling their grandchildren later in the century about the artist lady who lived on a strip of an island who made an open-air tunnel of love for them. He told himself the couple could have that future. The war was over, wasn't it? The kid wouldn't get drafted. Maybe they'd hang tight to one another and everyone they loved would stay alive, and maybe their nights would slip by in quiet sleep filled with happy memories of glowing swans and hearts and roses.

None of that resembled his own nights or his own memories, but he could hope that for others and try, try to believe it would happen for them, if not for himself. Otherwise, what had it all been for?

Was Emily thinking about the same things, for herself, he wondered? He considered her, standing beside him, copying his posture against the railing. Would she and her darling Gil have their happily ever after? Children and romance? Or would Gilbert be always hiding from a killer? Had Emily's dreams died, too, in Reno this spring?

"I know it's not your fault you can't think clearly, but this quest of yours is going to be very inconvenient for me," she said softly when it was just them again. "And that irritates me."

"So, no chance of a dance now? Or a kiss?"

"I can't take advantage of you that way. You poor man."

Drew couldn't stop the grin again. "Is it that? Or are you ... involved with someone else?"

"No, no one else," she said simply.

His heart sank. *She's a natural liar.*

She went on, "You know, it's funny, but I've never floated through Lovers' Canal with anyone. I grew up with it, but I've always been up here on land, looking down." She sighed, turning away from the view below and looking at him now. "How does this work, Mathison? Do I have to give you my schedule or something? And how long does it go on? A couple of days?"

"We'll see how things go. For now, just ignore me. I'll keep an eye on you."

"I don't like any of this."

"I've noticed."

"What if you can't keep up with me?"

It felt like a challenge, so he decided he'd better try to catch a few hours of sleep after he'd poked around in the marina storehouses.

Chapter Twelve

The Buckeye Lake Beacon
Monday, June 10, 1946
Council passes cycling ordinance

Emily woke groggy on Monday morning with the uneasy feeling she'd suffered from nightmares all night long. As the sun streamed in through the lace-framed windows of the barge, though, she realized that uneasy feeling was yesterday in general. No nightmares, no dreams of falling off roller coasters, really — just the dregs of a not-so-normal Sunday.

She wrapped herself in a robe, tying it a little tighter than usual. She made herself a cup of coffee and shuffled around blowing on it, peering out each window cautiously. Sunbeams decorated dew on flowers. The hammock was still, the light catching a new spider web stretching from its top to the maple. A cheerful boat horn barked out a greeting from the otherwise quiet water. She saw Hickory talking with a family out by the bay at the marina, across the canal. They'd probably just arrived for a week of vacation. Tom, the new part-time help, stood near him, nodding.

Everything was calm, a typical Monday on the west side of Buckeye Lake, and Emily tried to cheer herself with the thought of a public records request to kick off today's to-do list.

There was always work to do.

Deliberately humming, she pulled on a breezy and comfortable skirt, packed up her satchel with what she'd need for the day, and only burned her toast a little before leaving with it. She paused to lock her door for the first time ever, though, humming a little louder to distract herself from the click as she twisted the key.

Of course, she was thinking about Drew Mathison this morning, as she had late into the night. For the first time in her adult life, she'd been strongly attracted to a man. She'd experienced the butterflies in the stomach that the other girls had always talked about. *Finally!* Her heart had at last been touched, only to have it all turn out ... confusing.

He hadn't seemed quixotic before last evening.

Emily tried not to feel foolish, waiting for word from her mother that might never come, starting to fall for a war hero who had turned out to be, at best, eccentric. Possibly delusional.

She tore off a bite of toast and shoved Drew out of her mind again. He had his agenda and she had hers, and that was that. As long as she understood her own, well, that was what mattered.

Emily waved farewell to Hickory as she accelerated up the parking lot. He raised his hand, his white brows drawn together. She was eager for that concerned look to leave his face. She figured it would, with time. Up at Loop Road, which ran in a simple circle around Liebs Island, she eased the car out to the right.

And was distressed when a partly rusted Ford work truck appeared in her rearview mirror.

She jerked in the driver's seat and saw Drew Mathison's hand wave to her from the truck's window. She sped up. *He's really doing this.* Tightening her hands on the wheel, Emily remembered her to-do list and the pep talk she'd already given herself once this morning. Her agenda had nothing to do with him. He could drive around behind her all day, for all she cared.

But she still caught herself biting her lower lip until she tasted blood.

Emily stopped at the post office to get *The Beacon's* mail. Drew's truck was parked just across the street. He didn't seem to be looking when she jumped back in her car, so she stuffed the classified ad envelopes and other mail into the glove box, whipped out of the lot, and took four usually un-travelled alleys and two side streets to get to the village hall.

She was dismayed to hear the truck chugging up behind her when she parked near the zoning office entrance.

Taking a deep breath, she slung her satchel strap across her chest, closed her car door and walked calmly back to his truck. Drew had a day's worth of whiskers she'd never seen on him before, but he looked relaxed behind the wheel in a fresh shirt. His bare arm was stretched across the door.

"You're following me," she told him, inanely.

His teeth were so white when he smiled. "I told you I would."

"What do you think I'm going to do?" She lowered her voice, leaned in.

"It's not about that. It's about what someone else might do."

"You're wasting your time."

"Maybe. It's my time to waste." He shrugged.

"Doesn't your family need you back at the business? In Philadelphia?"

"They got along all right without me for the last couple years."

"You could be making money over at the park."

"Gunn and I have an understanding, but it's nice of you to worry about my finances. Just carry on, Emily."

Emily pursed her lips to keep from losing her temper when he was so infuriatingly non-confrontational. Determined to go about business as usual, she greeted Carol, the zoning clerk, and settled in with a copy of an environmental group's objective report on the bog acreage. The zoning commission kept denying possession of the report, but here it was! Now they could read the highlights in *The Beacon* with everyone else.

She spent hours on the report, imagining Drew hot and bored in the parking lot. She walked across the street and left a message for Dottie at the park office. Then she moseyed to her sister's studio to check on photos from the regatta, to find Rosie still somber about the apparent "danger" in Emily's life.

The one thing Emily was not keeping secret since it wasn't real.

Back on the boardwalk, she saw Drew Mathison leaning against a light pole.

She wished the butterflies in her stomach would get the message from her brain that he was off limits now.

"I hope you had time for some breakfast or something," she told him sweetly as she strolled past, not bothering to stop.

"Your concern is touching."

He stayed put, and Emily met with the leads of the show diving team back in the park office. She paid them from the Civic Association's coffers and discussed the coming week's schedule. When one of them complained that someone had shot off a bottle rocket in their direction while they performed, it was easy to refer them to Drew.

"See that guy out there leaning against the light pole?"

"Yeah."

"He's a cop. Tell him exactly what happened. Tell him I said you need a *detailed* report about the incident on file and that we'd all be grateful if they'd keep a closer eye on the discharge of fireworks within the park."

Grinning, she waved to him and proceeded to check on Sub Man at the end of the pier. She stopped smiling when she had to wait ten minutes for a conversation on the under-water telephone while a group of young women flirted with him.

"It's that accent," one of them sighed. "So dreamy."

"I might go broke," another one said, handing off the phone to the next in line and paying the attendant her dollar, "but I think he might marry me at the end of summer."

Emily verified with the attendant that all was well, that the association was making good money from this silly gimmick, and then she spent a few minutes on the phone, sorry that she herself was indifferent to the accent.

Emily checked her watch. Moving quickly because the zoning business had taken longer than she thought, she returned to the office for a new notepad. She was meeting the city solicitor for lunch at Captain Jake's, a quick trip up the North Shore. She wondered if Drew Mathison would get a table next to them or if he would just go hungry.

That was when she spotted her bicycle, the one she'd ridden so faithfully during fuel rations, propped in the back of the office. She kicked around an idea.

It was a lovely day for a bike ride, and a little exercise might be just the thing for the headache she only just realized she had developed. So, she slipped out the back door, pushing the Schwinn until she reached an alley, where she hiked up her skirt, hopped on, and pedaled up residential back roads to get to Captain Jake's.

There, she celebrated her cunning escape by treating herself to imported shrimp and some sparkling conversation with Roscoe Morris about sidewalk ordinances the council wanted him to draft. He asked her if she wanted to see a movie that coming weekend with him, and she thanked him for the invitation but told him no, as she always did.

Heaven knew she had enough on her mind without worrying about another man right now. She insisted on paying for her own shrimp. She told herself Morris had agreed to the lunch interview because he respected her as a professional and not because he'd been looking for another chance to ask her out.

Emily decided she was safe to bike back up the main Lake Road and enjoy looking at the shops with their colorful displays. She'd always found them cheery, with the bright umbrellas and striped beach towels in every color. She was pedaling out of the restaurant's lot and onto the street when she heard a strange, small siren whoop behind her. Baffled, she applied the brakes and looked over her shoulder to find herself being "pulled over" by none other than Officer Drew Mathison on a cop bike with a ridiculous little siren and spinning light perched on its handlebars.

If she thought she'd felt embarrassed earlier, this was on a new level.

Gritting her teeth, she stood beside her Schwinn as he approached, his hat tugged low so his face was partly in shadow.

"I hope you're finding this as humiliating as I am," she told him.

"Maybe. It's a great day for a ride, though, ma'am." He took a small booklet out of his pocket. "How was your lunch?"

"Delicious. You should try the shrimp sometime. It's been a pretty quiet morning, yes? Not much cause for alarm?"

"Not much."

"Has it occurred to you that these villains paint threats against me when I'm not *with* them? Shouldn't you be staked out at the office or the island? Squatting in a bush or something to keep watch?"

"We'll see. I'll adjust the plan as I need to. Your lip is bleeding a little. What happened?"

She licked at it, making a mental note to stop chomping on it in moments of agitation.

"You didn't stop back there, when you pulled out of the restaurant and onto the road," he went on soberly. "I'm trying to decide if I should just give you a warning or a citation."

"*Please.*" She huffed out a breath. A car full of schoolmates Emily had grown up with rolled by slowly, waving and pointing at her, pulled over with a bicycle by a bicycling cop. The sore part of her lip protested as she clamped down on it again with her teeth.

"It seems like you're trying to elude me."

"And it seems like you're … angry with me. Underneath whatever else you say this is."

"I'm trying to protect you. I'm being professional."

Emily decided not to debate that. "Listen, Mathison. This is ridiculous. I don't even care anymore that you can't help that you're deranged. Please back off, or I might call the real police."

"I'm as real as they come," he said, scribbling out the ticket and offering the wide, white smile she'd only seen twice since the day they'd met.

~~~~~

And so, it went on that way.

For a week. Underneath every move she made was the conviction that she didn't really understand what Mathison was really doing as he "guarded" her. And underneath every move *he* made lurked a strange kind of tension that felt, for all he denied it, like anger.

Emily accumulated, on average, one citation a day for bizarre infractions, promptly tossing them into the trash can. She was cited for loitering while waiting for the school board to come out of executive session. She got another citation because one of her brake lights on the Cabriolet was burned out, though the bulb had been mysteriously replaced by the time she got up the next morning. When she tossed one of the paper citations at the trashcan and the wind blew it out onto the sidewalk, Drew Mathison was there to immediately cite her for littering.

She had snapped at him after that, which wasn't as satisfying as she'd hoped. He insisted he was doing his job. She insisted he was out of his mind.

"Are you committed to protecting me or to throwing me in prison for something?"

When he couldn't offer a clear answer to that, she vowed to ignore him completely in the hope that would make him go away. He needed to be locked up somewhere, himself, until he could think logically.

She was successful at ignoring him for two days.

On the third day, Drew started working on replacing the dock boards at the marina alongside Hickory and Charlie. She could hear the masculine rumble of voices out her window while she made tea to help her sleep.

The tea did not work.

On the fourth day, Emily realized she couldn't eat dinner with her family anymore because Drew was there for meals. They *liked* him. Hickory admonished her for not being more hospitable to a man determined to keep her safe from these vague threats she'd been receiving about the resort. Because she couldn't manage to be gracious to their new "guest," she ate condensed soup in the barge house kitchen while Drew played rummy with her family and feasted on Rosie's baked chicken.

Suppose he fell in love with Rosie? She would make an amazing wife, after all. Her maternal skills were already obvious. Emily vowed to talk to her sister about the drawbacks of marrying a crazy man, no matter how handsome he was.

The next day, when the sun came up, it occurred to her she hadn't truly slept in a week. That evening, seeing him sitting behind the wheel of the Ford when she was on her way to the dumpster, she went with her gut and flung a sack of garbage at his windshield.

Afterward, she wasn't sure why she had done that.

"That was childish," Drew confirmed, his head resting on the back window, his eyes partly closed.

So, suddenly breathing hard, she retrieved a half-rotten melon from the ground where it had rolled and burst it on the truck's hood with all her might. Had anything felt that good in months?

"Are you done?"

"There haven't been any new threats," she huffed.

"I feel like *you're* threatening *me* right now."

"Seriously. I don't know what you think this is, but I'm going to Gunn. This isn't reassuring or sweet."

"It's not supposed to be sweet. Maybe no one is threatening you because you're protected now. Has that occurred to you?"

"Go away."

But he didn't.

Then, on Friday morning, when Emily returned from getting her third cup of black coffee of the day, she found Drew Mathison inside her newspaper office instead of inside his truck.

"*What* is he doing in here?" she demanded so ungraciously that it silenced the entire office. She plunked her cup down on her desk and marched toward the back, where he stood in his short-sleeved shirt and shoulder holster, hugging a stack of at least fifty newspapers. She drilled her index finger into his bicep and forced herself to pull it away after the contact. "What are you doing in here?"

"I invited him in to help me address and stamp the papers for delivery, dear," Cookie said, in a tone that implied Emily was the crazy one. Like Hickory and Rosie, Cookie was reassured by Drew's tough guy presence. Whoever this FH Resorts was, the rest of the family knew Drew could handle their shenanigans. When it came to Emily, they could finally relax for a while.

They hadn't realized how dangerous Emily's life was until he'd invented new danger and told them all about it.

Cookie affectionately patted Drew's arm. "He was just sitting out there, working on keeping you safe, and there are more copies this week … I just thought it would be nice to have some help."

Drew put on a docile expression and moved the stack to a back table, where Cookie was supposedly counting off un-addressed copies for each drop location. Emily stood indecisively for a minute. He smelled like aftershave. Emily suspected Hickory was letting him bathe in the marina's office at night. Cookie pushed in.

"He's a strong one," the old woman crooned, smiling up at Drew. "The kind of man who could carry a woman to safety without breaking a sweat. Don't you think so, Emily?"

Emily rolled her eyes. "I suppose. To be fair, though, I've never once been in a situation in which I needed to be carried to safety."

"Let's hope that remains true," Drew said.

"And as for you, Officer Mathison. Just remember that justice can't keep a man warm at night."

Sammy looked up from his desk, made eye contact with Emily, and laughed out loud.

"I don't know," Drew said thoughtfully.

"Anyway, Emily was top of her class," Cookie was telling Drew now, out of nowhere. Emily made a sound that wasn't exactly human. "She scored so high on her entrance exams to college that she skipped almost a whole year, didn't you, sweetie?"

"Cookie knows the way to a man's heart," Walt said from his desk, which made Sammy laugh all over again. "Tell us about her *magna cum laude* again, or whatever it's called."

"Cookie, please," Emily said, wishing the floor would swallow her. She would simply go to her desk. There was always work to do, of course, and it was really a big office. There was comfort in that.

"Emily, I'd carry you to safety any time," Sammy put in, winking at her over his glasses as she passed. "Even with my heart murmur."

"Thank you, but no one is carrying me anywhere. I'm going to go write some news."

"Have you read Emily's writing, Sergeant?" Cookie asked. "She's brilliant. You should have seen her when she was sixteen …"

"Cookie, please," Emily said again helplessly, hating that her cheeks were on fire.

"I've read *The Beacon* cover to cover since I arrived here," Drew said dutifully. "I can't argue with Miss Graham's brilliance."

"She can't cook well though," Walt told Drew, enjoying himself.

"She *can so*," Cookie hissed. "You don't know anything, Walter. Have you ever tried one of Emily's apricot muffins?"

"Have *you*?" Walt wondered.

Emily turned around on her way to her desk and smacked the corner of Walt's. "Make sure you leave room next week for a Help Wanted ad to replace both of you morons immediately. I'll double what I'm paying you if someone with actual talent would apply. And, Cookie. *Enough*. I'm not being auctioned off to the highest bidder." Emily thought she saw Drew's shoulders shaking but couldn't be sure.

The bell on the door rang, and she was actually relieved to see Dot enter.

"Good!" Emily cried. "A sane person! I've been trying to cross paths with you about the parade, Dottie."

"Hotter than Hell's pepper patch out there."

"Dorothea Berkeley!" Cookie yelled from the back of the office. "Watch your language!" But she was laughing and fanning herself. "I like what you've done with your hair, Sweetie!"

"Some of it just slipped out of the bun, is all," Dot grumbled, squinting back at Cookie and Drew as she eased a hip onto Emily's desk. "Heard about your private security." She arched a brow. "What gives?"

"He's helping sort papers," Cookie called. "Isn't he strong?"

Dropping into her own chair, Emily couldn't help but smile. Drew was starting to look as embarrassed as she herself felt, like some kind of circus display for the single ladies of Buckeye Lake. Served him right.

"Are you seriously running that environmental report about the bog in the paper?" When Emily just smiled, Dot growled. "No one wants to read that stuff."

"That's strange. I'm sitting on dozens of letters to the editor praising our coverage of that issue."

"It's not an issue. It's our property, and I can do what I want with it. I'm selling the beach. This is America, Emily. Just get out of my way."

"I love it when you throw your power around. Look, the report is public record. And this week's paper is back there ready to hit the stands, Dottie, if you want to read about it."

Dot issued an unladylike grumble that delighted Emily. "*You're* the one throwing your power around. As a friend, I'm begging you to stop."

"Why? Because you want to get richer by destroying the lake's last natural place of beauty?"

"Oh, stuff it, Emily."

Cookie was up front now, and she smacked Dot on the back of the head with a rolled up paper. "I said watch how you talk, young lady."

Then she lovingly handed her a cold bottle of soda. "Heaven knows you've got more money than you need. It's your fault Emily has to have a bodyguard now, as it is. You ought to be ashamed."

Dot stopped with the bottle halfway to her pretty, pink lips. She looked back at Drew, down at Emily. Blinked. "What is she talking about?"

"I thought you heard about my private security."

"Yes, but for *what*?"

"Emily's being really brave about it, but we all know she's been threatened," Cookie went on a little angrily. "Why, you're practically threatening her right now."

"*What?*"

"What is this community coming to when its newspaper can't report the truth without death threats?"

Emily knew her friend would never have been behind any of those messages, and nothing about death had actually been mentioned. Just blood. Still, she rocked back in her chair, content to let Cookie make up whatever nonsense she wanted, which proved amusing as Dot sputtered denials.

Emily glanced back at Drew, who was obediently counting off stacks of papers into piles like the muscle-bound pet he had become.

Soon, she thought, he would grow weary of how crazy they all were and head on back to Philadelphia to be crazy himself at home. She just needed to out-wait him, was all.

Chapter Thirteen

The Buckeye Lake Beacon
Saturday, June 15, 1946
Post-war vacationers mean boom for marina business

The woman worked *all* of the time.

Drew wasn't sure exactly what she was doing from one minute to the next, but every one of those minutes had other people in it. She never held still, darting in and out of places, back to her office, back out to some event, back to her office. He understood now why Hickory Graham held so firmly to not allowing any work on Sundays; Emily was like a wind-up toy, sputtering out just in time to drop into that hammock after church and then winding back up for the next week.

Tonight, she'd come home early for once, disappearing into the barge house after some kind of early Civic Association dinner, so Drew had changed into his work clothes and settled in at the marina for the evening. He had taken to tearing up old docking and replacing it when he had a minute, in exchange for the kindness Hickory had shown him. Besides, when he was at the marina, Emily could not leave the towpath without him knowing. He figured it was a good way to keep an eye on her and keep busy at the same time.

He pried a rusty nail out of a board, knowing he should call to update his parents. But he couldn't bring himself to report the truth.

After several days of close observation, he was no closer to figuring out where Emily was hiding the coward who was supposedly the love of her life.

He'd been through the marina that first night, of course. He'd checked every nook and cranny of Hickory's house, under the auspices of security. The newspaper office was so full of activity at every hour, it would be the perfect place to hide someone in plain sight, but Gilbert wasn't there. Rosie had happily shown him her dark room and studio. Drew had poked around Emily's beloved Chris-Craft boat, but it didn't even have a cabin, and he'd even made up an excuse about wiring problems in some of the buildings to wander through Dot Berkeley's offices at the amusement park, where Emily sometimes went. Of course, she also sometimes went to the school board's office, the town hall, and every stinking business around the lake to pick up ads or get quotes or whatever she did.

He pried another nail out, slid it into a pouch on his tool belt.

Actually, it had been strangely satisfying to read last week's paper, Drew had to admit. He was able to connect the tangled path he watched Emily travel to stories and advertisements on every page. He could read in black and white exactly what she'd been doing at the watercraft office, at the zoning office, at her lunch with that dog of a village manager.

But *where* was she interacting with Gilbert Reese?

"I'm gonna help you again," little Charlie Graham announced as he barefooted his way down what was left of the dock boards. "Can I help you again, Drew?"

"I could use the help."

Tom, the part-time help, managed some work on the docks during the days, but he was often in the marina office. The man was quiet and mildly lazy. Drew got a lot more done in a shorter amount of time.

"I just took Aunt Em that leftover gingerbread," Charlie was saying.

"That's nice."

"She looked like she was crying." Charlie peered up under his dirty fishing cap at Drew, who rose to his full height. "She told me she wasn't crying, but I don't believe her."

"She doesn't cry much, I 'spose?"

"Never. That I know of." Charlie maintained eye contact. "You didn't make her cry, did you?"

"Son, I haven't said two words to the woman all day. On my honor." Drew tried to concentrate on the conversation. Why was Emily in the barge house crying on a Saturday evening? Clearly, she wasn't ill, or she'd have told Charlie. Drew looked over at the flower-fringed barge, considering.

He wasn't exactly earning her trust. That would be a problem when he did track Gil down. In truth, as much as he was beginning to understand her movements and her sense of purpose, he felt further and further away from knowing *her*. She'd written him off as delusional. And why wouldn't she? From her perspective, this made no sense.

But why had she been crying?

"You're just keepin' her safe, right?" Charlie seemed worried, scratching at his neck.

"That's right."

"I sure wish I knew from what. Then I could help, you know?"

Drew swatted at a fly, deciding on a half-truth. "Well, Charlie, you know how those newspaper reporters can be ... always stirring up swarms of stinging insects sometimes best left alone."

Charlie laughed, his voice cracking. "Oh, man. You should try that line on her some time and see where it gets you. 'Sometimes best left alone.' That ain't the way Aunt Emily sees things. She don't think *anything* is best left alone."

Drew smiled, considering the truth in that as he bent to pick up the board again. He directed Charlie to help him, and the kid shouldered the plank. Together, they carried several pieces of freed, warped board up to the burn pile beside the beach, making lopsided trips that slowed Drew down a little. Taking it easy on the kid, he squinted up at the barge house again and, again, thought about Emily. He didn't like the idea of her crying. Should he go and ask her what was wrong? The problem was, he figured he knew what was wrong. What was the point in asking?

Maybe if he just sat with her on the little stone step of her barge, she'd open up to him again, as she had about her mom.

Was that what had her crying?

Charlie had said he wasn't aware of his aunt crying much. Drew could well imagine that being the kid's perception, though it stood to reason there had to have been plenty of tears. The nation and its vibrant Aunt Emily had just been through a war. Sacrifices had been made.

Had she cried with Gilbert? Drew tried to be open-minded, but the preacher's son had proven himself to be selfish. What kind of husband would he make her, if he lived to take those vows? Sure, the kid had grown up alongside the girl, but had he grown into the man an idealistic woman like Emily deserved?

"So, anyway," Charlie said, grunting under a fresh board he was helping tote down to the end of the dock with Drew. "Anyway, if you need a break from keeping Aunt Emily safe all the time, I can do it. I'm here most days."

They set the board down, and Charlie swiped some imaginary sweat off his forehead.

"Appreciate that." Drew nodded, thinking again about the grown-up Gil Reese and how he wasn't half as noble as this skinny boy.

When Charlie accidentally dropped Drew's favorite hammer off the dock, the pair called it a day and spent the rest of the evening on the dock drinking Coke and talking about what made girls so weird.

Chapter Fourteen

The Buckeye Lake Beacon
Wednesday, June 19, 1946
Top Ten picnic destinations at the lake

By deadline night, Emily was in her office, even more annoyed by being hours behind on the stack of dummy sheets than she was about the hulk of a man who had been following her around doggedly for days.

"I shouldn't leave you," Cookie told her, arms crossed, chewing worriedly on her heavily wrinkled and bright pink lower lip. A family trait, Emily thought. She looked disapprovingly at the clock and then at Emily, who was changing the ribbon in her typewriter.

She mumbled, hair coming out of the comb with which she'd tried to tame it. She'd shed her jacket and shoes and had ink on her left forearm.

"It's just that we're booked more than full at the inn tonight, honey," Cookie groaned, sliding her purse strap further up her shoulder. "I told Burt I'd be home hours ago."

Emily's head came up, typewriter back in action but still feeling far from relaxed. "I think I'll be fine." She blew out a breath that parted the straggling hair from in front of her face. "Of course, you should go. You should have gone a long time ago." She flitted over and pressed a quick kiss on the rouged, papery cheek. "Not my first deadline crunch, Cookie, and hopefully not my last."

"Hopefully?"

"You know this is what makes it fun." A grin split her weariness, and she pushed the older woman toward the door. "Get back to your guests before Burt starts some kind of midnight accordion celebration and puts you out of business."

Cookie dug in, grabbed the counter and turned around. "You know I hate leaving you here so late, alone."

Emily snorted. "That's the problem. I'm never alone," she said, peering out the glass at the pickup parked on the far side of the lot. Drew Mathison would be in it, she knew, waiting for nothing. His apparent lack of desire to make any contact with her was making the whole scenario even worse. She would have thought he'd had enough of this game by now.

"I guess he's got it under control," Cookie said skeptically. She shouldered her enormous purse. "You could be nicer to him, you know.

He's a fine man."

"Be sure to offer him a kiss goodnight on your way out," Emily suggested with an amused wink.

"Wouldn't be a hardship," Cookie admitted. "But Burt might not like it. You know how jealous he can get."

Emily laughed. "Plus, we can't have that public servant falling head over heels for you, only to have his heart broken. Off with you now, Cookie. Sleep tight."

"Finish fast," Cookie called as she left. "And lock the door behind me, anyway!"

Emily waved and obediently moved to lock the glass front door after Cookie left. Turning back, she let out a breath and considered the messy sprawl of the newsroom before her.

It was small, windowless except for the front wall of the storefront. A massive, wooden front counter was surrounded by newsstands, all the front walls collaged with flyers and posters as the community's open pegboard. Behind the counter, an ugly but high shelving unit made the only wall-like structure in the open space, and it was stacked with past issues of *The Beacon* dating back to 1934. Sometimes, alone on a deadline night as she was now, Emily could walk over and pull out a copy of the first issue in which she'd appeared on the masthead as "staff reporter," which would inevitably lead to an unproductive hour sitting cross-legged musing over her favorite stories in those early weeks and years. It was fun to track her own learning curve as she'd mastered the craft of journalism. She could point to the first headline she'd set and then to the first *good* headline she'd come up with. The first page she'd laid out.

There was no time for an inky, smudgy stroll down memory lane, though, on a night where nothing had gone right.

The back half of the office was empty now of the rest of her small staff, none of whom Emily could quite tolerate in eighteen-hour doses. That was why, their individual responsibilities met, they all went home on deadline night while she stayed. She preferred the relative silence of the newsroom this one night a week, when it was just her and her paper and, occasionally, if things went very quickly and smoothly, Cookie.

For the next hour, she lost herself in the quiet and the design of the front page. A fan whirred at her from the top of the shelving unit. Rosie's photos traveled to and from Newark Engraving by bus each Tuesday, returning to her as zinc engravings on wooden forms that would slide right into the steel frame for printing. She typed all the stories on her typewriter, then designed the layout on the dummy pages, indicating how many inches where and how the photo engravings would fit with the text. Tonight, the Pataskala weekly would churn out its own pages, and a fresh linotype operator would be in at dawn to set *The Beacon*. She just had to make sure she had the stories, the dummy pages, and the photo blocks there before he arrived.

The photos from the traveling circus spoke for themselves and needed little text, she thought as she arranged them. Kids dodging elephants to pick up gumballs rolling along the bricks of Yacht Street, a pubescent juggler whose eyes were about to pop out of his sweaty head, a trapeze artist swinging the rather heavy mayor by his hands over a strong net.

They were ridiculous, Emily thought with tenderness as she laid them down, and they were the community she loved. Rosie had captured them faithfully.

Emily's back was killing her. A glance at the old clock Burt had left behind on the wall, the one with the pinecones hanging from it, told her it was nearly midnight, and she reminded herself to drink something. One day last summer, she'd foolishly worked too long without water and had paid for it with a far more severe headache throughout the next day than was usual on Thursdays.

Having retrieved a glass from the fridge in the far back of the room, Emily stood contemplating the unfilled dummy sheets.

The typed stories and column inches were the hard part. The ads were easy enough to measure out and cut and paste onto the bottom of each page.

She glanced toward the door, sipping water, knowing *he* was out there. The fact represented its own special, irritating distraction. What did he do in that truck all day long as she raced about her own day, she wondered. Read? Sleep? She dismissed the notion of him sleeping almost immediately because, after all, he was always aware of any movement she made. Last night she'd tried to sneak out of a township trustee meeting, get to her car, and hit the road before he noticed she'd left, but there he'd been, three cars behind her on the thoroughfare.

Emily considered Drew fully capable—physically, at least—of cutting and pasting a pile of typed and scribbled ads. Even delusional people could probably do it, she thought now. It was time to put the man to work.

If she couldn't pretend her problems away, her problems would have to step up to at least lend her a hand.

Giving herself no time to think over her next move, Emily pinched some color into her cheeks, tried in vain to bring order to her hair, and slid back into her shoes. She told herself it didn't matter how she looked, really, since *he* must be disheveled in the extreme by now. But there had been that night on the pier, that dance in the shadows, that heat. It seemed like another lifetime, another man and another woman, but it was still there. So, she pushed yet another strand of hair behind her left ear, and

107

she marched out to his truck.

~~~~~

Drew watched her stumble a little outside the door. She leaned down, adjusted a strap on her shoe, and kept coming.

He did not move from his slouched position in the truck, wondering what she was up to this time, wondering what kind of food might come flying at him. His windows were down, of course, so he could hear the clicking and crunching of her shoes on the gravel, louder as she got closer. Then he smelled her. Lemons and girl soap.

She smelled good, but she looked awfully tired.

"Busy?" she asked. She was chewing gum again. Chewing with great purpose, the same way she walked and talked.

"My mama taught me never to be too busy for a beautiful woman." And then, because she had become so much fun to rile and because he'd missed actually getting to talk to her: "What's wrong? Commode clogged? Is there a mouse in there? Can't get a jar open?"

She didn't miss a beat but did narrow her eyes. "I have this darling little thing called a newspaper to put together and some brainless work that needs to get done and a desperate need for at least three hours of sleep before the chamber meeting tomorrow morning."

"You mean this morning. It's after midnight."

"This morning. What d'ya say, Deputy? Help me out? I don't see what you're accomplishing out here." She blinked tired blue eyes, probably never realizing that small gesture, the strange vulnerability of it, was what had him nodding. Watching her from a distance hadn't yielded any finds, so he told himself maybe getting closer would help.

And here she had invited him closer.

The door of the truck squeaked like a gunshot in the stillness of the late hour, and Emily stepped back to let him exit. He followed her in silence back across the parking lot to the office door.

"You lock it?" he asked gruffly. "The door? When you're in here alone like this?"

"I didn't figure I'd need to, what with my own personal police officer spying on me around the clock.."

"I mean typically."

Emily nodded. "I'm not a stupid girl, Drew."

Something in his stomach leapt any time she said his first name so casually.

He took in the clutter of the office with fascination because somehow it managed to look more vital than messy, like it was alive with stories.

"Do you know anything about the composition of ads in a newspaper?"

"Now, why would I?"

"Point." She cleared her throat because her voice sounded as tired as her eyes looked. "These are the ads that ran last week, already cut out. They're the easiest to start with ..." She showed him how to peel them off the old dummy page, find the labeled area of the fresh page, and literally paste them on as a guide for the printers.

"They go in a stairstep, sort of. Like this. Bigger ones on the bottom. It's like building with blocks, see?"

"What will you be doing?" he asked, curious.

"The stories. They'll go on top." She looked up at him. "Do you want something to drink? I have drinks back in the fridge. A few Cokes."

"Coke," he decided. "But I'll get it. You get started."

A huge blackboard hung slightly askew in the middle of the room with what he figured must be story ideas scribbled over it, along with dates. He read over them as he walked to the back.

Drew snagged the Coke from the door of the fridge and popped the bottle top on the edge of a small kitchen table that was cluttered with more junk. He drank deeply, watched Emily move papers around on her desk on the other side of the room. She wore a light-yellow dress with a belt of the same fabric, but he noticed she had shed her stockings and worked in bare feet. He figured the bruises under her eyes were well earned, after what he'd watched her do today alone. Meetings, interviews, typing, long phone calls, rushed trips from one side of the lake to another. He'd thought police work was unpredictable and tedious, but how did anyone survive at this pace?

And *how* did she find time to communicate with Gil Reese?

And *why* had she been crying at her house the other night?

Drew picked up a page and followed someone's lines to cut it out.

They worked together for almost an hour, under only the sound of the ticking clock and the soothing whir of the electric fan. Over that whir, Drew thought he heard Emily's stomach growl. Looking up, he considered suggesting she stop to eat. Who knew as well as he now did how sporadic her meals were? Especially today, facing this deadline. By his calculation, she may have eaten something before leaving the barge house at seven. She'd dodged in and out of businesses throughout the early morning hours but was never in one long enough to eat anything. He'd seen at least four different cups of coffee in her hand. She'd holed up in the office in mid-afternoon with her entire staff, but there had been no sign of food that he had seen.

Suggesting she get something to eat now seemed absurd, though, because she was working furiously on a story with that little line of concentration between her eyes. Besides, what would be open in the middle of the night?

Drew stretched, weary to the bone himself, and walked to the fridge again. Poking around, he found half a block of cheese, half a sandwich that looked questionable, a bunch of carrots bound with a rubber band with their leaves still on top, part of a small bottle of milk, and two shelves of glass bottles of Coke. On top of the fridge was the tin of crackers he had hoped for.

~~~~~

Emily forgot Drew was there until she heard him clear his throat. Startled, she straightened, her spine making little popping noises as she found him sitting on the very corner of a plaid stadium blanket that he had spread across the floor behind her. In the middle of the blanket was a plate filled with cheese and crackers and two open bottles of Coke. He gestured in invitation.

"People don't have enough two a.m. picnics," he said gruffly, apparently now slightly embarrassed at the display he'd created. He had the start of a beard growing. He crossed his arms and shrugged. Instead of the defined muscles of those arms this time, Emily zeroed in on his silver-gray eyes. He might be delusional, but he could be very kind.

Also, for the first time since the day he'd come to the towpath, he was looking at her in that certain way he had before. As though he not just knew her but liked her.

And just like that … just the same way a person might spill part of a cup of coffee on her shoe when she wasn't paying attention … Emily accidentally slipped a little bit into love.

"Oh, no," she said out loud. *Is this where those initially tingly feelings ended up?*

"You're hungry," Drew insisted defensively. Blindly, Emily's hand moved to her stomach, and she realized this was true. She was, indeed, hungry.

She sat on the corner of the blanket opposite the corner he had claimed and reached for a cracker, unable to meet his eyes. *Say something,* she told herself. She took a bite instead and, looking for further distraction, reached for one of the Cokes.

"Thank you." It was all she had, either because of the hour or because of that unfortunate little slide into something foreign. She was too far at sea to know. The attraction had been confusing enough. This was some kind of layer on top of that.

"You're welcome." Drew popped a cracker in his mouth and seemed more relaxed, for his part. When he was done chewing and had taken his own swig of soda, he said, "The ads are all pasted up."

Emily nodded, glancing at the stack of dummy pages. "They look great. I'm five minutes from done with the community calendar page, and then we're all set. Again, thanks so much for the temporary truce."

"You don't need to keep thanking me. I always wondered what all went into 'putting a paper to bed.' Now I know. Do we get to go home soon, then?"

Something about the way he suggested they "go home" tugged again at that alien part of her that she hadn't realized wanted to snuggle into a shared life. She yawned, too tired to agonize about her heart. "Um ... not exactly. Not yet."

His eyes widened. "What more could you possibly have left to do? Can't we clean up tomorrow?"

Emily pointed this time at that stack of finished dummy pages on the table beside them. "Those pages? Those blocks with engravings? Do they look like a newspaper to you yet?"

"I do not like where this is going. Is this why you drive down Route 40 in the middle of the night?"

"That's right." She picked up another cracker. "That's where they lay out and print our paper. Saves me having extra staff and equipment for that."

"And then you drive back to the same building around lunchtime tomorrow?"

She nodded, noting that he had her schedule down by the second week. "They have the galley pages done about then, and I have to proof them. They edit type while I stay and give it one more look. Then it's Burt who drives back later tomorrow night ... I mean, tonight ... to grab the printed bundles. You've seen the addressing and distribution process from there."

"Early Friday morning." He nodded, looking up at the clock again. "We *have* to go to Pataskala tonight?"

"We?" She cocked an eyebrow at him. "They start it at dawn, so yes."

He gave her a wry look, which of course made him even more devastatingly handsome. His short, coarse, dark brown hair managed to stick up on one side.

"You know I'm not letting you out of my sight. I don't think we should take two cars."

Sobered by this reminder that this wasn't a soul mate hanging around just to make her office picnics, she asked, "Aren't you bored following me around, Drew?"

"One more Coke, and I'm good to drive you over," Drew offered, ignoring her. "You, you look like you're going to drop. Ten Cokes wouldn't help you."

That was insulting, she thought, though probably true. "You don't look too perky yourself, pal."

He shrugged. "Cops and soldiers are used to not sleeping for days. I was on a stakeout once that lasted three days, not a second to so much as blink my eyes. I can drive you to Pataskala and back."

Polishing off a fourth cracker and feeling full enough, Emily nodded. "I won't fight you on that count." She brushed crumbs off her fingertips. "Though I'm afraid you'll be disappointed not to find anyone lying in wait for me, ready to roll me up in a printing press."

He ignored that and bent to pick up the blanket. "Heard anything from your mother yet?" he asked casually.

Emily experienced her usual desire to apologize for Lillian on some level, but why would she possibly owe that to Drew? "No, I haven't. I'm hoping she's just getting things settled."

"That would take her a minute, especially if she's out on bail and can't leave yet."

"That's what I thought," Emily said.

Twenty minutes later, Drew carried a flat box full of carefully arranged dummy pages, typed pages of text, and engraved photo blocks out across the parking lot to his truck. He helped her up into the passenger side and, when Emily shivered a little in the damp night air, he wordlessly leaned across her to the middle of the seat. He still somehow smelled good, like fresh air, and his closeness had her breath hitching. Drew came up with a rough, beige blanket that smelled like a mix of him and his truck, and he draped it over her. Pausing, he cranked her window closed, closed her door, and made his way around the hood.

The driver's door creaked open in its turn, sounding louder in the still of the early morning hours. So did the springs of the seat as they registered his weight, and the engine cranked to life. Emily was acutely aware of Drew two feet away, the box of weekly newspaper ingredients all that separated them in the darkness.

"Left?" he asked in that unused, gravelly voice that was almost enough to make her lightheaded.

She explained the route.

Streetlamps provided the only light through the usually busy main streets of Buckeye Lake village, the homes and fishing cottages dark with slumber all around. This wee hour chill, this sense of being the last survivor of some kind of holiday holocaust, was familiar to Emily.

"It'll rain tomorrow. You can smell it in the air," Drew remarked casually.

Unused to company, she studied his hands on the wheel. They were large and sun-browned. She wanted to know everything they had done, imagined that they'd operated nearly every type of construction tool, sanded nearly every type of wood, pulled triggers on weapons she could only guess at, and cuffed the wrists of people who had hurt others.

"I have a theory," she said, drunk with fatigue. He made some sound of curiosity. "You're actually in love with me, but you're bashful, and this all was the only way you could think to spend time with me."

"Following you around day and night in my truck?"

"Yes."

"Honey, if that were the case, if I were doing it because I'd fallen for you ... that would be stalking."

"*Is* it stalking?" She enjoyed his soft chuckle in the darkness.

"Believe it or not, I've never had to resort to that to spend time with a woman."

"Just a theory." Disappointed and confused, she leaned her forehead against the cool, vibrating window glass and relaxed into sleep.

Chapter Fifteen

The Buckeye Lake Beacon
Thursday, June 20, 1946
Lake levels rise with early summer rain

Emily lost the battle against exhaustion again the following afternoon. A few hours at home, in her bed, were the equivalent of waving a white flag.

She'd stalked out early that morning to offer Drew a large thermos of hot coffee as thanks for driving her across the county and back while she'd slept. He'd gruffly thanked her and followed her back into town for the chamber meeting as dark clouds rolled across the sky. She had driven back to proof the galley pages in the pouring rain but, after a cup of soup for lunch, had given in to the quiet patter of the rain and her now perpetual headache.

Emily hadn't paid attention to whether Drew followed her back out to the island or not. She had simply trudged across the bridge, dripping, and collapsed on her bed. Then she soaked her pillow, between the rain and crying herself into a nap that lasted late into the afternoon.

The whistle of her tea kettle woke her. The rain had stopped, and Emily stretched and yawned loudly.

Though the sun was not out, the world outside the windows of the barge house was post-storm silent, broken only by the arrhythmic tap of stray drops trickling through the leaves of the trees as a breeze rustled them. A muffled hammering joined now and then. From the vicinity of the kitchen, Rosie's soft humming and rattling around replaced the sound of the kettle. Vaguely, Emily remembered giving her sister free reign to finish the wallpaper in the kitchen area of the little barge.

Scrubbing her hands over her eyes and face, she shuffled out toward Rosie's song and found her previously drab, rugged, barge of a kitchen area ... half pretty. As promised. The paper Rosie had chosen was the softest yellow, with pink and blue flowers connected by whimsical green vines.

"I love it," she said with warmth.

Rosie turned an equally warm smile over her shoulder as she pressed the edge of a piece of the wallpaper into place behind Emily's toaster. These feminine touches should have been done long ago, but Emily had resisted until Rosie had declared she was simply taking over.

"Tea's ready," Rosie announced, casting a satisfied look around her.

A few comfortably quiet minutes later, the sisters slid onto opposite sides of the old knot-freckled table to drink their tea.

"How's it going with the vandalism and threats and such?" Rosie said with a British accent, extending her pinky finger like a fine lady as she sipped her tea. "Any more bloody typewriters, love?"

Emily grinned. "No, nothing really."

"Any reaction to the environmental report you published?"

"Strangely quiet, now you mention it."

Rosie hummed around another sip of her tea. "I'd expect the developers and some of the town to be hopping mad about the habitat information. Or about you printing it, I mean. It makes a strong case for protection of the bog."

"To people with sense. I'm afraid this is probably the calm before the storm."

"Dr. Lamb called to tell me to tell you 'well done.'" Rosie assisted the OSU botany professor with Cranberry Bog research. "We're heading out to study and sketch some of the moss segments early next week. Sketches are better than photographs for moss."

"I'll take your word for it. And tell him I'm glad he liked the story."

"You think your Sergeant Mathison out there has discouraged all the vandalism and nonsense?"

"I don't know. I think I'm even more full of nonsense than usual, actually."

Now Rosie smiled. "You know what I mean. Maybe having him around shows people you're not to be trifled with."

"Or it sends the opposite message. That I need a big, strong man to protect me."

"You and I both know you don't need a big, strong man to protect you. But do you *want* one?" Rosie made her brows dance playfully.

Emily considered answering honestly. *Want* was new. She met her big sister's eyes as she blew softly across her tea and sipped. It was lemony but still very hot.

Rosie didn't wait for Emily's tongue to stop burning. "You *do* want Sergeant Mathison."

"Shhhh." Emily glanced around as if he might materialize beside her. He had a way of doing that. "He could be anywhere."

Rosie laughed. "He's been out working on the marina docks since the rain stopped." Emily started to rise, eyes toward the kitchen window, but Rosie shook her head and pressed down on Emily's hand on the table. "No, don't look. It won't help with whatever you're going through. His *shirt* is off, Em. I've been fanning myself with bits of wallpaper for quite some time now."

At a loss, Emily stayed seated and dropped her head into her hands. She sighed and laughed at the same time. Another white flag needed to be waved, she supposed. She thought about the way Drew had asked about her mother the night before, how nice it had felt to speak casually with him about that situation. To have him hoping for what she hoped for. Was that what he'd meant about God bringing people into a life to share burdens?

Her telling him about it on the stoop that night had not changed the situation at all. But she felt lighter, just the same.

"I don't know how I feel about him," Emily bravely announced to her sister. She let the words hang there, an offered gift. God had given her Rosie, and though she didn't want to bother her with *all* the struggles she was facing, Emily figured this feminine stuff was a good way to hold her off. And she really could use some advice.

Maybe Rosie could make sense of what she was feeling and then translate it for her so she herself could make sense of it.

"Are you two … involved?" Rosie asked.

"No."

"He's been completely professional about this whole bodyguard thing?"

"He really has. In fact, before this all started, I thought we had a chance to … you know." Rosie's silent sip of tea and eager expression demanded she continue. "We sort of kissed. Right before he declared he was going to protect me, I mean."

"*Sort of* kissed?"

"We were interrupted. First by a vomiting heron and then by your son."

Rosie lifted a brow. "That sounds just unromantic enough to be true."

Emily heard the distant rhythm of the hammer in a new way now, knowing it was Drew out there a few yards away, laying down new planks on the dock. Helping Hickory. Without a shirt on. Imagining the way his shoulders and arms looked *in* a shirt, she figured Rosie was right. She probably shouldn't look. Emily considered how much Drew's muscles factored into her complicated feelings.

And, if they did, were her feelings really that complicated?

She wanted to say she was unaffected by the man's appearance. That she was deeper than that.

"I'm attracted to him," Emily confessed, growing bolder.

"Of course, you are. You'd have to be crazy not to be."

"But I feel funny around him. Like I kind of want to melt into him. Does that make any sense? Is this the way people *feel*?"

"Is this your first time experiencing that?"

"For sure."

117

Rosie's smile was full of both love and condescension. "I really hesitate to point this out, but you're the only one of us who has been engaged to a man. And you're saying you've *never* felt this way before?"

Emily looked down. She avoided talking about Gilbert. Much like she avoided talking about anything personal. "It definitely wasn't like this with Gil, Rosie. And besides, we were only engaged for a few weeks."

"But you kissed Gil, right?"

"We ... tried."

"Emily! How hard is this? How are you *almost* kissing all these men?"

"Gil and I started ... I don't know. Laughing. When we tried to kiss because we figured we were supposed to, we started laughing."

Rosie enjoyed that. "Why am I not surprised? The two of you never took anything seriously. That's why I was so surprised when you announced you were getting married."

Emily wanted that to be one of the things she forgot in old age. That whole engagement business. A youthful indiscretion that just faded with other memories like the collection of yarn bracelets that had consumed her when she was thirteen.

"Why didn't you say something back then?" Emily insisted. "If you knew I was being crazy?"

"You don't like it when I say that."

"Do you think I'm crazy now?"

"No. I'd be more concerned if you didn't find Drew Mathison attractive. And, besides, there's something about the way he looks at you."

"I *know.*"

"The whole business with Gil just shook your faith in yourself in matters of the heart," Rosie seemed to decide.

Like others, Emily had gotten caught up in the drama of the war. One weekend, there had been a send-off party at the ballroom in honor of Gil and two other boys from their school. They had all been dancing, laughing, trying to live a lifetime in one night. Between dances, Gil had confessed he was afraid. Emily assured him she would pray for his safe return. They had reminisced about the good times they'd had, from grade school on, until they both were crying and holding one another. She was afraid, too. What if her childhood friend, the one who knew her better than anyone, was killed by a German gun?

When Gil had suggested they get engaged, it seemed logical, somehow, on that emotionally charged night. "Engaged" just meant a fella had a girl to come home to, right? Someone who was praying for him. Someone who wrote him letters. Folks had been asking why they weren't engaged yet, anyway, they both reasoned.

Emily had imagined herself the heroine of a great war love story that evening, comforting her soldier with promises of devotion. There was no ring. No plan to formalize anything. Just the romance of childhood friends turned sweethearts, linking hands against a war machine.

Their crowd of friends had toasted them, back on the dance floor. When Dot had asked if they were going to tie the knot before he left, the panicked look Emily and Gilbert sent one another probably was the first clue they had rushed into a wrong decision.

They had vowed to write letters every day.

That lasted for a week. Three days on his part. In her remaining weeks of the term and then her quiet winter break at the lake, Emily was suddenly left imagining what would happen if Gilbert Reese returned from war alive and well. *When* he returned, she'd amended. She tried to picture herself walking down an aisle to him, promising God to love and obey him all her life. That was when she developed a nasty nail-biting habit. When she pictured the pair of them having some kind of honeymoon, she started to get an ulcer.

In the end, she had gently suggested in a long letter that they un-engage themselves, that they had perhaps been a bit hasty. She got a letter back from Gil immediately. He agreed wholeheartedly, which made the ulcers heal almost as soon as they'd come on. They quietly broke the engagement, telling their families and hoping news would just trickle out that way around town. Emily was loath to be the "Dear John" letter writer when the community had just embraced their eventual marriage with such glee. How could she explain that the couple was more enthusiastic to see it come to an end?

"Do you enjoy his company?" Rosie asked, pulling Emily back to the sound of the hammer and new, very recent memories of Drew Mathison sitting on a picnic blanket at two in the morning. And a very different feeling.

"Yes, I do." They had laughed together, too, in their brief acquaintance. But even that was different from the way she had laughed with Gilbert. It was better. "I think he's a really decent person."

"And sad. I think he's sad," Rosie said.

"Oh, yes. I can't figure out if it's the war or his brother getting murdered. Probably both."

"Maybe that's why he's so worried about you. He cares about you, and he couldn't protect his little brother," Rosie reasoned.

Emily shrugged. "What should I do, Rosie?"

"What do you mean?"

"You've been asking me to open up to you. Now I am. So, tell me what to do."

"About finding a man attractive? What do you want me to say, Em?"

"I'm not sure if how I feel is normal. Or if *he's* normal. To me, it seems like he's overreacting to some mild vandalism and threats."

"That's all in how you look at it, I guess."

"That's how I'm looking at it. And, looking at it like that, there's nothing about this man that my head should like or want to get so close to."

"What *isn't* for your head to like, Emily? The man won medals in the war, for crying out loud."

"I didn't know that. We haven't talked much."

"True. Since you don't eat dinner with us all anymore, the rest of us might know him better than you do," Rosie said with a grin. "I *know* you want to go look out the window."

"No, I do not. I'm finishing my tea before it gets cold."

Rosie got up. "He's made a living out of building things and putting bad guys in jail and protecting good people. He doesn't talk too much, but he's not stupid when he does decide to speak. He's persistent. I guess the only thing not likable about him is that he doesn't ever smile."

"He smiles sometimes," Emily said.

"I've never seen it."

When Rosie shifted toward finishing touches on the wallpaper, Emily stretched and moved to help her. In the kitchen. Near the window.

She sighed to find evidence of Drew's handiwork but no sign of the man himself on the dock. The hammering had stopped.

On one dock stretching west into the lake, there was an obvious torn up line where the old, rotten planks stopped and fresh, even pine began, framed by small piles of carpenter's tools. Movement from the over-water garage had Emily perking up, but it turned out to be Tom, the new guy Hickory had hired to help fix the place up. He was a short, lean man with dark hair, lugging some of the rotten boards out and around to a dump site near the other side of the parking lot. He must have been inspired by Drew to finally put in a day of work.

The pile of old boards was growing, it seemed.

"Hickory will be hosting a bonfire and hog roast before we know it," she said to her sister.

"Your hero must be off cutting more planks." Rosie hip-bumped Emily and turned to clean up wallpaper paste. "Don't give up, though. It's worth the wait."

Chapter Sixteen

The Buckeye Lake Beacon
Monday, June 24, 1946
Council considers zoning change; bog damage report in

The rain started again and only let up for a few hours at a time in the days that followed. The weekend was a washout that kept crowds at bay, so Emily hunkered down with Rosie to finish her kitchen and add some more lighting over the dark mass of the table.

She even let herself be talked into inviting Drew Mathison in for fried chicken Sunday evening to celebrate the minor renovation. During the meal, she'd been baffled and charmed by the closeness that had developed between Drew and her nephew. Then she'd been entertained, alongside her family, with his stories from Europe. Mostly, she realized she had avoided one-on-one interactions while she tried to sort out what to do about him and, in doing so, had ended up missing a good deal.

Emily's hammock nap had been rained out, but she'd sat thinking about Drew Mathison as raindrops gathered on her screened windows late into Sunday night.

He was still on her mind the next day. She was thinking about how respectful he was to Rosie. How his large hand looked when he messed up the top of Charlie's sandy hair. She was thinking about the way he genuinely seemed to like listening to her grandfather's stories. Emily certainly *wasn't* thinking about the editorial she'd written last week about Council President James Chapman as she approached town hall Monday evening, but later she would reflect she should have been more ready for his reaction.

Instead, she'd been forcing her mind toward this week's issue of the paper after a day of distraction. *Photos have to be on the bus to the engraver's tomorrow,* she thought as her heels clicked across the damp parking lot in the twilight. She ran through a mental inventory of what she had and where it would go. Some storm damage and light flooding photos had turned out to be powerful, so she figured she'd lay a couple of those out above the fold with a jump of a smaller print inside. Page ... six. There was an ad on six for the bait shop, and she figured that would be some good exposure. Beauty pageant prelims on the bottom of one, along with the start of tonight's town council story, which might be a doozie based on the number of residents streaming in now.

Emily made her way through the thick wooden doors toward the meeting chambers, damp shoes squeaking on the tile, when she heard her name being called to the left of the foyer. Mentally changing gears, Emily was unpleasantly surprised to see Chapman waving her over toward the back hall. She didn't have to see that his face was an unhealthy dark red color to know he was less than happy with her.

The editorial she'd penned about him last week made it easy to know why.

Still, she followed him out of the foyer and into the administrative hallway that ran behind chambers. She took a deep breath and squared her shoulders. It wouldn't be the first time she'd been taken to task by a paternal local politician for telling the truth. The hallway was low lit with evening and smelled like bleach.

Everything about Chapman's body language and stilted greeting exuded a little more fury than she'd expected.

She hadn't pulled punches in the editorial she'd published alongside the environmental report. In it, she had accused Chapman outright of abusing his office to pave the way for the resort developers who would destroy the bog and a section of North Bank. The company negotiating with the Berkeley family was owned by a relative of Chapman's, Emily had learned, and Chapman himself was promised a large, beautiful lot adjacent to the site of the proposed resort, courtesy of the company that sought to own the rest of the stretch of waterfront property. The promised gift of land had preceded a series of illegal meetings meant to secure the zoning change needed.

She'd simply written the truth. And now, it looked like tonight's meeting was a little more crowded than usual.

Emily wasn't surprised by Chapman's anger. She was very surprised, however, when he whirled around in the empty hallway and grabbed her hard by both arms. Her satchel strap slid off her shoulder at the impact, and she heard the bag fall to the ground.

The air in her lungs rushed out in a painful whoosh. Nonsensically, she thought about the small jar of honey she'd stashed in her bag to give to the village clerk after the meeting. What would a broken jar of honey do to her notepad?

"Listen to me," the big man ground out between clenched teeth. "You troublemaking, stupid ..." He called her a few other things that Emily was relatively certain no one had ever called her before—at least not to her face—as he backed her against the wall of the hallway. Emily felt her heart pounding in her ears. She was always up for a verbal sparring, but this ... this was on the edge of scaring her.

Okay, it was over the edge. She was scared.

"Let go of me," she demanded, trying to sound calm and turning her head to escape his breath. James Chapman was a fit man in his forties, and she'd never guessed until tonight that his teeth must be rotting right out of his head. She tried to pull her arms out of his painful grip by jerking her shoulders. "And don't *ever* call me that again."

"You're going to hear from my lawyer regarding the lies and accusations you published. Hope you're ready to pay."

"Involving a lawyer sounds a bit civilized for a brute who's manhandling me outside council chambers," she spit out. "I said let me *go*." Emily struggled, but his hands grew even more punishing, and he pushed her harder into the wall. Once, twice. She remembered the blue heron breaking the bones of the fish so it could swallow it more easily. On the third push, she heard the back of her skull rap hard against the wall before she registered pain with another gasp.

"You think you're a real hot shot," he was saying, a wildness in his eyes she did not like. "You publish so much as a *word* about me again, and you'll pay. Not just money."

"You're threatening me now. And not in an original way." She tried to breathe normally. "The typewriter was more creative."

"What? What typewriter? You don't think I can carry through? *Watch me*. I can destroy your little business, your grandfather's business, everything you love. I'll make it my life's work." This was punctuated by another very personal insult that stung.

"I thought your life's work was destroying the lake. Ow! Stop it!" She yelled now, hoping someone would hear. How had she managed to forget this scene was playing out in a public building?

"You never know when to shut up, do you?"

"She's not the only one."

Drew Mathison. Finally. Emily could turn her head just far enough to see him striding down the hall fast, badge out. It was only when she spotted him that she felt herself trembling.

"I'm going to tell you just once to get your hands off her."

He looked intimidating. Even bigger and broader than Chapman, shoulder harness and gun exposed, strides that ate up the floor, and a look of fury that no man in his right mind would challenge. Certainly, Chapman wasn't ready to because he dropped Emily's arms like handles on hot skillets. She leaned back hard against the same wall that had been so painful a moment before, battling to catch her breath. She rubbed her hands over her arms where they ached.

"There's no problem here," Chapman was telling Drew, still trying to sound authoritative. He smoothed back a lock of hair that had fallen over his forehead. He was breathing hard, and his voice gave away some sudden anxiety ... either that he'd been exposed as the bully he was or that Drew would smash *his* head into the wall.

"Give me one reason why I shouldn't lay you out right here," Drew ground out coolly, his large right hand curled into a fist.

"That, that badge. That's the reason."

Drew looked Emily up and down, assessing for damage, she realized. His eyes, as cold, hard, and gray as the concrete floor beneath them, met hers. "You're all right?" At her nod, he focused again on Chapman. "This badge says I can deal with thugs who assault and threaten women in empty hallways. That I *must*, in fact. But I don't need a badge to deal with you."

Chapman raised his chin. "Try it and you're fired."

Drew laughed, a frightening sound. "You overestimate what this job is to me. Anyway, I report to Chief Gunn and the mayor."

"Chief Gunn and the mayor work for *me*," Chapman said.

Emily saw a change move over Drew, knew before he pulled that powerful right arm back that Chapman was about to get his nose rearranged, and she somehow managed to step forward on her shaking knees.

"No, Drew. Drew, this isn't necessary." She didn't want him run out of town just when she was getting used to him. Especially now that she wondered if she might need a bodyguard. "The pen has always been mightier than the fist," she said with a calm she didn't feel. She reached back and placed an ice-cold hand on Drew's warm arm to draw strength. She felt his muscles twitching. "Now it's my turn to make threats, Chapman, but I assure you they're not empty. Everything you say and do that is unethical and unprofessional will absolutely end up in print, and *The Beacon's* circulation is getting bigger every week. So, you can try to toss tiny buckets of water at a raging forest fire, or you can start acting like the representative of the people you are. And, if I were you, I'd turn around right now and go get ready for your little meeting before you end up bleeding in this hallway."

Chapman mustered the most foreboding look he could, glanced behind her at Drew, turned around, and stalked off toward the back entrance to the chambers. She thought she heard him mumbling about how it wasn't over. *Still* unoriginal, she thought.

The pair of them stood alone in the very quiet hall. For a moment, there was only the sound of both their hurried breaths echoing in the emptiness. Emily turned around then, and it was a very natural thing just to lean into Drew. His arms came up around her. Face pressed into his shoulder, she took deep breaths and, irrationally, thought how nice it was, for whatever reason, to get to be close to him again. Another reprieve.

"You're okay? You're sure?"

"Mmm-hmmm. Just need a minute."

His hands moved firmly up and down her back, as though he were trying to warm her, and it worked. When he spoke, his voice was gentle and deep, and it rumbled beneath her ear.

"Things like this happen to you often?"

"No, not like this," she said on a sigh. "Usually, it's an irritated demand that I leave something alone. Just words. No one ever tries to hurt my body."

Drew let out a deep, deep breath and mumbled frustrated words about James Chapman that Emily figured he must have picked up on construction sites and in MP barracks. "Sorry," he said when he was through.

"'S okay." She chuckled, stepping back a little and rubbing the back of her head where it ached. "I was thinking all those things a few minutes ago, myself."

Reluctantly releasing her, Drew bent to pick up her satchel from the floor. Instead of handing it to her, she noticed he pulled the strap onto his own shoulder and proceeded to examine her upper arms beneath the short, lacy sleeves of her blue blouse. Emily's eyes followed his fingers and his glare.

"You're going to have bruises here."

"Another badge on my journalistic vest," she said, hoping to dispel anger with lightness. But it didn't work on either of them. She was shaken. She could not let her family know this had happened.

"Let's go fill out a police report. Press charges. *Then* you can write about it."

"Now you're catching the spirit! But no. Not yet. Let's see how things turn out tonight. I don't want to miss it." Emily heard some commotion in the large council chambers adjacent to the hallway that probably indicated the meeting was getting underway with the Pledge of Allegiance. She looked up at Drew. "Thank you," she said, reaching over and tugging her satchel back onto her own shoulder.

"Don't mention it." He swallowed, and Emily thought he looked every inch a hero. Someone she'd been able to trust so far.

"I need to speak with you after the meeting," she ventured.

"You always know where to find me."

~~~~~

Throughout the meeting, Drew could be found at the back of the chambers, arms crossed, alternately glaring at the council president at his table in the front of the room and watching Emily Graham scribble furiously in her notebook in the second row.

The room was crowded, and he'd deliberately chosen to stand rather than take the last remaining seat beside her on the old pew that made up the public seating in the meeting room. There wasn't nearly enough room there to keep them from pressing against one another, and Drew figured the brief but close contact with Emily's hair and skin and silky blouse out in the hallway was enough to mess him up for days to come. He didn't need to feel her thigh snug against his.

He figured he really had it bad for her when he found himself entranced by the way she held her pen as she wrote. She was constructing what looked to Drew's untrained eye like a web of inky sticks and swirls all over those pages. He imagined gently peeling that pen out of her fingers and raising each knuckle to his lips. What would her skin taste like?

And what did she want to speak with him about? Drew ticked off agenda items as the meeting progressed, bringing him ever closer to the meeting's end and to whatever she wanted to say. Was she going to tell him about Gilbert? Ask for his help? He hoped so. She'd seemed more relaxed around him over the fried chicken and after the deadline night.

Drew had spent some time yesterday talking on the phone long distance to his parents, who were begging him to let go of his obsession about Jamie's death and just come home. He'd told them he couldn't do that. Not yet. Not when he felt he was close, when he knew Gilbert was nearby. He was still reluctant to try filing paperwork forcing Emily to comply with his investigation because he was afraid of the Contis finding out she was involved with Gilbert. He couldn't afford to accidentally invite them to this confusing party.

"Motion to delay discussions about zoning changes until next meeting," James Chapman said from his post next to the mayor.

"I'll second that motion," a skinny old man said from further down the table of officials.

A grumbling arose from the crowd of residents, and Drew watched Emily slap her pen against her notebook in subtle frustration. She leaned back in the pew, and he caught sight of the mottled yellowish-brown bruise forming on her arm, just below her shoulder.

Drew despised men like Chapman.

"Can the public still comment?" demanded a fellow in a tie who Drew was surprised to see sitting next to none other than Rosie Graham on the other side of the room. Emily's sister looked like a beautiful thunder cloud beside the older man who had spoken.

"Sir, you do not have permission to address council at this time," Chapman declared arrogantly. He had studiously avoided looking at Drew throughout the meeting. "You may speak during public comment time if you wish."

"Actually, for the sake of time and our intention to strike the zoning agenda item, I move we also do away with public comments this evening," the lone woman on council suddenly said.

"I'll second that," said the same skinny old man at the end of the table.

"Wait, wait." This from the clerk on the mayor's opposite side, who was also furiously scribbling notes throughout the meeting. She struggled to be heard over rising protests from the residents. "We already had a motion from Mr. Chapman we still need to vote on. It was seconded by Mr. Forrester."

"Call the roll," Chapman barked.

The vote went four to two, as did the subsequent vote forbidding residents from addressing council at all this evening. The two nay-sayers, who Drew figured were eccentric enough to be on the town council to serve the residents, looked as frustrated as the crowd in the pews.

"Order," the mayor boomed, picking up his gavel. The crowd quieted a little. "If I need to, I will have Officer Mathison back there escort you from the premises."

Great, Drew thought. *Make me your stooge.* He instantly resolved to provide no such service. He looked down to see Emily looking back at him over her shoulder, obviously struggling to quench a smile. He winked at her and watched color wash into her cheeks.

The crowd that had grown silent out of fear of the grumpy looking man with the gun in the back of the room got loud again when the meeting was adjourned, and Drew watched Emily rush the council members before they could disappear through the door behind their table. *Jumping right back into the fray.*

He stayed within sight of her until Chapman left.

Strolling just outside the open doors and into the fresh air, Drew saw Rosie waiting on the steps outside.

"Tell me you're not the mayor's personal muscle," she said. It was the most she'd ever reminded him of her younger sister.

"Nah. I was just here looking out for Emily. It was a convenient thing for him to say."

"Is there some specific danger here? Besides pigheaded public servants?"

"With her, one never knows," Drew answered evasively. He nodded in the direction of the man in the tie who, up close, had dark hair in need of a cut, with a touch of gray at the temples, and a studious air about him. He was carrying a portfolio. "Who's your friend?"

"This is Dr. Maxim Lamb," Rosie said, angling toward him. "Dr. Lamb, this is Drew Mathison. He's … um, a police officer here in Buckeye Lake."

Lamb extended his hand, clearly withholding judgment after what had just happened inside.

"Dr. Lamb is a botanist at Ohio State, Drew. He's documenting the non-native plants that grow on Cranberry Bog."

"Ah." Drew nodded. "A pleasure to meet you. I understand from Emily that Rosie sketches as you classify?"

"Yes, and sometimes she takes photos. She's an amazing artist. I hope to get our work published by next year, but it's tricky. Have to work around my teaching schedule and her studio. But we'll get it done ... as long as no one chops the bog to pieces to build boat docks for a resort in the meantime."

"He hopes our project will help get the bog classified as a nature preserve, get it protected by the government."

Emily emerged from the doorway of the town hall. Spotting Drew and her sister, she jogged down the steps with her satchel, already shaking her head.

"Can you *believe* that bull?" she exclaimed in her casually irreverent way, shoving the notebook into the satchel and automatically gravitating to Drew's side. He wondered if she noticed she'd done so.

"Don't say 'bull,' Em," Rosie scolded. "Hickory lectured me all morning about the slacks you wore yesterday. He thinks they're making you crass."

"It's not the slacks doing it. It's Chapman and his band of crooks."

"Are you honestly surprised?" Rosie asked. "They're all about themselves and their own interests. Like most people."

"That's dark. Anyway, we'll just see what happens in November's election," Emily said. "How are you, Max?"

"Irritated," the botanist replied. "Came all the way out here for nothing."

"Well, not nothing," Rosie corrected. "We did get quite a bit of work done this morning."

"You staying at Cookie and Burt's too, Max?"

Drew didn't know why she said "too." He hadn't been back there for more than a change of clothes in some time. He was cultivating quite the back problem, sleeping on the seat of the truck. It needed to all pay off soon. He needed his witness.

"Yes, but I have to head back early tomorrow," Dr. Lamb said. "I've got a lecture at two."

"Why don't we all go have coffee?" Emily asked. "I've got a few things to finish up, and I'll meet you at the diner in a bit. What say?"

"Sounds good to me," Rosie said. Dr. Lamb also agreed, and the two of them strolled off through the parking lot, talking about moss.

Drew, likewise, followed Emily around the side of the building where he'd watched her park earlier. It was darker there, the sun having set completely during the abrupt council meeting as more clouds rolled in. Emily seemed to be bracing herself for something, he thought, watching her clutch her satchel close to her chest, her shoulders tense as she walked slowly. She turned when they reached a tree next to her car.

"Thanks again for helping me out tonight, Drew."

"Like I said, no big deal. Maybe now you'll stop trying to file complaints against me for harassment?"

She smiled. She *had* done that on an impulse the week before, and Chief Gunn had predictably done nothing about it. "I suppose between the late-night drive to the printer's and tonight's actual bodyguard move, you're finally coming in handy."

She turned around and placed her satchel in the Cabriolet just as it started to sprinkle again. The top had been in place for days. She gestured into the car and moved around to the driver's side just as the rain got heavier. Drew folded himself in. Her car smelled pleasantly of her perfume. He took in her cheeks, which had been pale after the incident in the hallway, but which were a riot of pink now. One of her lashes had a raindrop on it.

"You said you wanted to talk to me about something?"

"Um. Yes." She looked down for a moment and then back up at him. "I have something to ... well, something to ask you. A favor."

He smiled a little. Sometimes he saw Charlie in her more than he saw the boy in Rosie. Except that, unlike her nephew, she had the kind of beauty a person might completely lose his mind over. "Okay." He nodded a "go on," knowing he would help her with anything she needed. If he weren't lucky enough for her to ask his help with Gilbert, he hoped she at least wanted him to break the council president into pieces with a ball bat or something fun like that.

"It's ... my mother."

"Did you hear from her?" Maybe she needed him to pick the woman up from the train station. But he was not expecting that to be the favor either.

"No. I haven't heard anything."

"I'm sorry. You're having quite the time of it, aren't you?"

"You have no idea."

"I'd like to." He watched her twist the strap of her satchel into little pleats. "What do you need, Sweetheart?"

She blinked at him in surprise. "I think I need to hire a detective."

"Ah." Drew met her eyes and understood. She had one. Probably more than she even knew.

"Lillian says she's in Fresno. That's where I've been wiring the money. I can't seem to find any information about her in the court system, though, so I guess I just need to know what's true so I can figure out how to move forward. I don't know how to find out where she is without asking for someone's help. And what if she needs help? And you're the one who might be able to help with that *and* who knows what a fool I've been."

Drew's heart squeezed. "You tried to help your mother. Stop thinking you'll be judged for that." He reached over to the hand that was twisting the strap and enclosed it in his own hand. Maybe it was the closeness of the front seat and the light rain running down the windows that made it seem right to do that. Maybe it was the fact she'd turned to him for comfort earlier or asked this of him now. Her fingers wrapped around his. "And you're right to ask for help, in turn."

Her eyes were a little damp. "Sorry. It's been a night."

"Are you sore? Does your head hurt?"

"I'm fine."

"What exactly would you like me to find out about your mother?" *Is this really it? All she's juggling?* He was starting to get an uncomfortable feeling that he was off base about her hiding Gilbert. He didn't think so, but he certainly hadn't seen any sign of his missing witness, and she seemed more preoccupied with her mother than she was with the mob.

The uncomfortable part now was wondering if he was lingering in Buckeye Lake just to be near her and her family.

"I just want to verify that Lillian is where she says she is," Emily was saying, "and I'd like to know what her situation is. I want to know if I'm doing the right thing by sending money or if I'm just throwing it away to someone who may not even *be* her, you know?"

"I know. Sure. I can help you find that out. And you don't have to pay me."

"I will though. And you still won't say anything to Hickory or Rosie?"

"Not if you don't want me to. I don't know how that would be my place, anyway. But I think you're selling them short, not trusting them to help."

"I'm not selling them short. I just don't want them to get their hopes up or be hurt in any way."

"Like you have?"

She shrugged. "I can handle it." Emily hesitated. She seemed to shake something off and asked, brightly, "Want to go get coffee with Rosie and Lamb?"

Drew sighed, thinking it sounded like a double date. He imagined himself snugged into a booth at the diner beside her, drinking coffee at an unreasonable hour, probably talking late into the night because Emily Graham didn't seem to believe in sleeping except on Sunday afternoons. Her eyes would get sleepy, though, like they did in his truck when they drove to the printers, and she'd probably lean against him a little in the booth like she had in the hall, and then he'd be several more days behind in breaking the spell she was weaving over him.

What he needed was to focus.

"Uh, no. No thanks to the coffee."

"I'll buy."

"That's okay. I'll keep watch from the parking lot."

He watched her draw back a little. "Okay, then. Suit yourself." Drew climbed out into the rain. She leaned over and said, "Thanks again for everything tonight, Drew."

He went back to his truck cab, numb, but he noticed the raindrops on his roof sounded lonelier than they had from inside Emily's car.

Chapter Seventeen

The Buckeye Lake Beacon
Friday, June 28, 1946
Boat sale through the 4th! Trade-ins welcome!

Emily brewed coffee in the kitchen of the barge house on Friday morning, watching dawn burst over the lake with heat and a brightness that reminded her she was still young.

There had been days lately when she thought she might never feel that way again, so she took her time dressing. The fitted button-up apricot blouse and wide belt over a blue-checked patterned skirt made her feel as bright as the morning.

She brewed enough coffee for Drew, as she had every morning this week. They'd fallen into a pattern, the two of them, after that night at the town hall. He made calls and sent telegrams, trying to track her mother in California or wherever she might be, while she worked in the office.

Then she'd stopped trying to elude him when she went out. He'd stopped issuing her tickets and citations. And she'd stopped trying to get him fired.

Since that night, Emily found a twisted sense of comfort in knowing Drew was always nearby. And if the idea of him watching her with those pewter eyes had put a little extra bounce and sway in her step ... well, if he liked to keep an eye on her, she told herself, she might as well try enjoying the game.

Still, she was surprised to find herself alarmed rather than relieved last night when she'd completely lost her tail.

Drew's truck had been there at the market when she'd gone in to pick up ad copy, because she'd waved when she came out. But she had not seen him back at the office at all, and when she'd swung by the police station for a robbery report — practically *begging* to be back on his radar — there was no sign of him. It was late when she'd left the school board meeting, and he hadn't been there either.

What if she'd had a flat tire on those back country roads on the way home? With no one behind her to have her back? Never mind that she'd done just fine for years without a constant guardian.

She told herself it was nice to be free, and she kept telling herself that all night, looking around for Drew.

Finishing her coffee this morning, feeling young once more as she welcomed the bright sunshine, she couldn't get him off her mind. Had something happened? Had Chapman exacted some kind of revenge after the incident Monday night? He wasn't the kind to let himself be bested or thwarted in any exchange. Why hadn't she warned Drew more? What if he was hurt somewhere?

Nonsense. This wasn't a Hollywood production. This was simply life. She peered out beneath the valance, but there was only the sunshine. Nothing ominous in sight.

Hurrying a bit now, anyway, she made short work of emptying the pot into a steel thermos. Sunglasses were in order, she thought. It was going to be a long day, so she grabbed a summer sweater, packed a lipstick in the satchel with her notes, and snagged two five-dollar bills out of a jar on the counter labeled Sugar.

Father, she prayed, hoping He wouldn't mind a prayer on the go. *Please guide me today like You always have and let me know what the right thing is, according to Your perfect plan. Don't let me get in the way of any of that, okay? With my stupid ego. I'm working on that with Your help. And please let Drew be all right.*

Emily was nearly to the footbridge before she saw him, and her heart gave another big flop, this time of relief. His old Dodge sat at an angle in the marina's lot, the hood propped open. She could see Drew Mathison's wide shoulders hunched beneath the hood. Hickory, standing beside him rummaging through tools, called out a cheerful good morning to Emily as she crossed over the old canal toward them.

She made herself take a deep, calming breath, wrapping her easy confidence firmly back around her shoulders. A mechanical problem was all. He hadn't gone away. Emily squinted over her sunglasses as she approached.

"What's up?" she asked, peering down at the workings of the truck as if she would recognize the problem.

"Our boy here needed a tow," Hickory said while Drew stretched beneath the hood. When he pried himself back out with a soft grunt, Emily noted his scruffy jaw and a streak of motor oil along his cheekbone.

"You're right," he sighed to Hickory, determinedly wiping his fingers on a rag. He looked Emily up and down with an air of appreciation, either for her outfit or for the thermos she handed him. She couldn't be sure, but she liked to think it was the skirt. He nodded his thanks for the coffee, his eyes warm.

"Ralph said he could be here with the parts by noon," Hickory assured him, rearranging the tools as he snapped the lid of the kit closed.

Drew still looked at Emily like he was trying to work something out. She figured he must be imagining her going through a full day without him behind her. How many times might she be assaulted this morning for not leaving well enough alone? And were they both, in fact, wondering that?

Hickory seemed to also be imagining it. She'd begged Drew not to tell him about the incident in the hallway from Monday, but he had anyway, so that Chapman couldn't go renting boats out here at Graham Marina ever, ever again. Also, it seemed like Drew was trying to keep a job he wasn't even being paid for. Another "see … she does need a bodyguard" reminder.

"Ralph and I can fix her up, no problem. Have her running again by dinner," Hickory said, patting the truck. "You go on, Drew. No use putting Emily here in danger."

"I'll be okay this one day, Hickory," she said, pressing a reassuring kiss to her grandpa's bald head.

"No. Ralph and I could handle this in our sleep. We've got Tom here, too, for the morning. Drew will go with you, honey. No arguments," Hickory insisted. "Do you want to borrow my truck, son?"

Emily tried not to roll her eyes. Sometimes Drew's coziness with her family was just as odd as his mission itself.

Also, Hickory's truck was in far worse shape than even this one. But Drew nodded, having no choice. Emily thought of the day ahead and the fun she anticipated today. She loved her job. There was just one very secret task she needed to take care of without him noticing today, but she figured she could maneuver that as she had been for weeks. Pretending to sigh, she conceded in Drew's direction, "C'mon. You can just come with me." The idea of it lit those secret, lonely places in her life like the sunshine. "We've got all this water, after all. We don't need wheels."

~~~~~

Emily didn't seem to think anything of grabbing Drew's hand in hers and tugging him behind her down around the barge house, not far from the little rise where her tree and hammock watched over the towpath.

Drew had wanted to speak with Tom, the part-time guy, about maybe starting work on this unstable footbridge today. In the end, though, he didn't trust the man to build it right. He'd get to it himself, he hoped, but then reminded himself he should be hoping for *less* time at Buckeye Lake, not more.

He followed Emily to the dock that fronted the barge house, where the boat he'd poked around in before still sat: simple, sturdy, and gleaming with the warmth of expensive wood.

"She's a beauty," he said.

"Of course, she is. She's a Chris-Craft." With athletic grace, Emily pounced from dock to boat, leaving him to follow as she stowed her bag under a seat, flipped switches, and checked gauges on the wooden panel. Everything brisk, no wasted movements, even in her skirt. She crossed to

135

the back, checked something and crossed back up, where she slid around him and into the seat behind the wheel. Squinting at him with a broad grin, she said, "I drive."

Her narrow wrists didn't seem strong enough to control the large, white steering wheel and thrumming power of the Sportsman, but she handled it. More than. Emily didn't need to tell Drew that she'd driven fast boats since she was a child. It was simply there, in the slight corrections she made to their course as she talked with happy abandon about the lake and about the day ahead.

He had thought she'd seemed at home on the pier among the crowds, thought she'd seemed born for that typewriter, thought the council chambers were second nature to Emily. But he knew as he watched her, boosting herself on one foot on her seat as she pushed the speed of the boat to its max over the open water, this was her real element. The wind made a short, golden cape of her hair, and her teeth as she smiled were as white and dazzling as the spray of wake she left behind them.

He would never remember what she'd tried to tell him over the hum of the motor and the rush of the wind. But he was happier than he'd felt in ages, alternately enjoying the view of the lake water and his driver, with her lacy blouse blowing against her.

After so much time watching her move through her day across the distance of parking lots, it was disorienting being so casually near Emily. He'd only just adjusted to her not running away from him, but now here she was, voluntarily beside him, like a celebrity from a poster that he had to keep reminding himself was a real woman. But she *was* real.

He knew her fingers were warm, he reminded himself, because he'd held them now. He knew the pressure of her rib cage against his arms as he'd held her in the aftermath of Chapman's hallway attack, as she'd sucked in air to calm herself and to tell him it was all no big deal. She was both real and fictional to him, human and imagined ... and she made decent coffee, too, for which he was grateful as she maneuvered the Chris-Craft into a dock at the east end of the lake alongside some fancy speedboats.

A sign read *Vacation Times Marina*. Emily's boat looked like a classy aristocrat next to the newer speed boats. She mumbled something about an ad and "just a minute" as she bounded out of the boat just like she wasn't wearing that skirt.

An ascot-wearing, middle-aged man she said was Geoffrey Joyce strolled down the dock to greet her, his arms outstretched. Drew sat back, drinking the steaming coffee, and watched the man apparently try to dodge a late bill for some advertising by making lewd comments about Emily's body. Old Geoffrey's eyes were everywhere.

He tried to talk her into coming into the showroom, but she resisted and waited for him to return with papers. He asked her out no less than three times while she maneuvered him as easily as she had the Chris-Craft and while Drew's blood pressure rose.

At last, Emily climbed back into the boat with a wad of back-owed cash and ad copy for a full-page promotion in the issue of the Fourth. She tucked both into her satchel, stuffed the satchel back under the seat, and met Drew's baffled gaze with an easy smile. "You're wondering how one marina can be so different from another," she guessed.

"Not really."

"Geoffrey even has a customer suggestion box, painted all gold with that razzle dazzle the rest of the place has," she went on, starting the motor up again. She tucked her left foot up under her rear end. "Can't you just imagine Hickory running his place like that?" She laughed. "He just asks you how the boat handled. Comes out with his hands in his pockets and checks on how your day was. Guess they're trying to draw a different crowd, though."

"That's not the biggest difference between Geoffrey Joyce and Hickory Graham," Drew managed. She glanced over at his tone. "How do you do it?" he demanded. "Put up with fellas like that, I mean?"

She blinked. "Oh." Then she shrugged, shifted out of reverse. "That's just part of it."

"Part of it?"

"Of being a woman doing things men usually do. I'm sure it happens to all of us. I just, you know … work around it."

"Men talk to you like that a lot?"

"Not all men, of course. But yes. Some of them do. Like I said, that's part of it."

"How many times do you get asked out a month?"

She laughed, apparently dismissing his question. "Hey, I meant to ask you if you wanted to drive this time, back to North Shore? Want a turn?"

"Later, I will."

She mumbled something as she steered through the no wake zone and settled in. "I don't keep count, Drew." She glanced over. "I mean, how many times guys suggest dinner or dancing or a boat ride. It happens a lot, but I know none of them mean it, so I don't pay much attention. I just keep trying to get what I need. That's what I mean about working around it. Hey, did you see that fish?"

His gaze followed where she pointed, but he was thinking. He could just imagine her daily life, based on what he'd just witnessed. He'd been watching it from afar but wasn't sure he liked all that up close. Nor did he care for the fact she thought that was just the way things had to be.

"I think they mean it more than you think they do," he insisted.

137

"No, they don't. They don't know me. Not really."

"What does not really knowing you have to do with it?"

"I mean, how could they be genuinely interested when they don't really know me?" she clarified.

Drew huffed out a laugh. "How have you survived in the world this long?"

"What?" She yelled it and then she deliberately opened the boat up, and the shining wooden craft leapt across the tiny waves as she laughed with joy.

Across the longest part of the lake they darted, the morning heat mediated by the wind, until the park came into view on the north shore and Emily slowed back down. Even from a distance, the crowds and activity marked the start of another weekend. The sounds slid across the water at them like a greeting, while the skeletal shadow of the coaster stretched and beckoned like fingers. The breeze gifted him with the wormy scent of the lake water, lemon snatches of Emily's light perfume, and the polish from the wood of the boat.

Drew told himself to, but he could not let it go. "Do you ever say yes?" Emily looked at him, confused, cheeks pink from the exhilarating speed even now as they'd slowed. "Do you ever agree to go with any of those men to dinner? Or dancing? Or on a boat ride?"

"Are you asking if I date often?" She sounded just like a reporter, pressing for clarity.

"Yeah."

She shook her head pragmatically. "No." But then she offered no more. She eased the boat nearer a section of public docks, not far from her sister's studio.

"Why not?"

"I don't know. I don't usually want to." She tied up, grabbed her satchel, and disembarked with the same lithe movements she'd employed getting in, but in reverse.

"You make it hard for a guy to be a gentleman," he noted, climbing out. "I can't seem to move fast enough to help you into the truck or into a boat or out of a boat or into a building or out of a building."

"Guess I'm always just a step ahead, Officer," she tossed back, eyes scanning the dock and pier ahead, probably unconsciously sniffing out news and activity just as he habitually scanned the area sniffing out trouble and danger. "I've got a few errands to run over here, but we'll stop in at the inn for a minute. Need to run a couple of things past Cookie." She consulted the narrow watch again, then looked over and smiled. "I do like to go out dancing with my friends if I have a free night sometimes," she continued. "I haven't had much time this season. Sometimes I find people to dance with there, casually, but I guess I'm just not keen on being someone's date, that's all."

He wondered about poor Gilbert, the fiancé.

If he'd known Emily Graham under different circumstances, Drew thought ... if she'd lived in Philadelphia before the war, when he'd been carefree and very good at showing a girl a good time, he'd have taken that challenge. He'd have asked her out, too, just like the others did. Only, *she would know* he'd meant it. Dinner at McMillan's, a carriage ride. He squinted sideways at her as they made their way along the pier, off the dock. Why hadn't anyone besides a hapless childhood friend genuinely tried to win that heart, he wondered. She deserved more than superficial flirting and sloppy invitations paired with comments about her legs.

Feeling guilty, he tried not to stare at those legs as she moved up the steps of the place where Drew technically still had a space reserved in a utility room.

Emily charged through the front door without knocking and remarked on how quiet it was between kisses first for Cookie's and then for Burt's cheeks.

"They're all out swimming, our guests," Burt said, wrapping his niece in a drowning bear hug and then all but tossing her toward the counter. "Hot today!" He clasped Drew's arm in two places and managed not to break it while shaking it. "How do you like our Buckeye Lake, son?"

"I like it just fine."

"Haven't seen you much. Cookie said you've been protecting our Emily, but she can't sniff out the details of what kind of trouble's brewing. Driving her crazy. I keep saying our girl might just be under official investigation. Ha ha."

"Don't you worry about it, Burt," Emily said as Cookie systematically unloaded half the contents of the fridge onto the counter.

"Maybe he's courting her," Cookie said, pulling her orange head out with a wave of cold air and wiggling her brows as she loved to do. "Here, have a plate. Fridays are busy when it comes to news, and I have *plenty*." She was piling hunks of cold turkey onto a small plate, which Emily took out of her hands and pushed at Drew.

"The market asked for two more bundles, so I told Clarence to run those down with the usual stacks," Cookie reported, apparently picking up a thread of conversation with Emily about the newspaper delivery. Emily took a hunk of cheddar cheese off her own plate and tossed it onto Drew's. The turkey was cool, overly salted and delicious.

What time was it, anyway? Certainly not lunch time. As the women continued a conversation that included numbers and businesses Drew hadn't heard of yet, Burt poured him a glass of tea from a pitcher with little sunshine patterns around its middle. The tea proved as sweet as the turkey was salty.

"Geoffrey paid half," Emily was telling Cookie with a shrug.

"That buffoon," Burt mumbled, sinking into a kitchen chair that looked too small for him. Drew followed Emily's lead, which was to stand, leaning against the countertop as she picked at the turkey. Her ease—and the ease of the older couple—spoke to a regular and unofficial dining experience at any time of day.

"Tried to entice me to pick up the second half of what he owes at dinner next week," Emily said with a grin. "Like he's dangling bait. Drew here didn't like it." She punctuated this by dangling a string of cold turkey in front of her mouth, then snatching it up in a quick bite.

"Oh, the romance! That old dog's a catch, love, make no mistake. It's time you settled down and had some little Geoffreys of your own," Cookie declared, cackling.

"I can see your family portrait. All of them in little captain's caps and ascots," Burt said, joining in the fun. "You can have the wedding here."

"Because we wouldn't walk across the street for it, otherwise," Cookie said decisively. "Don't let him run that big ad for the Fourth 'til he's all paid up, dear."

"Already gave him the ultimatum. His eyes bulged a little. We'll see. I might bump him to page eight this week, so he knows I'm serious."

Emily announced she was running down to the park office while Burt had Drew taste-testing wine he was making in the cellar. "Let's meet in front of … the bowling game in a few minutes?"

Drew had to do a double take to realize she was addressing him. "Thanks for the tip on your whereabouts. You're making my job easier these days."

"I've given up hope of losing you in a crowd." Not affectionate words, but she managed to deliver them, somehow, with a sort of warmth that sent a thrill through him.

The three who remained in the kitchen heard the front door of the little inn shut a few seconds later, followed by the faint gallop of sandals down the front steps. Then a beat of silence.

"Well, then?" Burt's extremely fuzzy brows plummeted over his eyes in something almost like disapproval. "Is she safe? What's the latest?"

"We've known Emily forever," Cookie said. "She has no secrets from us."

Drew knew this not to be true, since he seemed to be the only person alive to know the young woman was being fleeced by the mother everyone assumed was still MIA while simultaneously hiding her childhood pal from the mob … which even *he* wasn't supposed to know.

Emily had been correct. Few people truly knew her.

"She's safe for now."

"We love her, though," Cookie insisted, clearly worried. "Surely there's something we can do to help."

Tell her to believe in me, he wanted to say. Short of that, what could anyone do? No one was more frustrated than he was himself. "I'll let you know," he said lamely.

~~~~~

Drew was waiting beside the bowling game when Dot Berkeley approached him.

He'd met the woman who managed the park for her father a few times since he'd arrived at the lake, and he understood enough background to know this was one of the friends with whom Emily had run wild most of her life. Dot was shorter than Emily, with curly, dark hair she wore up in a tidy, business-like arrangement. And she seemed irritated with Drew without bothering to hide it.

"Tell me the truth," she said without preamble, crossing her arms under her chest in a stance clearly meant to be intimidating. "You're no bodyguard."

"With all due respect, that's between Emily and me, ma'am."

"It involves me when folks are saying she's being threatened and harassed over the Lily Point sale and that bog, Mathison." She blew out a furious breath that he was close enough to feel. "That's *me* selling that property and *me* trying to push through the stupid zoning that she's basically blocking. Don't tell me it's *not to do* with me."

"Sounds like you have a hankering to harass her yourself, Miss Berkeley," he said with barely concealed amusement.

"That's not funny."

"Look, I don't know that much about any of it. I don't do politics."

"Well, I do. And *no one* is threatening her."

"I've got a stack of reports saying otherwise."

"Well then, it's not *me* threatening her. We've been friends practically all our lives. Where is she, anyway?"

Drew shrugged.

"You left her unguarded?" Dot gasped dramatically. But she seemed to relax a little with his lack of response, and she sagged back against the corner of the shooting range that was next to the bowling. A kid ran by with a balloon that smacked her in the face, but she merely sighed. "I really am getting tired of Em making FH Resorts look like bullies. They're going to make this place bigger and better. And they'd no more stoop to painting messages on her stupid car than I would."

Drew believed her, absolutely. He knew exactly why he was following Emily around, and that it had nothing to do with any resort proposal. And only a little to do with painted messages on her car.

"It's a respectable company that would build a gorgeous property. It would end up helping us all out. It would bring more people to the lake," she went on, as though Drew cared. "More advertising revenue for our little newspaper princess."

"I don't care much about it one way or the other," Drew maintained again. "But it doesn't seem to me like she's all that swayed by money, that princess of yours."

Dot laughed. "She's not mine. And, no, I guess money isn't her thing." Her lashes moved as she inspected him, more at peace now. "Do you have a cigarette, Mathison?"

"Afraid not." He considered how this woman had changed since the spring dance picture in the barge house. "So, you and Emily have been friends all your lives?"

"That's what I said."

"You must know her other old friends, too, then. Smokey Black? Gil Reese?"

Now Dot looked up at him. "Sure. We all grew up together. Rosie and Smokey were in my class. Em and Gil were a year behind us. I can see how you might've run into Smokey, but Gil's still out West."

"Is he? You haven't seen him?"

"Gil? No. He's stationed at Stead." She shook her head almost with disinterest, and Drew didn't see any of the suspicious extra information Emily's eyes sometimes gave away when he tried to bring Reese up. It destroyed his theory that Emily had some well-connected accomplice here. Specifically, Dot. "Em didn't mention him coming home, anyway. Is he headed back or something?"

"Not that I know of. Smokey had mentioned him, that's all."

Dot snorted. "You've seen Smokey? He pretty much never leaves his trees and pumpkins, as far as I can tell. And he isn't exactly up on news or gossip. You're barking up the wrong tree there, unless it's a Christmas tree." She seemed privately amused by herself for a moment. "Why aren't you asking Emily this stuff about her past?"

Drew shrugged, feeling like he'd boxed himself in.

"Are you interested in her?"

"Me? No. I'm just ... working."

"Which brings us full circle. And I do not buy for a minute that she needs a bodyguard. Not over the development, anyway. About some other hairbrained mess she's gotten herself into, maybe, but not the development. I mean, we're talking about a chunk of land along a manmade lake in Nowhere, Ohio. No one's threatening *any*one over that."

"Tell that to Chapman," Emily said, swooping into the shade beside them, her cheeks still bright from the heat, her eyes bright from ... whatever it was that kept her going.

Where Dot's hair was slicked back into a bun and she wore a classy, summer business suit, Emily was all lace and plaid and disarray, the light knit sweater she'd tied around her waist loosening and hanging half to the ground. Drew bent to pick up the sleeve so it didn't snag on the boardwalk.

"Chapman?" Dot asked. "What about Chapman?"

Done refastening the sweater at her waist, Emily pointed to the yellowed bruises at the tops of her arms. "He didn't like the editorial I wrote."

"He put his *hands* on you?"

"A nasty little scene before the meeting the other night."

Dot's eyes flashed fury. "I'll say something to him. That's nonsense."

"Drew filed a report on my behalf," Emily said, tidily moving the incident into her past. "Anyway, I want their contact info. The developers, I mean."

"What other threats are we talking about?" Dot demanded. "No way you're scared of Chapman, and people don't hire a bodyguard because someone squeezes their arms too hard. Besides, Mathison was here before that. People are talking about this whole bodyguard business, Emily, and you being in danger. I mean, for crying out loud. Do you know what you're *doing* to me in this town?"

"Maybe Drew and I are seeing one another," Emily said lightly, challenging her friend with a sparkle in her eye. "You know … romantically."

Dot shot Drew a look, and he studied his feet. "If you think that's true, Em," she said wryly, "you might want to inform your boyfriend here. Didn't you *just* say she's just a job, Mathison?"

That created a heavy pause.

"I didn't say …" he began lamely.

Emily simply sniffed and raised her chin with comic pride. "Well, I haven't exactly got my claws sunk into him just *yet*, mind you, but I'm working on it. I'm … using all my wiles."

"Your *wiles*?" Dot arched a feminine brow. "Please let me have a front row seat for that."

Drew was grinning outright because he couldn't help it. He'd like to see it, too, come to think of it. Emily swatted his arm with the leather satchel. "I've got to get to the office, Romeo. Come on."

"How will he ever resist you?" Dot called out. "You covering the dance-skate marathon tonight, Em?"

"Of course. Get me the card with the developers' info on it," Emily called back.

Chapter Eighteen

The Buckeye Lake Beacon
Friday, June 28, 1946 ... later that night
Dance-Skate Marathon to be broadcast nationally

"We're on the air again in four minutes!" Sherman Racer, the short, wiry DJ from XVH Columbus managed to both shout and wink at Emily without missing a beat. "Let me interview *you* this time."

Emily frowned, hoisting herself onto an unused speaker behind his broadcasting equipment in a corner of the Skateland rink. She reached down and slid a sandal off, rubbing her heel as her eyes scanned the thrumming room. "You're not interviewing me, Racer. I'm not the news. I report the news."

She thought back to Drew asking her, on the day they met, if she manufactured news.

"C'mon. Just say 'Woo woo' and scream and wish everyone out there in the great State of Ohio as much fun as you're having here at the lake, the lake that never stops, the lake that bee-bops and hops from bottom to top ..."

"You couldn't pay me enough to say that."

"Three minutes. You want me to talk to the French guy underwater again? That went over big an hour ago. Still got the line hooked up."

"Nah, it's good. Leave it."

"What's wrong? It's not even midnight. Want me to dance with you after the next live talk?"

Emily made a non-committal noise and sighed as she dug her fingers into the arch of her right foot. She'd been dancing and skating off and on for hours. The lights, the music, the crowds, the atmosphere ... everything was perfect. What could she say was wrong?

Certainly, she couldn't tell Sherman Racer of XVH that she'd had her female feelings hurt by the big, scary law enforcement officer who had been stalking her for weeks. He'd told Dottie he wasn't interested in her. *Fine*. But, also, Drew Mathison wasn't exactly sticking close to her tonight.

In fact, she'd spotted him dancing with the woman from the lemon squeeze stand over an hour ago. Actually *dancing*! Hadn't he claimed to her only days ago that he hadn't danced since before the war? Hadn't he been reluctant and uncertain that night out on the dock when Emily had practically begged him for a dance?

Another slap to her pride.

She'd also spotted him skating beside Meg Saunders from police dispatch.

What if something happened to her while her bodyguard was out getting fresh with Meg and Lemon Squeeze Girl? Hadn't he learned earlier this week that someone could come up and smash her head against a wall at any moment?

Slipping her shoe back on and acknowledging to herself that she was pouting a little, Emily tuned into the DJ's excruciatingly upbeat radio poetry into the microphone. A subset of screaming young women had gathered on the other side of his table, waiting for their cue from an assistant to squeal and cheer for weekends at Buckeye Lake ... since Emily had refused.

She loved the lake, but she didn't love squealing.

"We're going on four hours now in the marathon that's expected to last as much as thirty-six hours! There are still too many folks on the floor for us to get a clear idea of who might be in it for the long haul, ladies and gents ..."

Emily had no paper number fastened to her skirt like the others. She wasn't sure if she was working or participating, which was hardly a new issue of distinction. But she felt naked, suddenly, without her reporter's notebook. She'd left it sitting by the music equipment with a small amount of cash for a soda banded to it.

When she moved back over and grabbed her notebook, Sherman Racer cued up the next song and grabbed her, too.

"Let's go show these kids how it's done," he crooned, handing his headset to the assistant. Emily had worked with Racer at the odd event before and even shared dinner a couple of times when he'd been in town. For all that he was a bit shorter than her, the man had some on-the-beam moves on the dance floor.

"I don't know. I want something to drink."

"I'm back on in seven, no, six minutes, Toots."

"Don't ever call a woman 'Toots.' Here, then, put the notebook in your back pocket."

"It'll slow me down." But he did it. And then he swung her out in commanding and efficient movements. Emily relaxed into whirls and hops, telling herself it could all be this simple. The music was loud, she had broken a sweat, and Racer, at least, looked happy to spend a few minutes with her.

In fact, she'd hardly been thinking about Drew Mathison when her reporter's notebook flipped right out of Racer's back pocket as he rock-stepped. The pad skidded across the floor to land at Drew's feet, though. Emily pulled away from her partner and walked over.

Drew picked up the notebook first.

When he handed it back to her, the cardboard cover flapped a little and a piece of folded newsprint fluttered out like a drab bird to the floor, exactly as the notebook had before it. Emily wondered what the little scrap could be. Drew, seeing her confusion when he met her eyes, bent once more and unfolded the paper.

Emily moved in close to him to get a look.

And recognized the cut-out image right away.

It featured Gilbert Reese and herself just days before he'd left for the Army, their arms around each other on this very dance floor. How and why had that found its way into her notebook? She'd certainly never cut it out to carry around. A caption, which she remembered Cookie drafting all too well, read, "Reese and Graham engagement announced." And, as a sub-head: "Childhood sweethearts to wed at war's end."

Drew looked at her, questions in his eyes.

"Well ..."

What must he make of this? His lips moved again, but she couldn't hear what he said.

The music changed, and Racer was shouting into his microphone while everyone around them cheered. Drew motioned for Emily to follow him toward the patio.

"Better keep dancing, you two!" a total stranger with crooked teeth yelled into their faces.

They had just reached the edge of the crowd when Emily noticed the red, slashing handwriting on the back of the news clipping Drew held. Sucking in her breath, she grabbed it from him and flipped it. In harsh ink, it read, "Mathison knows you've got him. Watch your back."

Emily's eyes slammed into Drew's. "Him" could only be Gil.

Drew's eyes watched Emily's. Then he looked around with a detective's gaze, pushing her back inside the dance area. His abrupt movements confused her even more. And here, she'd thought *she* was the one with explaining to do.

"What's this mean, Drew?"

"Let's not be quite so out in the open, honey."

"Don't call me that. Who are you?" Her breath was coming in small gasps, and his eyes were darting in every direction as they moved.

"Not the one who's threatening you, that's for sure."

Emily hardly knew how they'd arrived at a concession, and she watched him plunk a coin down for a couple of cola bottles.

"What's this mean, Drew? *Explain*."

"Emily. Drink."

She stared at the condensation on her bottle as Drew's eyes kept tracking the room. She could hardly manage a sip.

He still wasn't looking at her when he said, "Your fiancé is in trouble. I think you know it."

There was a roaring in Emily's ears apart from the music, and she didn't realize the sweating bottle had slipped through her hand until Drew bobbled it, just saving it from hitting the floor. When she tried to suck in air now, it was a slight wheeze.

"Are you all right?"

"Yes. But who ... who are you?"

He looked very professional, suddenly, and not like someone she'd spent the day flirting with.

Now he bent toward her. "Gilbert witnessed a murder. Now he's being hunted by gangsters."

And this detective had been following her, hunting her, too, only far more cleverly.

"You've been *playing* me."

"And you've been hiding him. Keeping him from testifying."

Drew Mathison wasn't some kind of protector. He was a spy. She tried hard to think what she might have given away. But she'd been careful. Clearly, she'd been careful enough, because she *did* know right where Gil was this very minute, and he *wasn't* with Drew Mathison.

Or whoever this man was.

Emily told herself she still had the upper hand, no matter how much she felt like running. Or crying. She pulled herself together, the crowds of dancers and roller skaters forgotten some minutes before.

"You want Gil," she said. And Gil would be counting on her to handle herself.

"Yes. They want him, too. The Conti family."

Emily flinched. It was so strange, having cherished this biggest of all secrets, only to hear the man she'd come to care about speak so familiarly about the details.

"I know you're the one hiding him, Em, and now it sounds like *they* suspect it, too."

"Back up. Why are you looking for Gil? Are you from Reno? A detective from Reno?"

"No. Your darling Gilbert saw one of the Conti family shoot Jamie Mathison."

"Mathison ..." Emily swallowed. Jamie *Mathison*. She had never paid attention to the victim's last name, maybe had never even heard it. "Your brother."

"That's right."

"So, you're working for ...?"

"No one. My family. We'd really like to see Jamie's murderers put behind bars, Emily, but only one person has the power to do that. And you're engaged to him."

Emily shook her head but couldn't speak. She'd been so focused on keeping Gil safe when he'd asked her to that she hadn't considered the victim's family. She hadn't considered this man.

She'd known he'd been mourning the murder of his brother. He'd said as much. How had she been so dense? But she knew the answer to that. Too many secrets, that was how. She was losing track of details.

"Jamie was killed just before I decommissioned, and no one in Reno is doing a thing about it since they're missing the witness who could bring down a crime ring. In fact, the cops there think the witness was already *killed* by the Contis."

"Maybe he was."

"He wasn't. He's in Buckeye Lake." Drew held her gaze.

"What would you do with him? If you found him here?"

"Take him safely back to Reno to testify."

"So they can kill him before or during or after the trial? I don't know much about mob violence, Drew, but I wonder if you've thought of every side of this."

"That's insulting. There are ways to keep a witness safe."

"Of course." Feeling betrayed and wary, Emily followed her instincts. "I'm … I think I'm leaving now."

He wouldn't like it, so she didn't wait for his opinion. Clutching her notebook and hating that someone had waltzed into this giant party to insert a photo into it, she rushed out the side door and up the pier. She wasn't sure if she needed to get away from Mathison or from whoever else had been watching her. She had meant to move quickly, not to run. But then she started running anyway, the slap of the wooden boards somehow soothing against her bare feet.

And it was *her* boat tied down by the docks, no one else's.

She'd known he would chase her down, of course. In truth, she hadn't been thinking at all, but of course there was no reason Drew wouldn't chase after her. It seemed like exactly what was supposed to happen as she heard his boots gaining on her. He was yelling at her about running from the law, which seemed absurd.

She wasn't running from the law. She was running from a man who had used her. From the man who had nearly kissed her. From the man on the picnic blanket in the newsroom. And maybe, now, she was also running from *the mob*.

"You're insane if you think I'm letting you get in that boat alone and jet off across the lake," he called, much closer now.

Both of them were breathing hard by the time they reached the docks. Emily knew there was no way she could leap into the boat, untie it, start it, and pull away before he was upon her.

"Leave ... me ... alone." She put her hands on her knees, trying to breathe.

"Not a chance." He was huffing too. "You ought to ... be glad it's me chasing you ... and not *them*."

There wasn't much to say to that.

Someone had touched her reporter's notebook. Left the five-dollar bill where it was and slid that clipping in. Intended only for her. It wasn't a message about a bog, either, or about anything she had written in the paper. She could not remotely construe it as some professional message. Where had they gotten that photo? That issue of *The Beacon* was years old.

She had to admit this faceless person did seem imminently scarier than Drew Mathison right now. Drew, after all, claimed to want to protect Gil, not kill him.

"You led them right to me, didn't you?" she said as she thought it through, climbing into the driver's seat.

"It was not a complex trail to follow, Em. It was always a matter of time."

She made her peace with Drew riding back to the towpath with her, but she welcomed the roar of the engine and the wind that gave her time to think.

~~~~~

The last thing Drew needed, he thought, was for her to engage that brain of hers. Emotion was far more telling. But the boat was too loud at this speed to lay it all out for her.

Who had penned that message?

He looked around over the dark lake as if for answers. The only people who knew he'd made the connection between Emily and her fiancé, who knew Drew's real purpose at Buckeye Lake, were three apparently good men: Chief Gunn, a lifelong lawman with a reputation for fairness; Pastor Skip, the beloved local preacher; and Smokey Black, a war hero.

Drew stared out over the black chop of the water, the wind swirling around them as they headed west. Who among those three would have the motive to write a warning like that to Emily? Someone who didn't want her to place Gilbert into the hands of the law, clearly.

Gunn didn't seem all that close to the Reese family and had, like Black, been less than surprised that Gilbert had been wrapped up in trouble of this kind. There was no reason the police chief would want Gilbert to remain well hidden. It stood to reason Gilbert's father, the preacher, would want his son safe, but he seemed to trust Drew to do that. In fact, he'd left a couple of messages suggesting places to check for him.

Only, he had never mentioned Emily to Drew. That still seemed odd, no matter what Smokey had said about the man's optimism that his son wouldn't involve his fiancée in something to do with the mob.

Which made Drew wonder about Smokey for the first time. He *had* pointed him in Emily's direction and believed his childhood buddies would certainly be likely to have their heads together about this. If he were in on hiding Gilbert, Smokey would never have had reason to mention that. Or had he mentioned it and then felt guilty? Like he'd betrayed an old friend? Was this Black's way of making it right?

He didn't seem the kind to be this secretive about it, though. His whole focus seemed to be on his farm. If he'd started feeling guilty about leading Drew to Emily, he seemed more like the kind who would have driven over to the towpath and told Emily outright that he was sorry and that her "bodyguard" was onto her.

So, both the guilty sentiment and the red warning message seemed entirely out of character for Smokey.

The possibility that upset him most, though, was the Contis. Specifically, Don Conti, Jamie's old "friend" from university, whom Drew had figured was the family's main hit man now. He felt sure that it had been Don who'd fired the gun in the alley. That it would be Don tracking Gilbert Reese the same way Drew had, back to Buckeye Lake. If he were here and also watching Emily, he'd have to have figured out what Drew was doing. Was Conti hunting Jamie's big brother, the detective, just as much as he was hunting Reese?

It stood to reason the man would lay low. Maybe he'd seen that Emily seemed to be spending real time with Drew now, that she was starting to trust him. And if Emily trusted Drew, Conti would assume she'd hand the witness over to Drew's keeping, which would be very bad news for the hit man's family. It was in Don Conti's best interest now for Gil to stay hidden away, if he couldn't easily find him to kill him.

In light of that, it made some sense for the note to have come from him. It was a possibility, anyway.

That possibility had Drew looking over at Emily as Towpath Island came into sight. She reduced the roar of the engine, and the wind stopped howling in their ears. It was breezy tonight, with a moon peeking in and out between clouds. In that unpredictable lighting, it was still easy to see Emily's posture, tense and straight and brittle. He thought he saw her swipe a tear off her cheek as she pulled up to the dock. Drew rose to tie the boat off as she shut it down. Wordlessly, they climbed onto the dock.

"We need to talk, Em," he said softly.

She walked ahead of him but didn't go to the barge house. There was no way she'd want him in her space in the middle of the night since she was back to not trusting him, he figured. And she couldn't take him to Hickory's, because if there was one thing Drew was sure of, it was that Emily had not told her family she was hiding a murder witness.

And Drew believed she *was* hiding the murder witness, now more than ever. Her reaction at the rink had been all but a confession.

She chose the base of the maple tree, finally, sliding down the trunk to the ground. She pulled her knees up and wrapped her arms around them. She did not invite him to join her, but Drew dropped down to sit in front of her on the cool, dewy grass. He stretched out, propping himself on an elbow, as non-threatening as possible. Fireflies were still flickering here and there around the lawn and the shoreline.

When Drew met Emily's eyes, more beautiful than the moonlight on the dew or the fireflies, they were sad. He decided to use the old detective trick of waiting for her to talk.

When she finally did, she asked, "What was it like?"

"What was *what* like?"

She swallowed. "What was it like, when you got the news that your brother had been murdered in an alley?"

Of all the things he was expecting her to ask for or ask about, this one had not registered as a possibility. Was that *compassion* he was seeing in her eyes? The panic at the rink, the frightened accusations, the look of total betrayal ... all of that had made more sense.

Not for the first time, the woman unnerved him so completely that he looked down and plucked at the grass to keep from meeting her eyes.

"My parents sent a telegram to the base. That's how I found out, after we processed through," he said. "They asked me to call right away. Said they had bad news about one of my brothers."

"And they told you when you called home?"

"I was so confused. The war was over. I thought Jamie was headed back from Reno, that I was the last one who would arrive. The others were back. I couldn't imagine how in the world Jamie had been involved in a battle, since he was stationed stateside, and the war was over. It took me a minute, I guess, to understand that we weren't talking about war. It was the part about the casino alley that finally got through the haze I was in, I guess."

"And what was he like?" She swallowed tears. "Jamie?"

How did he explain the kid to someone who hadn't known him? Someone who never would? It occurred to Drew, like just another emotional punch in the gut, that Jamie would not age, that he'd always be the way he'd seen him two years before.

"He loved numbers."

"Like Charlie."

"Yeah. Like that. He was a little shorter than me, wiry. Curly hair." Drew smiled a little. "He was so funny and laughed so loud. He liked to play pranks on people. Never anything mean, but he just loved the possibility that a good story might come out of it, you know? You'd have liked him."

"Sounds like I would."

Drew chuckled. "I hate to admit it, but you'd have liked him a whole lot more than you do me. Most people did."

Emily made a non-committal sound. "I can't imagine thinking I was coming home to be with the people I loved and end up ... end up losing Rosie like that." She sniffled and wiped her nose on her kneecap, which he found oddly adorable.

"What was it like for *you*?" he asked in return.

"What was what like?"

"Your fiancé showing up with the mob on his tail."

If Drew had been unprepared for this line of questioning from her, he was utterly shocked when Emily, with no warning, leaned forward and pressed her lips to his. He leaned, too, on instinct. She tasted like tears, and her lips felt just right. Nothing passionate. It was too slow and tender for that. But the zing that lived between them was there beneath the gentleness.

When she pulled back, he decided he didn't care if she'd been trying to distract him or that she hadn't answered his question.

"I'm not engaged to Gil," she said simply. She watched him with those lake-colored eyes. Drew tried to process that information. "I don't even know where you heard that. It's true that the two of us were once engaged, like in that clipping, but we haven't been for some time now."

"But Smokey said ..."

She huffed out a frustrated laugh. "I guess Smokey doesn't know. He's been entrenched out at the farm since he got back from Europe, and he's never been one for the latest gossip. He just must not know we called it off a long time ago."

Drew had to admit no one else had indicated a fiancé. He'd thought it was odd that Cookie was always suggesting he and Emily get together when she was supposedly planning a wedding to someone else, but he figured she was just an eccentric old woman (which was still probably true).

"No matter what else happens, Drew, I can't have you thinking ... that I ..."

"What? That you what?"

"You know. That I danced with you that night and that I ... that we almost ..." Her gaze, full of emotion, landed firmly on his lips. He felt his lips tingle, almost like she'd brushed against them again. "That we almost kissed," she said in a quiet rush. "That night on the pier." She took a shaky breath. "I can't have you thinking that I would have been that ... I don't know. Free? With someone if I were truly engaged to someone else. I'm not like that. I don't even act like that with men. I'm not sure why I do with you."

She shook her head and let out a frustrated laugh, pushing her hands through that crop of hair, and suddenly Drew, who had never been good with subtext, understood what she wasn't saying. Emily Graham wasn't a flirt. But she'd flirted with him that night on the pier. And since then. *On purpose.* She'd been interested. More than interested, and the almost-kiss had meant something to her, or she wouldn't have felt uneasy about the idea of him believing her engaged to another man.

Which she was *not.*

She was not engaged to Gilbert Reese.

Her heart belonged to no one else. If anyone, it seemed like her heart had angled itself toward *him.* A lightness rushed through Drew that made him forget about almost everything else. She'd been interested. Which made him want to explore the whole kissing thing again, but for now she seemed eager to explain herself, and he needed that, too.

"Gil and I grew up together, you see," she rushed on, a blonde wave still sticking up on top of her head like a trail of agitation from her hands. "We ran around together all those years, with Smokey and Rosie and Dottie and all our friends. But mostly there was Gil and me. We were the troublemakers. And then he was my date to school dances because everyone just assumed we'd go together and then, when he signed up for the war, everyone assumed we'd get engaged before he left. So, we did." She laughed a little, shaking her head. "It was such a mistake. I do love him, Drew. The boy I grew up with. But I never loved him like *that,* and he didn't love me like that, and we knew it was a mistake right away. Something was just ... missing. You know? That ... thing."

Drew nodded but couldn't speak. He knew what that thing was. He had to talk himself out of that thing every time he laid eyes on Emily.

"So, we ended it in a few letters, not long after he shipped out," she went on. "We're still friends, of course."

"But you're not going to get married to Gilbert."

"Never. Ever. No."

"Okay."

"I can't imagine what you've been thinking of me," she said again, shaking her head.

"I've always had the utmost respect for you, Emily."

This had not gone the way Drew had expected. But, as much as he wanted to sit here with Emily Graham forever and watch this maple turn golden and drop its leaves and bud again in an endless cycle ... there was a matter of life and death to tend to first.

"You need to tell me where Gilbert is, Em." When she looked away, he sighed. "Look, the most important thing you need to know is that I have every reason to keep him safe. I just really need his testimony to put the creeps who killed Jamie away for good."

"You haven't said anything to my grandfather, have you?"

"No, of course not. Not to Rosie either. They don't know he's back here, do they?"

She still stared out toward the lake. Far away, the faint sound of the all-night skate and dance marathon mingled with the occasional bark of a dog. Seeming to come to a decision, Emily turned back to him.

"If I did know where he was, I couldn't tell you," she said simply.

A thrill ran through him. She did know, for sure. He'd been on the right trail.

"Couldn't or wouldn't? Which one?"

She seemed to respect the distinction with a small nod. "Would not."

"I'm the most charming person who's going to come looking for him, you know. The others will be mean."

That was putting it nicely.

Emily smiled. "You haven't been all that charming, Drew."

"This isn't a game. If I tracked him to you, the Contis will. Or have."

"You think they wrote the note."

"Do you?"

"I don't know."

"What if they did? I don't care for the idea of my witness being in grave danger. But the thought that *you* might be ... that's even less acceptable to me. You need to let me do my job."

"Look, it's been a long day, and I need some sleep."

"Emily."

"Another big day tomorrow. We can talk more then, okay?" She rose and, just as she'd fled Skateland abruptly, she strolled off toward her barge. Drew followed her, hating that the person standing in the way of all he cared about in this season of his life was also the person he cared about too much to force.

Without a word, Drew entered the barge house before her, drawing the gun from his belt. He heard Emily muttering something behind him as he moved through each room, clearing the closet under the stairs and then going up. When he was finished, he obediently walked back out the door.

"All clear. Lock it once I leave."

"Thank you."

"I'll keep *him* safe, too, Emily. I promise."

"He said you'd say that," she whispered.

Chapter Nineteen

The Buckeye Lake Beacon
Saturday, June 29, 1946
Golden Bass lures anglers with prize money

Drew's truck was fixed, thanks to Hickory. By unspoken agreement, he drove separately into town the next morning when Emily did. If she needed a little time to think, he'd do his best to give it to her. As long as she did it fast.

The sound of the dance-skate marathon was garish in the early hours, with the sun just risen.

"What's on the agenda today?" he asked Emily as casually as he could in the parking lot of *The Beacon*. He wanted coffee from the diner, since she hadn't brought him a thermos this morning, but he didn't dare leave her alone in that office. There was no phone at the barge house, but there was certainly one here. And things had changed for her last night.

How would she communicate that change with Gilbert Reese? Or with someone who would communicate it *to* him? Drew knew he needed to be extra vigilant today.

"I've just got a few things to catch up on at my desk. Nothing interesting. Figure I'll head back over to Skateland later on."

"Want to walk over and get coffee?"

"I already had some, but you can go."

And wouldn't she just love that?

He did without coffee. In a gesture of good faith, he used the morning to make a few calls to California. He was closing in little by little on Lillian Turnbull Graham, and he didn't mind making the calls in the otherwise empty office. It was Emily's business, and he wanted her to hear that it mattered to him. That what mattered to her mattered to him.

In the way of an experienced detective or even just an average, thinking human being, Drew already had a feeling about what he'd find was true about Lillian. And he hated that he'd have to be the one to break the news to her daughter. How did Emily hold onto such hope about a person or an outcome, he wondered, with so much evidence to the contrary?

But wasn't he doing the same thing himself, about his brother's death? He insisted he could be honest with himself as he guzzled a Coke to make up for the coffee. He propped the door open and stepped outside.

Wasn't he also caught up in some concept of poetic justice that might never come? He needed someone to pay a price—a price that would never be high enough—for taking Jamie from his family. Emily needed—wanted—some kind of normal family life. Or what she imagined normal was.

He couldn't help but wonder if telling Emily her mother would probably never be coming home would turn her against him rather than build trust. So, he tried to stay optimistic.

Having spent time with Pastor Skip, Drew had started praying somewhat regularly again, if only because he believed in discipline. Prayer was a discipline, Skip kept insisting. Feeling the sun warm on the back of his neck, Drew bowed his head and talked to God about all those unknowns. About Emily's stress and about the weight of her trusting him with this thing she hadn't shared with her family. These *multiple* things, actually. He prayed about his family and his own attitude. He prayed about justice because God was in the business of justice, and Drew didn't see how he could be anything but aligned with God's will there.

God's will be done.

Even so, when he turned back into the office with a weary "amen," he wondered if God would just let the whole thing shake out the way He'd meant it to all along. Discipline of prayer or not, God was God. Drew told himself accepting that fact was a mark of spiritual maturity.

So why did it make him feel so helpless?

He picked up a copy of the latest newspaper off the front counter on his way in and was struck again by the Saturday quiet.

"What does your band of merry men do on Saturdays?"

"I make a point of not asking," Emily said, blinking owlishly above the typewriter.

He spread the newspaper on Cookie's desk, across from her.

"Now you're really set," she said. "Caffeine and the best doggone newspaper in the county."

Her half-glasses were perched on the tip of her nose, that little concentration line between her brows as she moved on with her work. There was some rapid-fire typing, followed by a lull while she flipped through a notebook.

She was used to him, he realized. It was funny what human beings could adapt to, given a few days' time. Drew wasn't sure he wanted to be gotten used to. He thought back to last night, to the tenderness she'd shown when she could have fought him. To the gentle kiss she'd shared after so many half-truths on both sides.

He longed for one day with her. One day in which they truly could be the man and woman they were without Jamie's death and Gilbert's escape hanging over them.

For now, though, he sipped energy and plowed through *The Beacon*, front to back. He learned that Rich and Wanda Tucker from Harbor Point had recently been blessed with triplets when they had been expecting just one baby, and neighbors had pitched in money for a second and third crib. The dance-skate marathon was expected to last until tomorrow morning, at which time the music would stop and a church service would commence on the pier. The state park watercraft office was cracking down on boats operating without a light after dark. Drew thought of the lovers floating through Rosie's canal lights in their dark little vessels. Then he dutifully flipped to the obituary page while explosive little rhythms continued to come from the typewriter across the aisle.

Someone named Harley Taggert had passed away, it seemed. Drew skimmed his birth location, his parents' names, his "preceded in death by" and his "survived by," but then he slowed as he reached the good stuff.

... it's Harley's life-long hobby for which he will be remembered by us all. Hundreds of children who have already grown to adulthood and will continue to grow here in the lake area were blessed with the gift of Harley's miniature, wooden tea sets: plates smaller than the nail on your ten-year-old pinky finger, itty-bitty tea cups perfect in detail that couldn't even accommodate a raindrop and complete with almost microscopic handles, little wooden tea pots with lids that somehow fit, though they were smaller than a single jack. He labored over them nightly in his appropriately tiny backyard shop, magnifying glasses strapped to his head ...

Drew thought about his brother Jamie's obituary again, short and stark, misspelled. It certainly wasn't this monument of words. He could almost hear Emily speaking as he read on.

There is wonder in the small stuff. Harley understood that. All over the lake area, generations of people on any given day can hold a complete, wooden tea set in the palm of their hands, wondering at the craftsmanship, guarding the pieces with a passion they barely understand. What they're marveling over, though, is the intricacy of Creation. It's the same thing that causes a shiver in the scientist peering through her microscope. It's the wonder of a fingerprint, unique in its patterns. There was a love of detail and for those who would appreciate it in Harley's work. It mirrors the intricacies of God's Creation and of his love for amazing us with power that is both universe-expansive and as small as a newborn baby's thumb. Harley Taggert had an eye for the Small Stuff. And that ends up being a very Big Deal to the rest of us who knew him.

The rest was about a memorial service. Drew's gaze slid off from there and over to Emily's desk, where the phone was ringing. She'd had a pen in her mouth and picked up the phone receiver upside down, righting it on its way to her shoulder.

"This is Emily at *The Beacon*," she said, somehow managing to start typing again. And then her fingers stopped. Her head straightened, causing her to reach up and take hold of the phone again. Drew snapped to attention. Everything was very quiet for exactly three seconds. "Yes. Of course. I'll be right there!"

She stood abruptly, and Drew felt her wink deep in his chest. "It's go time, sidekick," she said with a smile, packing up her satchel. "We get to be photographers today, too. Grab that bag. The big camera case there."

"Am I allowed to ask where we're going?"

"Someone caught the Golden Bass!"

~~~~~

Emily missed traveling with Drew in the Chris-Craft, plowing through the water with the engine and wind too loud for conversation.

Instead, he insisted on driving around the lake back to the watercraft office and docks, and it was far too easy to talk in the cab of his truck. She could not think of an excuse to drive separately, so she hummed to fill the silence and kept her attention firmly out her side window.

Of course, Emily knew exactly where Gil was. If her mother's requests for cash were weighing down one of her shoulders, the pressure on the other was her childhood friend's terror and need to stay hidden. It occurred to her that, in just a few weeks, detective Drew Mathison had managed to find out the entire web of secrets Emily had been weaving for a year.

Well, almost the entire web. She knew, without a doubt, that Gil was tucked away safely.

Then she told herself this really was a game of sorts, even if Drew said it was not.

She tried not to think of the way Gil had cried when he'd called her over behind the barge house late one night in early May. She hadn't seen him in ages. He'd been trembling, desperate. *Changed.* A few months of total disappearance, he'd assured her, and then he'd be okay to be on his way. She would be saving his life, quite literally.

She didn't like to think about sweet, awkward Gil being in a life-or-death situation. She didn't like being responsible for keeping him on the life side of that situation. If Emily could keep telling herself it was a game, then she could remember one important fact: she generally won games when she played them.

She simply had to figure out how to play *this* one, now that it had grown more complicated.

Drew's little brother had been murdered. Emily remembered Gil crying so hard, talking about his friend, Jamie, and details of the shooting she still wished she hadn't heard. Poor Jamie, whose only way out of a numbers racket had turned out to be death.

"They're not messing around," Gil had told her, his nose running as he'd cried. "They know I saw. He *saw* me, Em. He saw me. He's trying to find me. You can't let him find me."

From the moment he'd uttered, "He's trying to find me," Emily had been so distracted by Gilbert's plight and by the need for total secrecy that she hadn't spared much of a thought for the family of this Jamie, the whiz with numbers, who had been shot dead in an alley. It could easily have been Gilbert, she thought, cut down in a city far from home, his life and death pushed aside because of another family's talent for abusing power.

Something uncomfortable nudged at her spirit. Wasn't her job to help *stop* the abuse of power? But this was not the kind of power she usually went up against, after all. Zoning violations and public record denials and good old boy politics, those were the things she'd been trained to fight against. This kind of abuse of power, by contrast, was about guns and cold-blooded killers. This was something to hide from, she told herself ... and hide other people from, when necessary.

She noticed how Drew's normal attentiveness to their surroundings had grown even more keen. So far, he'd been careful with her today. He hadn't brought up the barrier that she supposed he'd known about all along but that she was only now seeing clearly. Only now thinking through.

"When did Smokey tell you?" she asked suddenly.

"The day after we danced on the pier."

She went back in her mind to that strange day he had appeared on her little strip of island, surprising them all with his decision to guard her from the evils of Buckeye Lake politics. It was finally making sense. "That's what I thought."

"Speaking of thinking," he said, making the turn onto Liebs.

"Chief Gunn knows," she interrupted.

"Yes."

"That's why he doesn't seem to mind that you come and go whenever you want from your duties at the park."

"I come and go with you, that's true."

"I can't believe he didn't tell you about Gil and me once being engaged."

"I asked him about it afterward. He had never known that, he said."

Emily blew out a breath. "He can be really clueless. For a policeman. I shouldn't be surprised, though. I mean, he doesn't even read the paper."

"I understand your need to catch up with all this, Em, but the clock is ticking here. I need to know where Gilbert is."

"It's not my call, Drew."

"Let me talk to him. Let me convince him, and then it can be his call."

Emily shook her head. "I need a day, okay? Can you give me a day or so?"

"I can until it's not up to me."

~~~~~

The Golden Bass was another Civic Association gimmick, Drew learned, as they made their way closer again to the lake. The association had tagged a bass with a golden tag on Decoration Day and released it back into the murky waters of Buckeye Lake. Catching it on the end of a line after that meant a fat check for the victor.

Charlie Graham had wanted to use the money for a fancy adding machine and some comic books, Drew remembered. But the angler who'd snagged it was reportedly eighty-two-year-old Gunner Frazier.

A hardy man in a brown-on-brown uniform was waving at Emily as they made their way toward a crowded dock in front of the watercraft office.

"I wouldn't let them start without you!" he shouted, moving toward them. "Emily, did I hear Louis Armstrong is coming in August? *The* Louis Armstrong? Can you confirm?"

"That's what I heard the other day from Dot, so it must be true," she said, yielding to his hug.

"Who's your friend?"

"Drew Mathison. Drew, this is Ed Sherlach, director and manager of the watercraft portion of Buckeye Lake Park."

Drew found his hand being engulfed in a grizzly handshake, everything about Sherlach reminding him more and more of a bear, right down to the texture of the man's shaggy brown hair, mustache, and beard. Even the back of his hand felt unusually hairy.

"Pleased to meet you, Officer Mathison. I've heard about you from Gunn. Says you're a good worker. Just back from the war, I hear?"

"Yes, sir."

"Europe?"

"Yes. MP."

"Well, we can always use law enforcement help here on the water, too, you know. If ever you're looking, I mean, and you don't mind patrolling by boat. I better go get this shindig started."

"I'll just be a few minutes," Emily told Drew before following Ed toward a dock of about forty people, surprising Drew by squeezing his forearm as she passed him.

Drew ambled closer to the dock as Emily wove her way through the crowd in Sherlach's large wake. People greeted her as she passed, and he noticed yet again how skilled she was at speaking with friends and neighbors while staying in motion. To move forward and make other people feel special all at once … that was a talent. He figured if she hadn't developed that skill, she'd either never get a single thing done or not be nearly as popular as she was.

A bird called from a tree nearby, screeching to be heard over the din on the dock. There were mostly older people in the crowd, but there were a few kids, too. They were already cruising on too much sugar, and it was barely noon. Parents chased them around, laughing with one another nearly as much as their children laughed together.

Drew couldn't have explained it, but something about this photo op made him uneasy.

In light of that, and knowing to trust his instincts even when he was tired, he took up his post at the very edge of the dock, back to a tree trunk, arms crossed, and scanned the area the way he'd been trained to. It was easy to spot the aged and overwhelmed little fisherman who was being heartily congratulated at the end of the dock. Gunner Frazier. Drew wondered if he'd be wearing nicer overalls this time next week, once he'd cashed his check.

There were other people Drew recognized milling about the dock itself for the presentation of the check. A couple of business owners, he figured, from the association. The mayor was out there, along with some members of the town council already in their casual, weekend clothes. No sign of Chapman.

Standing off to one side of the dock were two men who looked out of place in expensive suits. They didn't seem to be part of the association crowd. Around thirty years or so, one of them blond and the other dark, they stood with their arms crossed. When Emily had moved down the dock, closer to the winner, both men's eyes had tracked her. Were they just interested because they were men and she looked like everything a man was naturally drawn to, Drew wondered, or could they have been sent here by the Contis?

Something didn't feel right.

Drew nodded to someone who greeted him but didn't take his gaze off the men as Ed brought the celebration to order. He produced a large, paper check to the sound of cheering. It was difficult to see Emily down there for a moment, but one of the men, the blond one, moved a little until he had her back in his sights. Drew pushed away from the tree, ready to move.

At the end of the dock, whatever Ed said had people clapping again. Emily obligingly arranged herself to take the picture, gesturing about the best way to stand. They laughed at something she said. Everyone shifted on the dock.

The two suits studied her relentlessly as she placed her camera back in its case, left it sitting on the wooden boards, and strode a few steps over, notebook out, to chat with Gunner Frazier. She scribbled but did not look away from the victor's face, that light, hospitable smile never leaving hers. Gunner seemed to glow in the beam of it, to puff himself up a bit.

Drew wondered, a little uncomfortably, if he looked that same way when Emily smiled at him.

The old man began to talk to her with animation, gesturing to the water and laughing like a boy, as Emily's pen moved across the notebook. She said something.

And, like Drew, the two suited men missed none of it.

They were going to have to have a talk, Drew decided, one way or the other. He was just stepping off to move closer when the blond one pulled away and sidled along the dock toward Emily. Surely he wouldn't hurt her here, not with the crowd, Drew told himself, feeling adrenaline flush his system. Now he had to keep an eye on both men in two different spots.

Emily looked up and saw the one who had moved toward her, who apparently said something to get her attention. Drew saw something like alarm flash across Emily's face, her eyes going wide, her face going pale. He hardly knew he was moving toward the pair until he nearly knocked someone over, picking up speed still more when Emily tried to turn away and the suited man reached out to snag her arm in a grip that she tried to break but couldn't. With the other hand, the man reached into his jacket as though going for a weapon.

Drew ran hard. Shoving through the scattering crowds along the dock, uncomfortably aware of the other man behind him even as he moved so fast, his feet pounded loud on the wooden planks. People started to scream.

The man who still had hold of Emily heard Drew's approach because he pivoted awkwardly, stumbled in surprise and, somehow, though he seemed to release Emily's arm, reeled just enough to manage to knock her right off the dock and into the lake. She cried out as she fell back, the gasps of the crowd mixing with the splash of her landing in the water.

Realizing he had caused her fall and baffled by the sight of Drew running toward him like a furious bull, roaring now, the man fought for purchase of his own on the dock, but it was no use when Drew plowed into him. The pair fell back into the lake water three feet beyond where Emily rose dripping below.

Shoulders and chest heaving, Drew regarded Emily just long enough to make sure she was okay from the fall, glanced back to find the second suited man above simply looking shocked, then made quick work of disarming the wet one ... not of a gun but of a heavy tube from his inside suit pocket.

"Hey! Hey!" The guy was dripping and furious, but he wasn't that strong. There was, still, a good deal of splashing and thrashing as Drew patted him down thoroughly and none too gently. When Drew raised him by the collar of his silk shirt, Emily was suddenly there beside them, saying something he couldn't hear over the protests of the worm whose ID was now in Drew's pocket.

"Stay back, Emily."

"Drew, I know who this is," she said breathlessly, honey curls hanging damp in her eyes.

"I wasn't *hurting* her," the man blabbered, still spitting water and choking. He maintained his soggy flailing, looking like a fool. "Let me go! Give me back the plans."

Drew craned his neck for the guy's accomplice, who was standing now above them on the dock, surrounded by the rest of the crowd, hands casually in his pockets … and a bemused grin on his face.

That struck Drew as inconsistent with organized crime.

"What's your name? Who are you?" he demanded of the soggy one, not releasing him long enough to study his ID

"Keith … Fairchild. I just wanted … to talk to her! Let … go." He cursed furiously then, fighting sloppily against Drew's size and strength and still unyielding grip. Drew felt Emily's hand on his arm, glanced at her just long enough to see that she didn't necessarily look afraid. Wet, irritated, disgruntled, resigned. But not afraid. Her words finally registered with him. She'd said she knew the guy.

Which didn't mean he wasn't capable of harming or threatening her, of course. But which also meant he was not likely to be a hired thug from Reno, after all.

"Who is he, then? How do you know him?"

"Keith's family owns the hotel here on Liebs Island, Drew," she said with hints of exasperation, as though soothing a hysterical child. She was still trying to catch her breath, herself. "I haven't seen him for years, but he's *not* here to hurt me. I'm sure of that. You can let him go, Drew. Keith, this is Drew Mathison. He's the law here, and I've been … threatened lately."

"I'm not going to hurt anyone. I swear it. I wanted to talk to Miss Graham."

Something was still off, Drew thought, as he released him. There was more than irritation at being soaked in Emily's eyes. There was hurt, too.

"You okay? Em? You're sure you're not injured?" Drew asked her gruffly over Keith Fairchild's blustering about "having this man's badge."

Emily assured him she was fine, and by the time they'd climbed back onto shore and moved to a picnic table away from the dock, Ed Sherlach had tried to step in to help with this unexpected drama on his shores. Then he'd reiterated his offer of a job to Drew, despite Drew's heroic assault being deemed unnecessary. Ed seemed to recognize "the Fairchild boy" and then left them all alone, returning to manage the small crowd of very suspicious folks who had simply gathered to watch an old man get a cardboard check.

Feeling guilty about the way Emily's clothes were clinging to her soaked body—and more than a little distracted—Drew unbuttoned his blue cotton shirt and wrapped it around her. Standing there in his undershirt, with his shoulder holster and weapon exposed, Drew found himself shaking hands with the only dry member of the group, the darker haired man who introduced himself as Gabriel Adams "of FH Resorts."

Resorts? Could this possibly have to do with that stupid development on the north shore?

Adams shook Emily's hand, too. "I'm sorry we're meeting like this, Miss Graham," he said smoothly, just a hint of Appalachia in his voice. "I know you already know Keith here."

Emily nodded but wasn't paying attention to Gabe Adams. Still pale, she stared at Keith, who had recovered from his shock enough to lean into his anger.

"Give me one good reason not to press charges," he told Drew. "You're a maniac. Give me back my blueprints."

Drew did. Then he pulled out his own wallet and Fairchild's at the same time, handing the one back, and opening his own to reveal the badge Gunn still let him carry. Combined with the weapon holstered against his middle, it seemed to calm the man down.

"Looked like an assault from where I was standing," he said.

"Dot said Emily had hired herself a bodyguard because *we* were supposedly threatening her over the zoning for the resort. Ridiculous. Now I'm *more* than offended."

"I can't believe this," Emily said from within the folds of Drew's blue shirt. "*You're* the developer for the resort at Lily Point!"

"I'm sure trying to be, Emily," he said with a familiarity that grated on Drew. "But I'm not buying the property from the Berkeleys if the zoning won't go through, and you're being a pain in the ..."

"We understand your concerns," Gabriel Adams said easily to Emily, eyeing his partner. "But this is no place to talk business, with you both ... dripping."

"I don't have any business to discuss with you," she snapped.

Drew felt a flash of annoyance. How could she be so passionate about a strip of land while justice still hadn't been done in Jamie's murder? Everything, he thought, pushing remaining drops of water off his hair, was turning out to be one distraction after another.

He walked down the dock and picked up Emily's camera bag where she'd left it. Slinging it over his shoulder, he walked slowly back in the direction of the truck to wait for her. Emily had said Keith Fairchild's family owned the hotel near the marina. Of course, she'd have recognized him. Wouldn't they, also, have grown up together?

Drew was so tired of envying everyone else's stories with Emily Graham.

"Let's go get some dry clothes on," Emily suggested as she reached the truck beside him. She made no move to take the camera bag back but slid her hand into his as though she needed the contact. Or the warmth. It surprised him, either way.

"Sorry you got pushed in."

"I told you it happens to me a lot," she said simply, climbing all wet onto the seat.

"That's right." She had mentioned it that night on the pier when they'd danced. "Charlie must take after you, too." Drew thought about Charlie dropping his favorite hammer and at least half a dozen other tools off the dock as they'd worked. Emily stared at him with an expression he couldn't read. "I mean, he's clumsy like you. I've seen him nearly fall off the docks a dozen times while we've been patching them up."

"Keith Fairchild, the guy you just tackled? He's Charlie's father, Drew," Emily said simply.

Drew hesitated with the keys on the way to the ignition, contemplating it.

Yes, it was there in the bridge of the wealthy man's nose, he supposed. The shape of his chin. His posture. He thought back to how young Rosie must have been when Charlie had been born. Add to that a fella whose family owned the hotel right next to the Graham Marina. The age was right.

Both Emily and Ed Sherlach had indicated "the Fairchild boy" hadn't been around for many years. And that "boy" — very much a man now — had been entirely focused on a resort development he was planning when he ran into Emily Graham after all these years. Entirely focused.

"He doesn't know about Charlie, does he?" Drew asked, looking over at Emily.

"No, he doesn't."

Her pale, stricken face made sense to him now. And, of course, this would be the man also trying to build the resort that would annihilate the bog and its habitats that seemed so all-important to Hickory Graham's granddaughters.

Unlucky coincidence for one Keith Fairchild.

In light of that, Drew wondered that Emily hadn't reached over and attempted to use his service pistol on Fairchild as he'd stood there dripping in his three-piece suit.

Chapter Twenty

The Buckeye Lake Beacon
Saturday, June 29, 1946
Round the Bend: voted best sandwich on the lake

Back in the barge house, Emily hung her wet skirt up to dry. She'd told Drew she'd meet him back at the dock in ten minutes, gratefully handing his own shirt back to him, and he had only nodded. Not for the first time, she wondered if Drew was dropping his clothing at the laundry in town or if Hickory was doing it for him. The latter wouldn't surprise her much. At any rate, the man always smelled like Laundry Day. And like the woods.

The incident with Keith and his friend had seemed to bring all of Drew's frayed nerves to the surface, to say nothing of her own. Emily was honest enough to admit to herself that she'd been shaken by the incident in ways that had nothing to do with taking a plunge.

Still, while Drew had been concerned for her safety, she knew her own shaken foundation had more to do with her family, her own circle. How, she wondered, did *so many* ghosts choose to make themselves known at the same season in her life? And how had this former construction worker-turned-soldier from Pennsylvania she'd met weeks ago become the only other person who knew about any of them?

Gilbert, her mother, and now good old Keith. All returned, in one form or another.

Keith Fairchild. The charming rich boy who might as well have walked off the pages of a twenties novel. Who else but Keith could have been behind the resort project all along, she thought. She wondered if she should be embarrassed that the name FH Resorts had not tipped her off on the development documents; the family must have branched off from Fairchild Hotels, which already had chains of upscale hotels in several cities, in addition to the quaint but luxurious one on Buckeye Lake's Liebs Island. A decade ago, young Keith had waltzed in for the summer and taken her sister's innocence, and this time, he meant to dance in and out and destroy a natural treasure of the lake, leaving with an even fatter wallet than the one Drew had tossed back to him this afternoon. If that were possible.

Feeling weary and a little jaded, she stripped off the rest of her wet clothes and stood in the small front bedroom that was also part living area, staring out at the lake as her bare skin dried in the breeze coming in from the window.

What would her sister do with all this?

Rosie had developed tough skin, but this might be a lot even for her heroic big sister. Though it had certainly always been possible that the owner's son would find his way back to the hotel next to the marina, Emily had never imagined that their paths would have to cross over a zoning issue.

And what about Charlie?

Charlie, who had latched on so pathetically to Drew Mathison, who was useless with tools and footballs but who so wanted to try. Keith didn't know the boy existed. Charlie certainly wouldn't know Keith if they passed on the island.

Half-panicked, Emily wondered if they already *had* passed one another.

Would Keith see himself in Charlie?

No, of course not. Charlie looked like a Graham. Mostly. But Rosie would need to know, so she wasn't caught off guard. Emily would pull her aside tomorrow for another cup of tea in the barge.

Or Monday.

Which was the right day to reopen that chapter of Rosie's life?

Emily pulled fresh clothes on slowly, remembering how young and vital she'd felt only yesterday morning.

Drew was waiting down by her little dock, his arms crossed. She thought back to the scene at the watercraft office dock today. Seeing him run like that, so aggressively, so focused on eliminating a perceived threat to her ...

There wasn't a thing about him that didn't quietly thrill her.

She wondered if she could convince Gil to let Drew take over, to make everything right. She wondered if trying to convince him was the right thing to do. Lives were at stake here. Still, if it worked, then Drew could be the one to keep Gil safe, and *she* could stop worrying about all of it. She felt sure Drew was equal to the challenge, now more than ever.

She wondered what he'd do if she simply refused to hand Gil over to him. He must have thought through his next move in this "not game" they played. For a wild moment, she imagined herself tied to a chair in a back cell of the police station while he tried to break her like a spy in the movies.

She hated the idea that Drew might be forced to give up on her after a time. He couldn't just remain her pretend bodyguard, living out of his truck, indefinitely.

Drew smiled at her, still apologetically, as she reached her boat. She wished he hadn't put another shirt on. She'd rather liked the way the simple white cotton had clung to his chest beneath the harness.

Even walking closer to him, just joining her space to his, made her feel a little steadier.

"Hi," she said.

"Hi. Where to now?"

The heat had only increased in the afternoon, rising like the waves of red-faced visitors pouring from the parking lot at the amusement park. They were a younger group than normal, here to get in on the last day of the dance-skate marathon. Emily, still armed with the camera, dragged Drew to a beauty pageant and to a diving clown show. She found herself charmed by his lack of interest in the young pageant contestants, decked out in their bathing suits. Instead, what little enthusiasm he showed was saved for a lemon ice that melted before he could finish it.

His nose and forehead were beginning to burn, she noticed, so she finally took pity on him. Leading him back to the boat, Emily decided he seemed numb, burned, and preoccupied.

"Thanks for saving me again today, Mathison," she said as they got situated once more against the sun-sizzling seats. She had gestured to the driver's seat, and he slid into it with the same reserved interest he'd shown for the lemon ice.

Why should she, who so loved words, be so attracted to this man's reluctant use of them?

He shrugged. "I didn't save you from anything."

"But you *thought* you were saving me, which is really all that matters. Just like the other night at the town hall, with Chapman."

He grunted this time and fired up the engine. "You needed me that time."

"You're not wrong about that. Anyway, the upside is that neither of these two rescues—real or false alarms—have had to do with angry mobsters. That's such a good sign, don't you think?"

He made no response to that, concentrating on easing the boat out amidst the traffic of the lake near the park. An old schoolmate shouted a greeting at Emily, and Drew said, "You're going to have to tell me where we're headed."

"I'm going to feed you." Emily pulled the scarf off her hair so it didn't blow off. "It's a little place called The Bend because of its location. Usually, only locals are committed enough to find it. Best burgers around. Cold, cold drinks. You look like you could use a cold drink or two." Drew mumbled an agreement, messing with the console. "But because I'm Buckeye Lake's ultimate tour guide at heart, I do want to show you something quickly, before we eat. The bog. It's on the way. Go left. Just up that way, where that sailboat is."

He opened the boat up outside of the wake zone, the breeze welcome but the air still heavy. It promised to be an especially hot Fourth this year.

She directed him to steer up to the bog area after a short jaunt along the north bank, just beyond the chaos of the public beach. "I can't have you going back to Philadelphia not having seen this gem," Emily said when he could hear her again.

She didn't love the idea of him going back to Philadelphia at all, of course. She felt like she'd known him longer than she had and wasn't entirely comfortable being without him, but neither of those feelings made a bit of sense, so she kept them to herself.

She almost, in fact, managed to keep them *from* herself.

"I know this looks like a misshapen island, overgrown with brush," she began, gesturing for him to shift down again at the same time, "but it's actually made of sphagnum moss. No dirt, Drew. *Moss.*"

"I take it that's odd for an island."

"We call it Cranberry Bog because it's loaded with cranberry bushes that everybody comes out to pick in season."

"You can walk on moss?"

"Sure can. It's like walking on a bouncy sponge. If you jump up and down on the ground, it squishes around your feet. We used to do it for hours when we were little."

"No kidding."

She studied him and the scruff that roughed his jaw. "Are you impressed?"

"I am."

"Okay then, head that way. Time to eat." She craned her head to get another look as they drove off. "This FH Resorts, they're not just going to build a resort. They're going to remove a large portion of the bog to build out docks for their guests."

"How is that allowed?"

"They've got a lot of money, believe me. And the town fathers love money a lot more than they love cranberries and prehistoric land movement. Also, no one ever did anything to try to officially protect it. There are no policies or ordinances in place." She thought about it for a moment and remembered Chapman's connection to the development. Keith Fairchild, she realized, connecting the dots, was the cousin of Chapman's she'd heard about.

Which meant Emily's sweet nephew was *also related* to Chapman. She must have groaned with the realization because Drew looked concerned.

~~~~~

By the time they'd boated to the out-of-the-way grill, the breeze that had been a vague respite from the heat all day had turned almost to a wind, but it was nothing fierce enough to keep them from deciding to eat outside. Drew understood why only locals might come here, since he didn't spot so much as a sign—not from the water side, anyway—

advertising that this was a restaurant at all.

Though a few old men with fish stories slouched at the bar inside, listening to a Reds game on a radio, the place was more or less deserted because of the party raging stronger than ever on the opposite side of the lake. From here, he thought, it was impossible to believe all that noise and expectation hummed just two miles across an expanse of grayish-green water.

Emily swiped cold glasses of tea off the bar, and they seated themselves at a weather-worn table on the patio. They had it all to themselves, and a stretched canvas over the patio provided shade and rippled softly in the wind.

Across the speckled lake water in the other direction from the patio, the hodgepodge of small homes was only just visible along a shore that twisted back toward the old canal and around again toward the main village. Everywhere was the chase of white gulls, dipping toward the shadows of the lake and silhouetted against the deep greens of the shoreline trees.

The wind had produced brown-green waves, small in size but rushing toward the shore beneath where they sat on the patio. The waves, he thought, didn't have a lot of say about the course their journey took. Trying not to think about choices and purpose, he decided he envied the waves and the white-bellied little gulls their carefree existence. Which made him turn in consideration of the woman across from him who was far from carefree and who was watching him with about as much patience as she ever managed. How did she seem *fine*?

"You're one of the ones who've got it all figured out, don't you?"

"This feels like a trick question." She sipped at her tea, intent on him. "If you mean what I'm eating for dinner, then yes. I do have that figured out. But I'm guessing there were deeper thoughts giving rise to that."

"Your place in the world. The newspaper, this community, your family. For all your long hours, for all the trouble you've shouldered on your own, you're still … I don't know … at peace."

She grinned, sucked on her straw again. "I'm no great example of peace. Just ask my family."

"I mean on the inside. When it comes to your place in the world."

"Oh, that. That's faith." It was simple, even accented with a one-shouldered shrug that Drew envied, too. "I'm where I'm supposed to be. I'm blessed that I love it. The troubles come and go and, I admit, feel big right now. Probably because I'm not handling them well." Another shrug. "And that's probably because I'm talking about handling them by myself instead of with God."

"If you asked Him to handle all of it, do you think He would?"

Emily paused, pulling her left leg beneath her in the chair, the same way she did when she was driving the boat. "Yes."

"What if it wasn't part of His plan, though? The way you wanted it handled?"

"Then, I wouldn't want it. He's smarter than me." She smiled her usual sunburst smile. "Drew … it only now occurs to me. Have you been coming to church because of what Jesus did on the cross or just to *spy* on me?"

"Spy is such an ugly word," Drew said with a wink. "But yes."

"Yes what?"

"Yes, I go to church because I'm thankful every day for grace. But also, I went to spy on the preacher, if I'm being perfectly honest."

Emily smiled a little but then quickly sobered. "Poor Pastor Skip."

"He doesn't know where his son is?"

"Absolutely not." She leaned forward. "So, what's got you shaken when it comes to God's plan?"

"Nice change of subject."

"We haven't even ordered food. Let's pace ourselves here, Mathison. What are you hung up on, anyway?"

"I guess it's life *here*. I don't know how to explain it." It was too much work to explain it, and he didn't want to change her opinion of him. In many ways—not all ways, but many—he was a doubter now.

"You don't mean life here at Buckeye Lake," she said. He glanced up at her searching eyes and then away again. "You mean life here on earth." She left it alone for a quiet moment, which was so unlike Emily, and it was long enough he started to think he would maybe get a pass. But that was too much to hope for. "You trust God with your eternity, then," she said softly. Drew nodded. He did, absolutely. "But not with your *day*, I take it? You don't trust Him with the details while you're here."

He would never have said it just like that. It sure didn't sound good when she said it that way, certainly didn't sound like something *a believer* would ever say. He couldn't deny the truth in it, but when he searched her face again, there was only understanding there. No disappointment. "Something like that."

"I've been there," she said easily. It seemed like she was as comfortable talking about this as she was about zoning regulations or a golden bass. "I was just thinking, earlier, that I guess I'm glad *you* know about … well, all the things no one else knows about in my life right now, Drew. Even if one of those things has us completely at odds." She dumped more sugar in her tea and stirred, almost visibly shaking off the specter of Gil between them. "I'm glad because I've gotten really, really good at not trusting the people God has given me, which is one more way of not trusting God Himself. You were right about that from that day on the step of the barge. So, I've got some work to do there." She reached over and squeezed Drew's hand, withdrawing it again too quickly. He found it oddly comforting that Emily was a little uneasy with emotion, since she seemed to be good at just about everything else. "But," she said on a bracing breath, "I'm glad to start trying out the whole trust thing with you. You know, in case I haven't *told* you that I'm glad about that."

Touched by her genuine tone, Drew still smiled, thinking about her throwing trash on his windshield and filing complaints against him. "I haven't heard a lot of thanks from you, come to think of it, Miss Graham." She laughed lightly, shaking off the heaviness a bit. He decided to use her laugh to his advantage. "So, you're saying you *trust me*?"

"But we're talking about trusting God," she clarified, obviously unwilling to go down the road that kept pulling them in separate directions. He needed her to trust him, and she claimed she did. It was hard not to insert Gil Reese into that context.

"You were talking about trusting the people God gave you. That's me."

Just then, the screen door to the grill sprung open and slapped shut, making way for a petite waitress who, unlike the small waves below, didn't seem to be in any hurry at all.

"Did'ja decide?"

"Burger," Emily told her. "Tomato, lettuce, the works, Annie. Oh, and Annie ... this is Sergeant Drew Mathison from the U.S. Army and now our police department."

"How d'ya do, honey? Welcome home. Whatcha eating?"

"Same as Emily. Thanks."

"He's most definitely paying for this," Emily advised. Annie nodded and sauntered lazily back toward the screen door. Alone again, Emily explained, "It's the price you pay for following me around."

"You said you were going to feed *me*," he protested. "And I've already paid through the nose for the privilege of following you around."

"You were asking me for spiritual advice. The cost is a burger. That's all."

"I never at any time asked you for spiritual advice."

"Where were we? That's right. Trust. Yes. I confessed I'm not good at trusting other people. I take on too much myself. From deadline day to, well, everything. I play that game with God, too, I'm sorry to say." She said it matter-of-factly and punctuated it with a sigh. "Now, it's your turn."

"My turn? To *confess*?"

She nodded, eyes sparkling, and then she threw in a wink for good measure. Man, did she pull at him hard. He wanted to rewrite their whole story in that moment, to have her just for his own, with nothing between them but a simple existential crisis.

Having finished his own iced tea and not remembering having done so, Drew reached over and took a long pull from hers, pleased when she allowed it.

Did he have things to confess? For sure. But not to Emily. Well, not many to Emily, anyway.

"You know you'll be in heaven one day," she prompted, visibly retracing their conversation as if for herself. "You buy that part, you say. It's the day-to-day that you're hung up on. Life here, as you put it."

Drew made a sound, which she took as encouragement.

"You don't think He's involved with the day-to-day?" She was a reporter all the time, he thought, and accepted it all over again. This was who she was, not just what she did.

"No, not exactly." He searched her eyes to see if she'd let him leave it there. "I mean, I think He's involved in the little stuff, but I don't think He's all that likely to change any of it if I ask Him to."

"Ahhhh. So … prayer. Now we're getting down to it."

"You know the whole *'Thy will be done'* part?"

She nodded, reaching to take her tea back. "Yes. We pray for God's will to be done in every situation … and you're struggling with wondering why you're even bothering to ask, then, if He's going to do it His way anyway."

"Mmm."

"I imagine that kind of thing comes to specific relief in a war, doesn't it?"

She had baited him with such perception, and he decided to jump right on the hook.

"All I'm saying is, if I pray and ask to be spared a painful gut wound but know all along God's will *will* be done … I have to find peace knowing that a gut wound might be part of His plan for me … but how much peace is there in that?" He watched for the shock and dismay to come over her, regretted having said it out loud even as he was saying it. He wished God hadn't heard it. But he pushed on. "There is no peace in knowing a gut wound might be coming, no matter what. Unless it's the peace in knowing it might land me in heaven with Him. But it sure will hurt *a lot* first, and then I'm right back to struggling for some peace again in my situation."

"Because it scares the life out of you."

When there was still no shock and dismay, he assumed she wasn't quite appreciating it. "After D-Day, a friend of mine lingered three days, Emily. *Three.*"

Her hand was on his again, and the understanding was in her eyes. But people didn't talk about that stuff, not back there in the war, and definitely not back here in victory land.

God knew it all, anyway. Three long days. It must have aligned with

His will.

And now Bax was in heaven with Him, along with so many others. Jamie was there too. All's well that ends well. But *three days*.

"I have a good imagination, and even I can't imagine how scary that had to have been," Emily was saying softly, and this time she didn't pull her hand back. She held on. Now they both regarded the small waves below, the gentle thud of a downed tree against the lower dock. "I can handle stories, you know, Drew. The bad ones, too."

"I know."

Her thumb traced a ridged scar on his knuckle. It wasn't from the war. It was a stupid construction injury, from when he was seventeen. Somehow that touch kept him from bolting, along with her voice, and her voice was moving on, thankfully. "My Grandma Louise ... have I talked about her?"

"Hickory has. And I read the obituary you wrote for your grandmother."

"Of course. I think Cookie has it hanging somewhere, doesn't she? Anyway, my grandma raised us. She used to say that, when we pray, God answers by either giving us just exactly what we asked Him for because He loves to give good gifts, or ..."

"There's always an 'or,'" he said lightly, feeling validated.

"*Or* He gives us something better than what we asked for." Emily smiled, a little sadly. "I always liked that. I had trouble with it a bit when Grandma Louise went home to be with Him, because I asked for her to be able to stay with us, and there was no 'something better' to her being gone. Not for us. But maybe ..." She stopped. "Maybe that's a whole other conversation."

"It is a nice thought," Drew offered, appreciating that she'd tried. "He either gives you what you asked for or something better."

"Which is still small reassurance when faced with a gut wound," Emily said, nodding and proving she'd understood all along. He didn't have to say it all again. "We're in a fallen world where gut wounds do happen. And I guess that's where the mercies come in."

"The mercies."

"Yeah. Jesus says not to borrow trouble, not to worry about the bad that's coming tomorrow. He says God's mercies are new each day. So, I take that to mean the bad things seem like something we can't handle today because we don't have the mercies to handle them today. Those mercies come on the day we need them. And there *can* be mercies, even in the worst of stuff. I've seen that."

Drew considered it. Thought back. If he looked at things through that lens, it was hard to argue. As much as he hated to admit it, there had been mercies, even over the three days Bax had lingered. Unexpected mercies.

Unconsciousness. Especially kind doctors and nurses, eventually. Plenty of medicine to dull the pain. A chance to say goodbye in a letter Drew had penned and mailed home for him. And then heaven.

"That's how we know God's already been there," Emily said softly, giving his hand one squeeze before withdrawing it this time, just in time for the burgers that preceded Annie the waitress back onto the patio.

~~~~~

Emily made herself tamp down on her entire nature as she watched Drew take bite after slow, luxurious bite. She wanted to ask him how he liked the sandwich. Sure, the answer seemed written right there on his face, but she did so *love* asking questions and hearing answers.

Be still, she told herself, which Hickory and the Lord had been trying to tell her all her life.

So, she was still. In the stillness, then, she got to watch the rise and fall of Drew's Adam's apple as he swallowed. Only in stillness could she surprise herself with a fantasy in which she tasted his skin, right there on his neck. She took in the happy sound he made with each new bite, somehow felt the sound in her own stomach. It wasn't unpleasant. His tongue darted to the corner of his lips to grab a stray bit of mustard, and she watched his lips as he chewed.

This was the cost of spending time up close to him, then. As the early evening grew noticeably warmer, Emily figured this wasn't what anyone had in mind in terms of stillness.

"Are you okay?" he asked, swallowing again.

She took another bite of her own so she could just offer him a nondescript sound and nod.

"You were right about these." He swallowed. "They're good."

She smiled, chewed. Was still.

Settling back a bit, Drew considered her. Evidently more relaxed now himself, he crossed his arms over his chest and let out a satisfied sigh. Emily chewed and chewed, imagined crawling right up into those arms, burrowing into that chest ...

"You're good at your job," he said, surprising her out of her increasingly wild thoughts.

"Thank you."

"I read that Harley fellow's obituary today, too. Feel a little like I know him now."

She glowed at that, told herself it was the praise that made her feel how warm her own cheeks were. "Thanks." She put her sandwich down, wiped her fingertips on a napkin. "I adored Harley."

"Did you have one of his carved miniature tea sets?"

"All of us who lived out this way did, yeah."

"Are the obituaries your favorite part of all of the job, then?"

She considered. "They were the first part that drew me in, I guess. A kind of story. I channeled all my heartache at losing Grandma Louise into learning the craft of it, all the different kinds of stories of people lost. Cookie and Burt kind of picked up where my grandparents had left off, so to speak, teaching me, praying for me. I was a wreck when we lost her, and I had a lot to ... work through." Thinking back, Emily saw the segue he deserved. "Rosie had a lot to work through, too. I was blessed because I had the newspaper business."

"Is that when she started taking pictures, too?"

"No. She'd always been interested in art and photography. No ... she found her solace back then in a sophisticated summer boy named Keith Fairchild."

Emily watched Drew make the transition. "Ohhh."

"Yeah. *Oh.* While I was so busy at the newspaper, imagining myself the next Nellie Bly, Rosie fell head over heels in love, as they say. I didn't even notice." Emily shook her head. She hadn't even thought about those days in so long now. And now so many parts of those days were back, right back in front of her. "Keith had come to the hotel on the island for the summer with his parents. He was older than Rosie by a couple of years, heading to college that fall, and he swept her off her feet. The usual story. She thought they were going to get married." Emily met Drew's eyes and knew he understood, saw the ache in his that must reflect her own. "When he left and ignored her, Rosie couldn't simply put the summer behind her like the growing experience it might otherwise have been."

"Because of Charlie."

Emily nodded. "I got a job at the newspaper that summer after Grandma Louise died, and Rosie got little Charlie. I know this isn't my story to tell you, but after what happened today, with Keith back at the lake ... I think you might as well know." She blew out a breath. "And it's nice to have someone to talk to, anyway. Because I *do* have to tell Rosie that Keith is finally back here. And that's going to be so hard."

Drew nodded. "This is you trusting me again, then. Just to listen to what's on your mind."

Emily smiled, coming back full circle. "Did I mention that I'm starting to be glad to have you around?"

"While we're on difficult topics from the past ..."

"Oh no."

"It's nothing. That's the problem. I don't have anything solid about your mother yet. I'm not stopping, but ..."

"I figured you didn't, since you hadn't mentioned it today."

"Something will turn up, Em. And, in the meantime, I can at least buy this dinner. Since I got all that spiritual advice and everything."

~~~~~

Drew figured it might be years since he'd been so relaxed. Sitting there, waiting for the check, talking freely with Emily Graham. She'd taken down so many walls today. One important one remained, of course, but he hoped it would be the next to fall. She had to be close to deciding she could trust him with Gilbert Reese. *She must be.* He watched her plow a path through some spilled sugar on the tabletop with her pinky finger.

"What made Rosie decide not to tell this Keith character about the baby?" he asked, knowing she'd allow the question just now but maybe not again.

"She did try to tell him. She'd tried writing him just because he'd told her to, after he left, but he hadn't written back from school. She even tried calling, once she knew about the baby, but he never returned a call, either. After that, she didn't want to keep trying because she didn't want him sending money out of some sense of obligation. She'd wanted his love, not his money. She never said it in as many words, but I guess she didn't want a father like that for Charlie."

"What did Hickory do?" Drew imagined the old man he'd come to respect, a fresh widower with two teenage granddaughters to raise, one of them unexpectedly pregnant.

"I think Hickory has always suspected it was Keith, but he respected Rosie when she didn't say." Emily was thoughtful for a moment. "I think the three of us have done okay. We've handled things."

Drew could see now how Emily had stepped into that direct, decision-maker role that had carried through into her professional life, as well. And maybe led to the same spiritual struggle she'd indicated. She had developed, from a young age, a knack for seeing a challenge or problem, seeing its solution, and telling everyone else what to do to make that solution a reality. The publicity stunts at the amusement park. Public records fiascos. The weekly project that was the newspaper. Drew had never taken the time to think about it before, but he could see how a relatively weak kid like Gil Reese would go running to a person just like this when his life was in danger.

"It's easy to see how you've become so convinced you can handle things on your own," he said softly. "Because you always have."

She looked up and smiled with such warmth, he felt it in his gut. "This was a nice talk, Mathison." And he understood that it was over now. He shifted, put one forearm on the table, and leaned.

"Emily, has anyone ever told you your eyes are the *exact color* of Buckeye Lake?" In response, those eyes widened, darted toward the lake in consideration, and the smile got a little larger still.

"Even if the water is a bit … murky?"

"Blue and green and gray. Lit up. Your eyes look like the lake looks in the sunshine."

Smiling and a little thoughtful, she excused herself to go wash in the inside restroom, leaving Drew seated at the table alone, sinking into an even deeper abyss than he'd been standing in upon arriving at the lake several weeks before.

He had come here broken, sorrowful, pensive, hopeless, angry.

Only to fall head-over-heels in love with a woman he first thought was another man's bride and who now, he realized, he could not build a life with anyway.

Not with the way things were.

How would that look, he wondered for the first time. A romantic relationship with Emily Graham? Would she sneak food to Gil Reese after they'd eaten dinner together?

Suddenly weary, he tried to hand Annie money for the food as she cleared the last of the plates, but she said Emily had already taken care of the bill inside. Then Emily came back out, chattering now about a Reds game, apparently drying her hands on her skirt. He followed her all the way back to the boat, watching the sway of her hips and the late evening sun making a warm, living thing of her golden hair.

Instead of bounding into the Chris-Craft like a twelve-year-old boy as she typically did, she stopped. When she turned slowly back to him, her lake eyes sparking attraction, she was all the things he only now knew he wanted. There had always been something magnetic between them at the core, he thought, something that made him dig deep just now for the code he lived by.

It was a code of justice.

He had to remember that. Couldn't afford to take his eyes off it.

But she wet her lips and moved closer, and she was all around him like a cloud so he could barely breathe. Against his will and against that code, Drew saw his rough hand rise to the softness of her cheek, watched her lean into the caress, heavy-lidded. Leaning toward him, into him …

He somehow managed to step back.

"Do you drive this time or do I?" he asked, trying for casual, fisting his runaway hand. That fist closed hard around his code and any hope he might otherwise have for a future with this woman.

She reeled like she might go right off the dock again, caught herself, and quickly dropped into the driver's seat, confusion in her face and in her movements.

He felt angry at them both.

It was silent on the ride back to the north shore, the easy camaraderie and friendship of dinner lost to them now. Knowing he was right was small consolation, Drew reflected, for being forcefully removed from all that warmth.

He'd hurt her, so when Emily eased into the only slip she could find anywhere near the thrumming, frantic boardwalk, Drew reached his hand out again to halt her. She pulled her arm away but looked over at him.

"I want to kiss you, Emily," he told her.

Her brows lowered, and she looked so vulnerable he ached. She stared at the shore. "You do?"

"I do. I want you in my arms. Badly." Afraid she might sway toward him again, he quickly continued, "But we both know that's not a good idea."

"Drew ..." Her gaze tracked the crowd now, still not him. "I told you I'm not engaged to Gil. You're not ... we wouldn't be breaking a promise or trampling anyone's honor or anything."

"Only yours and mine, Em. I'm a detective. Have been for years, only now it's personal." He ran a hand hard over the back of his neck, not able to look at her now either. "And as much as I've had fun pretending to be your bodyguard, I'm still here as a detective."

She grunted an acknowledgement.

"That's why I can't kiss you. Because you'd always wonder if I'd just used you to get what I wanted. If you let me kiss you and hold you and then you gave Gil up to me because of this ..." he gestured futilely between them "... because of what we have between us ... you'd wonder if it were all a means to the end I've been counting on."

Now her head swung toward him. "Is it?" she demanded, still a reporter every bit as he was still a detective. "Is that why you'd be kissing me? To break down my defenses or something?"

"Honestly?" Did he even know any more? He looked away, afraid he wasn't quite sure of what was true inside of him anymore. Had this obsession with justice and retribution simply taken the shape of Emily Graham for him? Was she the key to indicting the Contis or the key to his whole happiness?

Whatever she was, she was also moving past indignation now. Straight to anger. And he still had no idea what the honest answer was.

What happened next was bound to. Emily hauled herself up to the dock, ducking into the strap of the camera before he could take it from her.

Drew just allowed her to move far ahead of him before he climbed out and made his way through the bold bulbs of twilight, now so familiar, leading up to the boardwalk.

Today had been a good day, he reflected sadly, his arms empty but the rest of him full. He'd do it all again, given the chance. He'd sweat it out all over again: every jet across the water, the ridiculous diving clowns and even his own mistaken dive into the lake, an overreaction over a perceived threat to a woman he might be in love with any time he got up close to her.

Which was no way to go about this, so he hung back. She was easy to track from a distance ... the hair, the way she moved. It was all just a matter of hanging back.

~~~~~

"Gil, we need to talk."

Emily told him all of it. He was still hidden, but at least one man was actively and persistently looking for him. She let that sink in.

"He's the one you *want* to find you, at least."

"I wish you hadn't just given the whole thing away like that," her old friend said, nervous and irritable.

Irritable made him a perfect match for Emily, the way nothing else could have made a match of them.

"If you only knew how much *more* information I want to give him, you clod," she snapped, then forced herself to take a deep breath. "Sorry." He made a nondescript sound in response. "Anyway, I'm not cut out for this, Gil. This is not me."

"Just a bit longer, Emily. I promise he'll lose interest. They'll *all* forget about me, if we can just hold on a bit longer."

"It's hard to imagine the amount of time it takes one to get over a brother's murder. I think you're underestimating it."

"It's not as though I killed Jamie."

"You can protect other people by letting Drew take you back to Reno, Gil. Is it truly enough for you to not have pulled the trigger? Don't you see yourself as having *any* obligation to help put the men who did pull the trigger behind bars?"

"No."

They were both quiet. Emily meant to wait him out, certain he'd come to the right decision if she left him alone with it again.

But then she thought of Drew's strength and sharp eyes and total focus on his objective. Though she'd resented it after dinner, when she'd wanted to be more to him for one precious minute than just the woman who knew where his witness was hiding, that intense focus would keep Gilbert safe through whatever lay ahead. Emily was certain of it.

Plus, Gil had *already* had a good deal of time to think ... while she'd sweated and worried and exhausted herself.

"You must trust me to some extent, Gil, or you wouldn't have asked this of me in the first place."

"You know I trust you. That's not what this is about."

"I've gotten to know Sergeant Mathison, and I know he can keep you safe. He's done a pretty great job keeping *me* safe this past week, and I'm just peripheral to all this. Don't you understand it's in his best interest to make sure you stay alive? And I'm telling you, he can make sure of it."

"Can he stop a bullet?"

Emily didn't want to think about that.

"Can he stop a bullet, Emily?"

"You can't live your life this way, Gil."

"For now, I sure can. It's the only way to hold onto my life. Then I'll work on becoming the man I'm supposed to be, once they've all forgotten."

"How many more people will die while you wait to resume your life?" She nearly despised him for not valuing the lives of others, so she tried another tack. "Doesn't it bother you that your father may end up in danger at any time now? What about little Delia? Will the Contis ignore her because of some ethical convictions? And Drew Mathison was led straight to my door after just a couple of days in this community, Gil. How long do you think before the Contis find me because of who we've always been to one another?"

They already had.

"All while you're waiting to work on becoming the man you're *supposed* to be?"

More silence.

"That was quite the speech," he finally said with his usual wry humor. "It's close to working."

"Gil, give him a chance. Please."

"I need some paper and pens. Let me write a few letters, Em. Just in case. Then maybe, when I'm done, I'll … let him have me. Maybe. But not yet. *Please.*"

Chapter Twenty-One

The Buckeye Lake Beacon
Sunday, June 30, 1946
Jazz draws crowd to Lily Point lawn

While Gilbert wrote his letters, Emily spent time studying Drew Mathison from the distance he was suddenly keeping and wondering if she could have both safety for Gil *and* something more with this detective who made her mouth water. From what he'd said, Drew seemed reluctant to mix romance into their already complicated dynamic, but Emily knew herself not to be reluctant at all.

And she couldn't be solely responsible for all this heat.

She wanted to know the story of that little crescent-shaped scar that stood out amidst the scruff of Drew's chin. She wanted the right to touch it. And she was beside herself, not knowing how to go about any of this.

Emily had always dismissed Cookie's assertion that the way to a man's heart was through his stomach. She'd been privately convinced that the way must truly be through good, stimulating conversation, of course.

The problem was, she and Drew had engaged in some pretty stimulating conversation, which had turned out *not* to be the way to his heart, after all. It was only the way to her own, she supposed ruefully. Instead, he was still hanging back, resisting her in the name of principle; and so, out of ideas and not yet able to hand over Gil (which she suspected was the real way to *this* man's heart), Emily decided to cook. And to bake.

Her aunt had better be right.

Emily had debated beckoning him into the barge house to watch her, wrapped in her most domestic looking apron, cooking just for him. She would bat her eyelashes and channel her inner Ginger Rogers, humming and stirring things alluringly as she danced around her tiny kitchen area. In truth, though, she knew she was not a very graceful cook, so she had resisted that idea. She tended to make errors and messes that might not be the way to a man's heart at all. No number of coy gestures with wooden spoons, she thought, would make up for burning the bottom out of a pan or splattering said spoon and its contents across the floor.

And so, there had been no nap in a hammock that Sunday. No, by Sunday evening, Emily just barely had time to pack away the contents of a picnic hamper full of homemade wonders when it was time to arrive at the Lily Point Jazz Concert. She wasn't working on a Sunday by attending

185

the concert. Of course, she wasn't. The concert was *play* ... but there might be something written about it for this week's paper, of course. By someone who happened to be at the concert.

A stage had been raised toward the edge of the point, the bog visible just beyond the large lanterns across the stage top. Some jazz band had already set up shop, smooth notes oozing out over the green lawn. Caterers rushed around tables where the wealthy laughed and sipped champagne. Emily had coughed up funds from *The Beacon's* shallow coffers for a corporate table, of course, but she had no intention of sitting with her staff this evening. Clutching her hamper, she nodded at an acquaintance and scanned the crowd.

Though she hadn't seen him around the marina all afternoon (she'd been busy cooking, after all), Emily was counting on Drew Mathison making an appearance of some sort at the concert, even if it was just to keep an eye on her. She was likely to be up to no good, after all.

"Ah, the other Miss Graham." It was Dr. Lamb, the botanist from OSU, who approached alongside a weary-but-happy Rosie.

"Have you two been out here working all day?" Emily demanded. She had sought out help in the kitchen from her sister earlier, as well as a chance to talk with Rosie about Keith's presence at the lake, but Rosie had been out, so Charlie had spent the day with Hickory and Tom at the marina. Emily's gaze skimmed the crowd again, and she was thankful not to find the Fairchilds anywhere among the guests. She did spot Dot Berkeley on the arm of that other man who had been with Keith, that Gabriel Adams. He must be representing FH Resorts here tonight, she figured, in league with the woman who had the power to sell.

But no sign of Keith, thankfully. For now.

She really needed to get Rosie alone.

"We've got the book project on fast-forward to try to push back as much as we can against the development," Lamb explained, clearly inspired despite the skin flaking off the end of his burned nose.

"I've drawn so many leaves and bark patterns these last few days." Rosie laughed.

"It'll work," Emily assured them with more confidence than she felt. The concert might have been another of the Civic Association's moves, but Emily had also been determined to let the beauty of this natural space fight for itself, in a sense, to the many members of the council and zoning commission in attendance. The lily pads made a carpet in the water, with the beauty of the lush bog framing the space in the distance.

"Who're you looking for? I smell chicken," Rosie said, poking at Emily's little woven hamper.

"I fried it," she said proudly. "Hey, Rosie ... we need to chat some time."

"Sure." She sniffed appreciatively. "Over dinner?"

Emily's eyes tracked to the edge of the dining area, where she finally saw Drew up on a little rise. He was dressed in his uniform tonight, and he was watching her across the lawn. She fought not to shiver under his gaze. "Actually, I was hoping you might do me a favor," she said, turning back to Rosie, feeling her cheeks heat.

Why didn't women make the moves in a relationship more often? It felt exhilarating, so much more active than simply waiting for a man to come to his senses.

"I need to go set myself up as alluring and irresistible and sort of ... domestic, and you're going to be my bait."

"Your ... bait?" This from the botanist who was blinking, appalled.

"Not you, Lamb. Rosie."

~~~~~

So, this was where the lake's elite gathered, Drew thought. While the poorer folk splashed around the beach or screamed their way through a roller coaster ride, the lake residents with money were gathered here, on the pristine, rolling lawn of Lily Point, with its picture-perfect frame of green pads and blossoms. They were dressed in white and tea-colored linens.

Drew wore his holster and gun openly tonight, badge clipped to the strap, working security at the festival as a favor to Chief Gunn. He owed the man several, and heaven knew it was easy work, "patrolling" the perimeter of the concert area, paying absolutely no attention to anyone, of course, with the exception a lean blonde in an elegant white dress that shimmered a little in the strands of electric bulbs near the stage.

The jazz music reminded him of Jamie, though. His kid brother had loved all kinds of music, but he'd played jazz albums until they wore out on those sleepy weeknights back at their parents' home. Their father, always sunburned and callused, would doze in his favorite chair. Mama, with her needlepoint and half-smile, would constantly drop in and out of their conversations to scold them while they went out of their way to exasperate her. Jamie, a percussionist at heart, had tapped out rhythms on the porch boards while they talked and laughed, the cadence of family stories and uneventful days and nights.

The memories, prompted by the music and the scent of freshly cut grass, had him feeling itchy and like he wanted to crawl right out of his skin. They reminded him that he was no closer to bringing his brother's killers to justice than he had been weeks ago. There were more pleas from his parents to come home, so that he was almost reluctant to call and check in these days. His mother thought he was obsessed; he could tell from what was said and unsaid. Maybe even unwell. She was a wise woman, and the way he'd felt lately ... maybe she was right. Maybe she was right, and he was unwell.

As he did any time he felt at sea, he homed in on Emily Graham, not because he thought she was up to anything, but because the sight of her somehow steadied him.

It was so much harder to watch her from a distance now.

Tonight, with the lazy jazz flowing, he was forced to watch a middle-aged man in a crisp linen lawn suit move behind Emily and slide his arms around her in greeting. Drew tensed at the blatant familiarity. If he wasn't free to touch her like that, it didn't seem right that anyone else should. He watched Emily laugh lightly and turn smoothly out of those arms to greet the man from the front. Some old acquaintance, clearly, who demanded another ten minutes of her attention. He was soon joined by another man, slightly younger, and she seemed to know him, as well.

Drew paced along the edge of the party as the emcee took the mic and stragglers moved to their seats. He felt so ... removed. And very working-class.

He wondered how he'd get Emily alone for a few minutes this evening, after spending the morning trying hard not to be alone with her. It couldn't be helped, he told himself; he needed to talk to her. He finally had the information she'd wanted about her mother, and he wanted her safe at his side, just the two of them, when he told her she'd been betrayed once again by the person who was supposed to love her more than anyone.

Would she cry? He did not like the thought of it.

How could Lillian Turnbull Graham help but love her girls? Drew could only imagine what Emily had looked like as a toddler, the way she'd have squealed with laughter and explored in exasperating ways and probably never took a nap a single day of her childhood. She would have been a beautiful child. She would *have* beautiful children one day. And this Lillian woman with her stupidity and complete indifference would miss it all.

But then, Drew figured he would, too.

One of the trumpet players spilled a folder of music from his decorated stand, and the stray sheets began to blow about a little in the same breeze that moved the umbrellas at the tables. There were exclamations and laughter as those on stage hurried to gather the precious sheet music, and the emcee was quick with a one-liner that had the crowd chuckling. Drew found himself listening for Emily's light laughter. Eyes tracking toward her table again, he found she was not there.

Who had those men been? They were gone too. His heartbeat picked up.

But she'd clearly known them, right?

"Drew?" Rosie halted his forward charge. She registered the urgency in his movement, apparently, because she said, "Emily asked me to tell you she needs you over that way, beyond the stage. It's not an emergency or anything."

Drew nodded his thanks and didn't hesitate to make his way around behind the table area, where she had gestured. Rosie had seemed calm. Emily must be fine, he told himself. Illuminated paper lanterns hung in strings along the back, providing warm light as the sun began its descent. She had recognized those men in the lawn suits, he reminded himself again. No way they'd have been sent from the Contis in Reno. They'd seemed like old friends. She was fine.

Emily was fine. Images of her being rammed against the hallway wall of the council building burned through his mind again as they had so often since that night. Walking faster, Drew was vaguely aware of the music starting again as he reached the strand of maple trees that lined a path between the slope of the concert area and the inlet of the lake.

What business did a little, out of the way place in Ohio have, being this pretty?

Or having someone that pretty in it? Because he spotted her then, sitting alone, and his first response was immense relief.

His next response was mild confusion because Emily was sitting demurely on a checked blanket along the bank twenty feet away, watching him expectantly. She wore one of the best of her collection of enchanting smiles, but there was no one else around. The basket she'd had on her arm earlier sat next to her now on the blanket.

Impossibly, she motioned for him, as if she had been waiting for him all along.

He considered the odds that a woman in a dress like that, with her golden hair and her successful business, would have laid out a picnic for a man with work-worn hands and uncomfortable memories of POW camps. All this should have been for one of the linen suit guys. Emily had a degree, after all, while Drew had crippling grief.

He was afraid of messing up all that perfection, but he crossed the grass to her anyway.

"Expecting someone?" he asked, hands shoved deep in his pockets. It was the only thing to do with them whenever he got near her now.

She looked startled by that. "You," she said simply. "I didn't figure I'd need to invite you for you to come find me. You're always close by. Or you *were*. Will you have a seat? I cooked today."

He just stood there, taking in her body in that dress.

"You're rejecting me again," she said on a sigh, tucking the dress further beneath her legs and staring down at the blanket in dejection. "You're hard on a woman's ego, Mathison."

"I didn't ..." He somehow felt like a bigger bumbling idiot than he

189

had moments before. Hands still in his pockets, he nodded toward the blanket. "What is all this?"

"You arranged our first picnic. I figured I owed you one this time."

"Our first picnic?"

"In my office, deadline night, cheese and crackers."

"Oh, sure. Sure." He ran a suddenly sweaty palm over the back of his neck. "I'm being a real dope here, aren't I? I can't seem to help it."

"Will you just sit down with me already?"

He did, deciding to give himself permission to enjoy that she'd cooked something for him. For him, not for the radio guy or the linen suit guy or any of the others constantly offering to buy her dinner out. He stayed at the edge of the blanket, where he couldn't touch her.

"Thanks," he said, forcing a smile. They could hear the music from here, he thought, and enjoy the view of the lily pads at the same time. Could that French water lily painter have done these things justice, Drew wondered. The green pads looked like elaborate dishware for the perfect white blossoms that sprung from them. "You can sort of imagine walking right across them to the opposite bank over there," he observed as he looked at them.

"You won't be able to attempt it after you eat what I've brought you," Emily responded enthusiastically, bouncing a little on her knees as she opened a smaller basket filled with fried chicken. She passed him a blue plate while his mouth watered, and he helped himself to a couple pieces. Then she unloaded a heap of yellow on his plate. "You like potato salad?" Then there were rolls and a bottle of honey, and an ice-cold bottle of Coke. "I prefer Coke to champagne when it comes to fried chicken, what do you think?"

"I think this is perfect. Did I ... say thank you?"

"Yes. But you're welcome."

Not for the first time, he wondered what things would have been like if they'd met under any other circumstance. "Why are you really doing this?" he asked, studying her.

She settled back and began arranging food on her own plate. "I remember you telling me you like me."

"I hardly think I have to tell you that."

"The thing is, I like you too, Drew. I think you also know that."

He told himself not to make too much of it. "Thanks. That's good, I guess." Why did he feel like she had him at such a disadvantage, on this blanket, holding a plate?

"I know we're at odds constantly because we're both after different things ... rather aggressively, I guess you'd say. But the fact you can like me, and I can like you even when we're pretty much irritated with one another every minute of every day says something. I wondered if we might call a temporary truce, like the other day. You from your spying ..."

"It's not spying when cops do it. It's surveillance."

"Right. But maybe we could just be together again. You know, like at dinner. Here I am, and here you are. So, let's relax. You know Gilbert's not nearby, unless he's the frog prince living on a lily pad, and maybe you can forget for a while that I'm being difficult. And I can forget ... well, all the things I've been trying to forget since May."

"Is that when he approached you? In May?" He dug into the delicious chicken and made a sound of appreciation, even as he filed the information away. He wondered if he could get her to slip up. "Where did the two of you meet up when he got back from Reno, anyway?"

She clearly hadn't been expecting this turn in the conversation, and he thought she seemed unhappy, probably considering what answering that question would mean. He saw her reach a decision. "He was hiding out on the towpath one night," she finally said simply, apparently having determined there was nothing damning in that. Which also meant he hadn't been there since, or she wouldn't have mentioned it. "What do you think of the chicken?"

Drew took another bite and mumbled compliments, his imagination at work. Where would Emily have taken him from the island? The marina made the most sense, but Drew knew every part of it now, and Emily was supremely unconcerned about Drew roaming around the island. Gil hadn't been hiding there. He knew more about how her mind worked now; he should be able to figure this out. Before he realized it, he was down to the little chicken bones, and he looked up and smiled.

"It's real good."

"You like it," she said, nodding, as if reassuring herself. She took a bite of her own.

Drew imagined Gilbert and Emily, huddled inside the barge house at that scarred table while spring blossomed in Ohio, thinking they could outsmart the law and mob bosses alike. Stupid. Stupid, clueless kids from a small town where everything had always been twinkling lights and calliope music. He pictured again what could have happened to Gilbert if Conti had tracked him down already, and his stomach ached. He pictured what Conti could do to Emily, and the perfectly fried chicken rose in his gullet.

Something else, something dark, also rose in him that he hardly had a name for, but it had to have something to do with the feelings he had for her and the idea of losing her to senseless violence, the same way he'd lost his brother. These weren't things he imagined *could* happen. They *did* happen. He'd seen the pictures.

When he set his plate down on the checkered blanket, his hand shook a little.

"How much longer, Em?" he asked on a sigh. She raised her pretty eyes in question. "How much longer before you decide about me?"

"Decide about you?"

"Decide if you can trust me with your buddy? How long before I pass all your tests and get on with what I need to do?" The perfectly laid out little meal blurred in his eyes, along with her hurt face.

She was going to end up hurt or dead, and *he* wouldn't survive that. Any day now there'd be a new message, or maybe the messages were done, and they'd had their chance.

"It's not my call," she told him sadly. She made a little sigh, as though regretting his determination to ruin this. There would be no truce, she seemed to realize. Not even for the length of a picnic. "Believe me, I trust you, and I understand that you think you can keep him safe."

"I *can* keep him safe. It's as important to me as it is to you or to him!"

"Like I keep telling you, it's life or death for him," she said easily. "For you, it's revenge for someone you love."

"That's not true. Not all the way."

"You have to at least admit it's not life or death for you, then!"

"It's my *brother's* life and death!" His voice was louder than he'd intended. He tried to rein it in. "And I can't believe that means nothing to you."

Emily blew out an irritated breath. Her eyes flashed. "You know … here we go again."

"Here we'll *always* go again because there's no happy middle ground on this. Admit you know where Gilbert Reese is hiding right now."

"I admit it. I hid him there."

Though he'd known that was true all along, the words were gasoline on a fire already burning.

Drew pushed himself up in one fluid motion. He ran his hand across the back of his neck again, this time in fury, and walked toward the lily pads, blind to the white blooms on them now. Behind him, Emily was packing up the remains of the food in choppy motions. He felt strung so tight he might explode. He heard her slap the lid of the basket down. He heard her bare feet crossing the grass behind him, felt only her nearness for a time, wanted desperately for their story to be completely different. He tried hard to breathe normally.

Her fingers, just her fingers, reached out on either side of him and caressed his arms. He shuddered. She pressed against his back. He felt all that warmth and energy seeping into him like exactly what he'd been waiting for. And always, this terrible feeling of being torn between intense attraction and intense frustration.

"I just don't know what else to do, Em." It was a white flag. Drew felt himself hoisting it, and the surrender that came with it was not one that two people could use as any sort of common ground. It was the kind of surrender from which there was no moving forward.

"I need just a little more time, Drew. *He* needs time."

His voice, when he answered, was calm now. "There's no time. You're not safe, and if you're not safe, neither is he. I wish you could see it." He turned to find her right there, and it was an easy thing to put his arms around her. Her arms circled his waist, too, beneath his gun, and she rested her head on his chest. He felt her trembling a little inside his arms. He wasn't sure if the two of them were keyed up with longing or with anger. Probably both, he realized. Whatever it was, he thought, it was the same for both of them.

He let the silence stretch, let her feel his heart beating hard against her cheek, wondering what she'd say next. What she could possibly say.

"You have to remember, he doesn't know you like I do," she finally whispered. "But then, do I even really know you?" He felt her lips move, her breath hot against his chest.

He kept his voice low, too. "Yes, you do."

"I don't know."

"Then *get* to. Get to know me. Ask me anything."

"You're pulling away, Drew."

"I've had to pull away to keep from touching you. Like this. How is this helping anything at all?" But even as he said it, he let his hand trail up her back, hypersensitive to the texture of the beading on her gown and, beneath it, the heat of her skin. "Besides, you *do* know me. When it comes right down to it, what you see is what you get."

She pulled her head away a little to squint up at him then. "What I see is what I get?" She shook her head. "That hasn't been true once so far."

"I'm more myself with you than I've been with anybody in a long time."

What more could he give her?

"Somehow, I do believe that. I do. I'm not *asking* for anything, Drew. You're upset because I don't trust you, and I'm upset because, I don't know, you don't seem to appreciate the other realities of this."

"Have you been talking to him?" When she didn't answer, when her blue-green eyes darted down to his shirt collar, he released her. Stepped back. His mind went in a hundred directions. "*How?*"

"This is his decision to make, not yours or mine."

He imagined her chuckling to herself as she communicated with Gilbert right under his nose, and he was helpless to figure out how she was doing it or where the man was. Had he, himself, talked to Gilbert Reese, in plain sight, and not even known it?

"You're obstructing justice," he suddenly accused. "I ought to just arrest you and be done with it."

Emily laughed but not with amusement, probably at the image of him cuffing her and parading her across the jazz concert crowd after having just held her with such tenderness. "I guess I hadn't considered that," she acknowledged, wiggling her brows a little. "That will make a fine headline, won't it?"

He narrowed his eyes. "It's a joke to you. You're playing a game you think you're winning, and you think it's funny."

"No."

"The law, the trial, a murder. This is a game to you." He took a few more steps away.

Her face went blank and pale. "No! Drew ..."

"I don't see the sense in playing it anymore." Beyond tired, barely knowing what he was saying or doing, Drew tossed the cotton napkin that he hadn't realized he still held in his hand down on the picnic blanket. Had he recognized that he'd been this angry with her all along? It had blown in, blown through him like a terrible storm, with all that stupid jazz music in the background. In its aftermath, he saw himself for the fool he'd been. "Thanks for making me dinner. Sorry the truce didn't work."

"Drew, don't go. Hey. We can talk about this," she said.

He didn't want to talk. He wanted to walk away and keep walking. This was a different kind of hurt and anger than what he'd grown used to from grief. This was somehow more personal because his pride was involved.

"I think we've both drawn our lines in the sand, so I'm not sure what more there is to talk about." He really did start to walk away. And then he stopped.

No, there was one more thing to talk about. Then maybe he could walk away. Not having to watch her live her life any longer felt both empty and freeing at the same time. But he just had to deal with this one last thing before he could make plans for moving on, for finding some other way. "I almost forgot."

"Forgot?"

"It's bad timing, I guess, but with the picnic and everything ... I did mean to tell you tonight. I've been in touch with some detectives and officials in Fresno and other cities near there, in California."

Emily visibly shifted mental gears, emotionally braced herself. He watched her draw a deep breath. "And?"

"And your mom hasn't been in jail. Not lately, anyway." His voice was void of emotion, matter-of-fact. "There's no need for the attorney's fees she's been asking for. There's no Lillian Turnbull in any jail there and no record of her being jailed for any length of time that they can find. No one meeting her description. But the detective did say there's a Lil Turnbull who works at a ... dance place."

"A dance place?"

"Not a good kind of dancing, Emily."

"Oh. I see."

"She manages the girls, the dancers, or something. I have the name and address of the place, if you want it. She has been in trouble with the law a few times, mostly over illegal substances, but right now the detective says she's just plugging away at this joint she's been affiliated with. He called the station for me. I found the message this afternoon, and we got to talk before I came over here."

"Oh. Okay, then."

"I'm sorry she lied to you, Emily."

"Well, I guess it's not a huge surprise, is it?"

"I'm sorry she left you and lied to you, because you don't know when to trust people now. I guess I'm sorrier about that than anything." He looked closely at her, even in his anger determined to memorize the flecks of her eyes, the freckles on her cheekbones he could only see up close. She looked so alone in the world, but, he thought, she only wanted others on her own terms. "Do you need help with the basket?"

She just stood there, looking confused. "No, I ..."

"Good night, then."

"I want to pay you for working on tracking her down, of course."

"Don't."

Tense with frustration, Drew turned and walked away from the lake and from Emily Graham. He had imagined consoling her over the news that her mother had been using her, on top of abandoning her, but he didn't know how that was possible now.

No middle ground for the two of them, he thought again.

If she'd been communicating with Reese all along right under his nose and she couldn't convince the darling boy to let her give him up, it would hardly benefit Drew to keep pursuing the whole surveillance concept. It was only making him crazy and heartsick.

But what next, then? If he couldn't follow the one person who knew where Gilbert was to Gilbert's location, how would he ever find him here?

Setting a brisk pace away from Lily Point, he considered that he could have Emily taken into custody. Not for the first time, he considered asking someone out in Reno to open the investigation, to issue a warrant for her arrest in connection with this unsolved case. If she could file a harassment complaint against him with his own boss, after all, and blatantly admitted she was actively responsible for hiding and secretly communicating with Gilbert Reese ... wasn't that a fair move?

But he dismissed the idea just like he always had. No sooner would the Reno cops have the information than the Conti family would, Drew had no doubt, and then all he'd be responsible for was Emily's sudden and probably permanent disappearance.

The thought chilled him.

In all his own surveillance, Drew hadn't detected any of the Conti family at Buckeye Lake, but he wasn't going off great intel. There had been no second tag on her. He'd been careful to watch for others watching him, as well, and hadn't picked up on anything. Though he had been reluctant to admit it, there was a thin possibility that the casino family had let this go, that they hadn't tracked Gilbert to the lake where he was raised, that they hadn't tailed Drew after he'd stirred up a ruckus in Reno. Maybe the message on the back of the engagement clipping was from someone local. Could the Contis really be letting it all slide on this one? Gambling, as they did so well, on Gilbert being too afraid to come forward with a testimony? It was a safe bet, Drew figured, given the guy's determination to stay hidden and look out for his own interests.

What had she ever seen in Gilbert Reese?

Chapter Twenty-Two

The Buckeye Lake Beacon
Sunday, June 30, 1946 ... even later that night
Study shows swimming improves health

Except for the illuminated glass of her sister's canal art, the rest of the towpath was made up of only shapes in the darkness when Emily arrived home to the barge. Restless still from her disagreement with Drew and then with her longing to talk to *some*one about her mother, she bypassed the barge completely and walked out to the stone step on the side of the little dwelling that looked out over the dark lake. There was enough moon to make any other light unnecessary, she thought. She watched it play here and there on ripples caused by fish moving under the water. The stray cat that had been hanging around lately rustled its way through the hydrangeas, rubbing against her leg and making her realize how uncomfortably warm she felt.

Hickory and Charlie would have turned in hours ago. Even Rosie's little studio on the second floor of the family home was dark. Tomorrow she and her sister would need to talk.

For now, it was hot and dark, and it had been too long since she'd had the lake all to herself.

Her shoes came off first. She placed them on the stone step, flexing her toes inside their stockings, feeling the dewy coolness of the midnight grass. The dress and silk slip were next. She pushed buttons through their holes and, with a shimmy, let it fall. The cat pounced on the material, shoving its head and ears beneath the folds even as Emily unclipped her stockings from their garters. She pushed them down her legs and then set to work on the summer knit girdle with its waist-hugging band, unzipping it at the side before peeling it off and leaving only her satin, peachy-pink panties and brassiere. Shoving her cast-off garments up onto the step with her shoes, Emily exulted in the cool night air on her stomach and thighs.

From the end of that dock, she launched herself unceremoniously into the night-black water of Buckeye Lake. As it closed over her head, she realized too late she hadn't removed her earrings and half-heartedly reached up to see if the screw-backs had survived impact. One did. With numbness rather than any real sense of regret, Emily kicked her legs in the water and hastily unscrewed the surviving ornament, letting it slip off to join its mate in a watery grave.

Then she dove under again, pushing herself deeper with her arms and a few strong kicks. She'd always been able to hold her breath longer than Rosie or Gil, and so she stayed down, listening to the whooshing beat of her own heart against the pressure of the water, letting the embrace of the lake soothe. She curled into herself, her rounded back floating back up toward the world.

Curled like that, weightless and peaceful, Emily thought idly of a babe in its mother's stomach, remembered vaguely the lazy afternoons pressing her own hands to Rosie's belly when Charlie had pushed and rolled within the space. At last, reaching the end of that stored breath, she let her head emerge from the lake to greet the comparative silence of night on top of the water.

Emily tried to imagine herself an unborn baby, wondered what Lillian's thoughts had been as she'd carried her second child in as many years. Had she lovingly stroked her swollen belly? Resented that belly for keeping her from dancing? Hoped for a boy this time around? Thought even for a moment about who that child would be one day, which parent it would resemble? The verse about being knit together by God in her mother's womb came back to Emily as her limbs enjoyed the press of the water, and she reminded herself that God had known the answer to all those questions even then.

It struck her how long He had known her and planned for her. She waited for the thought to comfort her, but she just couldn't feel Him in the silence.

Sometimes things just ended and with no explanation, driving Emily's mind back to her mother leaving and now, stealing her own child's money. Almost like a physical cramp, Emily cringed at the way she herself had been so gullible. Fated an optimist. Knit together in her mother's womb in that very way.

Well, no more. She'd changed a bit lately.

Drew's eyes and jaw had been hard when he'd told her the truth. Though she understood he'd been angry with her at the time, the way he'd delivered the information about her mother had done nothing to soften her shame. She needed to be angry, and Lillian simply wasn't around for that, so she let herself be angry with Drew Mathison's lack of sympathy.

Restless with herself again, Emily flipped over and kicked hard and strong in the opposite direction. Using her arms, she covered distance with certain force. She ate up the area where she'd floated for so long in four hard strokes. She reveled in the motion and in her own body, in the freedom of her bare muscles in the water, in the power of her own legs.

Unladylike. The word seeped in but caused her no regret or compulsion to mitigate those kicks.

She knew she was considered unladylike by the definitions of many. Unrepentant for all that, Emily still wondered how it had happened, anyway. College? Had she lost track of ladylike virtues somewhere in the musings of the Transcendentalists? Granny Louise had been a feminine ideal: habitually well put together, tidy, graceful, nurturing, domestic, sweet tempered, gentle. Granny Louise had been walking Scripture, Emily thought, pushing air from her lungs and loudly sucking in more as she swam. Patience, gentleness, self-control. And certainly, Emily's own mother had been her own kind of feminine ideal, if perhaps a more worldly one. Emily knew from photographs that Lillian had been staggeringly beautiful, everything a talented artist of dance would be expected to be.

Neither of those women who'd had a hand in making her, Emily reflected, would have been swimming so hard, mostly undressed in a public lake in the middle of the night. Would either have given thought to the power of her own limbs for no other reason than that it felt right to cut through the water with speed?

But she had been knit together by God, in just this way. As just this kind of woman.

Abruptly and finally tired, Emily turned and swam toward the vague shape of the dock, slowing and catching her breath on a sigh. She drew herself up onto the wood in one swift motion and stood there, the night blessedly cooler. She let her underclothes drip in the moonlight as she wrung out her hair with her hands.

A sound from near the barge house startled her, and she squinted into the darkness. She couldn't see anything. With wild hope, she wondered if Drew had changed his mind and come back on watch. Dropping her hands from her hair, she peered hard for the shape of broad shoulders on land. And what if he were there? What if he could see her now, standing on the dock? Would he walk out toward her? What did she want from him, anyway?

No one seemed to be there, anyway. It was probably the cat up there by the house, she thought with mingling relief and disappointment, and she shuffled back to retrieve her things from the stone steps so she could go to bed.

Chapter Twenty-Three

The Buckeye Lake Beacon
Monday, July 1, 1946
Local photographer hosts gallery open house

"I don't understand," Rosie said Monday afternoon in her dark room. She had just rinsed a proof and blinked up at Emily through the horn-rimmed eyeglasses she wore for extreme up-close work. The scent of the chemical bath and the darkness surrounded the sisters. "*Keith* is the one trying to buy the Point? But under a different name?"

"This Gabriel Adams has his name on everything, like a manager or something, but it's Keith's company. They changed it to FH Resorts from Fairchild Hotels, from what I can tell. Or it's a different branch of the business. I'm not sure. But Keith's in charge. Keith and his father, I suppose."

Rosie turned back to the print, her hands steady. "And you say he's here, at the hotel?"

"I saw him Friday on the island."

Rosie made a thoughtful sound and kept working. No real reaction. Emily had rarely seen her easy-going sister react dramatically to anything, which made her a great mom but a puzzle of a human being.

"Are you upset?" A sister shouldn't have to ask that question to another sister.

"I don't like his connection to the resort development," Rosie finally said. "But otherwise, I don't see how it should affect me."

Emily watched her pin the print onto a length of rope and blinked. "You aren't worried about seeing him again after all these years?"

"I doubt he'll seek me out. It was nothing ... I was nothing to him."

"But it was something to you."

"Not now, it isn't."

"What if he sees Charlie?"

"Charlie isn't even on his radar," Rosie said with an odd little laugh. "Keith's self-absorbed. Always has been. Why would he give a second thought to another ten-year-old boy running wild on the island?"

Emily gave an exasperated huff. "He looks a little like him, Rose. Charlie does, and you know it. I didn't realize how much until I saw Keith again."

Rosie waved that away. "Like I said, he'd never look at someone that closely unless he wanted something from him. I appreciate you giving me a heads up, though."

Emily paced the tiny space while Rosie continued to work, restless. She had longed for a confrontation, some reckoning, for one bloody loose end to get tied up in this crazy thing called her life. She'd imagined standing by Rosie's side while Rosie demanded Charlie's college tuition money. Keith would weep with regret and guilt for having used Rosie and for ignoring her calls and letters. He'd settle the whole thing quietly with the Grahams, and then his discomfort would compel him away from Buckeye Lake, withdrawing his bid for the Lily Point property so he wouldn't have to be faced with his own sin and carelessness.

But then, how many things ever worked out the way Emily wanted them to anymore? Emily thought about Drew and his anxiety about God's will.

"You seem disappointed," Rosie said wryly, pushing the glasses up on top of her head. She went back to the tub and looked over her shoulder at Emily with a little smile.

"I'm not going to lie. I wanted us to kick him around a little, Rosie. Make him squirm."

"I know."

"But I did not want you to be sad."

"I'm not, Em. That seems like another lifetime. I just want to go on the way I have been. Charlie and I do just fine, thanks to you and Hickory and the good Lord. I don't want to complicate that." For a moment, she leaned back against the sink and crossed her arms over her apron, watching Emily pace. "I promise I'm okay. But I still don't think you are. What else is bothering you?"

"Everything's bothering me," Emily snapped, annoyed that she'd snapped. Rubbing her temples, she followed it with her usual: "I'm fine." She heard that hollow phrase like an echo, as well, though.

Wasn't that her problem? Telling everyone she had it under control, that she'd be fine? Rosie was the only person she could talk to about this, besides Drew, and he was hardly an option now. She stopped pacing and looked directly at Rosie.

"I think he's gone. Drew, I mean."

"The picnic didn't go well, then?"

"He got mad at me. Not exactly the reaction I'd been imagining when I was frying all that crummy chicken."

Rosie's brow knitted. "He got mad? *About chicken?*"

"Sit down. On your stool there. Sit down for five minutes while I tell you something."

When she obeyed, grabbing her cup of water, Emily pulled her own stool closer. Her sister had handled Keith's return the way she might have handled the return of a stray dog.

Let's see what she'll do when I drop this bomb. At any rate, some secrets were hardly starting to feel like secrets anymore. Emily was finding shedding light on them enormously freeing.

So, she laid it all out for Rosie in detail, from Gilbert's connection to Drew's murdered baby brother to the Conti gang in Reno, from Gil's request for help from Emily to Drew's determined surveillance. In typical low-key, Rosie fashion, her sister just sat there, brows drawn together in concentration, nodding.

"Wow," she said into the silence that marked the end of Emily's tale, which happened to involve Drew following her around issuing her tickets and driving her to the printer's in the middle of the night. "*Wow.*"

"Yeah. I don't know what to do, Rosie. Tell me what to do."

Her sister just sat and processed, blinking into her cup and then blinking at Emily's pale face.

"So ... Gil ... Is he *here?*" Rosie looked around her own darkroom with new eyes. "I mean, is he on the towpath?"

"You don't think I'd be that big a knucklehead. We're talking about trained killers here, sis. Give me a little credit."

"Emily, listen to yourself," Rosie hissed. "Then where? Where did you hide him?"

"*Not* a riddle for you to solve."

"C'mon."

"That's something I'm not telling you." She held up her hand before Rosie could take issue. "It's not because I don't trust you. It's just that this is dangerous business. Right now, the only person in the whole world who knows where Gil is would be me, and I'm keeping it that way." Emily ran her fingertips nervously up and down her thigh. "If I were to tell *any*one ..."

"It would be Drew?"

Emily shrugged and nodded at the same time, which made Rosie smile a little.

"Do you think he can keep him safe to testify and then ... after?" her sister asked.

"I don't know! I don't know! Do I tell Drew or not? *Can* he keep him safe? Or will Drew and Gil *both* be the targets of cold-blooded contract killers? Oh, Rosie." Emily privately wished for Dot and one of her forbidden cigarettes. "Rosie. There's no way of knowing how this turns out. Which way is disaster? Or is disaster inevitable?"

"You've prayed about it?"

"Of course."

Had she prayed hard enough, though? Had she been brave enough to ask for God's will to be done? She thought about Drew, as she always did now.

"Hmmm." Rosie sipped at her water, calm and collected. Just as she had been when she'd announced she'd be having a baby alone at age sixteen or when she'd declared her intention of opening this photography studio at the park by herself. "I do see that you're in a bit of a pickle here, Em. I don't envy you."

"Thank you for admiring the problem."

"On the one hand, you've got our childhood buddy counting on you keeping his whereabouts a big secret, possibly for a long time. On the other hand, you've got what seems like a doggone good guy who wants and needs justice for his brother and possibly others, which hinges on Gil's testimony. And Gil's testimony hinges on whether or not you're willing to gamble his safety on the protective skills of a stranger."

"That's pretty much it."

"Is Gil all right? I mean, he's not hurt or anything?"

"He's fine. He's fine. I just talked to him early this morning."

"This *morning*? How in the world do you do that?" Rosie briefly tried again to solve the mystery. "You promise he's not on the island at all?"

"Promise."

"You told Gil about Drew?"

"Yes. He's still scared. Almost as scared as he was when he arrived."

"And you want him to make the choice."

"It's his neck on the line."

"Yours is too. But if he tells you to turn him over to Drew, you're absolved of responsibility if it all goes south, aren't you?"

Emily nodded. She tried not to think of alley shoot-outs. She'd seen *The Earl of Chicago* and *Bullets for O'Hara* in the theater. How would the pair make it all the way to Reno and through the trial safely?

"But Gil's still too scared," Rosie continued. "Did you explain how Drew's committed to guarding him? That he's the best of the best?"

"Gil said he'd think it over. He has lots of time to think things over. Unlike me. I have nothing but work and deadlines." Emily sighed. "I think all Drew wants from me is Gil. And he just thinks I'm playing a game. I know it's serious. I *know* it's not a game, but he's mad."

"Oh." At that, Rosie stood and laid the next sheet in the tub. She rocked it for a time, letting it soak.

"That's it? *Oh*?"

"Are you actually surprised that he's getting mad about it?" Rosie's glance at Emily was loving, which was the only thing keeping Emily from leaving. "I'm not saying you're wrong, Ems, but what did you expect?"

"I don't know."

"You figured he'd place his brother's murder aside, take you into his arms, and live happily ever after with you, eating your fried chicken, while Gil stayed hidden wherever you've got him hidden?" When Emily opted for silence, Rosie laughed softly. "Sheesh, Ems. Only in your imagination is that possible." Waving the dripping print under the light, she tilted it. "Does this look focused here to the left, or did I over-expose that part, the part with the horse?"

"It's fine."

"You didn't even look."

Emily looked. "It's fine."

"You need the horse stuff for tomorrow?"

"Yeah. Yeah. Whenever."

"Where's Gil hiding, anyway?"

"Rosie, please, please." Emily sank down on an old, hard stool. "If I could tell you, I would. I don't need this from you, too."

"Okay, sorry. It would just help me help you, that's all."

"I don't remotely see how that would change anything."

Rosie made some sound that indicated she was momentarily lost in the next photograph in its tray, and Emily let her head fall back against the cool wall behind her. The dark room, with its eerie light and isolation, was not normally her favorite place, not even normally a place Rosie allowed her sister to spend time. But she'd come here today, after another sleepless night, desperate to be somewhere no one could find her. She'd found Rosie busily working on prints for this week's paper.

This week's paper. Emily sighed and looked through the black ceiling as if to the heavens beyond. *Do I have to? Can't I just curl up for a while and sulk?*

I'm sorry she lied to you, Emily. Though Drew's voice seemed to come through a ringing in her ears, Emily cringed at the way her name sounded on his lips when he'd said it that last time. No husky, tender "Em" that she'd grown used to. She was *Emily* now. Was the change because he was mad about Gil or because the woman who'd given her life was so seedy and corrupt? Weren't they both, Emily reflected, mother and daughter, borderline criminals to him?

It stung all over again that the wise and venerable Hickory Graham had always said Emily reminded him of her mother. She wondered how much that was true and—not for the first time—questioned her own honesty, integrity, moral courage. The works. Especially in light of everything Drew had said yesterday.

The weight of her mother's dishonesty was as constant as the weight of Drew's words. Briefly, she considered sharing the truth about Lillian's current situation with her sister, but she simply couldn't see the point in it. Love and kindness were things she passed on to people she cared about. *Pain?* Pain was a thing she shielded them from as much as she possibly could. She believed that.

Here was one critical way, at least, she was different from Lillian Turnbull Graham.

It occurred to Emily that Rosie would probably take news about their mother in stride, though, just as she had Keith Fairchild's sudden presence or Gilbert's scary mob connection.

Rosie raised her head from more gentle swishing of the next tray, nudged the glasses down again in satisfaction. "So now you say the delicious Drew Mathison has stopped spying on you completely?"

"Surveillance. When cops do it, it's called surveillance, not spying."

"Yeah, but surveillance makes you sound like a criminal or something."

Emily snorted. "I think that's pretty much the way he sees it. And yeah, he's gone. He's not following me around at all today, anyway."

"Sounds like what you wanted. Why do you sound disappointed, then?"

"Because I *like* him." Emily didn't hesitate. Perhaps she couldn't unload on her sister about the burden of their mother, but she could open up about this. "I like him. He's just basically incredible." And he really was. It felt good to say it out loud, like surrendering at the end of a battle she just didn't want to fight any longer, one in which the casualties and the price were getting too high. Not that she could put into words what it was about him that got her so crazy.

But Emily could close her eyes and see him in her mind, a glowing negative in the dark room. In spite of how angry he was with her, and how brisk he'd been about her mother, she couldn't help but like just about everything about him.

"He's actually kind of funny and patient, though there are definitely limits to his patience." *Like me. I'm a limit to his patience.* "A bit sad and noble and brave and tough and lonely. I really, *really* like him, Rosie. I've never felt this way about anyone. That's the problem. I can't give him the information he wants, and he can't get past needing it. You're right. Who can blame him? This is about justice for his brother. He wants me to trust him, and I suppose I do now, but it isn't entirely my call. It's really Gil's. And Drew's fed up with waiting. And now he just ... *leaves*? Now I don't know *what* to do. I can't help but wonder if he was Gil's best and only chance for safety all along and maybe I made the wrong choice leaving it up to Gil, anyway. I mean, Gilbert has been remarkably stupid about this whole thing from the beginning, don't you think?"

"To be fair, Gil's been remarkably stupid about a lot of things over the years." Rosie finished clipping the latest print up on its little rope line and adjusted the scarf holding her hair back. She stopped work for a minute to examine her sister. "I'm sorry, dear, but you can't blame Drew for cutting you loose."

Emily gaped. This was not what she'd come here for. "Yes. Yes, I can! Doesn't he *care* about me at all? Is it just about the information, so that he can barely tolerate me apart from that? I guess that's what hurts."

"Look, it probably hurts him, too." She turned back to the sink, hands busy, but kept her eyes on Emily. "Think about it. Here's this guy who's vowed to protect and serve, first his country and then his community. He probably sees himself as a trustworthy protector above *all* other things, and that's the thing you won't give him." Rosie wiped her right hand on her apron. "Do you still have chewing gum, Em? Put half of that stick in my mouth so I don't have to touch it, will you?"

Emily obliged, feeding her sister a rectangle of spearmint. Rosie chewed it a few times before she spoke again.

"Anyway, I know how much it's chafing *me* not to know where you've got Gil hidden, and I've only known about the situation for a few minutes. *And* I'm not the great American Hero. Trust is probably a big, big deal to him."

Emily shrugged in acknowledgement of a good point. Was the personal aspect of this deeper than his murdered brother? Had she called into question his entire definition of himself and what he had to offer? To society? To her?

Trust was an awfully big deal to God, too. There was no denying that, nor that Emily was only making baby steps with that, too.

"I'd say you need to stop stringing the guy along." Rosie stretched her neck from side to side and, reaching up, dropped her glasses into her apron pocket.

"I am *not* stringing him along."

"Call it what you will. It's decision time. You either trust him or you don't."

"Look, like I said, there's another party involved. I'm kind of ... waiting for Gil to give me the green light. And I think things will move pretty fast when I do."

"What kinds of things?"

"The trial, everything back in Reno. Drew will have to take Gil back, set everything up."

"So, both of them are effectively out of your life at the point you turn Gil over to him. Have you considered the possibility *that* might be part of what has you hesitating?"

A deep chill settled inside of Emily, and she shook her head instinctively. "Nuh-uh. No." She thought for a second and shook her head more decisively. "No. Look, Rosie. That would make me a horrible person." Emily told herself again and again that this thought had never gone through her mind, that it wasn't a factor. Of course, Drew would go back to Reno for the trial and then to Philadelphia. He had always been going back. His family was expecting him. He couldn't just follow her around at the newspaper and paste up ads forever. "That would make me a truly, truly horrible person."

"You said it, not me." Rosie blew a tiny, ladylike bubble with the gum and laughed softly to take the sting away. "Or it makes you a woman in love." Walking over to the stool, she wrapped her baby sister in a fragrant hug. Lavender and developing chemicals. "Hey, check out this shot of the sun setting over the lily pads. Isn't that lighting something? You want me to frame an extra copy of that print for your office?"

"It's exceptional. But no. No, thanks, Rosie." Because when she saw those lily pads, Emily would forever think of what it was like to watch Drew walk away from her.

Chapter Twenty-Four

The Buckeye Lake Beacon
Wednesday, July 3, 1946
Benches added for lakeside services

Drew watched Pastor Skip fill out the Missing Person report in a cluttered kitchen that needed a woman's touch. His already frayed nerves felt deeply each thud of the kickball little Delia sent hammering against the outside wall of the house from the yard.

Skip made little weary sounds as he moved from one block of information to the next, occasionally asking questions. Drew hoped he was doing the right thing, moving ahead with the Missing Person report. He needed a paperwork trail, if only a very careful and secret one, to start moving Emily along in a formal way.

"I don't know if I'm indebted to Emily or want to strangle her," Skip had mumbled as he started. He said he'd tried to wear her down, too, but nothing he said could convince her that her shoulders weren't strong enough for this burden.

Drew could commiserate.

Skip pushed the completed papers across the table. "Well, there we go. He's officially missing. What next?"

"Just like I said. It's time to force her hand." Drew didn't move to leave though. "Your part is done. Just keep an eye out, like you have all along."

"What if you take Gil back to Reno but don't get the trial?"

"We'll get a trial. We have a witness to go along with the crime scene reports. Supposedly that's all they needed. I don't know how the department there looks the other way when someone saw the whole thing."

"What if they don't get convicted? These Contis?"

"I can't think like that."

"Sometimes things don't turn out the way we think they should, like they do in the movies," Skip pressed on. "Sometimes the hero does everything he's supposed to, but he doesn't win."

Drew thought of Emily, praying for years for her mother to return, never losing hope, even after she'd been fleeced out of thousands of dollars. Where was the justice in that? Lillian wouldn't be back, Drew thought. Some people didn't have all the pieces of family in place and never would, and that was just the way it was. The thought of simply going on without Jamie and without any sense of *right* attached to his death was not a thought Drew could stand to entertain for long.

"Sometimes God's justice looks different than what we'd imagined," the pastor continued, "and I wonder if you can trust in that?"

"That seems like more trust than I can manage just now," he said, his voice gruff. But his words sounded a lot like Emily Graham's, not quite trusting *him* this past week.

And so, he guessed he understood God's frustration, too.

Hadn't Drew done everything he could to show Emily she could trust him? It hurt that he could help her and that she wouldn't let him.

What we asked for or something better.

Those promised mercies.

It's how we know God's already been there.

Drew opened his own hands on the table and looked at them, thinking about the way things had gone as he'd done them his own way. Hadn't all the things he'd come through been in God's hands, even the ones that hadn't turned out the way he'd have liked? Did he really think he himself understood the big picture enough to alter it, if he could? Who else was there to trust, in the end?

"God's still my best bet," he said out loud, wishing he had said it with more conviction. But it felt right, however he said it.

What we asked for or something better.

"It's the kind of thing you accept entirely on faith when you're young, when it's easy," Skip agreed. "But as you get older, you know from experience. Let this situation be one of the times you look back on that way, Drew, the next time you need to remind yourself to trust Him. Because He has a better plan for this than you or Emily do. And much, much better than whatever my son has in mind."

Chapter Twenty-Five

The Buckeye Lake Beacon
Thursday, July 4, 1946
Police staff up for holiday coverage

Drew watched Gunn chew sunflower seeds and spit the shells into a paper lemon squeeze cup. The chief stood at a smudged window, watching the streets already filling with people. Every now and then, the older man scratched an itch on his lower back.

July the Fourth, and buses had been depositing at the amusement park station more visitors from the city than it had seats for. The parking lots along 79 overflowed. Well-supplied for a long holiday weekend, the crowds trailed along the walkway in front of the tiny station the department kept adjacent to the enormous parking lot.

It made sense to keep this tiny sub-station near the water's edge and near the crowd, however, partly because crime and injuries tended to follow crowds and partly for storage of the rescue boat and dive equipment, including two sets of Davis Submerged Escape Apparatus the police shared with the volunteer fire department. The department's black patrol bicycles were tucked away at the back of the building next to an enclosed bunk area they sometimes used for double shifts and for harmless, drunk park patrons who needed to be temporarily kept in custody for their own safety.

Gunn had asked Drew to meet here at the station to discuss some work they needed to do to get a flat barge ready for setting off fireworks after dark. Drew had countered, for the second afternoon in a row, with his insistence that Gunn arrest Emily Graham.

So, as it stood now, the fireworks would be set off from the barge, no problem.

The arrest of the local newspaper woman on obstruction charges, however ... well, it still hadn't happened.

They'd kept the Missing Person report here at the station but had not posted it, and the warrant for Emily's arrest for Obstruction of Justice was also "under the radar" so she wouldn't be in danger from anyone they couldn't trust. This was the only way Drew could go about forcing her to hand Gil over without letting the Contis in on her involvement with the witness.

"Let's just get it done," Drew said impatiently. It had been a terrible week, a week almost entirely without Emily. He just really, really needed the chief to be the one to arrest her.

Spitting another shell forcefully into the cup, Gunn turned back from the window, swatted at a fly with his free hand, and shook his head.

"All right, all right. I guess I'd better go and do this thing," he said at length, but he looked hostile and did not move. Drew rustled the paperwork on the metal desk. Gunn blinked and shook his head again. "I just hope nobody's there to see it happen to her. Poor kid."

"This is bigger than her embarrassment."

"I know, I know." Gunn popped another seed in his mouth and chewed like a squirrel. "It's just that I go to church with that girl. Known her all her life. Hickory's going to have my hide." He spit the shells into the cup. "Tell me again why you don't just do this yourself."

The very thought of shackling Emily and leading her to the station, of having to touch her like that and smell her hair, made Drew uncomfortable in ways he didn't want to discuss with the police chief and that were very different from Gunn's own reservations.

"Things are too complicated between us. Anyway, she's mad at me."

"So, you want her to be mad at *both* of us, huh? Spreading the good cheer."

"She won't fight you like she will me. Time's wasting, sir. Both she and Gilbert could end up in danger."

"I agreed to do it, and I will," Gunn said, straightening. "Just promise me her life returns to normal after she gives you Gilbert."

Because Emily had a holiday to cover and a paper to crank out, there was clearly no doubt in the chief's mind that Emily would do anything to avoid being locked up in the detention area. Gunn's vision had Emily coughing up Gilbert's whereabouts within minutes of her arrest. Drew, on the other hand, wasn't as certain. The chief might have known her since she was a kid, but Drew figured he still had her pegged just about better than anyone.

"You're making a more optimistic leap there than I'm willing to make," he told Gunn, gently. "But assuming she ever does turn him over, I'll take *him* into custody, and she can go on about her life. We can drop the charges. Don't file any of it. She'll forgive you. Tell her I threatened to sue your department if you didn't cooperate. Whatever you want, I don't care. I'll be gone anyway, and it won't matter." He said it like it didn't matter, like he didn't care if he ever saw her again, even though he was aching after four days.

Gunn grunted but still didn't move toward the door. Drew supposed that, even in his impatience, he didn't blame the man. Having Emily Graham irritated with them really wasn't what anyone would call a good time.

But the chief's thoughts had taken another turn entirely. "Once it's all said and done, I s'pose you'll go back to working construction with your old man, then?"

"With my brothers, maybe. My father's looking to retire in the next year or two," Drew explained. "Says there are birdhouses waiting to be built."

"Hmm. Good for him." Another couple of shells plopped aggressively into the cup. "Just seems like the loss of a good detective to me."

Drew was half-sitting on the desk, which was on the far side of the room, and he managed a cynical smirk as he shook his head. "Some detective."

"Aw, you can't look at it in that light. If I'd known from the get-go Emily Graham was *responsible* for hiding that boy, I'd have told you to settle in for the long haul. She always was a stubborn kid."

"I feel like I *have* done the long haul, Chief, and it's gotten me exactly nowhere."

Instead of moving, Gunn wanted to review all the hundred-and-five places Drew could be looking for Gilbert right now. They'd been through this before, and Drew recognized the stall tactic. If he hadn't moved to arrest her in another quarter of an hour, Drew was going to have to do it himself, regardless of the rest of it.

Still, he couldn't shake the feeling that a man should never have to read the woman he loved her rights.

"No, no sign of Gilbert while I was staying at the inn, anyway," Drew told the chief again with forced patience. "I figure there's a chance she's talking to him on the phone at the office during the day, in a sort of code so no one knows? That's all I can come up with. I'm requesting records from the phone company, to see if I can track down his location that way by recognizing a pattern in numbers called, but they're not furnishing those very quickly. Or there could be a messenger, a go-between." Drew had briefly entertained the idea of her using Hickory, Rosie, or even Charlie for such a task, but he was certain she wouldn't involve them in anything risky. She didn't even want to confide in them about Lillian's extortion for the sake of their feelings, after all. Involving them in mob violence seemed preposterous, in that light. And he'd eaten enough meals with them to dismiss the possibility.

"Well, I'm plum puzzled." Gunn turned back to the window, still rubbing his chin. Then he reached around to re-tuck his uniform shirt more tidily into his trousers, as though finally getting ready to go do his job.

Drew straightened, as well. "Thank you for your help in this, Chief," he said with sincerity. "Right from the start."

Gunn nodded. "We'll help you see it through, absolutely, son. You've been through hell, no doubt about it, these last few months. Though I wouldn't wish that on my worst enemy, I'm sure glad your path brought you here to my station for a short time."

"I thank you for that, and for ..." Drew never got to thank him again for trusting him with a temporary badge because just then the door of the station house burst open to reveal a winded old woman in a woven, summer-weight shawl, moving in a way that no old woman would ever actually have been able to move.

Sharp motions, speed. In one wild gesture, she ripped a gray wig off her head to reveal the subject of most of their previous conversation. *Emily Graham.* Drew's heart pumped one hard, painful beat.

Gunn, merely baffled where Drew was shocked, managed a chuckle. "And the prey strolls into the trap before it's set. That's what I call an easy day on the job. What's this get-up all about, now, darlin'?"

Golden hair in disarray from its time under the wig, cheeks a splotchy crimson mottled over corpse white, eyes wide and wild. It took a split second to know something was wrong, less than a split second for Emily to rush past the police chief at the window to get to Drew, who was standing now.

She seemed beyond speech, which Drew found more alarming than her appearance. Wheezing, she simply thrust a quarter sheet of paper at him and shoved the fingernail of her right pinky finger between her teeth, nibbling almost manically even as she tried to catch her breath.

"What's that?" Gunn demanded, pushing closed the door Emily had left standing open. "Why are you dressed like your late grandmother, child?"

She seemed not to hear Gunn at all. "What do we do, Drew?" she breathed with urgency around her fingertip. "What happens now?"

Drew re-read the brief note pasted together from bits of newspaper ads, trying to make sense of it, feeling sweat break out on his brow.

"Where'd this come from? How'd you get it?" He searched her eyes and, seeing her pupils, wondered if she were prone to fainting. Doubting it, but unwilling to take a chance, he whirled her around and hauled her onto the desk where he'd been sitting. He kept his hands on her upper arms. He registered that she smelled mildly of moth balls. "Did someone hand this paper to you? When? Where?"

"What's it *say*?" Gunn demanded.

"It was stuck to the middle ... of the office door ..." she sucked in air, "...when I got back from the park office a minute ago."

Drew yielded the paper to Gunn's eager grasp, and the chief read it out loud.

Obituary. Emily Graham, dead at twenty-four, killed from being shot.

*Along with her family. She could have avoided it by bringing Reese to
the state park dock on the north shore at midnight tonight. Alone.
P.S. She had quite the little swim Sunday night before her death.*

Gunn looked up at them. "I assume you don't want me to arrest her
just yet."

Drew answered with a murdering look, processing the fact Emily had
run straight to *him*. That caused a warmth in his chest that he didn't have
time to enjoy. He would allow himself to relish that morsel of instinctive
trust once the danger had been dealt with.

And the danger, now, was very real.

The Contis had figured out not only where Gilbert Reese was but also
who was likely to be hiding him, whether they'd been behind the last note
or not. As Drew had feared all along, if it had been relatively easy for him
to get the information, they'd have had it as soon as they'd arrived.

Hearing Gunn mumble his way through the note a second time,
Emily visibly shuddered and hopped off the desk again. "We've got to get
to the towpath. He's watching my family. What if he's already got them?
What are we going to do now, Drew?" she asked again, already in motion.
She flattened the gray wig with the bun in it back on her head. Drew took
a second to appreciate her disguise and her foresight, even in her panic, to
visit him here as an old woman rather than as the newspaper publisher.
"I slipped out the back of the office, came up the boardwalk," she
explained, following his eyes as they tracked her unlikely dress. "I didn't
want him seeing me rush to you when I saw the note. Didn't want to set
him off. What if he hurts them before tonight?"

Drew adjusted his gun into its holster and was out the door beside
her, Gunn locking up behind them. "Who was there in your office when
the paper appeared?"

"No one. No one was there."

"My truck's over this way. So, you came straight over here from *The
Beacon*?"

"I didn't know what to do."

"Shorten your stride, Granny. You look like an Olympic athlete. Did
you go in the office? Did it look like anyone had tried to get in?" They
were weaving through vacationers at a relatively fast trot, Drew playing
the gentleman and pretending to guide the old woman by the elbow.

"Don't mow down any pedestrians, Mathison, got that?" Gunn
called. "I'd give you an escort with lights and sirens, but that seems like
the worst idea, given the circumstances."

"Yeah, right," Drew called back. "No cop cars."

"Why don't you go grab Burt and his boat, Chief? Make it look like a
social call? We may need you out at the towpath," Emily suggested, panic

still in her voice. She seemed to be imagining a disaster. Drew couldn't, in good conscience, persuade her that wasn't the case.

"I'll cut across in the boat, then, and meet you there," Gunn agreed, on the run. "Permission to explain everything to Burt?"

"Yes. Yes!"

Grateful for the extra support, Drew tossed Old Lady Emily up into the passenger side of his truck and jumped in the driver's side at a run. It occurred to him it was the first time he'd had a chance to help her into a vehicle without her leaping in on her own.

"Hurry, hurry," she was chanting, approving rather than resenting his handling of her. "The note. Does Chief still have the note?"

"Yeah." His tires squealed as he pulled out, but Drew was quickly blocked by an ice cart. If the blast from the truck's horn wasn't enough to get the cart's operator moving, the threat he belted out the window was. They rushed out into the main road.

"So, everyone's out of the office for the holiday?"

"I sent the rest home at lunch," Emily gasped, hand on the dash as she bounced on the springs of the seat. "We don't go to press for our issue of the Fourth until Friday night because the printer's closed for the holiday. My staff's got tonight and tomorrow off."

"How'd he know *you'd* be there, then, I wonder?"

"I don't know. I don't know."

Drew thought it over. "Walt, Sammy. They've been working there longer than the last few months, right?"

"Oh, yeah. Years, Drew."

"Hmmm."

"What are we going to do?"

He took a moment to appreciate her use of "we." Jerking the truck's wheel, he whipped passed a green Windsor and sped up more.

"We're going to check on Hickory and Rosie and Charlie," he said in a calm tone that contrasted with his driving. His cop's mind could only see an old man, a woman, and a little boy sitting vulnerable on that island. And an invisible enemy who didn't play by the rules or even stick to flimsy "deals" typed as crummy obituaries. He mentally ran through every weapon he had on his body.

"They're okay," Emily said out loud. "They've got to be okay. Who would hurt them?"

She didn't know the Conti family, Drew thought, and figured it was better that way. Except if she did know what he knew, she'd have turned Gilbert over to Drew at the get-go, no questions asked. He saw her trembling on the seat beside him. Glancing over very briefly, he took in the way she'd tossed the light-weight shawl over a patterned cotton dress that would have been way too roomy in the bust ... if she hadn't stuffed it. Her now matronly bosom, made of heaven only knew what, bounced with the springs in the seat, as well. It was mesmerizing, but not in a good way.

"You're right. It's going to be okay," he told her. He allowed the grin that her stuffing evoked, in spite of everything. "I like your getup, by the way."

Emily glanced down. "Comes in handy for work now and then." Her hands shook as she smoothed the mothball material. "We're fine. We're okay." Saying the words until she believed them, she cast Drew a look still just this side of panic. "Drew, I'm sorry. I really am. What Gil thinks doesn't matter any longer. About you. About his own safety. I don't care what he thinks about telling you where he is, I mean."

"Sweetheart, we'll get this under control. Just breathe."

"I'll take you to him. It's going to be ... complicated though."

"One thing at a time." Drew reached over to squeeze her hand. It was ice cold.

"I won't sacrifice my family. Gil's got to stand up and do the right thing. That's all there is to it."

It had only taken her a week to catch up with him, but she was there now. He told himself that was all that mattered.

Drew took the remote turn off to the island on two wheels, barreling along the winding road bordered by feed corn. His truck rumbled over the connecting bridge before he was forced to slow down by a gang of young children in swimsuits headed for the canal bank. Emily used the time to rip her wig off. She wiggled out of the flowered wrap and shawl, revealing the secret to her fake bosom: two stockings, filled with something crunchy like grains of rice, knotted together around her neck. She caught Drew's raised brow as he shifted gears across the bridge. "I keep this stuff in a box for when I need it," she explained. Instead of a box, her costume got balled up in the center of his truck seat this time.

As they reached the parking lot, they immediately spotted Hickory leaning outside the door of the marina. He waved, relaxed as ever. Drew took a steadying breath of his own. Emily visibly unwound, if only just a little. The old man looked confused at the cloud of dust shooting out from behind the truck, but he was whole. Safe and whole.

"Where are Rosie and Charlie?" Drew shouted to him out the window of the truck when he came up close enough.

"Rosie and Charlie? They're over on the towpath. Why?"

"Meet us over at your place," Drew said. The old man watched the boat approaching across the sun-drenched lake with the chief and Burt in it and registered increasing agitation. He turned to his part-time help, Tom, with a request to take over.

Emily, meanwhile, had already vaulted from the truck and was running across the rickety bridge to their home. It occurred to Drew there wouldn't be time to fix it now. Soon, God willing, he'd be back in Reno helping the prosecution build their case.

But he had to leave the Graham family safe, or he could not leave at all.

Drew followed right behind Emily.

Charlie was whittling something from a block of wood, sitting dirty and happy in the lengthening shadow of the big, white house on the island. Rosie walked out onto the porch in response to the sound of raised voices. She had flour on her hands, rather than any art supply. She was clearly also safe, simply interrupted in holiday supper preparations. Emily slid to a halt.

They were okay.

He heard Emily wheezing a little beside him, overcome.

Drew didn't leave her side during the next hour. His mind sifted through plans to keep the family safe and to keep Gilbert safe while his hand kept firm hold of Emily's in the tense living room. There, she suffered Hickory's angry disappointment, Rosie's worry about her son's safety, and Charlie's pale silence. Mostly, there was the underlying anger.

"I'm sorry," she kept telling them, numbly. At one point, she'd torn her hand out of his grip, loped outside, and been sick off the railing of Hickory's front porch. Drew was the only one who followed her out. As he'd wrapped her in a hug and pushed the damp hair off her temple, it occurred to him that all the conflict between them went back to her instinctive desire to keep people safe. Wasn't that something with which he could identify?

And he knew how it felt when it all got away from him. He certainly knew how that felt.

By late afternoon, the Grahams had disguised the evacuation of the family from Towpath Island as a pleasure boat trip in Burt's cruiser. The hapless Tom was left in charge of the marina and its holiday crowd, which worried Hickory, but there was no alternative. Hickory, Rosie, and Charlie would spend the holiday hidden in the Strouts' inn, while Emily and Drew worked to get Gilbert Reese safely out of town.

They'd called Pastor Skip to join them, and they'd all held hands as they always did at dinner, to pray about the situation. Skip had harnessed parts of Jehoshaphat's prayer from 2 Chronicles: "We do not know what to do, but our eyes are on You."

Drew promised Hickory a few dozen times he would keep Emily safe, but Hickory seemed to regard Drew suspiciously now, as well. He had trusted the young man from Philadelphia who, like his granddaughter, had given him half-truths for too long.

There were no cheerful goodbyes when the others pulled away from the dock. Only a worried silence.

"I can take you to him, but we can't get him out immediately," Emily told Drew solemnly, turning back to his truck. "This is going to take some planning. And it can't be me who takes you there. It has to be the old lady. Otherwise, it's obvious where he is."

Back in the truck, Drew helped a much calmer Emily fling her rice bosom back into place and don her gray wig. "I'm afraid to ask where you've worn this before and for what purpose," he murmured, tucking a golden lock of hair up into the netting. She was chewing on a piece of spearmint gum. "How's your stomach now, sweetheart?"

She looked sheepish, wouldn't meet his eyes. "Sorry about that."

"No need to apologize. You're having a rough day."

She reached up and took hold of his wrists. "I'm so sorry, Drew." He fussed with her shawl while she watched him intently with those giant, wet eyes. "This is all my fault, and you told me. You told me, and I didn't believe you."

"Now, when did I ever say any of this was your fault?"

"No, you said they'd come after Gil and come after me. You told me that. You were right. I didn't believe you, not really. I thought I could handle it, just like everything."

"First of all, all this is only the fault of thugs from Reno. And, believe me, being right doesn't mean a lot to me right now."

"No. Not with Gil in terrible danger."

"Gil?" He let the back of his hand trail down that impossibly soft cheek again. "I care a lot more about you being in danger, Em."

And those soft words were how he ended up with what looked like an eighty-year-old woman curled up in his lap on the front seat of his pickup, her head on his shoulder. He nestled her closer while trying to avoid the wig that kept scratching his chin.

"I know we have a lot to do, but ... I've missed you." She let out a deep breath, which came out shaky. "I could use a lot more of just being like this with you."

"Me too. I hated not seeing you this week." He thought of the paperwork, the Missing Person, the obstruction of justice charges, unnecessary now. "Let's do what needs to be done, and I promise you ... the next time you're in my arms, it will last longer than a few stolen minutes. Deal?"

She managed a smile. "Deal. Anyway, this shawl is hot. I've never worn this get-up in the summertime."

She wouldn't tell him where they were going. She said she had to *show* him where Gil was.

A short time later, Drew escorted the feeble old lady through the crowds on the pier, past the Dodge 'Em cars, his discomfort growing with a sudden and unsettling certainty about where his missing witness had been hidden. Duped, he resisted the urge to toss the little bewigged troublemaker beside him right into the water even as he wanted to keep her firmly beside him.

Emily, carrying a packet of food she'd snagged at the civic association's storefront, motioned to the young man who stood guard next to the phone that hooked up to the underwater sub at the end of the pier. "I need a minute, Donny," she said, cutting in front of dozens of angry people. She took off the phony old lady glasses. "It's me."

"Oh. Oh, hey, Emily ..."

"Shh. Zip it."

Donny was clearly a college kid with a summer job that included standing out at the end of this pier, baking in the early July sun while teenage girls giggled and pushed in line. He stared at Emily's sagging bosom for a moment in puzzlement before shrugging.

Did the whole community just take it for granted she was odd?

Drew pushed at the tingling on the back of his neck as Donny went over to prompt a pair of red-haired twins that their time talking to Sub Man was drawing to an end. Sub Man, Drew thought, was ingeniously hidden, would be impossible to extract on the busiest day of the year, and was vulnerable ... essentially, for the man who wanted him dead, Sub Man was the equivalent of shooting ducks in a barrel.

But he'd been very well hidden, indeed. *French accent ... my rear end,* he thought.

"All yours, uh ... ma'am," Donny said, dragging Freckles One and Two away.

"Have you met my friend, Deputy Drew Mathison, Donny?" For the first time, the kid's eyes tracked to Drew, who stuck out his hand. Emily opened a stainless-steel tube-like structure that extended into the water. The phone line ran down it, and there was a basket-like contraption Emily placed the food packet in before lowering it.

"Pleased to meet you, Donny."

"Yes, sir. Thank you. Nice to meet you, too. I think I recognize you, sir, from patrols and such."

"We're going to have a word here, if you could keep the girls back away, Donny?" Emily commanded gently rather than suggested, as she picked up the phone on the stand and pushed a button. Drew stood where he was while she turned away from him and spoke softly into the receiver. He waited, giving her space. Finally, she turned to him, eyes haunted, and offered the phone receiver in a hand that shook.

"Drew, there's someone on the other end of this line who wants to speak with you." Of course, he knew before she said it, and he felt like a fool for not guessing in the month he'd been here. She told him softly,

"This is my old friend, Gilbert Reese."

Chapter Twenty-Six

The Buckeye Lake Beacon
Thursday, July 4, 1946
Star-spangled boats on parade

Emily had to dig deep for the charm that garnered them a table at the diner for supper, where crowds lined the sidewalk, eating hot dogs to go because tables were so scarce. "I'll run your specials free this week," she had told Roscoe so no one else could hear. Roscoe had squinted at her suspiciously in her old lady getup but had escorted them to a table.

The sun was still bright, the sky cloudless, which boded well, she thought absently, for the fireworks display that would start in a few hours.

"Eat," Drew told her later, over the din. As he'd predicted, the shouts of the servers and cooks and the boisterous, sometimes inebriated conversations of the patrons gave them plenty of privacy, and Emily had resisted returning to her office just now.

The note describing her death had left her feeling violated.

She sipped her soda, the wig in her lap and the bags of rice hot and itchy against her skin, and she wondered if Drew had finally reached the end of his questions. Was there any point to the basket of chips if he was going to press on as he had for the last hour?

"You need something in your stomach," he urged her, glancing at his watch as if to signal the end of the interrogation. Numb, she watched the tendons and muscles of his forearm flex with the gesture.

She picked up a single chip. In the end, it had been a relief to explain how it had all unfolded. Before today, only she and Gilbert had known the full extent of their secret.

Emily had explained to Drew how Old Man O'Hara out at the scrap yard had managed to finagle a small model of an early sub that had been used for testing just before the war. One of the town council members and a member of the civic association had supervised modifications to the little sub as the initial publicity draw, which Emily had been apprised of late the summer before, long before any trouble had gone down in Reno. The original plan was to be able to submerge and withdraw the thing with paying tourists in it, giving folks in rural Ohio possibly their one chance in a lifetime of experiencing a real, submerged submarine. O'Hara devised a pulley system at the end of the pier that could bring the sub up and down in a spot that was deep enough.

The logistics were ultimately a problem, however. The space inside the sub was so small that only one visitor could fit in it comfortably at a time, and the raising and lowering of the contraption was so laborious that just one person couldn't be paid to do it all day. So, it ultimately couldn't be justified as a paid attraction. The ticket prices would have to be outrageous to cover O'Hara's expenses and two operators all day, and it was regretfully determined to be more than most visitors would pay for the experience.

By late winter, she told Drew, Emily had tried to salvage the plan by proposing they intrigue those visitors by keeping someone *in* the sub for the summer. It was the same ridiculous philosophy as any of the dance marathons or the high wire cyclist ... *could someone last that long?* This someone would convey thoughts from the bottom of the lake while people paid for the novelty of communicating with him somehow. Corporate sponsors would chip in, too.

Stranger things had been done for publicity, after all. The civic association had loved the idea.

About the time Gilbert had returned in early spring, desperate and in danger, Emily had arranged with the association to make the Sub Man spectacle the baby of the local newspaper almost entirely. She was named chair of the project. She and her staff would handle publicity, obviously, but would also secure the Sub Man, "pay" him, and arrange round-the-clock security, which, happily, the association agreed to help fund.

"So, the photo and bio of Sub Man that runs in *The Beacon* is a complete hoax," Drew said, stating the obvious. "As was the French accent."

"Every bit of it. It was kind of fun to make up that guy in the sub. It's no wonder all the women are in love with him. I made the man perfect."

Drew rolled his eyes, but Emily figured he'd been as jealous of the fictional Sub Man hero as any healthy, real man would have been. The imaginary Sub Man had been an Adonis, if she did say so herself. Far from the reality of the real man in the sub who'd gotten tied up in so many mistakes.

"I don't see how you got Reese down there without everyone seeing or recognizing him." Drew had worried over every angle of a security breach, doubtful how such a bizarre scheme could truly have worked for this long. The vulnerability of his witness, now that he knew where he was and that Conti knew Emily's connection, was making him crazy. "It seems like there must be a handful of people around here, at least, that know him and know the truth."

Emily shook her head. "Our buddy O'Hara is a mere two-year resident of the lake area, which means Gil is no one to him. Gil's been gone as long as O'Hara has been here, you know? And Old Man O'Hara is the one who helped lower the sub, early one morning, with zero publicity and no one else even knowing it was happening."

"How did the civic association like *that*?"

"They didn't. They wanted to make a big thing of it. I don't blame them. I used the photo we ran of the random man with the bio, cut it out and glued it onto the picture of the sub just before O'Hara lowered it. Ran it in the paper. No one really said much, in the end, about not being there for it. It was before the big season opening."

Drew grinned in spite of himself. "Crafty."

"The folks at the engraver's probably looked at it funny, but they're the only ones who could tell the photo was doctored. I told them we had a glitch in the dark room and had to make do. That happens."

"And this submarine fellow, he didn't think it was odd he stuck a red-haired kid in the sub rather than the swarthy-looking guy in the picture?"

"It was half dark, and Gil had shaved his head close, anyway. O'Hara didn't seem too interested beyond what I paid him to come out at that ridiculous hour to lower the thing. Later, some of the guys from the scrapyard came over with him to take the pulleys back over until we need them again. All along, the plan has been to remove Sub Man on Labor Day weekend with a big celebration. I've been trying to figure out a way around that since the day we put him in there, but now it's not an issue. You'll have Gil by this time tomorrow." Emily sipped her Coke again and stared into it, imagining headlines amidst the swirling ice. "We'll close the attraction for a few days and say Sub Man is sick, headed back to France."

"Good grief."

"Anyway, I'll publish an apology saying that he needed to be removed suddenly to get some light medical attention. Something like that. Sorry for the inconvenience, folks. That kind of thing. I'm not afraid of taking the heat."

And that was where they'd left it, both of them plotting distractedly.

Emily crunched a chip. Drew pushed the remains of his bread crust around on his plate with a fork and occasionally admonished her to eat. Emily marveled at how small a normal fork looked in his large, work-worn fingers. The other hand picked at the edge of his napkin on the table. She thought about how gentle those large hands really were, and she couldn't resist reaching out and touching his fingertips on the napkin. He stilled and let out a breath, half laughing.

"Sorry, sorry. I guess I'm not very good company, am I?"

"It's okay. You've got a lot on your mind."

"True." He nodded, abandoning the fork with a soft clatter and turning his attention to his coffee cup. "I've got a place for him, a place to keep him until after the trial. There's no problem there. I can keep him safe."

He had assured her of this several times.

Emily was relieved that Gil seemed to have mollified Drew's anger a bit on the phone at the end of the pier, when he confirmed that he could, in fact, identify Jamie's killers. His disembodied voice had revealed there were three men there that night, all of them having pulled the trigger more times than necessary. Though Drew had flinched at that, Gil had promised to say as much in court, at least now that he had no choice in the matter. And Drew had assured Gil in no uncertain terms that he had no choice in the matter now. Because of his time with the books in the casino, Gil even knew two of the men's names and could easily pick the third out of a lineup.

An apology had also been issued from the bottom of the lake to the man on the dock. Emily didn't know if it had made Drew feel any better, but she felt a little better about her childhood friend than she had this morning.

Could it possibly all turn out okay?

Gil couldn't flee the sub without help. Drew had quickly decided on a plan to extricate him in the pre-dawn hours of tomorrow morning, July 5th, when Buckeye Lake would be sleeping off the riotous party scheduled for tonight. Before that, there would be no getting him out unnoticed. The holiday crowds were too thick.

Emily looked up, startled by a large, dark figure suddenly looming over their table. She jolted out of her chair, ready to flee herself, but was relieved to see another old friend rather than a hitman ... *this time.*

"Smokey!" She let out a shaking breath, and she wrapped her arms around him automatically, grinning. "You left Festival Farms on a holiday? Will wonders never cease?"

"You're not aging well, Emmie," came the familiar baritone that matched his size. He plucked at the hideous wig she'd stuffed under her arm and smiled down at her lumpy figure.

"You're the last person I'd expect to comment on my gray hair," she said. Smokey, after all, had inherited his nickname back in high school, when some genetic fluke had turned his hair from dark to gray at roughly the same time he was winning the state swim meet and breaking girls' hearts throughout the heartland. Since then, he wore his namesake gray hair buzzed shorter than military short over a sun-browned head. "Drew, this is ..." She turned. "Wait. You two know each other." Emily dropped back into her seat as Drew whipped the empty chair beside him around and into the aisle. "I forgot, Smokey, you're the one who told Drew that Gil and I were engaged."

"You *were* engaged?"

"Not now."

"I can't keep up with you. Never have been able to." He stretched his hand out to Drew's for a firm, one-pump shake. "Anyhow, this guy's why I'm in town on a day this crowded."

"I called him from the station," Drew explained to Emily. "He's going to come in pretty handy, I think."

"Heard our boy Gil got himself into some hot water again," Smokey said softly to Emily, leaning forward and helping himself to the rest of her food.

Emily looked over at Drew.

"He knows," he said to her, then turned to Smokey. "Into some hot water and *under* the water. That's where you come in."

"You said you've got two Davis apparati?"

"Over in the substation, yeah."

Smokey nodded. That was when Emily remembered what her friend did in the war. Frogman for the Navy, an underwater demolition expert or something like that, she thought. But it was Drew she looked at with new respect. The man was a thinker, and that he'd won the loyalty of a man like Smokey in such a short time spoke volumes.

The plan that unfolded in the diner was simple enough, if dangerous. Somewhere nearby, one of the Contis was waiting for Emily to hand Gilbert over at the north shore ramp at midnight, when the park would be far from deserted. Drew didn't want Emily anywhere near there, of course. So, Emily and Drew would go out on the water with the thousands of other boats on the lake for the star-spangled spectacle of lights, a crowd that wouldn't clear until almost the midnight deadline. She would drop Drew off on the north shore, and he would pretend to fish from the ramp there, watching to see if he could spot and take out of commission a Conti who looked familiar to him from what little he knew from Reno. If that worked, they would buy themselves important time.

Emily didn't ask what it meant for Drew to "take him out of commission."

If that didn't work—and neither man seemed optimistic about a gangster materializing without catching sight of his witness or Emily— Drew would rendezvous with Emily at the boat slip by the inn after passing one of the dive team's rebreathers down the chute to Gil on his way back. He would signal Smokey with a bandana on Cookie's mailbox. Drew and Emily would stay afloat further down the shore, until 3:30 a.m., when Smokey would enter the water under cover of darkness from the inn, swim around the pier, and extricate Gil by opening the hatch on the sub and flooding the capsule, both men in breathing masks.

Swimming, Smokey would return Gil to the dock at the inn, where Emily and Drew would be waiting to whisk him off to safety.

From there, Drew had a plan in place, formulated all the way back on his original drive to Buckeye Lake from Reno.

"There are three guys in the Reno force I know can be trusted. One I trained with as an MP. He grew up with the other two, so he trusts them, and I trust him. He knows the power the Contis have and that they've got to have inside guys in the police department. He'd gotten himself named lead on this investigation by the time I'd left the city to find Reese. He just needs the witness. I *do* know I can trust him. Once we get there, the Contis will know we have our witness, sure, but I don't anticipate dangerous leaks because no one else will know where we've got him."

Emily, naturally a curious person, wanted to ask for specifics about the secret location. Even as she understood the logic of such secrecy, she also understood it would soon be her turn to be on the wondering end of her friend's location. And Drew's location, for that matter. As a person obsessed with control, she couldn't think about that yet.

"Thanks so much for helping us out with this, Smokey. I know you didn't have to get involved," Emily told him when he stood to leave them. "See you in the middle of the night, I guess."

"You won't see me," he said with his easy grin. Nodding at Drew, he left.

Emily looked across the table, where Drew offered her a wink with one weary eye. An unfamiliar tenderness washed through her, and she recognized the irony of the protective feeling *she* had for *him*, the man with the sidearm and probably several other weapons strapped all over his fine body. She desperately wanted to hide him somewhere, while they were going about hiding people.

"You don't have to worry about Gil," Drew assured her, clearly misreading her concern.

"I know. You'll keep him safe. It's just …"

"What?"

"What if something happens to *you* while you're trying to keep him safe?" Emily thought in headlines, had thought in headlines since before she'd attended her junior prom. And she knew, with an ache in her heart, that the destruction of a decorated and heroic Good Guy like Drew Mathison in the line of duty would read like a siren's song to the post-war American public. The thought brought a wave of nausea that had her regretting what little she'd managed to eat.

"If you knew what I'd already come through in France, you'd know God's keeping me alive for some reason."

What if the reason was to get Gil to the safe house? What if He's done with you then, and wants to bring you home to Him? She didn't say it, of course, but did feel compelled to send up a quick prayer to God as it burst from her heart. *I'm not! I'm not done with him, Father! Please!*

She hoped that mattered. She thought of what Drew had said, about trusting God with eternity but not always with the events of the day ahead. Hearing her own wisdom rattling inside her head, she drew a steadying breath. He seemed more at peace now. She had better catch up, herself.

But a bottle rocket went off somewhere just outside the diner, causing them both to jump a little. Turning her hand in his, Emily glanced at the narrow watch on her own wrist and smiled at a second mild explosion.

"It begins," she said.

"One more thing." Drew tightened his grip on hers. "I can't very well cart Gilbert off to a safe house under the cover of darkness and leave you and your family here, vulnerable. I don't like it."

"We'll be okay, Drew. We agreed to all hide out at the inn with my aunt and uncle for a few days once you and Gil are on the road, until the Contis know Gil's back in Reno. I'll wait for the all-clear, I promise. I won't so much as go out on the porch."

She might go insane sitting indoors doing nothing for that long, but sanity was usually low on her list of priorities.

"I just can't guarantee he still won't come after you for information, whoever this guy is. And I don't see him being very polite about it, once the meet doesn't happen."

"I have a crazy idea. Let someone else keep Gil safe," she decided, giving his hand a squeeze. "You stay here and keep following me around. Plan?"

That brought a smile to one side of Drew's mouth, and Emily reflected on how she adored his reluctant smiles. Part of their magic was that they only seemed to be for her.

"Tempting," he said. "You have no idea how tempting. Except I promised Gilbert—and *you*, I might remind you—that I'd personally guarantee his safety through the trial."

"If your plan is to send some other badge to bug the daylights out of me, I'd rather you didn't. I've only just gotten to where I can tolerate *you*. I can't break another one in."

"That's just what I need, one of my colleagues falling head over heels for you, too."

She batted her lashes again, exaggerating it. "That's now the sweetest thing you've ever said to me."

"Just watch it, Lois Lane."

"Who?"

Now he blinked at her. "Superman? You've never read the comic?" She shook her head, wondering why Charlie had taught her about Captain America and not this Superman. "Never mind. I've been sitting here hatching yet another plan, actually," Drew told her after another gulp of coffee.

"My, you're fast about those ideas."

"It's only if I can't locate Conti at the North Shore. It has to do with a diversion. We can talk about it later." He pulled out his wallet and tossed money on the table, which started a short battle about whose turn it was to pay.

"I want to talk about how you said you can't have someone else falling for me *too*. What did you mean by that? By the word 'too'? Does that mean you've fallen for me?"

"You're dressed like my late granny, so we can talk about that later as well."

Together, they wove their way against the diner's line and out into the equally loud village, the sidewalks filled with families heading to the boat parade. They picked an older, smaller camera from the office to shoot the fireworks because Sammy had the nice one at the parade. Black and white photos of fireworks weren't all that interesting, anyway. Then they drove back out to the island and loaded the Chris-Craft with everything they'd need for a night of crime fighting ... at least, that was how the narration went in Emily's head.

"This old boat is starting to feel like home," Drew told her.

"I can think of worse places to live." Emily noticed Tom had closed the marina office already, on the busiest day of the year. She decided not to tell Hickory until all of this was over, and then she'd advise her grandfather to fire the useless man. "Wanna drive?"

"I will," he said. "But the water is a madhouse."

Emily smiled, appreciating this view of her lake, crowded with boats long before sunset. There would be no real accelerating or speed this evening. She dropped onto the seat and flinched at the heat lingering on the leather from a day in the sun. That was when she decided it was past time for the costume to go, since she was out of the center of town. Wearing the outfit she'd started the day in with the old lady layers over top was suffocating. She shrugged out of the little woven sweater, shaking out her real hair, which had curled up in damp rings again along the edges.

"Here, let me," Drew said, leaning forward to unbutton the formless cotton dress, one slow button at a time. Stirred by his nearness, Emily tried to regard him with the humor the situation deserved.

"Young man," she cackled. "What do you think you're doing? *Young man*?" She pretended to squint at him and at his fingers unbuttoning the housedress that made up her billowing, stifling outer layer.

"Shhh." His big fingers worked at the little pearled buttons her grandmother had sewn so many years ago. His head hovered closer. "I'm concentrating."

She tried not to think about what it would be like to belong to this man, to allow him true access to real buttons. Try as she might, Emily was having trouble breathing by the time she turned away to remove her rice bosom, welcoming the comparative coolness of her checkered, sleeveless top and soft, faded capris. "I was way too hot in that," she mumbled, sucking in deep breaths and letting them out slowly, moving over in the passenger seat. Once there, she also tried not to think about the fact Drew Mathison would be gone by this time tomorrow.

Chapter Twenty-Seven

The Buckeye Lake Beacon
Thursday, July 4, 1946
Holiday Big Bang

Later, Drew would look back at that warm July Fourth as being one of the longest nights of his life, with moments stretched out like pastel taffy.

Maybe, he thought, it was because he'd stumbled into love and was still trying to catch onto the rhythm of the woman who had managed to take him there for the first time. The entire evening was overlaid with that dizzy rush of feeling he got from touching some innocuous part of Emily Graham or the feeling he got when something he said brought her blue-green gaze slamming into his with sudden, soul-deep understanding. Maybe it was that.

All those messy feelings combined with waiting for the holiday to wind down so he could go claim his witness from beneath the lake. He would *finally* be taking the first real and satisfying step toward justice for Jamie.

On edge, he thought the day felt more like Christmas than the Fourth of July. Only, he couldn't decide whether the gift he'd been waiting for was Gil Reese or the woman beside him.

Crawling through the colossal boat traffic on the water, he spun the wheel to avoid yet another low-speed collision with a runabout packed full of inebriated patriots. One of them yelled something unintelligible but with a good-natured laugh. Drew debated killing the motor entirely and just letting the crowd *bump* them closer to the coveted center of the lake.

"Oh, no you don't!" Emily sang in amusement when he slowed. "We can get closer than this, Captain!"

"You're enjoying watching me sweat."

"Yes, very much."

"A person could actually walk across the entire lake, from boat to boat," he said, marveling at the idea. He thought of the lily pads far on the opposite end of the water, about how he'd thought the same thing of them.

"I know," Emily was saying. "Isn't it splendid?"

The clothing that had been under her disguise looked like America: a cream-and-crimson checkered pattern on a shirt that tied in a little bow at her waist above soft, form-fitting pants. Her hair and skin glowed in the late evening sunshine. Drew thought she looked like everything they'd been fighting for in Europe and in the Pacific. Every awful memory shifted in his mind, took on a different hue, and would always be worth it. *She* was worth it, and so were nights like this.

Drew had said the boat felt like home now, but what he meant was that it represented the only place he ever got to just be with Emily Graham alone. Any other time, it seemed he had to share her with *someone*. Business owners, the high wire cyclist, her former Campfire Girl leader, the owner of a local restaurant who claimed her friendship, one of the council member's wives who wanted to put a plug in for something her husband had done that Drew didn't care one lick about, a pleasure boat captain, and even some infatuated youth from Skip's church named Moe.

Here, despite the hull-to-hull boats, it was just the two of them, and she seemed surprisingly relaxed, given the afternoon they'd had and the evening they were facing.

He supposed not being solely responsible for Gilbert any longer had to be a relief, on some level.

When a group of twenty-somethings in a Hacker Craft recognized and hailed Emily, he nodded toward them in a friendly way and promptly angled the Chris-Craft in the opposite direction. *That* was all he needed, he thought: a dozen pals taking over Em's boat like good-natured pirates and squeezing him out.

Drew figured he might be just a worn-out, soldier-slash-construction rat and frustrated detective, but for a few hours, the newspaper girl was going to be all his.

"Maybe this is as fine a place as any to settle," she said when he'd maneuvered a little deeper into the nautical abyss. A bottle rocket whizzed by his ear when he turned to look at her. She offered him a lazy grin and a wink. "If you push another twenty yards in, we'll meet up with two boats yonder full of my former high school teachers and their spouses."

"Heaven help us." Drew promptly killed the motor and was surprised when Emily Graham slid lightly into his lap once more. Only, this time, she was not in costume. The unexpected weight of her there, as well as the weight of the move she'd made, had his heart flopping madly in his chest. "Well, hello there."

Her arms slid up around his neck, her face deliciously close. Suddenly the crowds of people didn't bother him at all. Nothing did. She was simply his girl.

"Nice driving, officer."

"Sergeant."

"Thanks for keeping me safe and being there when I needed you today."

"Believe me when I say ... it's been my pleasure."

"And for taking care of Gil."

"Probably won't be quite as much pleasure as this."

He felt and heard her take a deep, deep breath. She half-sighed, and her lids half closed. "I do like the smell of you."

"Emily?"

"Hmm?"

"How many of the people in the boats immediately around us right now babysat you, taught your Sunday School class, or paid you to mow their lawns when you were a kid?"

She glanced around and grinned. "None. That's why I told you to stop here. Now, if you'd like me to locate someone ..."

And then Drew finally got to kiss her. For real. It was easy and right, just as it had always seemed like it should be. He merely moved a fraction into her, pressing his lips against hers the way he'd wanted to the first day he'd seen her on the boardwalk and the way he'd wanted to when she'd danced with him on the pier and the way he'd wanted to every blasted time she'd given him that look that even vomiting herons couldn't render unappealing.

His hand snaked up into the warmth of the curls on the back of her head and he felt her shiver against him. She tasted like the golden summertime, like hot sun beams and iced lemonade and maybe the juice of a cantaloupe broken open in the garden.

The kiss got deeper, and Drew was sure the woman in his lap must feel his heart pounding hard against her as his hands sought purchase in the fabric of the back of her blouse. Somewhere, dimly, he registered the sound of people hooting and whistling. A boatload of people.

Please, he thought vaguely, *don't let it be her former teachers.*

Having heard it too, Emily tore her lips away and grinned. Drew was helpless but to drink in the look of her, lips swollen and pink, cheeks glowing with two red splotches of color.

"Well," she breathed, blinking, studying him as he studied her. She seemed startled and then said, "My goodness!"

He wanted to smile at her declaration but couldn't because she leaned back into him and made another project of his mouth. She kissed, he thought through waves of desire, like she did everything else. With energy. Another bottle rocket whizzed by, and a loud series of crackling exploded from somewhere to their left. Emily ended this next kiss with a playful nibble on his top lip, her breath shaking out around him like the falling firework embers.

Sitting there with her still on his lap, knowing for sure now what he'd always expected would be true about the power of the two of them together ... Drew realized this boat was entirely too small an area for them both to occupy for the rest of the evening.

Sanity and good behavior here were going to depend upon space. And there just wasn't enough of it.

Muscles quivering a little in his arms, he lifted Emily off his lap and took a careful, desperate breath. He ran his hand over the back of his neck, not surprised to find it damp. Emily stood there, looking at him uncertainly.

"Soda," she said suddenly and with efficiency, and she stepped away from him quickly to her trusty picnic basket in the back of the boat. It wasn't very far to the back of the boat, Drew thought with a shuddering breath, but she was at least out of arm's reach.

Dazed, he stayed in his seat and really took in his surroundings for the first time since shutting the boat down. Now, with the motor off and with a desperate need to avoid looking at Emily, he was struck by the almost comical array of humanity as far as he could see.

Boats of every kind had turned the lake into a solid parking lot of decks. Colorful explosions arched into a blue-gray sky that would soon give way to twilight. People leapt from canoes to aluminum fishing boats, from speedboats to rafts, a sandwich in one hand, a bottle of soda or beer in the other. The noise was a steady hum of laughter that pooled above the lake and stretched to the shorelines, which were also alive with parties and bonfires. Music mingled with laughter. A band was playing on a distant pier, beside the yacht club. Someone strummed a guitar on a nearby boat, and the chords mingled with that distant music.

Then the sound of an opened soda fizzed and mixed with all of it, and Emily was there beside him again. Her color was still high, but she seemed almost as composed as she ever was, and she handed him a Coke.

"You're a good kisser, Mathison."

She always surprised him like that. He watched her shake a few peanuts still in their shells out of a paper sack and into her palm, and he tried to think of something to say that wouldn't sound stupid. He ended up sounding stupid anyway.

"Um. Thank you."

"Maybe I'll write a review on it for next week's edition." She winked at him, picked up her own Coke, and perched back into her seat. He could tell she was trying to break the tension. But her leg brushed his, and he told himself not to touch it. That way lay madness.

"Don't write about it. It would bring competition."

"True. But I feel like I can hold my own."

"Oh, you can certainly hold your own." The very memory had a drop of sweat chilling a path down his neck and back. He chugged half the Coke. She watched him.

"So, when can we do it again, Drew?" she asked, leaning toward him.

"Kiss, I mean?"

He groaned.

"Why did we waste so much time *not* kissing?" She sat back again, looking around. "Oh, right. You didn't want me to think you were trying to *romance* Gil's location out of me. I've got to admit to you though ..." She popped a peanut in her mouth and crunched. "I would've given him up in a heartbeat if you'd just kissed me like that at any point."

"Emily, Emily."

"I loved it."

"Can we not talk about it right now?"

"Why not?"

"The boat's just ... not big enough."

She blinked at him and looked around. "I don't know what that means."

He was drowning, that's what it meant. Sitting right in the middle of a boat in the middle of a lake, drowning. She looked at him skeptically, and Drew was reminded what a strange mix of street smarts and total innocence she was. He changed the subject by reaching for the peanut bag. "Good call, bringing these."

Emily sliced him that look that let him know she wasn't done, that this wasn't over, but she granted him the reprieve, just the same. "I've got a sack of blueberry muffins back there, too. I figure what we ate at the diner won't stay with us all night."

The way she'd said "all night," followed by a comparatively dainty sip from her bottle, made him just about throw in the towel.

"Hey, Drew?"

"Yes?"

"I meant it earlier when I said I was sorry about all this." When he shrugged, she pressed on. "And I meant it when I said thanks for giving me information about my mother."

"I'm sorry I wasn't ... smoother. When I told you what I'd found out."

"You had every reason to be angry with me. I mean, there I was, trying to win you over with fried chicken and pretending I wasn't just completely in your way."

"I never thought of you as being in my way." At her glance, he clarified. "Well, I didn't *always* think of you like that. Anyway ... you were trying to win me over with that chicken?"

"It didn't work." She laughed at herself, rocking back and tossing a palmful of shells into the water. "I thought maybe you'd put your convictions aside and kiss me if I fed you well. The way to a man's heart ... All the old ladies were wrong."

"Turns out all you had to do was climb all over me on a crowded lake."

"Who knew?" She munched again, thoughtfully. "No one gives good advice about love, it turns out."

"I guess it's different for everyone." He reached for another peanut and wondered how they could find themselves chatting casually about love. He'd never talked about love with a woman in his life.

"I guess Rosie's not the worst at advice, but I don't think she's been in love since Keith," Emily reflected. "If then. She'd tell you it was infatuation, but I'm sure she thought she was in love."

"Did you tell her about Keith being here?"

"Yes. She took it stoically, the way she does everything." She tucked her leg up under her. "I was kind of disappointed she didn't want to take him to the cleaners over Charlie."

"Is that what you were expecting?"

"No. That's what I would have done." She flashed him her Cheshire cat smile, as he thought of it, as she went on. "I figure it's on Rosie to tell Hickory. And I hope Hickory doesn't, you know, kill Keith or anything."

"That is very hard to imagine."

"You could probably make the charges go away if he does, right?"

"For you? Anything." Drew winked at her, finished his drink. "Can I say one thing without *you* killing *me*?"

Emily narrowed her eyes. "That sounds dangerous."

"This Keith character. He went Ivy League, I'll bet."

"Yale."

"Written all over him. The guy's a heel for leaving for Yale and not calling or writing your sister, Em. I mean, after what happened between them. I'll give you all that one hundred times over."

"You bet he is."

"But is it really fair to hold the fatherhood thing against him if he didn't know about Charlie? Is it fair to assume he *wouldn't* have done the right thing if Rosie had given him the chance?"

"You mean if Rosie had *been given the chance* to give him the chance?" Emily's eyes flashed, and Drew wondered what in the world he was doing. "Are you trying to talk me out of disliking him, Mathison?"

"No. Absolutely not."

"Anyway, would *you* want to be strapped to a life with someone who was only with you because it was the 'right thing' to do, instead of for genuine love?"

"No. No, I wouldn't."

"Rosie didn't either. He wanted her or he didn't want her. He chose the latter. Charlie wasn't part of that initial equation."

Drew raised his hands. "I'm not arguing. I just figure it's best to sentence him based on the crime he knowingly committed, not the one he didn't know he committed."

"Can I sentence him based on the resort development?"

"If it makes you feel better, I'll allow it."

"Just as long as you are in no way taking that fat head's side."

"I wouldn't dream of it. Can I get you to eat one of those muffins?"

"I don't feel hungry."

"You were pretty keyed up at the diner, spilling your submarine story and everything. I know you hardly ate a thing today besides those couple of peanuts. Maybe split a muffin with me?"

"Tell me that because we shared a colossal kiss that you don't somehow think you need to take care of me now?"

"To be honest, I've somehow thought I needed to take care of you since the first time I saw you."

The admission caused something to visibly soften in her face.

"I'm going to interpret that as sweet, Mathison, rather than patronizing. Free pass."

"So, you'll have a muffin?"

"For you? Anything," she said, tossing his words from a few minutes before back at him as she unfolded her legs from the seat. She amused him then by obediently retrieving a blueberry muffin from her bag, tearing it in two, and tossing him one of the halves.

The time between their snack and nightfall passed in a sort of haze of easy conversation. They spread a blanket and stretched their legs out on the deck of the Chris-Craft, backs propped against the back seat. He talked about his family, this time without the specter of Jamie and guilt, and a little more about the war when she asked questions. Emily told him stories about her college years that made him laugh. Former Fourth of July celebrations. They compared likes and dislikes.

All the while, Drew worked very hard to keep his hands to himself, but he didn't protest when she reached over and linked the fingers of her right hand with the fingers of his left. The minutes ticked by slowly as the entire population of the lake watched the sky for the first firework. Lightning bugs and stray explosions from the shoreline kept them entertained as they waited.

"Sometimes I think waiting for things is better than the things we wait for," Emily said on a contented yawn.

"I follow you."

"This is a nice time we're having."

"Yes."

"It's funny. When I think about spending the day at the amusement park with my friends when we were kids, I remember standing in line waiting for the ride more than I remember the ride itself. The laughter and the talking, the horsing around. It's the same with waiting for the town council to come out of executive session and back into public session. There's nothing to do but sit there and wait, never knowing how long you'll be waiting, and so you end up just sitting and talking to people you'd never get a chance to talk to otherwise. You know? I've come out with so many feature stories just from being forced to wait with people and talking to them. I'm going to start making myself be very happy about the prospect of waiting."

Drew thought about the separation looming before them, of all the waiting. Would they get to be together again? He had no idea, suspended in time here in the best boat of them all, what lay before them, so he couldn't make a single promise. And he desperately wanted to make promises.

"Waiting for fireworks with you makes me very happy," he said instead of saying the things he was thinking, like about not wanting to wait for anything when it came to her.

"For sure. The Bible's full of all that 'wait upon the Lord' business, which I admit has never seemed like much fun to me."

"So few things in the Bible regarding self-discipline turn out to have fun as the objective," he mumbled. Emily looked at him and grinned hugely.

"You're pretty wise." He yawned and nodded, and Emily went on. "I guess the waiting is part of the point. Maybe we're not truly ready for the thing we're waiting for until we've ... waited."

"Because I'm wise, I think you're saying we're going to be subtly different people by the time these fireworks begin, that we'll get more out of the experience than we would have even two hours ago."

"Yep, yep. You get it, Mathison. A giant metaphor for life." Another stray firework from someone's home on the shoreline exploded red overhead, and there was a smattering of applause from the boats. Emily sighed, happily. "Want to hear something strange?"

Drew grunted affirmation.

"Somehow, even with everything up in the air and danger around every corner, I actually feel better right now than I've felt in a very long time."

"Maybe because you've learned to lean," Drew said softly, and she rewarded him by leaning her head on his shoulder.

Apparently, he didn't need to explain what he meant. "You're right about that," she said softly.

It felt good to have both Emily and Gilbert trust him. Drew had been impressed with the things the kid in the submarine had said through the phone line this afternoon. He had apologized and compared himself to Jonah in the belly of the fish. Drew supposed he'd been learning his own lessons about trust, but the test of it was still to come. He'd been surprised to hear a bit of Pastor Skip in the voice of Gil, surprised by the apology he'd given. Perhaps Drew would want to protect him for more reasons than justice for Jamie.

Drew tried and failed to feel jealous over the relationship between Gilbert and Emily that had stretched over so many years. And yet, somehow, he couldn't imagine them together.

He scrunched his neck to look down at her now, so close beside him on the boat, and he said, "I want you to know that I think I like your pal Gilbert, even though he ran scared when he should have faced the truth. Who knows but that I wouldn't have done the same thing in his shoes?"

"You wouldn't have," Emily said with a quiet certainty that stirred him. She looked down at their joined hands and rubbed the pad of her thumb over the back of his. "How long do you think it will take for the trial to start, once you get Gil to wherever you're taking him?"

Drew shrugged. "I wish I could tell you. I'm going to push hard to get it going fast. I think the court will agree, given the safety issues."

"You don't seem to have any doubt that they'll indict."

"Now that I've talked to Reese, I'm more certain than ever. He can corroborate all the evidence. His story gels entirely. We could already place him on the scene, and we even have a witness who saw Jamie and Gil leave the club with the Contis. The judge and jury will know without a doubt he saw the murder. All he has to do is point his finger."

"I'm glad those men will pay for what they did to your brother, Drew."

"I'm glad they won't be able to keep doing it to other peoples' brothers." He leaned over to press a kiss to the top of her head. "Thank you for that, on behalf of all the victims they hopefully won't make victims. I guess, in the chaos of today, I never really thanked you for introducing me to your oldest friend."

She waved that away.

"Have you thought about what you'll do when the trial's over?" she asked casually, but he could feel her hand twitch a little in his. "I mean, are you going to keep doing detective work for the Philly PD or Reno or somewhere, or ... or will you go back to work with your dad?"

He noticed she didn't add a third option.

"I haven't thought past tonight. Or, I should say, early tomorrow," he lied a little. "Thoughts of getting Gil out of that sub undetected are keeping me plenty busy. I guess I'll just let God do what He wants with me after I finish this job."

She nodded and sighed. "That's smart."

Drew wished he knew what to say. Because he didn't, he asked her the same variety of question. One to which he knew the answer, but he asked anyway.

"How about you? Are you going to run *The Buckeye Lake Beacon* for the rest of your days? Or are you ever tempted to move to the big city?" *Philadelphia, specifically*, he wanted to say. Maybe cover the police beat. Lois Lane to his Superman. Maybe live happily ever …

"Oh, this is my place," she said with quiet conviction. Just as he knew she would. "I've never doubted that." Did she sound a little sad about that now?

"I think you're right about that." And she was. Hadn't he envied her that sense of purpose all along? Drew's stomach churned with obligation and with the will of a Creator in which he was never a hundred percent sure he was planted.

Then the warning shot went up from a barge to the west of them, a pale ball of fire streaking toward the apex of the gunpowder-colored sky. It exploded and rained white sparks down in an umbrella, and a cheer went up from the lake that would build until it was louder than the grand finale. Emily unfolded her legs and readied her camera, a smile on her lips. Drew remained stretched out, watching her switch so seamlessly into the role of documenter. The camera was pressed close to her face. She shifted positions periodically.

He wondered if she consistently saw life laid out on a broadsheet, if she thought about the world around her in headlines. He almost suggested she put the camera away and simply watch the intense explosion of the finale through her own eyes, that she cherish it for herself instead of documenting it for others, but Drew knew that the woman he'd fallen for was made for this. Any request like that would be like a minister's wife begging him to lounge in bed with her on a Sunday morning or a detective's girlfriend trying to convince him to stop chasing the bad guy and just stay safe with her.

Emily would never ask him to do that. And he would not ask her to put the camera down. That, Drew figured, was love in the light of purpose.

Chapter Twenty-Eight

The Buckeye Lake Beacon
Friday, July 5, 1946 ... early morning
Overnight security added to parking lots

Hours later, it was clear that Plan A — as Drew thought of it — had *not* gone well.

The north shore boat ramp had still been packed at midnight, and if one of the Contis had been there for the meet with Emily and Gil ... well, he had not stepped forward and announced his gangster status in any way Drew could make out from beneath his fisherman's hat disguise, in the limited light of the lot.

So, it was on to Plan B.

Gil still sat, clock ticking, in the sub. And Emily's boat was anchored a quarter mile out on the water from the inn and the north shore. Drew sat in it again now, leaning back against the back of the driver's seat, legs stretched before him, Emily beside him, waiting for people to finally get tired of celebrating their independence and *go home*, for crying out loud.

Where had Conti headed when the meet hadn't happened? Drew squinted at the distant shoreline as if expecting him to materialize. Would this be one of the men who had shot Jamie full of holes? *Almost certainly.* Would this next phase of the plan he had plotted with Smokey and Emily end in justice?

It had been the one thing he'd asked God for in the aftermath of Europe. When he'd returned home, he'd asked for quick justice for Jamie. It was all the consolation to be hoped for at such a point. Drew hadn't been surprised when God had been silent on that, when instead of swift justice, he'd found Reno to be thick with corruption. When he'd ended up tracking a preacher's kid back across the country. When the case had been of no interest to anyone but himself. It certainly hadn't felt of interest to a distant Creator who had set a Plan into motion and then left them all to pray about it while the Plan rolled out the way it always was going to.

Now, as the cool of the dew settled on them, Drew thought about what Emily had said about God either giving them what they'd asked for or, if He did not, giving them something better. If he'd gotten what he'd asked for — that swift justice — Drew would have gone his whole life never meeting Emily. His path would never have crossed through little Buckeye Lake in rural Ohio, with its lovable residents and its stunning sunsets and the oceans of corn that bordered the water. If he'd gotten what he'd asked for, even now Drew would be tucked in bed in some apartment near his parents' place in Philadelphia, having barbecued the afternoon away with his remaining brothers, sleeping now in preparation for another day at the job site. Looking forward to … what? A beer with the crew after work? Mama's banana nut bread? A sore back?

Instead, he'd met Emily. He now knew there was a woman like this in the world, where he might only ever have wondered. Having her mop of golden hair resting on his shoulder in the darkest hour of the night was not something he'd have thought to ask God for. Swift justice had given way to waiting, and Drew thought of the way they'd waited for the fireworks. The way Emily had decided to think about waiting. This was something he wouldn't have asked for, no, but it was better. He might not have dared to pray for this, but God had had it for him all along … had her for him all along. Drew believed that as one plan gave way to another, as Plan A gave way to B. He knew there was a verse about good gifts, about God giving good gifts to His children, but it was hazy on the edge of his tired mind.

Drew figured once he'd looked at a thing like justice through a lens like this, it was hard not to pull out some other things and examine them under the very same lens. And it was starting to look like it had taken brokenness to know the life God really promised, to know God at all. When God had seemed silent, when His Plan went seemingly unaltered by Drew's earnest prayers, so much so that he'd stopped asking … he could see God now in those places, too. If he revised history as he'd have shaped it himself, some men would be alive again, but not alive in Glory, not at peace with their Lord. Some tears would not have been shed, but Drew wondered how he'd see things on this night if not through the eyes that had shed them.

The challenge of Plan B, of Reno, of this vow to keep Gil Reese safe, was tempered now with the knowledge that, however this went, God would work even the painful parts in a way Drew might not have recognized he needed them to work.

~~~~~

Emily was running through the fallback plan in her mind, Drew silent beside her. She watched as lights finally went out along the shoreline, the expanse of black water clearing of boats in the sleepiest hours of the night.

There had been no sting operation on the north shore docks. So, the game grew more dangerous.

The safe, quiet life she'd led stood out in contrast to what this night held, she thought. Even what she'd always thought of as her trials — the death of a father she hadn't been old enough to know, her mother's abandonment, Grandma Louise's return to Jesus, the censure that had never quite cleared for any of them with little Charlie's arrival—seemed rather tidy in comparison to a killer willing to do whatever he had to do to eliminate Gil and preserve a family's criminal empire.

Plan B, Drew had called it. Get Gil out of the lake safely and quietly. Out of town. So, they waited. She ran through it again and again, though. A rendezvous with Smokey and the breathing device at the inn. Soft, dark movement of the boat out to the end of the pier. Water rushing in. A silent extrication, and ...

Emily pressed closer to Drew. Even the best and most successful scenario meant saying goodbye within just a few hours. And then what?

Suddenly the lake felt a little less like home, with even the idea of his absence. She smacked a mosquito and already felt the swelling itch on her thigh. How long did a trial take? Caution would be paramount through that, but what would happen when it was over? Would both Drew and Gil have to disappear for a time? And for how long?

She asked questions by both nature and profession, but she couldn't ask these. She did not want to hear them spoken. Instead, she held Drew's left hand in both of her hands in the darkness and memorized the trio of freckles beneath the joint of his thumb that looked a little like a clover leaf, letting her fingers run over calluses.

Even without those questions, there were things they should probably say, she thought. She was in love with him, for instance, and that was something it seemed a person ought to know. Emily was no longer perplexed by the unfamiliarity of what she felt for him. Something had clicked into place, and it was a peaceful something.

Maybe, she thought as her feelings mixed with the details of the fallback plan, she would get to tell him she loved him as he prepared to leave with Gil in the pre-dawn. She might work with Cookie to pack them a basket of buns, and she'd pull him aside at his ugly truck, and instead of goodbye she'd simply say, "I love you." She felt he would know without her telling him that she had not said it before to anyone else.

For now, though, there was the soft movement of the wooden boat on the water, like a sort of cradle. And his scent—familiar now so it smelled only like what she'd call "safety"—and the strength of his shoulder beneath her temple. The warm cotton of his shirt. The rise and fall not just of the boat but of his breath ...

Emily didn't mean to nod off, but she must have.

Later, in the days that followed the headlines of this night, she would only remember the next hours in fragments. Later, she would wonder what would have happened if she'd only stayed awake ...

The whole boat lurched, and Emily gasped, thought she was falling. The shadow of Drew and his sudden movements disoriented her, bringing alarm even before she could make sense of his urgent orders. She heard him say her name, scrambled toward a seat as the engine powered on, deafening in the night ... until the sound of sirens invaded her senses at the same moment as the leaping orange flames on the horizon.

The pier was on fire.

The pier was on fire!

It was engulfed in flames, the worst of them at the end—the end where Gil was—and lurching like an angry monster up the dry wood, toward the main park. The roof of the Dodge 'Em cars was catching, mesmerizing in its speed, but Emily's eyes kept tracking to the end of the pier, which had broken off now into the dark waters that reflected the flames.

"Gil," she heard herself say stupidly.

"I know," Drew said firmly. "Almost there. I've got him."

Lacking more words, hardly able to hear him at this speed, she glanced over at him at the wheel. Her hair slapped at her eyes, but Drew looked like the soldier he was just now, cool and determined, handling the boat like some unforgiving tank as he sped toward enemies all the more real for not being visible.

Emily thought wildly of the tube that went down to the submarine, of it breaking off into the water with the rest of the burning pier, of wood crashing down over the hatch and then water rushing in without Gil being prepared. Leaning forward, her hand held the glass of the windshield like everything might shatter.

"He knows Gil is down there," Drew shouted. "Conti. He figured it out. He's smoked him out."

Had the man followed them earlier, when she'd been in disguise? Guilt stabbed at her as they drew closer, both of them peering urgently at the water, looking for any man. Criminal or old friend. Firetrucks had arrived at the park now.

The water around the flaming posts was still. No bubbles. Nothing and no one bobbing in it, outside of what seemed to be charred wood. There was no kind of path from where the sub had been toward land, and on land there was no obvious, menacing figure waiting for Gil to surface.

Drew pulled Emily over to the driver's seat, quickly shedding shoes. He tossed his watch at her, barking out, "Get back to the inn. See if Smokey's there with the breathers. We need air. We need the tools. Go, fast. Come back, fast. Get Smokey."

And, before she'd had time to make sense of these instructions, he'd made a sharp, powerful dive into a lake full of flames.

Paralyzed for exactly five seconds, Emily made herself say, "Breathers. Tools. Smokey." And then she was jetting to the shore and the inn.

Smokey would be there, she told herself, looking over her shoulder back at the disappearing pier. Sirens were everywhere now. Drew and Gil would be okay, especially when Smokey joined them, capable, experienced, and waiting for this boat.

Please let them get to him first, Lord.

The faceless enemy waiting for him was what had her shaking so hard, she told herself as she came in way too fast at the little inn's dock. And, sure enough, the figure of a man was waiting for her there. But his movements were not Smokey's crisp, military movements. Emily's heart stuttered a moment until she heard Burt call to her. He'd been in a lawn chair at the end of the dock.

"Out," he said gently, bending to tie the boat off.

"I need to go back out. I need Smokey." She fumbled with Drew's watch to check the time, but it was so dark. She couldn't see her own either. The smell of burning wood was everywhere, and Emily noticed residents and guests milling around in alarm on the walkway to the park.

"No." Emily resisted as Burt reached down to pull her up into one of the hugs she usually loved. She pushed at him, looking for Smokey Black.

"Stop," he said softly. "It's okay. Breathe." His face swam before her in the shadows, and she heard herself breathing too hard. "It's okay. Smokey's been here and gone, Sweetheart. He saw the fire right away, right when it started. He was in a sprint and in the water before I knew what was what."

Emily let that sink in. Smokey was out there, ahead of them. He had the other breather. He hadn't waited around for the boat. *Why would he?*

"How long?" she huffed. "Did he ... did he take the equipment? Drew needs his help. They need air."

"He had a pack. Now you get some air, too, you hear?"

Emily turned back toward the fire, watching in horror as the Dodge 'Em cars sank, almost in slow motion, into the water. Each car slid off into the orange lake like they were some of Charlie's toys, swallowed up by the blackness.

We will never get those out of that muck, she thought pointlessly. *How does any of this turn out okay?*

"Hickory, Rosie, Charlie?"

"Everyone is locked up tight here. They're waiting for you. Come on." Burt moved her up the yard from the dock, pocketing the key to the boat.

"But they need the boat."

"They've got what they need. The boat will only draw attention. You get inside here with the others where it's safe. The Grahams are in hiding for a bit, and you're a pretty important Graham. Got it?"

Emily nodded.

"No gawking. Inside."

~~~~~

Emily never went inside, after Burt took off to lend a hand at the park. She made a decent show of it, and it was a testament to Burt's urgent desire to be useful that he believed taking her as far as the porch would work.

She gave him a three-minute head start before she crept off the porch and sprinted down the alley on the town side of the houses, alert now as she hadn't been before. She wasn't sure what she was looking for ... a stranger making off with Gil?

Cutting back up to the midway, Emily realized there was no getting down the fiery pier. Only firefighters were out there now, some of them moving hoses down the severed planks, working to save the ballroom on the other pier, as well.

Emily was jostled by the crowds. She saw Dottie run past, her curls unbound. People poured out from everywhere, it seemed, the vacationers to stare and the residents to find some way to help. Emily tried to get to the ballroom pier for any kind of view. Her eyes scanned the water, helpless. Half the park seemed to be floating in there now. Some of it was still on fire. Everything looked like a body, and she felt dizzy as she whispered a request to God not to let anyone be hurt.

Then there was a soft sound from the water below. A voice. She thought she heard her name.

Emily lowered herself and leaned over, only to see a young man in the shadows, half clinging to a piling. "Donny!"

It took just a split second to imagine how it had all gone down, even as she removed her shoes. Their mysterious enemy creeping out on the pier after the crowds had gone, intent on setting the wood to blaze. Where would he have waited for Gil? Had he thought Gil could get out on his own, or had he understood collapsing the pier would drown him? Regardless, he'd have had to do something about young Donny at the end of the pier.

"I'm coming, Donny! Hold on!" The water wasn't her usual Buckeye Lake water as it splashed around her, warm and cluttered with debris. She hadn't realized how loud the air was — the sirens, the shouting — until that water closed around her head with the silence of only her heartbeat.

The noise crashed around her again as she broke through, pushing through charred wood toward Donny, who had just been trying to make some extra cash for college.

"You're okay," she told him, gasping, commanding it to be true. He was clearly weak, bleeding from his head. "How did this happen?" she asked him, wrapping her arm around his skinny torso. "I've got you."

"A man," he murmured, unashamedly attempting to cling to her and doing a lousy job of even that.

"The man who started the fire?"

Donny made a sound of affirmation, but Emily knew this wasn't the time for questions. She pushed off, channeling everything she had learned from Hickory about how to swim while carrying another person. Growing up on a lake, they learned and called it play.

Breathing hard, Emily swam-crawled toward the shoreline, working hard to keep Donny's head above water. He was no help with that. She couldn't afford to talk more, to tell him to hold on. She couldn't afford to look around here in the water for Drew, for Gil, for Smokey. In fact, she was starting to wonder if she'd make it in, but that was hardly an option. Donny was innocent of all this, after all, far more than she or her stupid friend Gilbert were. Donny had to be okay.

She slipped below the water, muscles burning, lungs burning, and it scared her enough to propel her forward again—slowly, so slowly. She tried to focus on her legs, reminding herself they were strong enough. Ears just barely above the waterline, she heard Chief Gunn up ahead, and he was calling her name just as Donny had. Except this time from the shore. *Thank You, God.*

Emily had trouble remembering being pulled the rest of the way onto shore with Donny. It was a blur punctuated by Burt's frustration with her, but Donny would be okay. He would be all right. They assured her of it. Chief Gunn had gotten him to the sub-station where he could get patched up.

When she'd wandered back toward the pier to look for the others, Burt was there, arms crossed in clear disapproval. "Don't even think about it."

~~~~~

When dawn came on the Fifth of July, Emily Graham had to face some sobering truths.

First, she was no match against the police chief, Burt and Cookie, and her family. They'd finally managed to trap her effectively inside the inn to watch the fire be extinguished from a distance, to watch that sunrise over a changed, charred Buckeye Lake.

Secondly, she had not been able to help rescue her childhood friend, after all, even though he'd begged her to do so months ago. Had he been rescued at all? She didn't even know. She had not helped catch an arsonist/killer who'd caused trouble for more than her friend, for more than her family. She could still see Dot Berkeley and her family, the loss reflected with the flames in their eyes. Had the Conti hitman been caught by anyone? She didn't know that either. And she wasn't even any kind of newspaper woman because here was the biggest news of her career in Buckeye Lake, and she didn't have a single photo, a single interview ... or a single care about any of that.

But she had been forced to trust in those hours just before dawn and after. Could she make something heroic out of that?

Cookie made a breakfast of bacon and waffles. Emily, hidden with her family in a back bedroom, couldn't force any of it down. Even not eating it, nausea was a real threat. Rosie forced a cup of black tea on her. Emily let it go cold after an obligatory sip.

Hickory had asked questions, and Emily's frustration only mounted when she had no answers.

Charlie, subdued, played with a train set Cookie had unearthed from their box of Christmas decorations in the attic. The acrid smell of its miniature engine smoke was overwhelming in the little room, especially when coupled with the heavy woodsmoke that clung to Emily's clothes and to the air itself.

Cookie, who talked too much any time she talked, was silent this morning, which was more disconcerting than any wailing and wringing of her dishpan hands would have been. Emily considered wailing herself, in the hope someone would free her from the room for sanity's sake, when a tapping on the door yielded the large, weary-faced figure of Smokey Black.

Her heart stuttering, Emily flew at him, nearly climbing him like a tree in her need for news.

"Ah, there, there," he said good-naturedly, always amused by her, even when they'd been young. "All is well, Emmie."

"But ..." She was having trouble catching her breath, somehow, though she'd sat all morning. "*All* is? *All* are well?" Was that what he'd said? She took in his dry clothes, different from what he'd worn at the diner yesterday, his calm demeanor. She felt soggy, sweaty and quite wild in comparison.

"I can't say much," he told Emily. To the room, he said, "I can say, you're okay to leave now and head back to the towpath. Everything is as it should be."

"Drew?" Rosie insisted.

"Alive and well. Everyone you care about is." He winked. "And now you can put this behind you." With that, he nodded, and turned the Grahams over to Chief Gunn, whom Emily only just now noticed also hovered in the doorway. The chief looked considerably less put together.

But Smokey ushered Emily out the doorway, down the hall, and out of the house as she heard Gunn talking behind them. She wondered if she should be embarrassed that, with his hand guiding her lower back, he could certainly feel the all-over trembling she hadn't been able to get a handle on so far today.

"Walk with me," he said softly.

She did, matching the lazy pace he'd set. He moved his hands into his pockets. Was he taking her to Drew? No. He led her out to the dock, where her boat was still bobbing quietly. Down the sidewalk toward the midway, Emily could barely make out people still milling around the wreckage. A pall of smoke hung heavy over the water like smelly fog.

"What is it?" she asked him. She scanned the shore, scanned her boat. "Are they really okay? Where are they?" Her ability to ask questions seemed to have resurfaced.

Smokey looked relaxed, leaning on a post. Not at all like a man who, by all accounts, had recently done some dangerous underwater work amidst fire. "Mathison doesn't want me to say much, for your safety," Smokey said. "But I know you won't settle for a simple, 'Don't worry.'"

Emily narrowed her eyes, and he laughed that deep, rich laugh that had always come so easily to him. "Both of your sweethearts are on their way out West."

Dizzy with relief, she half-heartedly slapped his arm, but her relief warred with sorrow. There would be no chance for goodbye.

"Listen," he went on. "Drew said he's got it under control as much as he can, but he asked for you to pray for them. For Gil especially, he said."

"Is he hurt?"

"He's worked up, but he's still willing to do what needs to be done. Things may take a bit of time now, Em."

"But they'll make it back there? And why are we fine to go back to the towpath? Doesn't it stand to reason this killer is still around here, looking for Gil?"

"No, he's not around." Smokey was entirely serious now. "I wouldn't tell you it's safe if it weren't. The man who was here to retrieve our buddy Gil is no longer a threat."

Emily searched his eyes for more information. "C'mon, Smokey. It's not like I'm writing a story or anything. How is that possible?"

"I got there just after he'd started the fire. When I was diving, someone attacked me. Tried to take me out. He obviously didn't succeed, and now he's gone. Drew got there and we got Gil out, and the attacker is no longer a threat. And that's about enough about that. Except Drew wants you to know, because you'd wonder ... it was Tom."

Emily blinked and felt a little dizzy. "Wait. Tom who was working at the marina these past few weeks? *Our* Tom?"

"The very one. Guess that's how he knew so much. He was basically waiting for you to reveal Gil's whereabouts just like Drew was, only possibly with a little less romance thrown in?" Now Smokey winked playfully, and Emily rolled her eyes, but the worry was still pressing close.

How had they not noticed that?

"So, the other Contis know exactly who we are and think we're still hiding Gil, though?"

"They will realize in very short order that the witness who can put them behind bars is no longer here, I promise. Long before they realize they haven't heard from good old Tom — or whatever his name was — in a few days, they'll be placed under arrest." He gave her a second to let that sink in. Emily wondered what had happened to Tom, but she couldn't manage to care. Smokey went on, "By the way, I'm sure you realize you've got to publish something believable about your Sub Man. The crowds are frantic, wanting to know how he is and everything. Gunn's feeding them a story — get with him on that."

"Of course." Emily rubbed at a headache over her eyes. "Gil is out."

"After I … took care of things with Conti, I was down there clearing debris from the hatch to get him out when your main squeeze swam up and scared me good." Smokey grinned. "We pulled Gil out fast, both of us working together. Mathison can hold his breath, I'll say that. We swam south, away from the hullabaloo and the fire. Gil had one of the breathers all along, remember. He's fine."

Emily's eyes sought the still-smoking carnage of the pier, the remaining rides still and silent, even amidst the somber crowds. She needed to head over there, to pull her mind back to this place and not to a pickup truck on its way to Reno. She squinted up at Smokey. "Drew didn't send me any other message?"

"Honey, be glad you didn't get some emotional goodbye with him. You look just awful." His eyes crinkled in the corners when she smacked him again. "And no. He just told me to tell you as little as possible so you'd be safe."

No message of love. No tender, scrawled note. Emily knew there couldn't possibly have been time. She was left regarding the wristwatch he'd tossed her the night before, hanging too large on her wrist, and wondered how he'd keep track of time on the road.

Chapter Twenty-Nine

The Buckeye Lake Beacon
Monday, Sept. 2, 1946
Reconstruction to beat first frost

"So, you're not even going to try to pull the Dodge 'Em cars out of the lake?" Emily asked Dot.

Rosie slid in beside them with a pitcher of lemonade. Sitting along the open counter of Dot's office at the Crystal Ballroom, the three women had a clear view of the construction of the pier that would replace the burned one. There would be a few upgrades to this one, while the Berkeleys were at it, including bump-outs for two upscale restaurants and several new rides. Even a second ballroom.

"What's the point of pulling them back out of the water?" Dot asked. "We can't use them. Best to respect their watery grave."

"It seems so strange, imagining them piled down there like toys in a sandbox," Rosie said, almost to herself. Emily figured her sister was weaving a fantasy about somehow capturing photographs of them down there, still colorful and tragic in the dingy lake bottom.

The sisters had just been out photographing the construction progress, punctuated by the mayor's speech about the resiliency of the park and its community as summer drew to a close.

Labor Day was upon them, the official end of another season, and Emily found herself strangely indifferent to the natural cycle of the year. School would start. Charlie would exchange his fishing bucket for a backpack, and Rosie would spend longer days out at the bog, the slower pace of the lake opening more time for dark room experiments and other studio work. Professor Lamb's book with her illustrations was scheduled to be published over the winter.

The newspaper would get smaller now, as summer businesses withdrew their advertising. Ads would be for the year-round residents only: grocery sales and automobile tires. Back to the usual stuff of life when life was not punctuated by big-name bands and tightrope walkers.

Usually, Emily rather dreaded the approach of autumn and winter. The quiet of the pace had never been the kind she loved, her energy only gratified in spurts by skating parties or ice fishing tournaments. Early nightfall had always felt oppressive when she couldn't swim in it, and there was little dancing to be had. The hammock would come down until spring. She'd shorten her office hours by half, deadlines met by suppertime, evenings punctuated by sleepy council and township meetings here and there.

But this year, she reflected, sipping at the lemonade that would soon give way to hot tea and coffee, she did not dread the end of summer. She did not feel anything, in fact, and hadn't for weeks.

Time passed, she did her job, she went home, and more time passed. And Drew Mathison was as silent as the ever-shorter days.

"A few things will still need to be finished on the pier come spring," Dot was saying, "but most of it will be ready by opening." Emily envied her friend's freshness today, the sophisticated upsweep of her dark ringlets, the little dimple that punctuated the perfect skin of her cheek. Dot was dressed for business negotiations, as usual, but she'd toed off her shoes as the three of them had slid onto the stools together.

Emily, feeling a little spinsterish and old and tired herself, wondered if her friend were in love or something.

"Ready by opening," she mused, picking up Dot's thread. "Is that what FH Resorts is promising?"

Dot shot her a look. Keith Fairchild's company had backed off on the resort development because of the damage the fire had caused to so much of the park. Though they had not entirely abandoned the project, the company's press release said they'd "put it in a drawer for later in order to assist with the rebuilds that would strengthen the community."

So, Keith's assistant or whatever he was, Gabriel Adams, had become a fixture at Buckeye Lake as he helped oversee and fund through partnership these upscale additions to the new pier. And his increasingly familiar face was increasingly seen near Dot Berkeley's.

"FH delivers on its promises, I'll say that," Dot said.

"Are you seeing this Gabriel Adams, Dot?" Emily asked.

"He's representing the company's interests in this partnership, so of course I see him a great deal."

"Outside of business?"

"Love is business, the way our Dottie goes about it." Rosie winked and smiled.

Dot's chin went up, but it carried a smirk. "And why shouldn't it be? Mr. Adams isn't such a bad … deal."

It was true the man was handsome, well-dressed, wealthy. All things that paired well with Dot Berkeley. And Emily figured Dot had to look like a lucrative "deal" herself, as heiress to the park and an astounding chunk of the north shore of the lake. What might an enterprising businessman like Gabriel Adams make of a romantic partnership like that?

What went unspoken over the lemonade was Rosie's shadowy,

haunted connection to FH — to Keith, its owner, in particular.

Dot, like everyone else at the lake and like Keith himself, still didn't know it was his son Rosie had born and raised for the past decade.

Rosie insisted Keith wouldn't even remember her, should their paths cross, but even Emily suspected the man was not quite that villainous. For her part, Emily couldn't help thinking that her beloved Charlie should have some share and eventual inheritance in posh resorts and developments. But Rosie insisted nothing had changed.

In fact, Rosie was gleefully entering the conversation about Dot's love life. "Does he treat you well?" she asked of Keith's assistant, Gabe, as though she hadn't a care of her own.

"He's a complete gentleman," Dot affirmed. "Took me to O'Neal's in the city last night. His taste in restaurants and wine are really something."

Emily, watching workers haul wooden planks out along the pier, thought of Drew Mathison. She could close her eyes, in fact, and see him working on marina docks, that belt of tools slung around his waist. The way he moved. The way he'd watched her, too.

"That sounds nice. Dinner and wine," she said, trying to strike a normal tone. "When will you see him again?"

"Oh, not for a week or so now. But he may phone occasionally from Columbus."

It all sounded very tidy, Emily thought. She tamped down on a wave of envy, sent up a desperate prayer once she identified it as envy. *Lord, please help me be happy for my friend and to cherish the blessings You've given me in my own place. I know Your timing is perfect.*

But … drat. God would certainly also know the not-easily controlled grumblings of her heart. Because her heart demanded Drew Mathison. Any word from him, even, would suffice. A cryptic postcard. She was bright, after all; she could decipher coded messages. Just to know he was out there, alive, thinking about her at all … was that too much to ask for, as well?

She now subscribed to the newspaper in Reno, *The Evening Gazette*. It ran no helpful stories of criminal trials, at least as of yet. Emily had no idea what was happening or if Drew and Gil were safe.

Sometimes she poured her heart out to God and sometimes to Pastor Skip, whom she had wanted to join in her frustration and impatience. But it was courtesy of him that she was adopting phrases in her prayer life like, "I know Your timing is perfect," so she prayed those and tried very hard to know it in her heart.

"Emily, are you all right?" Dot wanted to know, startling her out of her sorry excuse for a prayer and making her wonder with alarm if she'd groaned out loud again or something. She'd been doing that lately.

"Don't lie and say you're fine," Rosie admonished her sister, clearly feeling a bit cheeky today, Emily thought. Miss Cool as a Cucumber. Miss Nothing Has Changed. That she had the nerve to tell *her* to be real ...

"Eh," Emily allowed. That should do it. That was honesty.

"Your eyes are all glassy lately, like you've got a fever or something," Dot was saying. "And you're pale." And here Emily had been thinking about how her friend was glowing. Dot pushed on. "You asked about my love life. I get to ask about yours. Is that what's wrong?"

"Some of it," Emily said. She'd been trying so hard to allow herself to lean on the people God had given her, to let others help her shoulder burdens. Recommitting to it, she told herself, *You don't have to handle this all by yourself.*

She wanted to say she'd found it freeing. And it was true that her secrets about Lillian, their mother, now shared, had made her feel less alone when it came to making decisions. She and Rosie had, together, sent a letter to their mother's last known address, extending love and forgiveness but no more cash, inviting her to the towpath to meet her grandson and her grown daughters.

There had been no response.

But Emily didn't have to quietly agonize about that now. She and Rosie prayed and hoped, and they shared the burden of accepting that things didn't always wrap up tidily in life. Not every broken relationship was redeemed.

"Sometimes you're born into the family you deserve, and sometimes you simply have to build that family yourself," Rosie had reasoned.

And, with those simple words, Emily had something new to imagine.

Meanwhile, she supposed there had also been a certain amount of freedom in handing Gil over to Drew's care, much as she resented knowing nothing now.

But it was this belief in the value of sharing challenges with others that made Emily admit to Dot now that she *missed* Drew Mathison. Dot had only known him as a police officer-turned-bodyguard who had disappeared once the supposed "threats" to Emily over the resort development had ceased. That entire falsehood, while necessary for Gil's safety, had done a bit of damage to Emily and Dot's easy and candid friendship.

"So, you fell for the bodyguard," Dot said with satisfaction, her eyes sparkling over her glass. "How delicious. How romantic."

Emily rolled her eyes, and Rosie smiled. Rosie, after all, knew the truth and was rooting hard for Drew. She told Emily just how much, often, talking about the way he'd worked on the docks with her son.

"Why don't you go find him and declare your love?" Dot suggested.

Because he is living with my ex-fiancé under the constant threat of murder just now. Instead, she said, lamely, "I ... guess I'm too busy."

Dot snorted. "And you Graham girls accuse me of being too business-minded for romance."

"We're all a bunch of career women," Rosie said playfully, looking every bit the free-spirited artist she was with her ribbon-woven, reddish braid. But, for all she played by her own rules, Emily knew her sister was as serious about her glasswork and her photos and her watercolors as Dot had ever been about managing the amusement park.

"Speaking of careers, I think I might be able to put some spring back in your step, Emily," Dot was saying, and it was her business voice now. Talk of romance was done. "The candy place on the main drag is moving out to the new pier."

That's what everyone was calling it: the new pier.

"Yeah?"

"So, there's a vacancy up front there, right on the midway." Emily's posture changed as Dot went on. "Seems like a logical, highly visible place for a local paper."

"Don't tease, Dottie. Can I afford it this time?"

Dot quoted a price, and Emily could, indeed, afford it. Especially since she was building her savings back up after emptying it for Lillian again and again.

She tried not to wiggle in her seat, but already she could see her logo, the lighthouse, on the current candy store. The increased interactions, the circulation.

She wanted to tell Drew about it. That was her next thought.

That evening, Emily let herself be convinced to celebrate the paper's move up to the north shore. As her friends made the toast, Emily told herself the autumn and winter would be just fine. She'd be busy with the move. There was so much to do and still a paper to put out each week, after all.

As she reached into her satchel to clasp Drew's watch in her fist, she whispered the time to him, as she sometimes did.

Time to come home.

She just hoped he knew *this* was home.

Chapter Thirty

The Buckeye Lake Beacon
Saturday, October 26, 1946
Beggar's Night scheduled for Thursday

Emily knew when the trial had finally started, following it in the papers and knowing, though others did not, the identity of the "unnamed witness."

At first, she'd known Drew was only thinking of her safety, and that was why no letters or calls came in. But by mid-September, when she'd begun to grow frantic from hearing nothing, her imagination racing with scenarios that removed Drew Mathison from the world, Pastor Skip had told her Gil had actually called him to check in.

"He's doing fine. He's safe," Skip told her with gratitude on the day she was packing the last of *The Beacon's* supplies for the short trip to the waterfront. She had frozen with a typewriter pressed to her bosom.

"How about Drew?"

"Gil said Sergeant Mathison is also doing fine. He has personal command of Gil's safety detail, and Gil said he won't let up a second. Complained about him, really, if I'm being entirely honest," Pastor Skip said sheepishly. It did sound ungrateful, which they both knew Gil could be.

Emily remembered similarly complaining about Drew's determination. What she wouldn't give now to glance out and see his truck. Or, for that matter, she'd give quite a lot for a phone call, herself. Certainly, it could be arranged if Gil had managed to call Pastor Skip?

And that was why, when September turned to October and the trial continued and she'd still heard nothing from Drew, Emily Graham began to doubt. Her doubts were few, at first. Then many.

She thought back now, to a decade before, to a time when Rosie had waited patiently for Keith Fairchild to call or write from college, how she'd excused the lack of contact for some time because he'd surely been busy with his new classes. This memory made Emily uneasy. Keith's rejection had seemed so obvious to Emily back then ... was she incapable of seeing the same dynamic now, in her own life? Was she making excuses?

She thought of how she'd mailed cash to her mother again and again, waiting for the telegram that said she was on her way or needed to be picked up at the station. Lillian had to tie up loose ends, Emily had told herself. It was bound to take some time, when you were moving clear across the country, right? Her own naivete gave her pause now, as the leaves turned multi-colored on the trees.

Then the trial ended with a guilty verdict, and the anticipated call or letter still did not come.

Pastor Skip didn't know what would happen next either, but he was disgustingly content to trust and wait.

Emily threw herself into arranging the new office, with plenty of help from Cookie, Burt, Hickory, and Rosie. This space, which would be more visible, needed to be arranged with more care, a more deliberate aesthetic, Rosie said. Emily tried hard to care about that, but she grew preoccupied re-imagining the moments of her time spent with Drew.

She saw them in a new light now, and it was upsetting her stomach.

Had he only been romancing the information he wanted out of her? The small, sweet gestures? Had they only been a detective's tools? Could she really have imagined the heat between them?

It had still been early October when Emily had taken a trip out to Festival Farms on the auspices of photographing some pumpkins to advertise a carving contest she'd decided to sponsor. But she'd ended up shamelessly trying to pump Smokey Black for information.

"They don't ring me up or anything, Em, but I'm sure they're fine," he'd said, hauling armfuls of dried, rasping husks over to a wagon. "Why don't you try tracking Mathison down in Philadelphia? Wouldn't he be headed back there to the family business after everything?"

"He did? He said that?"

Smokey blinked. "I remember. He said they're contractors or something."

Emily had wandered off without her pumpkin pictures, a sharp pain in her chest that made her wonder if she should see a doctor.

She also was embarrassed about the way she sniffled back tears as she wound his wristwatch each night, a ritual that accompanied her prayers.

~~~~~

Emily approved Cookie's arrangement of a newspaper-reading scarecrow in the shiny front window of her shiny new office. Inside, the space was still looking more skeletal than anything else, and not in a seasonal, spooky way, but Emily knew they'd get there. It was a matter of organizing shelves.

She left Cookie in her element, still decorating and promising to lock up once she'd prepared for Beggar's Night.

"I mean it," Cookie called after her as Emily made her way down the boardwalk. "You get yourself some supper and eat plenty of it!" The woman's thinning hair was the same color as the jack-o-lantern that had been the winner in the carving contest. That winning pumpkin had been arranged on a bench out in front and would be lit after dark. "Emily? You hear me?"

"I will eat supper, Cookie. I promise."

She dug half-heartedly for her keys and drove slowly along the shoreline and out to the towpath. The sun would set soon. It was still warm enough for a cracked car window, the scent of the water mingling with the dusty scent of stump-filled corn fields, harvested and ready to be worked for beans. It would be a warm Beggar's Night, she thought. No need to cover clever costumes with the dreaded coats, as Charlie had pointed out. Better photos, surely.

The giant maple that shaded Emily's end of the towpath all summer was more easily seen than ever because it had turned a bright marmalade color, made richer still in palette by the ball of sun sliding toward the horizon.

Emily's shoulders ached from all the lifting the move was still demanding, and she suspected she'd pulled something in her lower back. In true old maid fashion, she'd even opted for comfort over style in her shoes today, along with a pleated pair of mud-colored slacks and a short-sleeved powder blue sweater. She stretched her neck, ear-to-shoulder, in a bid to work out the kinks as she slid out of the parked car at the marina.

She shouldered her satchel, stuffing keys back in it, and trudged across the bridge. The lights were coming on in the canal below, but instead Emily pondered the lights in Hickory's windows, wondered if she still had soup in her own fridge or if she should make an effort to join the rest of the Grahams for whatever better thing Rosie had concocted earlier this evening. They would certainly have already eaten, she considered, deciding she was more inclined toward a hot bath in the barge house. There was the cat, zipping at her from the dock where ...

... her head jerked up ...

... she'd stowed the Chris Craft in the marina two weeks before.

But there, at her dock, was a small boat.

A rowboat, in fact.

With Drew Mathison sitting in it, smiling that rare smile he only let out when he absolutely couldn't help it.

Emily dropped her satchel, just let it thump to the grass from her shoulder, and made her way down to the dock, not feeling anything but a tingle from head to toe. No sore shoulders, no twinge in the back.

He looked good, she thought. She promised herself she was never taking her eyes off him.

Grinning up at her as she made the dock, he asked, charmingly, "Will you take a little ride with me, Em?" As though they'd seen one another only the day before.

Emily placed her hands on her hips, heart thumping, and leaned back on her heels. She couldn't stop the foolishness of her own, answering grin. But she was no fool, and he'd come back as she'd known he would, of course. She had not mis-labeled or imagined all that had been between them.

He'd been coming for her all along. Of course, he had.

She hadn't expected a rowboat, but he'd come for her.

It turned out a woman really might just trust her instincts when it came to a man who looked at her the way Drew looked up at her.

"I thought you might let me row you through the Sweetheart's Canal," he said. "Your first time, I believe?"

"I've gone five times just this past week with other fellows, I'm afraid." She burst out laughing and motioned for him. "I'll go, I'll go. But you'd better climb up here first to me. Otherwise, I'll flip that little boat for sure when I pounce on you."

He was up and out in seconds, laughing with her, vaulting up as the boat rocked, and then he was rocking her, too, in his arms. The latching on, the desperate quality of the embrace, kept them from kissing for a length of time that surprised them both.

But then they did get around to the kissing, too.

Breathless, on her toes, Emily tore her lips from his to taste his jawline and the heat of his neck where his aftershave mingled with the rest of him. His arms nearly crushed her, and they *still* weren't close enough, she thought a little wildly. He was whispering. Little endearments she barely registered, one hand moving through her hair. She reacquainted herself with the fit of him, the way they lined up, sinking back into a kiss until their breathing sounded like they'd both run the distance of the months that had brought them back here.

She pulled back. "I didn't know. I didn't know if you were coming back."

"Of course, I was coming back." His voice was rough again, like when they'd first met, like he hadn't said a word to a soul in weeks. "Of course, I'm back."

"You didn't say. You never said you were." To her horror, tears pooled. She felt a fat one make its escape and reached up as though she'd keep him from noticing. But his lips were there, instead, and the crush of his arms turned tender.

Here he was, and the nights of winding his stupid watch alongside her stupid doubts were being soothed away by his fingers and some soft words.

When he had Emily down in the rowboat at last, the sun balanced right on the edge of the lake and the sky exploded pink around it. He nearly ended up tipping them, after all, as he hauled her nearly onto his lap.

Drew didn't pick up the oar yet, but only pulled her tight, and she did her part by melting into him.

"I had only one thought," he finally said. "Well, two. First, the longing to talk to you. But, more than that, the need to keep you safe. Tell me you understand that, Em. I had you off their radar as soon as I rolled into the city with Reese. The last thing in the world I wanted was you back on it. Tell me you understand."

She nodded against his collar bone. "I could have decoded something though."

"Decoded? Like ... secret messages?"

"Yes. I checked the classified section of the Reno paper every day looking for a coded message from you."

She loved the warm sound of his chuckle beneath her ear, the feel of his hand on her side.

"Coded messages? You're giving me too much credit for imagination, Sweetheart. I'm a simple man."

"You're not so simple."

"And what did you want these secret, coded messages to say?"

"I guess it doesn't matter now."

"I need to be taught, clearly."

"Well, that's true." She tipped her head back to look up at him. "I needed you to tell me you were okay, Drew. That you were safe."

"Hmm. Sorry about that. I took it for granted you'd assume I was if you hadn't read about my death. I just didn't know how without putting you in danger. I'm really sorry."

"You should be. And you could also have put a message in there for me to de-code about ... I don't know. About how you were thinking about me a little."

"I thought about you every minute. I'm telling you that now. I mean every minute."

She re-tucked her head under his chin and took a shaky breath.

"And maybe you could have somehow found a way to tell me how you felt about me," she prompted. "So I wouldn't wonder all this time."

With a press of his fingers, he edged her face back up to his. "You wondered about that? *Really*?"

She shrugged, but it wasn't effective in this position. "You never said. Before you left, we never had a chance to come right out with it."

"That we love one another?" His gray eyes searched hers, and she knew again she had been wrong to wonder. "I do love you, Emily. No codes necessary. I've loved you almost from the beginning of all this. I'd have sworn it showed the whole time."

She smiled. "From the beginning? You nearly wanted to strangle me from the beginning."

"And I will want to again, no doubt, but I love you." He ran his hand, bigger than her whole head, over her hair. "Your hair got longer," he observed, a little gruffly again, like he resented the months that had passed.

"I guess so." He hadn't changed at all, she thought.

"I think you love me too," he said.

"Yes." It was gentle and simple. All this time, he'd known, she thought, and she envied his confidence. They sat and enjoyed it for a time, while darkness fell. She breathed a prayer of thanks.

Then, she found he'd thought of everything. There was a plaid, woolen blanket that he pulled over them before retrieving the oars. "Okay, it's getting dark. Let's see the canal the way it's meant to be seen. And I'll feed you some treats in that basket and answer all the questions I suppose you're trying so hard not to fling at me."

"You know how to speak the language of my heart, Mathison." The oars bumped softly against the side of the boat as he rounded the tip of the towpath. "I've always wanted to do this, but with the right person," she told him, enjoying the easy rhythm of his pull on the oars.

"Gil's safe," he offered casually, slowing his approach to the canal. It was almost as though he knew her memories of this spot were filled with scrawny little Gil, swinging out over the water on the maple tree's rope and dropping with a splash here.

"Can you tell me?" she asked, realizing she'd be content with his answer either way.

"Buddy of mine from the Army. He has a ranch up in Canada. Gorgeous and remote. Gil is settled there." He pulled on the oars a few times, switching sides. "I stayed a while with him, making sure he'd be okay, lending a hand. Definitely couldn't contact you from there, of course. There's no trail of breadcrumbs to that place, and we're keeping it that way."

"What about Pastor Skip?"

"There's a convoluted way for them to send letters, but they can do it. Until it's safe for Gil to leave. If he chooses to."

Emily tried to picture her old friend working dawn to dusk in an unfamiliar place. It would probably be good for him. "What's he think about it all?"

"He's content, Em."

"That would be a first for him."

Drew breathed out a laugh. "He might not be the same man you knew before. Sounds like he changed a bit on the bottom of the lake."

"Maybe you know him better than I do now."

Drew made a sound. "Either way, then or now, I can't picture the two of you together. He wasn't right for you."

"I did know that, yes." Amused, Emily sat up beside him on the bench so she could face him. "You are, though," she said earnestly, with a determined nod. "Right for me."

"You bet I am."

She let herself just drink in his features again, feeling proprietary. There were so many things she wanted with him, she hardly knew where to begin. He angled the rowboat into the canal now, and there were lit doves to their right, but Emily kept watching Drew. "You handle yourself pretty well in a boat, Mathison." She considered her words. "Everywhere, actually."

"Guess that's a good thing," he said. "Since I just took a job with the Watercraft office."

Now she sat up straight, the blanket falling away. "What?"

"What a follow-up question, after I've gone out of my way to give you the exclusive story." He smiled big this time. "I work for Natural Resources, here on the lake. Still an officer, but on the water. A manager position with the Watercraft folks. It's a good gig, and they made me a nice offer."

"Drew ..." Emily's heart was pounding. He'd be working *here*? Right here on her lake?

"My brothers and dad have the construction business running fine, and they support me taking the position here." He searched her face. "Please say you're okay with it. I told the Watercraft folk it's contingent on you being okay with it."

She laughed now, and with such joy that she didn't have to confirm it was okay. She leaned, rocking them, to kiss him again.

"You're missing the pretty glass," he mumbled, letting the boat drift. That was about when Emily heard a familiar voice from somewhere above them.

It was Charlie, and he called down excitedly, "Did she say yes, then, Drew?"

Emily twisted her head back around and found all three of them there—Charlie, Rosie, Hickory—peering down over the railing of the footbridge and into the rowboat. Even in the dark, she could see them practically vibrating with excitement.

Emily laughed hard, couldn't help it.

"Since she was kissing you, she said yes, right?"

In a crowded, confused moment, Emily could clearly imagine Drew asking Hickory for her hand in marriage earlier today, as she'd hauled boxes wearily around her new office.

She turned back to see Drew laughing, too.

"Didn't exactly get around to asking yet," he called, his eyes still on hers, and Emily knew she'd remember this moment forever, even more so than the apparently grander one about to come. This moment was filled with everyone's laughter, bouncing around the canal, and then by Charlie's sounds of humorous distress as his mother scolded him. Everyone Emily loved was right there, laughing and lit by soft spotlights.

When the laughter died, Drew did get around to asking if she'd please consider being his wife.

She told him she certainly would. She told him she'd pour even more energy into being Emily Mathison than she'd poured into her newspaper.

Drew said that frightened him a little, and Emily thought that was reasonable, indeed.

The End

About the Author

Kim Garee worked as a newspaper reporter before going into education. Now she's a 6-12 school librarian and has been married to her husband, a high school principal, for twenty-six years. The couple have three grown children and three grown pets. Kim is also a portrait artist and miniature enthusiast who will hike and bike with anyone willing to go with her. She welcomes connections at www.kimgaree.com.

Watch for *Packed Together*, Book Two in the "Together" series in December 2024:

After a blizzard strikes during her sister's wedding, Rosie Graham finds herself snowed in with the very people she most longs to avoid. Still, it's Christmas at the lake. No amount of stubbornness on her end will be enough to stand up against a very unlikely romance punctuated by no power, nosy relatives, a stab wound, and a nativity scene carved from soap.

Patched Together, Book Three in the "Together" series, releases in September 2025:

The wholesome fun of 1947 Buckeye Lake Park stacks up against staggering guilt for Dottie Berkeley. She has been the "princess" of the park her whole life, but her involvement in a local tragedy wrecks her reputation and leaves her to find redemption in the last place anyone would look for her: the fresh-tilled dirt and back-breaking work of a local farm. Plus, both she and the man who owns those acres of pumpkins and evergreens were looking for very different people to love.

THANK YOU!

Thank you for reading this book from Mt. Zion Ridge Press.

If you enjoyed the experience, learned something, gained a new perspective, or made new friends through story, could you do us a favor and write a review on Goodreads or wherever you bought the book?

Thanks! We and our authors appreciate it.

We invite you to visit our website, MtZionRidgePress.com, and explore other titles in fiction and non-fiction. We always have something coming up that's new and off the beaten path.

And please check out our podcast, **Books on the Ridge,** where we chat with our authors and give them a chance to share what was in their hearts while they wrote their book, as well as fun anecdotes and glimpses into their lives and experiences and the writing process. And we always discuss a very important topic: *Tea!*

You can listen to the podcast on our website or find it at most of the usual places where podcasts are available online. Please subscribe so you don't miss a single episode!

Thanks for reading. We hope to see you again soon!

Printed in the USA
CPSIA information can be obtained
at www.ICGtesting.com
LVHW031015260424
778524LV00012B/1083

9 781962 862219